RUTHLESS

The Completionist Chronicles Book Five

DAKOTA KROUT

ACKNOWLEDGMENTS

I'd like to thank my readers for their unceasing support. At the time that this book is going out, there is a global pandemic that is keeping a large portion of the world in lockdown. Knowing that you are supporting me helps me to push harder to complete my projects. I hope that my words can bring you joy and entertainment.

To my Patreons who are supporting me directly, thank you all so much! Especially to Justin Williams, Samuel Landrie, William Merrick, John Grover, Kyle J Smith, Dominic Q Roddan, Mark R, Carrie Crumsey, Arthur Gschwind, Phil the Strange, Chioke Nelson, and Mike Hernandez. I will drink a large pot of coffee in your honor!

The completion of this novel would not have been possible without my lovely wife, PhD Danielle Krout, CEO of Mountaindale Press. Thank you for all the work you do, not only in making things happen, but in giving me a daily reminder of what matters most in life.

PROLOGUE

Zone Alert: To the Unified Race, Humans, congratulations on your achievements this far! As of this moment, the path to the next Zone has been opened. The entrance to the Bifrost is located on the Eastern edge of this Zone.

The current Zone has earned the designation 'Midgard', the abode of mankind. If all else fails on other Zones, Midgard will welcome your return.

Take heed! Use of the Bifrost means stepping into an energetic field. If you have not achieved a second Specialization, also known as a Third Tier Class, there is a near-certainty that you will not survive the use of this mode of transportation.

A small group of well-armored humans stood next to a beam of colorful light that rose as a column into the sky. The largest of them, clearly a tank, nodded and strode forward. "I don't know about you guys, but I'm ready to taste the rainbow."

"*Seriously*, Sponge?" An archer-type shook his head. "It *literally* opened three hours ago, and it tells us that we'll die if we use it!"

Sponge grinned at the archer. "Nah, it said there is a *near* certainty of death. I'm level eighteen, and I have fourth-tier constitution. If anyone can survive this, it's me."

"Why is one hundred and fifty-five constitution tier *four*?" A fighter questioned him, stepping into the light. "Ooh. That tickles."

"Right? It's the fourth threshold, that's why! Ten, fifty, a hundred, then one-fifty points in a single stat. Tier four. That's as high as it goes in this Zone, so it's time to move on," Sponge stated knowingly. "C'mon, guys. Even if we don't survive the trip, I bet we get a title for being the first to use it!"

That argument was more persuasive than anyone wanted to admit, and after a few reluctant moments, the rest of the group was standing in the crackling rainbow. "Alright… you guys seeing the same options? I see 'Zone Two, unification unresolved'. Go for 'group transport'?"

There were a few muttered replies, but the overall tone was agreement. Sponge pressed 'activate', and the group vanished, leaving behind a puff of smoke that smelled of burnt hair.

The five screamed as they shot through space at speeds they could barely comprehend. Sponge looked down and saw Midgard vanishing into the distance, and was shocked to find that the entire Zone was a single massive disk. That didn't seem possible… but he supposed that they weren't on Earth anymore.

A sound like popcorn popping came from his right, and Sponge turned to find that the group's Assassin had vanished. He scooped up the dagger that had continued flying in the light, determined to return the loot to his fallen teammate. "How's everyone else doing?"

Pop.

There went their combat medic. Uh-oh. Sponge was starting to feel… *queasy*. The light of the stars darkened for a moment, and he turned his attention upward. There was something blocking the… the *new Zone*! He continued rocketing onward, travelling up the static-charged rainbow; the Bifrost. Odd… there was something different about this Zone.

Pop.

Another teammate gone. It took Sponge a long moment to figure out what he was seeing. By the time the truth dawned on him, he was at the top of the overly energetic rainbow, and he began to descend.

**Pop*.

Now it was only him remaining.

He was looking down at a landmass that was twice the size as the first Zone, but that was not what had been messing with his head. The fact was, there were two disks that had converged upon each other. They were rotating, and it was clear even from this height that there was a war raging wherever the disks touched. But from here, it was just an amazing lightshow. At least, it *was* just a fun show until a small asteroid tore past him, following a beacon of light toward the distant Zone. "Now we're talking! *That's* a power level I haven't seen before."

Sponge kept dropping, and found that it was getting harder and harder to breathe. That… that was… "Ow. Oh… *ow*."

**Pop*.

A pair of smoking boots landed on the ground near the active combat zone of the two disks, and a long-eared man grimaced at the boots and rainbow in disgust.

"Toads looking at swan flesh… they are a hundred *years* too early to challenge *this* Zone. Perhaps that one dying a dog's death will enlighten others!"

CHAPTER ONE

Boom.

Joe settled on the ground with the rest of his Coven as the ritual completed, finishing a dense black wall that encircled the core buildings of the Wanderer's Guild. "Thanks, everyone! I know it was an early morning, but I thought that this was the best way to avoid getting in people's way."

Class experience +400!

"Taka, Kirby, Robert, Big_Mo, Hannah, I'm going to go over your suggestions for more Ritualist classers, but please remember that we are making a tight-knit group. We aren't trying to make a sea of people that can do what we do. The more people that come into the class, the more likely it is that we get downgraded in rarity, and then there is less incentive for people that we actually *want* to join us."

Hannah nodded at him, grinning at how Joe preempted several incoming questions. They had been bugging him about getting more people involved. Robert waved and walked off with Taka and Kirby, while Big_Mo looked at the wall they had just built. "Whew. Looks kinda sinister, right? I mean... it's a wall, but that looks like something that surrounds an evil lair or terrifying dungeon, not a Noble Guild."

"To be fair, it *is* a wall that used to surround a terrifying dungeon," Joe pointed out. They watched for a few minutes as the guards in the area climbed the wall and took up positions. "Hey, look, Jay gets to get off the ground now. Jaxon is going to miss having easy access."

"I think he heard you." Big_Mo nodded at Jay, who nodded vigorously and made a 'victory' pose when he saw that he had their attention. "Makes sense to me, though. Jaxon is a little over-exuberant."

"He just loves what he does; can't fault him for that. The rest is the system messing with him." Joe laughed as he remembered how Jay got an extra strong dose of Chiropractic Services whenever Jaxon saw him. "Also, Jay might be running, but he can't hide *forever*!"

The last bit was shouted up at Jay, who shrugged and mimed stabbing with his spear. The guard then stood perfectly straight and focused on watching the people that were up at this early hour, which looked to be mostly trappers and a few rogues off to pursue dark deeds. Joe rolled his shoulders and started walking. "Alright, Big_Mo, I'm gonna head out. Let me know if you need anything."

"Doing good, man. Let's talk about a ritual I'm thinking about after I get about… four more hours of sleep." Big_Mo walked off toward his bed. "I'll find you; don't worry about me."

"See ya!" Joe moved through the gate of the new wall, getting a once-over by the guards. They seemed to enjoy having a specific area to guard instead of a vague 'the area'. "Time for a breakfast burrito. Yum yum."

"Did you see the *notification*?" Jess shouted over to Joe as soon as he came around the corner toward the coffee shop. The acoustics were excellent in the area, and most people were just getting going, so her raised voice made a few people dive for cover.

"Jess, it is *way* too early for that." Joe winced as he looked around at all the weapons that were suddenly in people's hands. Weeks of combat and *preparation* for combat made everyone a little paranoid, even with the mind-soothing that everyone was getting from this world. "Of *course* I saw the notification. Everyone did. That's the point of a *Zone* notification. We even had to dismiss it, or it didn't go away. One moment. Coffee. Large. Black. Espresso if you have it. By chance, do you have any burritos?"

Jess watched as Joe ordered his coffee from the suddenly-empty space in front of the coffee shop. As the team's new logistician, she was always looking for ways to prove herself useful to the group at large, and hadn't found much opportunity recently. Perhaps *this* was a place that she could help. "You know, Joe… you are getting a bit of a reputation for being dark and mysterious, and not in a good way. You need to boost your public image, or it is going to come back to bite you."

"What are you even talking about?" Joe started to turn toward her, but the barista on duty handed him a large mug, *way* ahead of the other people that had already been waiting in line.

"H-h-here you go… Elbow." The barista gulped as Joe turned dark eyes upon him. Joe was *certain* that this guy knew his name and was just playing up his role. "P-please come again."

"Mate. A boost here?" Joe continued staring daggers at the sweating Barista. A dark blob poured down his shoulder and hovered over his coffee before pouring half of its body into the drink. Then it rolled up his arm and flattened, making a black cuff at the end of Joe's sleeve. Joe took a sip of his drink and nodded at the Barista. "Thanks for this… *I'll see you tomorrow.*"

"You see, that is exactly what I'm talking about," Jess told him as they walked toward a table. "You have a *terrible* reputation. Everyone thinks you are trying to be all 'edgy', but you're strong and scary, so no one wants to do anything about it. Like tell you, or slap you until you stop. I'm volunteering for that."

"I have literally no idea what you're talking about. I was

trying to give Mate a rest, but the coffee they gave me was weak." Joe said over the rim of his cup. " As for the guild, I have done nothing to the guild and its members except *help* them, time after time. Look at *that*!"

Joe pointed at the towering egg-shaped Pathfinder's Hall. "We get a huge boost to learning skills near that. I also made the Evergrowth Greenhouse—which is the only place that is a sustainable food source—the housing that's keeping people out of sleeping bags at night, and the wall that just went up to keep monsters away from the doors! People should *love* me."

"Right. *You* made all those things. You also made them in the dark when no one was looking. You need to *involve* people in things, make a public spectacle of this sort of thing." Jess leaned forward. "People want to feel *useful*, Joe. If you give people too much, too fast, they are going to rely on you for things that you *can't* give them. Like security. Leisure. Power. When you can't do it, or you start needing help in the future, people are going to look at you in a different light *really* fast."

Joe shrugged as he sipped his fragrant coffee, responding flippantly, "Perhaps a ribbon cutting ceremony? Cake! People love cake."

Ignoring his attitude, Jess pressed on. "You need to help people rely on themselves to give them purpose, or you need to involve them in the process *now* while it is in the beginning stages. If you don't... if you make everyone *need* you, either you'll not be able to do *anything*... or you'll go too far. At the end of the day, they are going to think that you will do anything to get ahead. They'll think you'll leave them behind, that you're *ruthless*."

"I'm being too *nice*? I'm helping too *many* people?" Joe shook his head, then drained his mug and stood. "I have work to do, Jess. I know that I can't do everything for *everyone*, but I'm going to do what I can to make *all* of our lives better."

'I Know Better' effect activated!

Joe paused as he was storming away and looked at the notification. He replayed his morning in his head, but he didn't know where he had gone wrong. He pulled up the active effects tab of his status, and looked at the effect in question.

Intelligence is two thresholds above Luck! Debuff added: I Know Better. Little Joey would soon learn that he did not, in fact, know better. Effect: 1% chance to make a terrible decision.

"That's just... *what* terrible decision did I make?" Joe looked at the four other debuffs that were in place, frustrated that simply focusing on one area had caused him so many problems. He had a five percent chance to decrease reputation by a full rank during conversation, a five percent chance that he would see someone *else's* plan as a terrible idea beyond redemption, a ten percent chance of not *moving* when there might be an easier option around, and finally a chance that any actions he *did* take would be ten percent slower than usual.

The worst part was: he would never be able to realize what was going on. He might not even recognize that he had *created* an issue, similar to how Jaxon - the low charisma Monk in his team - couldn't recognize that he was making constant social faux pas. The system would make *sure* they couldn't recognize their mistakes, and that - more than anything - worried Joe. There was no opportunity for growth if you couldn't see the issue in the first place.

Before he could follow his circular logic down into the drain, another voice shook him out of his reverie. "Joe! You seen Jess? We gotta' get inta the greenhouse if we wanna beat the lines today!"

"Good morning, Bard. Oh, hey, Alexis, Poppy, Jaxon. Wow, the whole gang's here, huh?" Joe looked around at the others, surprised to see everyone out and about this early. "What's going on with the greenhouse?"

"Morning, Joe. Jess has been keeping tabs on the growth and respawn rate of the food in there." Alexis explained after covering her mouth to hide a yawn. "Apparently, there's a good chance that we can get Uncommon or Rare ingredients if we get in there in about ten minutes."

"Wait, you saw her already, right? She came to get you." Poppy looked past Joe into the dining area. "Everything okay?"

"Yeah, just... it's early. Hadn't had my coffee yet." Joe hedged, not wanting to explain his current sour attitude toward Jess.

"Well, let's get going." Alexis saw that Joe was floundering and evidently decided to help him out. "How's your day so far?"

"Oh... ah, between this wall going up and the work I did getting the Arena set up for the Kingdom, I'm sixty points away from leveling up my class. I can build practically *anything* and level up. So, pretty pleased with that. Otherwise? Uhh... good, I guess?"

"Great!" Alexis saw Jess and waved her over. The group made their way to the strange star-shaped Greenhouse and walked past the double guards at the entrance without needing to wait in line. The perks of an early-riser.

You have entered the Evergrowth Greenhouse, a building owned by Joe of the Wanderer's Guild. There is a 70% collection tax imposed on all goods harvested. Caution! There have been reports of Weeds in the area.

"Oh, they figured out the tax system?" Poppy blinked away his notification.

"Yeah. I transferred administrator control over to the guild a while ago. They figured this out yesterday, I think?" Joe waved at the notification that had appeared in the air for all of them. "They had been trying to collect by relying on the honor system, but..."

"Wasn't working very well?" Poppy smirked at his bald team leader.

"Not at *all*! I couldn't *believe* the estimates they were showing me." Joe rolled his eyes. "For how rare spatial bags and such are *supposed* to be, a bunch of people sure seem to have them."

"How does the tax collection work?" Alexis plucked a head of lettuce out of the planter, watching to see if a chunk of it would suddenly go missing. It did, and she had to scramble to catch the suddenly much-reduced vegetable as she stepped out of the doorway. "Ah. Yup, system just takes it."

Jaxon nodded at the head of lettuce, seemingly still waking up. "What an *interesting* way to make a chop salad! I wonder if it can do shapes?"

The group delved deeper into the building, which had its own subtle spatial magic. There was far more space on the inside than the exterior would suggest, and the entire greenhouse was filled with a rich, earthy scent. They made it into the last wing of the building when Jess pointed out what she was after. "There! Those are the rare fruit, 'Floodwater Grapes'! They are apparently really hard to get outside of here, and usually only grow in very specific areas. Super delicious, and a rare ingredient for winemakers! You would never guess it though; they are *really* prolific here, for some reason."

Joe gulped when he saw the sheer number of grapes in the area. They had taken over a ten-foot by ten-foot space, and the vines were coated with thick grapes. He started to wonder if he had made a mistake by placing the glass that increased fertility in the growth rack. "Yeah… maybe the soil is just really full of… nitrogen, or something?"

CHAPTER TWO

"Joe!" Mike called out just as Joe was swallowing a grape. The bald man had to pound on his chest to force the grape out of his airway. It landed on the ground with a wet **splat** and deflated like a sad balloon. "You okay there? Sorry about that; I've been practicing my stealth."

"I can see that. It's fine." Joe managed around a cough. "Hello, Mike. What's going on?"

"Ah! Yes!" Mike whipped out a paper and handed it over. "We're finally getting ahead on the layout of new buildings and planning. Here is the layout and the order we are hoping to build the buildings in."

Joe took the paper and looked over the list of desired construction, wincing as he saw some of the more complex designs. "Hey, I'm really happy to do this, but there are a few things that I am going to need. I recently found out that my skills are less effective when working out issues with pure math, and was informed that being taught properly would make everything work better."

"What are you trying to say?" Mike gestured impatiently for Joe to make his request.

"I need classes on architecture," Joe explained easily, getting a furrowed brow in return. "Here is why: I can scan a building, or I can work from existing blueprints. I *can* scan a building and make alterations to the blueprint, but if I screw up, I won't have a working blueprint anymore. That almost happened with the greenhouse, because I didn't know what I was doing on a few fronts. Also, I can't make my own blueprints from scratch. If I *could*, I could fix some of the glaring issues I see with this list."

"Issues? What do you mean?" Mike looked at the paper Joe held as the problems were explained.

"Here. It might make sense to have cattle and such, and it makes sense to have a butcher. It makes sense to have a tanner as well, which is why I think you want these three buildings to be together, right?" Joe waited until he saw Mike nod. "Right, well, you want these three buildings near housing, so people have easy access to fresh meat, leather armor, and whatnot. But how will the tannery and butcher not stink the place up? How will the cattle *not* keep everyone awake at night? Also, they stink too, so add that to the first part of the 'cons' list."

"Ah. Perhaps the city planner is still a little too used to Earth, and-"

Joe cut Mike off. "That's actually perfectly acceptable here. I've seen a blacksmith that has a sound-dampening enchantment, and I think that is something I will be able to do as well. *Eventually*. But if I could get classes in architecture, I could create soundproofing for walls, or filters for the smell. All of this could be added afterwards, of course, but until it *was* fixed, people would be very unhappy."

"Hmm. You may have a point." Mike took a long look at the paper, clearly trying to think through different ways of setting the area up. Finally, he sighed. "Alright. I'll see what I can do, but you're going to have to meet me halfway. Since it's beneficial to your class, I'm gonna ask you to pay-"

"Mike." Joe gave him a flat look and gestured at the protective outer wall that hadn't existed the night before. "I haven't asked you for rewards, because we have a deal. Tell you what…

you can finish that sentence, *or* you can repay the fees of the four people in my Coven that work with me on rituals. They get paid per ritual completion."

"As I was saying, I'll see what I can do." Mike winked at Joe and flounced off. This was very out of character for the ex-military man, so it forced a chuckle out of Joe. "I'm glad that Towny McTownface now has a solid fallback location! Thank you, Joe!"

"Glad you're having a good morning, Mike!" Joe called after the whistling Sub-Commander. Joe looked at the sheet again and grimaced. As far as he could tell, everything listed was set for maximum efficiency... on Earth. In Eternium, there were magical equivalents of things that would allow for the same amount of processes to be done in only two-thirds of the space. That was how millions of humans had lived in a single city before they had Shattered the Wolfmen race. He decided to take a look at who was doing the planning, and if they were actually doing research like they should.

When Joe reached the general hangout area, the mood was far different than it had been only minutes before. Joe looked around, and saw that people were eating and drinking just fine, so he had no idea why things were so grim. He sat next to a stranger and offered a smile. "Hey! What's got everyone so down? Things haven't been this, uh... depressed... since the notification that Earth was closed to us."

"You haven't seen the...?" The man looked up, almost excited to be the one to share the bad news. "It's pretty fresh news. Guild's in trouble. Someone posted our location to the message boards, then told everyone that we have unlimited food and supplies that we are hoarding and refusing to share. Clearly a lie, but there are going to be a lot of people that believe it anyway. The thought is that we are going to get swarmed by hungry or angry people soon."

"Yikes, that *must* be recent. I just got done talking to the Sub-Commander, and he was in a *great* mood." Joe looked off toward the Guild Hall. "Well... I mean, that doesn't really change much for us, does it? I'm sure the guild was prepared for this…?"

"Joe!" Mike came running into the dining area, spotted Joe, then sat down heavily across from him. "Something just happened that we were totally unprepared for! We need you to come-"

"Mike." Joe leaned forward and banged his forehead on the table as nervous chatter started up all around them. "You have horrible timing."

A short while later, Joe and the other guild officers were assembled in the Guild Hall. Aten entered the room, and everyone stood from their chairs. Joe followed along a beat later, confused as to why the group was acting so militaristically. He hadn't needed to stand at attention when someone entered the room since his military days.

"At ease," Aten barked, and everyone sat back down. Joe winced at the blatant attempt to place military practice in place, and he hoped it wasn't going to become a 'thing'. "We're in crisis mode. As far as we can tell, either the Nobility, or—more likely—a Noble *Guild*, has released our location to the general population. They are trying to rabble-rouse, and get us swarmed by low-level people. There is a good chance that there will be others in the mix that are here to steal or sabotage us if there is a large enough gathering. Thoughts on how to handle this?"

The first reply was nearly instantaneous. "Do we know the location of the other Noble Guilds? Let's make *them* go public."

"We don't." Aten looked around, gesturing for people to start throwing out ideas.

"Can we petition the King-"

"No." Aten shook his head. "The price of being away from the Kingdom is that we need to solve our own issues, but we don't need to adhere to the strict rules that are *in* the city."

"Why doesn't *he* do something?" Someone pointed at Joe, who raised an eyebrow.

"What would *I* do?" He blinked around the room, finding that everyone was staring at him. "What?"

"You always seem to have the answer we need!" The same Officer tried to smile, but it looked like it was painted on.

"Alright... uhh... we go find a hornet nest, poke it, and make them *really* mad..." Joe trailed off as people shook their heads in disgust. "What? What am I going to do against a giant mob of potentially *thousands* of low-level people? I'm good at making buildings and taking down very large, very *slow*, single-target creatures! I don't do anti-personnel!"

"You could..." Someone else started, trailing off after a moment. "You know, I don't actually know what your range of abilities is."

"Making buildings. Taking down single-target, *slow* creatures." Joe spoke in a serious tone while maintaining eye contact. "Everything else is just critical thinking and game logic, guys. C'mon. *Some* of you were gamers, right?"

Silence filled the tent, and Aten cleared his throat. "Most of the people gathered here were either in the military before this, or were investment bankers that helped fund the Guild at the start."

"Ah..." Joe realized that he had no idea how the Guild had survived this long. "So... I'm sure you all have some impressive skills in logistics, coordination, and long-term planning. Take this as you will, with all due respect, but *seriously*, Aten? Get some gamers in here. We need *creative* solutions to this. *Game* solutions. Stability is great, but I wouldn't be surprised if our location was leaked because someone decided to run a public relations marketing campaign!"

Hammerwords has taken effect! You have lost a full rank of reputation with someone!

There was some nervous shifting, and Joe noted a few winces. If there *hadn't* been a marketing plan, there was one that had been *about* to go out. "Aten, I'm sorry, but you need to take a look at this Guild from a different light. Stable is good, yes.

Smart, even. But we need people who will test the limits of what is *possible* in this new world."

"I thought that was what *you* were for." A snide comment sounded out, though Joe didn't see where it came from.

"If that's true, *if* I am the only one doing this, I need *way* more resources than I'm getting," Joe replied calmly, though his blood was boiling. "I also need the *authority* to make expensive calls, and I need to know what the limits are. Another thing: there's a good chance that if we start acting like the military, we are going to lose our top guild members. Knock that junk off. Here is how you all need to look at things: the most powerful people in this world are likely going to be min-maxing introverts. They will spend every single day getting better at *everything*, because this is their *dreamworld*. Talk to them, get on their good side, and *respect* them…"

Joe glared in the general direction the snide comment had come from, "Then, when we give you advice, listen carefully to that advice. It's gonna be strange, but that's *game logic*. You treat this place like Earth, and all of us are going to fall behind."

Aten nodded seriously, clearly understanding what Joe was talking about. "Fair point. I'll ask around, but please make yourself available if we need something from you."

"That sounds fine, but don't expect me to actively attack a mob of weak, hungry people. I won't do it," Joe bluntly told him. "I'll work on defense, but I'm not taking the fight to them."

Aten nodded again, and the meeting continued. "I want to talk about setting up large standing stones around town that are numbered. This way, they can be used as a reference for navigation. Since we don't have street signs…"

Joe supported that plan, and the next, and… by the time the meeting was *finally* over, he was in a foul mood. He went off to find some lunch and sat with the first person he recognized. "Hey… ah… Crim, right?"

The cleric nodded, his mouth full of sandwich. He swallowed, then spoke, "Hey. Joe, right? Good memory for names."

"The bright red robes help." Joe admitted, looking over the other man's red clothes and hair. "What are you up to today?"

"Mm. Lunch currently, then back to testing out my skills," Crim told him, excitedly clenching his fists. "I just got to level fifteen. Got a *beautiful* spell: Wave of Flame. It starts enemies on fire, and sends their allies into a directed rage against opponents. Kinda hard to test out of combat, though."

Joe sighed and groaned. "Man… can I vent to you really quick? I really have a hard time trusting people with this sort of personal information, but…"

"I mean…" Crim took a big bite of food and waved at his plate. Around the food hanging out of his mouth, he said, "Captive audience, go fer it."

"Alright. I feel like I'm reaching a point in my growth where I'm running into trouble. Specifically, I'm having issues getting all set up and going with new or interesting spells or skills. I'm getting frustrated, and I'm unsure what to do."

"Can you elaborate?" Crim quizzed him. Joe couldn't tell if it was because Crim wanted to hear more, or because he wanted to focus on chewing, but either way, Joe decided to go for it.

"Alright… so… I feel like I'm lacking in abilities and ways to go about learning or doing new things. Everyone else seems to be getting all sorts of cool, unique powers and abilities, and I'm over here spending a week at a time learning a new aspect of what I can do." Joe shrugged helplessly. "I mean, it makes the skill ranks increase really well, but everyone else just *gets* abilities when they level."

Crim considered for a moment. "Well, what sort of cleric abilities are you getting? If you are picking things that work together, you'll have an easier time leveling all of them up."

"I've gotten *nothing,* man! Everything I *do* have is basically a skill evolution from level one." Joe scowled as he thought about his healing skill, Mend, as well as Cleanse. "I keep finding new and interesting ways to apply them, to make them do what I need. You know, *great* for skill levels… but I was supposed to get

Cleric abilities as I leveled, like *you* are. I guess I messed that up pretty badly somehow."

Crim slowly chewed his bite, swallowed, then spoke."Uh… I mean… when was the last time you went to an altar and asked for your skills?"

Joe went as still as stone. Over the next minute, Crim finished his sandwich, then poked Joe hard enough to shake him out of his shock. "Hey. You okay? Did you hear me?"

"Please tell me that you were making a joke."

"What?" Crim started eating his fried vegetables. "You've really never gone and *asked* for the abilities? Why do you think Clerics are always hanging out at altars and such? For funzies?"

"You're *kidding* me."

CHAPTER THREE

Joe stood in front of the altar of Tatum, glaring through the flickering light at the unassuming book-shaped pedestal. "Alright, Occultatum. I know that you gave me hints in the past that I needed to use what I already had, but I really thought that you were talking about ritual stuff, or my Jumplomancer abilities. Would it have been so hard to say 'Come and get these abilities'?"

He sighed when there was no answer. There *shouldn't* be, as Tatum was locked away, but an answer was something that he had come to expect when he was at the altars. Still… this was a class thing, and he should still be able to get his abilities! Joe placed his hands on the book, and said, "Please give me my Cleric abilities."

Greetings, Champion of Tatum! Your Cleric class level is considered equal to your character level, as you started as a hidden class! As a Cleric, you gain an ability or spell every third level. Calculating… level is fifteen! You are owed an ability from level three, six, nine, twelve, and fifteen!

As you are a Champion, and not a standard Cleric, you get to choose the school that your Cleric abilities come from! As Occultatum is a 'Neutral' deity, you can choose 'neutral', 'good', or 'evil' aligned abilities from the school of your choice. Would you like to choose your level three ability? Yes / No.

"Yes; yes, I would." Joe sighed and watched as the stone book in front of him started to shine. In a moment, several glowing words awaited him. "Alright… Abjuration, conjuration, divination, enchantment, evocation, illusion… necromancy? Finally, transmutation. Any tooltips, help on what these mean? No? Alright… I think I mostly understand them, anyway."

"I think abjuration is something along the lines of auras or buffs; conjuration means to create something; divination lets you either look at something or tell the future. Enchanting should be as straightforward as putting an effect on something; evocation… is that spells like a Mage would have? Illusion, mess with people; necromancy deals with the dead. Gonna avoid that one. Transmutation means to transform one thing into another." He stared at the options, then touched Abjuration.

Would you like to select an Abjuration ability? This choice cannot be changed. Yes / No.

"Ah. Don't get to see the options, huh?" Joe thought about it for a long moment, then selected 'no'. "I need a new way to deal damage. Evocation it is."

Evocation is the act of calling upon or summoning a spirit, demon, god or other supernatural agent through the power of your will, mana, and potentially various sacrifices. Choose a spell.

Spell options available for evocation: Dark Lightning Strike. Heavenly Lightning Strike. Purge Invisibility. Radiant Ripple (locked). Searing Light. Seething Darkness. Sunshine. Zap.

"Locked? Why is that locked?" Joe touched the spell, and it luckily expanded into a description. "Release a ripple of divine power that damages anything within fifteen feet hostile to either you or your deity. Locked, as your deity has… no divine energy to spare. Well, poo. Yet another reason to finish that quest up."

"Sunshine is out, only makes things glow. Might be good against vampires, but nah. Zap is a bolt of electricity, seems to be neutral. Mmmkay. No need to get the purge invis, seems pretty specific. Heavenly Bolt… can only be used in a storm?

Nah. Searing light or seething darkness? Kinda already have the dark; could I combine that with the light, or would that make them both useless? No... Dark Lightning Strike is the winner here." Joe looked over the skill description one last time, then accepted it as his spell.

Spell gained: Dark Lightning Strike (Novice I). You raise your hand up towards the sky and issue a request to Occultatum to strike you and your enemies with dark lightning. The sky summons a massive bolt of black lightning to hit anyone within a 5+(n/4) foot radius of you, then spreads out across the ground an additional 10+(n/2) feet where n = skill level. The lightning bolt deals 10n dark damage to all affected beings OR 5n dark damage if impacted by the ground spread. Cost: 100 mana. Cooldown: 360 seconds.

"Yeah... this would have been *really* handy at level three," Joe sighed as he read the spell. If he had been using it over the last few weeks, the spell would have been *amazing* by now. "Ah, well... it'll get there. At least I am able to work on it *now.*"

For his sixth level spell, Joe took an abjuration option, and gained 'Antimagic Aura'. For his ninth, he took an enchanting option; acquiring an intricate knowledge of the enchanting spellform for 'Zone of Circumlocution'. At twelve, he took a transmutation ability called 'Corify'. For his final level fifteen choice, Joe took 'Knowledge (Occultatum Exclusive)'. As he stepped back from the altar, the glow faded and Joe found himself smiling happily. That had been *wild.*

"Hey! That took a long time; what's the holdup?"

Joe yelped, turning with a bolt of darkness on his fingertips ready to be unleashed. "Crim! You scared the *abyss* outta me!"

"Right, sorry. What didja get?" Crim ignored Joe's dark-coated hand and leaned in to hear the juicy details.

"Ah. A lightning strike, an aura ability, an enchanting ability, and a couple other things," Joe distractedly rattled off.

"*Details,* man!" Crim demanded boisterously.

"No real point in details for most of them just yet; I'm planning to combine them with other skills." Joe pulled open his

Soul Forge and started placing abilities together. "Want to help me with that?"

"I mean…" Crim paused, then shrugged. "Your funeral, man. Hope they don't turn into trash. You'll let me know if the combos work?"

"Yeah." Joe perused his large sheet of abilities and sighed. It had been getting out of hand, and a bunch of new skills wouldn't help him keep everything organized. "I'm planning to take the aura skill and combine it with two of my healing abilities. I think that they will complement each other well. As soon as I got the aura ability, a reward I gained from my skill 'Cleanse' went off and let me know that they had high compatibility. I'm going to use that and 'Group heal' to make a healing aura that dampens magic and removes debuffs."

"Hmm." Crim's tone made Joe pause. "Well… I've heard that order is important. If you want it to remain an aura, make sure that is the first thing added. Then I'd suggest the order of what is important to you."

Joe nodded, adding in Antimagic Aura, Cleanse, and Group Heal. He looked over the list and tried to decide if there was anything else he needed to add in. He decided that, since he was at an altar, he would use 'Query' to ask Tatum. As soon as his skill activated, his eyes landed on 'Channeling'. The word seemed to glow, and was extra bold for a bare second. "*What?* No way, I use that for practically everything!"

There was no reply, which wasn't a surprise at this point, and his skill was now on cooldown. Joe grumbled and tossed the skill into the mix. The worst outcome was that he would need to relearn how to channel, and the Mage's College could make that happen. Joe accepted the loss of the four skills and a chunk of gold; then was notified that his skill would appear in forty-eight hours. Instantly, he felt weaker as the four skills vanished.

"Ugh. I'm going to have to drink *water* again." Joe grimaced at the thought. He had gotten used to simply *hydrating* himself when he needed a pick-me-up. Needing to rely on drinking plain water again turned his stomach. "I'll need to *shower* too! No! I didn't think this through! Give me my skills back!"

"Trouble, Joe?" Crim caught Joe just before he could fall into despair.

"Just… I'm fine." Joe sighed and looked at his other skills. He decided to clean up some skills that he didn't often use, though he had no idea if they would work together. With a thought, Speech, Acting, Reading, Teaching, Drawing, Staff Mastery… and after a long moment, 'Medic', were all tossed into the mix to see what would happen. Thirty-two hundred gold loss and an eighty-four hour wait awaited him as he pressed accept. "That helped… still have a ton of skills I don't use though. It's just so *expensive* to clean them up."

Crim wrote down the skills and the order Joe put them in the Soul Forge, then made a copy for himself. "Tell me more about your skills from Tatum!"

"Swear not to share with anyone else?" Joe stared Crim in the eye, and the other man solemnly agreed. Now that Crim would gain a Warlock title if he told another person, Joe felt comfortable discussing the skills. "I got a spell called 'Corify', which adds a chance equal to skill level to make a creature solidify a Core upon death. Sounds cool, but if I use it on a regular creature, that would still only get me a one percent chance to get a trash-tier Core. Good for grinding it up, but it costs a hundred mana per cast."

"Yikes." Crim winced. "What's your spell stability looking like?"

"Pretty awesome at fifty-five percent." Joe grinned at Crim's shocked expression. "I got a spellform for enchanting, but I'm not sure how useful it'll be. Listen to this. 'You create a thirty-foot-radius zone. Beings within the zone that attempt to say something rude, vulgar, or hostile are compelled to say something positive instead.'"

"That seems kinda…" Crim paused as Joe continued speaking.

"This effect extends to any *text* which includes rude, vulgar, or hostile language. Creatures who attempt to make rude gestures end up making some friendly gesture. Paintings and drawings which would be considered vulgar change to become wholesome. This does not stop hostile actions from occurring. The enchantment must be placed on an object that is not easily moved, or it will not function. Examples include anchors, spikes driven into the ground, large stones, a bar countertop, a table too large to fit through a doorway, or any permanent construction."

"What in the actual abyss are you going to use *that* for?" Crim's face was bunched up in disgust.

"No idea… it would have been an amazing addition to a cafeteria in my old high school, though." Joe chuckled along with Crim, and the two of them started walking toward the exit. Joe's eyes gleamed as he looked over the final skill he had acquired.

Skill gained: Knowledge (Occultatum Exclusive) (Novice I). You tap into the System, searching for the secrets of this world. When you cast this spell, you gain one level of Lore in a chosen Lore skill, up to the maximum of the tier of this skill. Current maximum: Novice IX. Cooldown: 24 hours. Cost: 2,000 mana.

"Overall, I think this was worth doing. Thanks for the advice, Crim." Joe stared at his final skill, eager to test it out for himself. "Gotta go find somewhere private…"

CHAPTER FOUR

"I have a dungeon I'd like to have the group run through." Jess ambushed Joe as he walked out of the Temple, and she was clearly still upset about his reaction that morning; if the way she slapped a sheet of paper onto Joe's chest was any indication. "Since you are a guild officer, I sent a couple people to secure it for us."

"Oh, nice!" Joe looked at the information on the paper, then frowned. "Oh. Totally unknown what the interior is like?"

"Yeah, I want to use it to train up my new class." Jess taunted him with the fact that he had no idea what her class actually was. "Hurry up; everyone else is already gathered."

"Are you seriously going to ask me to help you train your class, but not tell me what it is? Nah. Tell me, or you can work on it without my help." Joe leveled a stare at her. He was *also* a little salty about their previous interaction.

"You suck. Fine… I'm a Necromantic Logistician." Jess waited for a reaction, but only got a blank stare in return. "Alright… I guess you have no idea what that means, so I didn't need to be so secretive. Basically, I am a support class necromancer, and I get experience for setting up trips. I can also use my raised creatures to scout out a dungeon or unknown area, and I can draw up a map. After the area is cleared, I get experience for how accurate my map was."

"Oh." Joe searched for something to say, but came up empty. "Neat. Yeah, we'll go ahead and do this dungeon in a little while. I am just on my way to meet with Aten. Can we go to the dungeon tomorrow?"

"Sure can. Everyone is already waiting, but I'm sure they'll be fine with disappointment." Jess gave a thumbs up as Joe scowled at her, "At least that'll give me more time to set up the trip, which means more experience in the long run."

"Silver linings everywhere." Joe walked toward the Guild Hall *again*. He had no idea why Aten had waited till he left to call him back. It was either a power play, or something else was going on. He was brought directly to Aten's office, which was now an actual enclosed room with *only* Aten in it. "Hi, Aten. What's going on?"

"Close the door?" Aten waited for the door to latch before waving at a seat in front of him. "Alright, man… we need to talk about the direction of the guild and what you want to see going forward. I probably don't need to tell you this, but you really upset a few people earlier when you basically told them that their ideas were outdated and useless in this new world."

Joe stared at Aten for a long moment before exploding, "Abyss those *debuffs*! I wasn't trying to say anything like that, I was trying to point out that we needed to look at things in game terms!"

"Debuff…? Oh… this 'Hammerwords' thing you were describing that no one else knows about?" Aten rolled his eyes. "You need to stop blaming other things and take action to better yourself. If this thing really does exist, then to fix it, you need to work on your charisma score, right? Take that skeleton man with you when you do, will ya?"

"Where is training available for charisma?" Joe ignored the slight and leaned forward eagerly. "I've been trying to figure it out, but the only thing I can think of is the Bard's College."

"They have a good program, but you can raise charisma by doing anything non-combat that is used to bring joy to others. Even if it isn't very good. Dancing, singing, art, carving, sculpting, pleasant conversations… stuff like that. Anyway, that isn't why I brought you here."

"Do tell."

"Alright, I'll get right to it." Aten took a deep breath and leaned back. "I need you to really focus on getting your next Specialization. We need to get ahead of the crazy amounts of people on… ah… Midgard… and start making a base of operations in the next Zone."

"I had planned on getting stronger as fast as possible, but what's the deal here?" Joe narrowed his eyes. It was sounding *suspiciously* like Aten was trying to get rid of him. "Getting pressured to keep only the extra-friendly folk around?"

"Nothing like that, Joe." Aten arched a brow, clearly understanding where he was coming from. "We know exactly how useful it is to have you around, and we certainly aren't going to throw you away for personal politics. No, what I am worried about is the absolute lack of resources that is going to be hitting the area. We have a food source secured, but when was the last time that you tried to buy up a Core?"

"I haven't needed to in a while." Joe thought for a moment and checked his storage ring and codpiece mentally. "I still have a half dozen common Cores, and one that is worth about five thousand experience. I forget the name, and I don't want to pull it out and check it."

"That was about what I was expecting." Aten nodded sagely, rubbing the beginnings of a moustache. "Everyone has a small personal stock, but the cost of Cores has doubled in the last few days due to the sheer *demand* for them. But it isn't just the Cores. Most resources have skyrocketed in price, which reminds me; thanks for the heads up on that a while back. We were able to buy up a lot of stock while it was relatively low-priced, so we're not suffering like some other people we know."

"Basic supply and demand, Aten." Joe bobbed his head. "Happy to do it, but what are you getting at?"

"I need to give you an *order*, Joe. As Guild Commander, I need you to gain your next Specialization, get to the next Zone, and prepare a safe haven for The Wanderer's Guild. If possible, I need you to start sending resources down to us so that we can get *more* people to their second Specialization." Aten looked Joe in the eye. "I would go myself, but my next Specialization is tied to the ability of my Guild and… ugh… Towny McTownface's town rank."

"What of the other guild officers?" Joe pointedly demanded. "I want to spend a good deal of time consolidating power here and making this town into an amazing city, and that's hard to do when I'm splitting my focus so heavily."

"The officers that I think can manage it? They are getting the same task." Aten leaned close and lowered his voice. "You know as well as I do that of all the people in the Guild… only a small percentage of them will use this opportunity as it should be used. Most will squander it, and resent us as *we* become powerful. Luckily, they will be in no position to affect us. The bankers, the lawyers, the trust fund kids that are our investors? They're likely staying on Midgard *forever*. So this is an order, but also a massive show of faith in your ability to make it happen. Get out of here and make it to the next Zone. I'll follow as soon as I can, and that is where our *really* talented people will group together."

Joe left the Guildhall with his mind weirdly whirling. Aten was giving out a secret task only to competent people? Should he trust that? Believe it? Or should he look into guild politics more deeply? No… if Aten thought he needed to go, he would take it as the compliment it appeared to be. Joe decided to take this as a turning point in his development, and realized that he needed to answer a major question. Essentially, "What do I need for my next rank up? Status."

Name: Joe *'Tatum's Chosen Legend'* Class: Jumplomancer (Actual: Rituarchitect)
Profession: Tenured Scholar (Actual: Arcanologist)
Character Level: 15 Exp: 134,813 Exp to next level: 1,187
Rituarchitect Level: 3 Exp: 5,940 Exp to next level: 60
Hit Points: 330/330
Mana: 1,590/1,590
Mana regen: 30.7/sec (Base 27.91/sec increased by gear)
Stamina: 295/295
Stamina regen: 5.67/sec

Characteristic: Raw score (Modifier)

Strength: 31 (1.31)
Dexterity: 40 (1.40)
Constitution: 38 (1.38)
Intelligence: 106 (3.06)
Wisdom: 77 (2.27)
Charisma: 31 (1.31)
Perception: 60 (2.10)
Luck: 30 (1.30)
Karmic Luck: 0

"Alright… looking good… but I have a long way to go before I can rank up. Sheesh. I need a total of forty-five *thousand* class experience, and I have only five thousand nine hundred and forty. I need to figure out how to boost that by a *lot*." Joe looked at his skill list, and his eyes landed on *Knowledge*. He shivered in anticipation, pulled out one of his two Mana batteries and held it to his chest. "*Knowledge*."

You have activated 'Knowledge'. Which Lore skill would you like to use Knowledge on?

"Ritual Lore."

Invalid target. Skill Ritual Lore is at Apprentice II, and skill Knowledge can only affect skills up to Novice IX.

"At least I know what it looks like." Joe muttered, putting

away his now-spent Mana Battery. "Gotta go get myself some lore skills."

He tried to think of what to do next, and came up empty. When in doubt, head to the library. As Joe walked toward the Pathfinder's Hall, he closed his eyes and listened to the magic in the air. His destination tolled in his ears like soft thunder as his Magical Synesthesia skill kicked in. All around him were the quieter, sharper sounds of enchanted equipment, but none of the screeching that he had started to associate with spells being cast.

"Mmm..." Joe opened his eyes, and they were filled with determination as well as excitement. "Time to do some research. I need to get to class level ten, start looking into new buildings, find material and Cores, and get some lore skills. Aten... you may have given me the kick I needed, buddy. I'll just have to hope that you can afford to devote the resources I'll need to power my way through the ranks."

A flash of light took him from the Temple portion of the Pathfinder's Hall into the main square of Ardania. After about twenty minutes of pushing through the crowd, he found himself in the library. There was a new man at the main desk, who seemed to recognize Joe. He didn't seem very happy, but at least he waved Joe through without stopping him, which Boris had almost always done.

"Common book area..." Joe walked into the largest room of the library and started toward the leftmost section. One of the benefits of setting up the organizational system for the area was that he knew where things should be. "Architecture... let's brush up on history, types of buildings, and anything else that might be useful."

He spent the rest of the day going through books and reading everything that was publicly available about the subject. He took meticulous notes, and at the end of the day, he had a thin stack of paper that he had devoted to the process. Mate, his coffee elemental, had spent most of the day on his lap. Joe found that it had habits similar to a house cat, enjoyed sleeping in warm spaces, and happily bubbled.

Joe *very* much enjoyed the creature. Not only was it giving him life-saving coffee, but as a non-combat familiar, it seemed that this thing was essentially a pet! He decided to look into how to take better care of it. Did it eat or drink; did it need anything beyond mana? He already knew that he could feed it beans to change the coffee flavor, but what else? All of this was information he would seek out, but for the moment he eyed his new skill with glee.

Skill gained: Architectural Lore (Novice II). Allows you to fine-tune Architectural blueprints that you find or create. Can increase the quality of structures or decrease the cost of building them.

"Knowledge, Architectural Lore." Joe felt his mana start moving instantly, but it was a… *strange* feeling. Normally when he used a skill, the mana would flow through and *out* of him. Right now… it was flowing *in* and *up*. Mana was drained out of the battery that Joe had pulled out, and a rush of power entered his brain. Suddenly, he *knew* more about Architecture.

Skill increase: Architectural Lore (Novice III).

Skill increase: Knowledge (Novice II).

"What in the *blazes* is going on in here? The library is closing; get out!"

Joe blinked away his notifications as Boris barreled into the room to find out why mana was surging in his precious library. "Oh. Hey there, Boris. Did you have the day off?"

CHAPTER FIVE

"No, I didn't have the day *off.* I was... why am I telling you this?" Boris shook his head and glared at Joe. "What are you doing, youngster?"

"Research." Joe waved at the table and nodded. "Trying to find out more about my class, get a few lore skills, and find my path to my next Specialization."

"Ah. Well... I can't exactly kick out a Tenured Scholar." Boris seemed as displeased by that fact as he seemed *happy* that Joe had that rank. "Is there anything I can help you with that will get you out of here faster? Truthfully, only so I can go to bed, but the offer stands. What are your reasons for looking into this?"

"I'm trying to find what I need to do to achieve my next Specialization, and I feel that lore is the way to go." Joe pushed his notes across the table and tapped his section headers. "As far as I can tell, there are three main categories of structure that I can make. The first is 'offense', or siege, which looks *amazing.* Buildings that can lob projectiles a quarter of a Zone? Resonating siege towers that cast and amplify a spell from a distance?"

Joe blinked as Boris's head bobbed; the older man was falling asleep. "Right, ahh… 'defense', which allows things like enchanted walls and traps. Also, massive stationary shields or magical auto-turrets. Finally, 'utility', which is mainly used as quality-of-life or support structures that help less *directly* with combat."

Boris glanced at Joe's notes and agreed with him. "These do look interesting. Is there any specific one that you are leaning toward?"

"Honestly… if I can find the path forward on one of these… I think that any of them will be valid. My real concern is that *I* am the class trainer for my class, so if I take something that isn't useful to everyone, there will be a lot of people stuck with my choices." Joe paused and licked his lips. "I'm actually pretty concerned with what I took for my first Specialization. I'm wondering if steering my class away from war was the correct path."

Boris nodded and put a hand on Joe's shoulder. "I think you are doing just fine. You can't decide to be responsible for everyone. If they want a different path, all they need to do is walk it. Now… I think I know of something that may help you."

Joe looked up, hope filling his eyes. Boris arched a brow and continued, "Don't get your hopes up too high. What I am thinking of is going to take a lot of research on my end. I don't mind doing it, because I still feel that the Scholars owe you something. I'll try to have some information for you in a week or two."

"Thank you, Boris." Joe shook the old man's hand.

"Don't run off now; I think that there is something you are overlooking." Boris gave Joe a flat stare over the top of his glasses. "You are a Tenured Scholar, and that is wonderful, but what have you taken for your other professions?"

"So far, I only have the one."

Boris shook his head in annoyance. "Then you are wasting your talents and throwing away experience and benefits. You have a profession that is *currently* based on gathering, so you should take another that is based on production or refinement. Or... it seems you are level fifteen, so take both! You can choose to synergize them well with your class and gain the most benefit from them. My personal recommendation would be something along the lines of paper production or bookbinding. You don't strike me as a blacksmith, for instance."

"Isn't blacksmith a *class*?" Joe quizzed the older man. "What's the difference here?"

"Easy enough." Boris cleared his throat and sat down alongside Joe. "You can have a *profession*, such as blacksmithing, that will give you anything from profession experience to skill bonuses for creating weapons and various metallurgy. Then, *separately*, you have the blacksmith *class*, which will give you things like weapon blueprints, class *and* experience toward your overall level, and will allow for much faster progression. Now, to maximize the potential, a blacksmith would likely take a blacksmith class *and* profession."

"I don't really see the difference there." Joe admitted. "It seems like they do the same thing."

"In a way, yes." Boris nodded, "But have you ever gained *personal* experience for increasing your profession? Or has it always been *profession* experience? I don't mean from quest rewards, of course."

"Honestly… I don't know?" Joe tried to think back, but couldn't remember the details.

"That's fine. The main difference is that a blacksmith *class* can reach say, level twenty, by crafting alone. No fighting required. *Nothing* is technically required, except smithing harder or more intricate items. A person with a blacksmith *profession* can make the same items, use the same tools, be *very* good at it… and be stuck at level one forever, because professions are only about skill. No experience is granted to the person." Boris waved away Joe's next question and pointed at the door. "My bed is calling, and the midnight oil is burning. I hereby rescind my previous statement that I wouldn't kick you out. Get!"

"Pff." Joe stood and helped Boris to his feet while chuckling. "Thanks, Boris. You gave me a lot to think about."

"Yes, yes." Boris waved his hands at Joe to hurry him along. "Out!"

Joe laughed and left with a wave, thinking through his next options. His profession was something that he should really look into, something that he should spend a lot of time researching… "Nah. I'll make Jess do it."

He chuckled as he teleported to Towny McTownface and found his bed. As Joe was disrobing, he heard a crinkle in his pocket. He reached in and pulled out… a paper crane? Was it a secret message of some kind? Joe pulled the paper to unfold it, and the entire thing glowed brilliantly… before exploding into shards of ice. There was a concussive blast that flipped Joe across the room and pinned him to the wall, where he lay feeling strangely lethargic.

Damage taken: 250 (125 x2 sneak attack damage!) Debuff: Chilled. Slowed, movement speed reduced by 25%! You take additional damage from cold damage until 'Chilled' has worn off!

Joe's teeth chattered, and he slowly reached his arm up and touched his chest. He rasped out, "*Mend.*"

Health: 245/330 Debuff: Chilled. Slowed, movement speed reduced by 25%! You take additional damage from cold damage until 'Chilled' has worn off!

"I'm really missing Cleanse right about now." Joe snarled in slow motion. "*Mend.*"

His health returned to full, and Joe slowly pulled himself out of the puddle of frosted blood that he had been lying in. His door slammed open, and a few guild guards looked around. "Joe! You alright there?"

"Jay? I've… never… seen… you… off… duty." Joe's teeth stopped chattering, and his motions became more fluid. The chilled debuff had finally worn off. "Was that a twelve second debuff on *one* spell?"

"Someone *attacked* you?" Jay pulled out what looked like a

riding crop and walked into the room, tossing open the small closet to see if someone was hiding there.

"It was a trap," Joe informed him. "Someone basically put a grenade in my pocket."

"There's a paper on the floor." Jay leaned down and picked it up before Joe could warn him off. "It says 'Wolfpack forever. Hope this helps you chill.' and it is signed 'S'. Know any people that are after you?"

"Way too many." Joe admitted stiffly. "Thanks for coming to check on me, but I'm gonna get some sleep now."

"Fair enough, take care." Jay stepped out of the room and closed the door behind him.

Joe flopped onto the bed, staining the sheets in an instant. "Ugh. I miss Cleanse. Alright… sleep. Figure this out later."

The night seemed to fly by, and far too soon, Joe found himself on the way to an unknown dungeon with his group early the next morning. He explained to all of them what had happened to him, and made his request for Jess to look at what professions would synergize well with what he was doing.

"I can certainly look into that, no problems there. It aligns well with what I am trying to research right now anyway, but let me know if anything changes." Jess got more information from him, focusing mainly on what he was building, the things he was trying to do, and where he saw himself going.

When all of her questions had been answered, Joe looked around at the others. "Hey guys, listen. I got ordered to make serious progress toward my next class, and I am wondering if you all need help as well. I don't want to have to leave Midgard without you, so if you need something that I can provide, just tell me."

"Sounds good!" Poppy was in a strangely good mood today. Joe didn't want to comment, so he focused on the road. "Did I tell you all that my girl learned how to do somersaults last night?"

Ah. That would do it. It was strange to Joe that the steely-eyed Duelist who was driven to perfect his skills with a rapier…

was also a doting doe-eyed father that could be put into a fuzzy pink mood for *days* after seeing his daughter. Joe certainly wasn't complaining. "That's *excellent*, Poppy! How's everything else going?"

"Mmm. Good. The Pathfinder's Hall allows for excellent skill sharpening, but I truly need to test myself in combat in order to consolidate my abilities with battle experience." Poppy gave Joe a dark glance that was *much* more his normal style. "Joe, we have seen neither combat nor time together for too long. More than needing resources, we need to make sure that we are progressing smoothly together."

"I fully agree." Joe nodded and glanced over at Alexis and Bard, but they were fully lost in their own conversation. Jaxon and Jess were arguing together, so Joe broke into their conversation. "Jess, will this be a good place for-"

"Jaxon, there *are* no other people with that skill! How the *abyss* am I supposed to help you find your next Specialization?" Jess ignored Jaxon and turned to focus on Joe, but Jaxon was having none of that.

"It has to be a cross between a tamer and a Chiropractor!" Jaxon demanded enthusiastically. "Or a *druid* of some sort!"

"Joe, we're here." Jess kept her eyes locked on Joe. She pointed at a hole in the side of a hill that was flanked by two guards from the guild. "Watch this, guys."

Jess pulled out a bag and started dumping snakes onto the ground. Bard yelped a curse and jumped back, but Jaxon's eyes lit up. They dimmed as he looked closer. "Aww. They're dead."

"Yup." Jess touched one on the head. "*Slither again. Become my eyes and ears.*"

The snake corpse started moving, then coiled up and looked at her. It remained unnaturally still until the spell was cast nine more times, creating more serpentine servants. Poppy started chuckling, and Jess looked at him with pure confusion. "What? This is *super* cool! They can scout! I even combined one of my rogue abilities that lets me use them to steal items out of people's pockets!"

"I'm sorry, Jess… it's just… you *raise snakes*. Ha! You can *steal* with your serpents? From people? Is… *hee*… is that skill called *pocket* snake, by any chance?" Poppy only laughed harder as Jess turned red. "The fact that you aren't answering the question tells me everything I needed to know!"

"You know *what*?" Jess growled dangerously, turning on the Duelist. He shied away, laughing, and she grumbled as she sent the snakes past the guards and into the open dungeon behind them. Jess pulled out a paper and a pencil, starting to draw a map out for the team while muttering, "Dirty minded… I better start getting some *respect* around here."

CHAPTER SIX

"Anyone know how to increase the luck stat? I remember something about games of chance, but I never followed up on that." Joe finally broke the lingering silence. The only sound for the last ten minutes had been the slow scratching of Jess's quill on paper, and the repetitiveness was starting to drive him crazy.

"Yeah." Bard perked up and scooted closer, leaving tracks in the dirt. "Ah'd be happy ta show yah. It's gonna cost yah, though."

"Are you seriously going to...?" Joe trailed off as a deck of cards appeared in Bard's hand. "What are you doing?"

"Poker."

"I'm in!" Poppy scooted closer, and Bard nodded before looking to see if anyone else wanted to join. One of the guards at the entrance to the dungeon was staring hopefully, but a glare from Jess made him go back to guarding with a sigh. Bard had Jaxon sit, and dealt him in.

"If I wanted to take your money, you would all just *hand* it to me. 'Oh, I need money to make *poisons* for you all'." Alexa pretended to swoon while speaking in a falsetto. "Pff. Yeah, right."

"...Right. We're gonna have a *talk* later. I somehow feel like I've been overpaying you." Poppy's narrow eyes were locked on a suddenly-sheepish Alexis, but only until the first hand was dealt.

Joe looked at his cards and tried to remember what everything was worth. "Can I trade these cards for another?"

"Nah, this is Texas Hold 'Em." Bard snorted, then waved at the empty spot in front of Joe. "Big blind, two copper."

The next ten minutes saw Joe losing hand after hand. He was *pretty* sure that Poppy was cheating somehow, but there was no way he could prove it. At the fifteen-minute mark, he decided to stay in even though he only had a two and a seven. Since he had been either folding or losing badly, both Bard and Poppy also stayed in till the end. Joe flipped his cards and sighed. "Two reds."

The others started chortling, then Jaxon nudged him. "Joe, you have a *flush*."

"Hey, no table talking!" Bard stopped laughing as the others leaned in to check. With a grumble, they let Joe take the coins.

Characteristic point training completed! +1 to luck! This stat cannot be increased further by any means other than system rewards, study, or practice for twenty-four hours game time.

"Nice." Joe grinned as the notification scrolled across his line of sight.

"Yeah, yeah. Blinds are up, now it is going to be two-" Poppy was cut off as Jess jumped to her feet.

"Done!" she walked over to Joe and proudly held out a detailed map. "Take and bind this."

Joe gingerly took the still-wet parchment and looked it over. It was decently drawn, and a prompt appeared as soon as he had looked it over.

Would you like to add the information from 'Uncommon Quality Dungeon Map' to your personal map? Durability: 1/1. Yes / No.

Joe selected 'Yes', and the map in his hand converted to ashes. He shook his hand to get most of the particles off, and grimaced as he realized that he didn't have his shield active.

Fifteen hundred mana poured into his Exquisite Shell, and Joe blinked as he realized something. He had fifteen hundred and ninety mana… which was exactly the amount granted by his intelligence score. If that was the case… he looked at his Mana Manipulation skill, and saw that it was no longer reducing the amount of mana he had! From now on as it ranked up, the stupid skill would *boost* the amount of mana he had! *Finally*!

"There goes an hour of work." Jess sighed as the ashes scattered in the wind, but she could only shrug and wave at the dungeon. "I *really* hope it helps. My experience bar is *hungry*."

Bard was still struggling to put all the cards back in their case. Jaxon patted Jess on the arm as they started walking to the entrance. "I'm sure it won't be *completely* useless. Chin up."

Bard tapped Joe on the shoulder, "Games o' chance. That's how ya train up your luck stat. Ya need ta have actual stakes, and ya need ta naw *cheat*, then play for a full hour. Pretty simple, compared ta other characteristics. Ya do tend ta lose ah lotta coin right away, but ya get increasing returns as yer luck boosts."

"Thanks, Bard!" Joe flipped one of the coins he had recently acquired into the air and caught it. "Poker, huh? Seems like a good way to relax at the same time as doing some training."

"Only reason gamblin's legal anywhere ya wanna go." Bard winked at Joe, then strode forward to the front of the group. He was their tank, and they didn't yet know what sort of attacks were going to be coming their way.

The party went past the guards, who saluted Joe before getting back into position. This dungeon was now owned by The Wanderer's Guild, and would have a rotating guard at all times to make sure no one else snuck in. As soon as they entered the open cavern, a small minimap appeared in the upper right corner of Joe's eyesight, and he *whooped*. "*Yes*! I got a minimap! I've wanted this since I *joined* Eternium!"

"What!" Alexis scooted closer, "Is it because of that map? It *is*, isn't it? Ahh, I *knew* that there was a reason people were quietly buying up all the maps they could get their grimy hands on!"

"Wait…" Joe's smile stretched across his face in a way that made Alexis compare him to Jaxon. "You mean to tell me that I can have a minimap all the *time* if I get a full map of an area?"

"Probably?" Alexis smirked as Joe started getting all wound up. "Dude, calm down and focus, please. You have the tendency to get all scatterbrained when you find something new to play with. We *are* in a dungeon, right? Oh, right on cue…"

You have entered a level nine recurring dungeon. Use caution, as self-sacrifice is the way forward but may require more than you can give. Keep an eye out for the resources, as well as the protectors! This dungeon will only remain until it is cleared, after which point the area will reset and be unenterable for twelve hours!

"So, are we always going to get vaguely ominous notifications whenever we enter a dungeon now?" Jaxon swatted at the air, likely swiping the screen away. "Is it just me, or have things slowly been getting more dangerous in this, um, Zone?"

"I *know* that I've seen a creature level up." Poppy offered easily, keeping his eyes on the walls as they walked. "It seems likely that we aren't the only things getting stronger. I heard a rumor about a boss encounter, in fact. People were trying to bum-rush it, so they just charged back in whenever they died. By the time they realized that it was getting stronger, there was no way anyone in the area could beat it. They had to call in an entire guild just to bring that bad boy down."

"Which means that the reward for actually beating it was almost worthless, I bet." Alexis chimed in. "Looks like there is a monster ahead?"

Joe flinched and checked the minimap. "Shoot, yeah. It's marked; I was just really getting into that conversation. My bad."

"Remember what I said about *focusing*?" Alexis archly reminded him. "What is that thing? Looks like an overgrown eye as a body with tentacles instead of limbs?"

Memories of playing DnD in days long past sprang up in

Joe's mind, and he let out a quiet whimper as the creature spotted them. Luckily, it didn't seem to be a copyrighted creature, but as it saw Bard... both the creature and the Skald had a slightly purple aura pop into existence around them. Jaxon ran at the beast, screaming, "Kill it with fire!"

He punched the creature right in its overgrown eye, but the beast didn't even blink. Bard, on the other hand, screamed bloody murder. "My *nose*! What hit me?"

"Everyone, stop!" Joe ordered instantly. "It isn't moving, and I'm betting that the dungeon description meant that the only way to hurt the enemies in it would be to take damage. Let me try my scan."

He stared at the creature, activating Intrusive Scan and holding it for the maximum five seconds that he could.

Everwatch.
Highest stat: Willpower
Ongoing effects: Levitation, Boneless Body, Damage Trade II, Instant Stasis, Self-Damage = only Damage.

Joe waited for the weak points to appear, but no red appeared on the body of the Everwatch. "Alright... looks like it has a 'Damage Trade' effect, and level two means that... it returns all damage done back to its target. It only takes half of the self-damage? Let's leave - *ahh*!"

He had turned around, and screeched when he found that Bard was covered head to toe in a blood red aura. It took a moment before Joe realized that he was currently seeing the weak points of the Everwatch. "Well... it's in stasis, so we can't hurt it. Let's just go around?"

"Joe." Alexis pointed at the creature's tentacle, which was wrapped around a small bronze key. "I have a feeling that this is as far as we go if we don't beat that thing."

Looking at his minimap, Joe saw that there was a door around the bend of the tunnel. He went and looked at it, confused as to how the dungeon could have been mapped out if… ah. "There's an inch gap under and over the door. Plenty of room for snakes to move around, plenty to stop us from going forward."

He touched the door, and a notification appeared.

You do not have the orange key!

"So, it's gonna be like that, huh?" Joe shook himself. "I can't stand it when dungeons *force* you to fight the monsters. What if I just wanted to sneak through and empty out the treasure room? That seems like it should be a viable option!"

"Can someone jus' *stab* me so we can get ah move on?" Bard demanded, taking off his armor so that it wouldn't get damaged by his teammates. Jaxon reacted instantly, punching Bard in the face hard enough that the Skald dropped to the ground and had his head bounce off the stone floor.

"Two hits for the price of one!" Jaxon crowed as a PvP aura appeared over his head. He pulled back his foot to kick the fallen Skald. "I hit you, *you* hit the floor!"

"Jaxon, stop!" Joe demanded. He was watching the Ever-watch, and his Dungeoneer title showed him that its health hadn't decreased at all. "Self-damage is only damage… Bard, you gotta do the damage to yourself, or it won't count against that thing."

"Oh, come *on*. Ah have'ta… gah, keep that healing spell handy." Bard pulled back his axe and swung it at his exposed leg, pulling it to the side at the last second. "*Ahhh* mah brain *sure* doesn't want me hurtin mahself."

"Now we know why the dungeon said that it 'may require more than you can give'." Poppy muttered to Joe, who simply nodded.

"If you can't-" Alexis started, only to be cut off as Bard closed his eyes and swung downward with a bellow.

CHAPTER SEVEN

"Gonna be honest wit' yah." Bard took and released a deep breath as he rubbed his legs and arm. "I am not ah big fan o' this dungeon. Ah know ahm gettin' healed, but ah feel like it's still bleedin'."

The group had gotten into a fight with two more Everwatch monsters, and had learned several not-so-fun facts. When you were chosen as the target of the self-sacrifice, you were the only one that got experience from the monster. The damage done was on a point-by-point basis, not percentage based, which meant that it *really* made sense for the tank to try to get targeted. Finally, the dungeon was a bust so far.

"I think that'll fade really fast here, Bard. Mental effects and all that. On *my* end, I can't believe that they haven't dropped a *single* item except keys yet." Joe was getting a little grumpy about the fact that they had agreed to come and try out the dungeon. He had been trying out his 'Corify' spell, but the stasis effect made the Everwatch immune. Not only that, but as soon as the monster was defeated, it seemed to rot at an accelerated rate; there was no way to get useful materials from the things.

"It's *fine*. Jess has been working her tail off, we can do this for her," Jaxon spoke up. The others looked around, then finally rested their eyes on the man. Had he just said something... nice? Helpful? *Normal*? Jaxon smiled extra-brightly at the attention, and the others slowly went back to watching their surroundings.

"Wait!" Joe's eyes caught on the floor, then checked the map again. There was a green outline indicated on the wall that had been tagged with a small question mark, and Joe's dungeoneering title and perception worked together to highlight an irregular crack. "I'm pretty sure there is a secret door here."

"*Please* let it be ah shortcut," Bard muttered gruffly. Poppy and Alexis worked together, running their hands around the outline until they found a small catch, and the door popped open. They stepped through, looking around cautiously. To their right was a hallway, while to their left was a large door with a skull on it.

"Oh, look," Poppy deadpanned. "A shortcut."

Bard beamed and yanked Jaxon into a hug, and together the group opened the door to the Boss room. It swung shut behind them with a *click*, and the boulder in the center of the square room *moved*. Specifically, it parted; exposing a massive version of the Everwatch monsters. Bard groaned as a red aura appeared around himself and the Boss. Unlike the smaller versions, it didn't stop moving; instead lifting into the air and slowly drifting toward them.

"Intrusive Scan." Joe stared at the creature, and it stared back.

Evan the Everwatch.
Highest stat: Willpower
Ongoing effects: Levitation, Boneless Body, Damage Trade III, Self-Damage = only Damage.

"It has Damage Trade three, but no stasis. Looks like we are going to have to-" Joe was cut off by an intense whipping sound.

Crack. The Everwatch hit itself, leaving behind a red welt that quickly faded and appeared on Bard.

"*Arther's* thundering *Seat* that hurt!" Blood started dripping out through Bard's armor, and Joe slapped a heal on him. "Joe, what *was* that?"

The Rituarchitect scanned the information on Damage Trade three, his eyes widening, then narrowing. "His version of Damage Trade makes it so that the first to strike themselves gives all the damage to the other! It switches targets, too!"

Indeed, the aura had vanished from Bard, but no one had been expecting or looking for it. Another resounding crack, and Alexis was clutching at her backside and yelping. Joe started glowing red, and instantly slapped himself in the face. He only did a single point of damage, but it was enough to make the aura vanish and appear on Jaxon.

Jaxon started poking himself in the wrist, and as a tentacle whipped toward the Everwatch, he took a breath and activated, "*Adjust*!"

There was a sickening crack as Jaxon's wrist twisted and broke, but the damage vanished in an instant; leaving behind only the memory of pain as the Boss's health bar dropped by a quarter. It wailed, and the target switching started happening faster and faster. As its strikes came down on itself, the aura kept shifting to a new target just before impact. If the team member was able to hit themselves first, the aura was interrupted and the creature's blows damaged itself.

Conversely, if the team was too slow, they often injured themselves without hurting the Boss. The fight quickly became a bizarre version of rock-paper-scissors, with every being in the room becoming heavily damaged rather quickly. But in the end, the Everwatch was a level ten beast, and the majority of the humans were at or near level fifteen. The humans also had Joe, who was able to keep them healed up. Inevitably, the Everwatch fell.

Experience gained: 400.

Jaxon walked up to the beast and shifted his hands into a pair of T-rex heads. "Lefty! Terror! Din-din!"

"Craw!"

"Nyah!"

Joe and the others looked on with complicated expressions as the Everwatch was torn into. A good amount of it was devoured before it could rot too much, and Jaxon babbled and cooed at his hands until the effect wore off and they shifted back to regular hands. In his left hand, he held a golden key, and he tossed it to Joe. "Lefty nearly *choked* on this mean little key!"

Joe grimaced as he caught the key, which was still coated in rotting meat and dinosaur saliva. "Um… thanks."

The door was opposite the one they had previously entered, and it swung open on well-oiled hinges. The key fell apart as soon as the door opened to reveal five small treasure chests. Poppy walked over to one and popped it open, pulling out a small skill book. "Huh. Look at that. 'Mass Riposte'. Never seen *that* before…"

Each person that opened a chest got a manual that was specifically useful to them, so Joe was *very* excited to see what was waiting for him. He pulled open one of the small chests, noticing a flash of golden light as he did so. It was likely that the treasure was added into the chest as it was opened, or just before. He *really* wanted to know how that worked. Joe pulled out his book and looked at the title in confusion.

"'Alchemically Enhanced Components'?" Joe read the information that popped up out loud, too shocked to stay silent. "Book *three* of *five* in the 'Basics of Rituals' series?"

He couldn't wait to see what information it contained; he had to know *now.* Joe pulled open the cover and read the first page out loud. "Foreword. This set of books is designed to teach the basic requirements for effective ritual usage, and it is recommended that you read and understand all five before beginning your pursuit of this particular arcane art. By the time you read this book, you should have read 'Ritual Circles and You' as well as 'Magical Matrices: Ritual Edition'."

Joe kept going, even as he realized that he was being led outside by the rest of his comrades. "After this, don't forget to study 'Advanced Enchanted Ritual Circles' and 'Micro or Macro: The Pros and Cons of Mega Circles'. Don't sell yourself short... make sure to read the 'Journeyman's Rules of Rituals' and 'Master of Rituals'... *series*?"

Blinking at the sudden light hitting him as he walked outside, Joe looked around woozily. "Guys, I think I'm gonna be sick."

"How was the dungeon?" Jess started excitedly, pausing and squealing softly as she was flooded with notifications. "Holy...! That *was* a secret door, then? That was worth nearly half as much as the rest *combined*!"

"It was an interesting dungeon that we all hated and will never visit again." Alexis took the lead since Joe had his nose in his new book and was mumbling nearly incoherently. "No rewards until you beat the Boss, but then each team member got a book that was useful to them. A skill book or a manual of some kind."

"We broke Joe!" Jaxon chimed in. "I'd come back if there was another reward at the end like that."

"Yeah, what's happening there?" Jess poked Joe, only to be met with a sparkling force that stopped her finger cold.

"As far as we can tell, Joe just found out that he has barely been using his rituals or something. He read off the titles to a few books, and it seemed that he almost fainted a few times." Poppy explained as he swung his rapier in a complicated new pattern.

Joe closed the book with a **snap** and looked around. "Everything I've been doing until now... just... it's all wrong!"

Jaxon gave him a few pats on the back. "You okay there, lil bald buddy?"

"I'm *fine*. Also. Jess. I don't need you to look for professions for me anymore." Joe took a deep breath and turned toward

Towny McTownface. "I need to get back and read through this. If I'm right about it, I am going to need to start hunting down the rest of this series."

"What do ya *think* it is?" Bard inquired as they started the walk back to the Guild.

"I... alright, you know how I could add in a health potion to that ritual that keeps monsters away? If I did that, then there was an extra effect of getting a rested bonus?" Joe waited for Bard to nod, then burst out with, "That's an entire *school* of ritual magic! It's called 'Alchemical Enhancement'. Not only can I add on potions and various pastes and such, but if I can figure out how to do it with this book... I can basically bottle entire rituals, or add on effects that make a ritual something completely different from what it was supposed to be."

CHAPTER EIGHT

Joe leaned over his book, staring down at words that were changing his entire understanding of rituals. "Purifying flame under a Gorgonsteel cauldron can enhance the potency of both earth and flame aspected components up to the fifth degree. The delta factor of the..."

"I have no idea what any of this means." He shook his head and sighed. After returning to the Guild, Joe had gone straight to his base in the Grand Ritual Hall and started reading. Unfortunately, the information was dense and multifaceted, going over concepts that seemed easy while containing many layers. He wanted ritual magic to be as mysterious and easy as it looked, but that should only be the case for those looking at it from the outside.

Reading this book, instead of twisting chants that would empower rituals through sheer magical language, he found graphs. Instead of searching for a mystical plant that would serve a panacea for his newfound potions, there was a chapter-long exposition on plant growth and harvesting techniques that were skills in their own right. He wanted to parse this information and solve a riddle or minigame that allowed him to make a ritual potion; but instead, there were heating and preservation charts.

Joe's attention slid, and he started thinking about the book series that he had just learned about. If the titles were any indication, there was a book about ritual circles. He was good at those; on Midgard, he was likely the subject matter expert.

'Matrices' had a few meanings, and he hoped it was just another name for math. Specifically, the definition that said they were 'arrays of quantities or expressions in rows and columns that are treated as a single entity and manipulated according to particular rules'. If that was where this skill was going, he felt that he would have a good handle on matrices and should be able to learn the information on his own. But if it meant 'an environment or material in which something develops, a surrounding medium or structure'... that could be anything from the placement of components to *growing* certain things for himself.

Enchanted Circles sounded pretty straightforward: add enchantments to the rituals to create certain effects. It was likely that he would need to use enchantments to create linked rituals like the ones he had found when gaining the blueprints to the Grand Ritual Hall. Until he found that book, Joe just wouldn't know for certain. Since he had only one *thick* book of formulae and concepts, there was only one thing that he could think to do.

"I need a teacher." Joe sighed and flopped down into his seat. He considered where to find a teacher, and came up with only a few options. "I'm sure that I could go to the Mage's College and take a course... but those are always stuffed with theory and bias. There's no way I would get any good hands-on experience in a timely manner. I could try to go the self-taught way... but that's gonna be really slow."

He sat up and rubbed his bald head. "Best try to find a tutor. Who would have better practical knowledge than an Alchemist with a shop? Let's go have a chat with Jake. Sure, he's creepy... but he seems to know his stuff."

Joe crept through the Pathfinder's Hall, keeping an eye out for Mike. The man had been popping up at inopportune moments and asking Joe to either work, attend *meetings*, or answer questions if it were at all possible. When he reached the temple without issue, Joe took a deep breath as he looked around the admittedly nifty room. Along with the lighting and heat sources, the river and shrubbery really tied the whole thing together. The shrubbery were actually young Tree Ents that would someday protect the temple if attacked, but right now they were extra pretty thanks to the flowers blooming on them.

"What's missing?" Joe spoke quietly, the area giving off a pervading sense of stillness that he didn't want to break. "Why do I *feel* like there is something missing?"

His eyes swept across the room, coming to rest on one of only two altars that was bare, blank stone. That would do it; the pantheon was still incomplete. Joe sighed, running a hand over his bald head in consternation. He didn't exactly want to go god-shopping, but it might be better than waiting around for something to approach *him*. Joe took a deep breath, and ever so slowly released it.

"I have time." He reminded himself. "I am digital now, and I can survive for hundreds or *thousands* of years. Let's learn all of this stuff, everything that I want to learn, but seriously… I gotta take the time to enjoy doing it."

Soul Forge complete! New skill acquired: Neutrality Aura (Passive).

"Has it already been two days since I did that?" Joe furrowed his brow, then realized that he hadn't yet read what the skill *did*!

Neutrality Aura (Passive) (Beginner IX): Remove all negative debuffs at double the rate of decomposition. Remove positive debuffs on hostile entities in range at double the rate of decomposition. Heal all non-hostile entities for 1n health per second within five feet, where n = skill level. Reduce incoming magical damage by .5n. Passive. This skill is doubly effective against poisons within a body, and will also pull moisture from the air to hydrate friendly targets over time. Range of aura is .25n feet. Reserves 8% of mana pool for use. Toggleable.

Instantly, Joe looked at his stained robes and sweaty skin. To his great relief, his 'filthy' debuff was starting to expire! He started to lose a headache he hadn't even realized he had… noticing only then that he hadn't drank any water the entire time that Cleanse had been gone. Joe had been fully reliant on the skill to keep him hydrated. Whoops.

"This skill is *amazing.*" The best part was that it was *passive.* He would be able to heal while focusing on other things, and using eight percent of his mana pool to keep it always active was a sacrifice he was willing to make. It wouldn't work on distant targets, nor would it be effective as quickly as the individual skills would have been, but there were a huge amount of new options that had opened up to him. The aura would work on anyone within four-and-three-quarters feet of him, basically the size of his standard party grouping, and that would only *grow* over time.

Joe sat down and waited a few long moments, keeping his eye on his active effects tab. He had been at 'Filthy III', 'Dehydrated IV', and 'Caffeinated V'. All but the last were slowly vanishing, and he could actually see his shriveled skin starting to become hydrated. "I *really* need to take better care of myself."

Wisdom +1!

"Bratty system!" Joe tried to relax, remembering that he needed to get his other stats up and over the next threshold. Yet *another* project that he needed to throw himself at. "Actually… what does my stat page look like right now?"

Name: Joe '*Tatum's Chosen Legend*' Class: Jumplomancer (Actual: Rituarchitect)
Profession: Tenured Scholar (Actual: Arcanologist)
Character Level: 15 Exp: 134,813 Exp to next level: 1,187
Rituarchitect Level: 3 Exp: 5,940 Exp to next level: 60
Hit Points: 330/330
Mana: 1462/1,590 (127 Reserved)
Mana regen: 30.7/sec (Base 27.91/sec increased by gear)
Stamina: 295/295

Stamina regen: 5.67/sec

Characteristic: Raw score (Modifier)

Strength: 31 (1.31)
Dexterity: 40 (1.40)
Constitution: 38 (1.38)
Intelligence: 106 (3.06)
Wisdom: 78 (2.28)
Charisma: 31 (1.31)
Perception: 60 (2.10)
Luck: 31 (1.31)
Karmic Luck: -4

That looked good, except… there were two things to fix right now. Joe activated his Exquisite Shell, dumping his mana pool into it. That reserved an additional one hundred and forty-six mana. The other thing… how had his Karmic luck dropped into the negatives? That was a tough stat that no one really understood, but research showed that it was fairly straightforward to either increase or decrease it.

Do actions that were considered 'good', and it increased. The opposite held true, and the only thing that he could think that he had done recently was going through the dungeon. Oh… self-harm? That would at least make sense, but it was frustrating to lose Karmic Luck simply by playing the game according to the rules. Perhaps there was another way to complete that dungeon…? He was sure *someone* would find out. Until then, there was no way he was returning to the area.

"Took five whole minutes," Joe stated as he watched his dehydrated debuff vanish. "Well… at least I don't have to worry about it again after this. Hooray for passives!"

He stood and walked over to the teleportation point, casting a glance at the empty altars just before moving to Ardania. He took a breath, nearly gagging as the scent of the city hit him. It had *never* been this bad before! The press of bodies had thinned over the last few days as people ventured out to find something to do with their lives, but there were still refugees from Earth appearing regularly.

Unwashed bodies, cheap food rotting, and even the clear fact that some people either didn't know where to find bathrooms - or didn't care to find them - hit Joe right in the olfactory organ. To his great delight, the smells reaching him dulled and eventually even vanished as his aura took care of the filth in the near vicinity. Apparently, his new aura even affected the air!

That settled it for him. He needed to do *something* to help here, no matter how small. Most of these people simply didn't understand what was happening; they weren't bad people. Joe made his way slowly between various groups, trying to get close to the thickest groupings of people. He stood in each place for a short while before moving on, leaving cleaner and healthier people behind. It wasn't much, but he knew that if he were in that position, he would be hoping for someone to do the same for him.

His slow pace caused him to arrive at the alchemy shop just after midday. He walked in and moved to the counter, pleased that his aura was taking care of the astringents in the air that had made breathing a pain in the past. "Jake? You here?"

A voice behind him made Joe whirl around. "Sure am. What are you doing to my shop? The air smells strange."

"*Clean*, maybe? **Ahem**. Oh… did I walk past you somehow?" Jake didn't answer Joe's question, so Joe simply moved on. "I was hoping to ask for a favor."

"No favors. Coin up front, always." Jake was feeling the edge of Joe's robes, glaring at something that apparently only he could see. "Coffee…"

"Not that kind of favor." Joe steeled himself. This would be as difficult as learning from an alchemist version of Jaxon. "I was hoping that you could teach me the Alchemist profession."

Jake's eyes shot up to lock with Joe's. "Trying to steal away my customers, are we? Hmm… tsk, tsk, Joe. That's not very nice at all."

"No, it's not that at all." Joe insisted, pulling out the manual that he had recently acquired. The cat was out of the bag on his rituals already, so he was choosing to be as up front as possible. "I recently found that my class is capable of far more than I've been using it for, and I want to fix that. There is a subsection of my class that focuses on Alchemically Enhanced Components, and I can't make heads or tails of the information."

"Book." Jake held out a hand, and opened and scanned through a few pages, nodding at certain areas and raising a brow at others. "Interesting. Very interesting… a ritualist, here in my shop. I do wonder if the old bounty is still active?"

"It's not!"

Joe froze, making Jake snort in response. "Only playing. Now… I will do one thing for you for free. Information. You don't want the 'Alchemist' profession for… this. It would *work*, but it would be like using a fireball to light a candle. The end result is similar, but one is incredibly wasteful. You need the 'Ritualistic Alchemist' profession."

"That exists?"

"There are few things in this world that you *can't* find a specific, more focused, or specialized form of." Jake handed back the book. "If you are only planning on making components for rituals, and not trying to brew cauldrons' worth of healing potions to save your guild a few silver coins, I can teach you. That is where I am going to need something from you, though."

"If I can do it, I will." Joe told the man carefully. It wouldn't be good to make a promise before he knew details.

"I'd like to align myself with your guild, as I am getting bored here. When you move to the next zone and make an outpost, you will build me a new workshop." Jake held out a hand. "Do we have a deal?"

Joe shook on it, "As long as my guild agrees, I'm in."

"No. You take the deal, or you don't. No negotiating."

"Then I take it." Joe stated firmly. He wasn't going to pass up a chance like this.

Quest received: Homebrew. Jake the Alchemist is looking to upgrade. Get your guild to agree to align with him, and make him a new workshop in your outpost on the next zone. Reward: Profession (Instant), Variable. Failure: hostility with Jake and other organizations. You have accepted this quest!

CHAPTER NINE

Joe was in the horse stance, grunting as flaming coals were dropped on top of the metal shield he was holding above his head. He found that strength and endurance training allowed him to free his mind to think of other issues in the background. In this case, he was going over what had happened with the Alchemist last night.

The 'instant' in the reward line meant that he gained that portion of his reward right away, which meant that they needed to train. Jake had brought Joe to the back of the shop and directed him to start reading through various primers. He had used the book Joe brought, found a section detailing recipes for ritual-only usage, and worked with Joe to help create one of the brews. The entire process had taken until *well* past sundown, even with Joe's enhanced learning speed. It was frustrating for him to find an area of expertise that he just wasn't instantly good at.

Joe focused on his brand-new second profession and grunted; partly from a coal that slipped and singed his skin.

Ritualistic Alchemist (Level 0): An Alchemist creates potions and elixirs that can amaze and astound the world. A Ritualistic Alchemist takes that in a different direction, focusing on creating components that enhance and alter rituals. By sacrificing the ability to make most things that an Alchemist can easily produce, the Ritualistic Alchemist is able to become a master at his craft in a fraction of the time. +25% chance to create ritual-specific alchemical items. +25% speed of production to ritual-specific alchemical items. -50% to all attempts to make non ritual-specific alchemical items.

On a very *positive* note, the hours of practice and lecturing had also allowed Joe to gain the 'Alchemical Lore' skill. That was going to be really helpful when testing new combinations or troubleshooting his failed projects.

Ritualistic Alchemy (Novice VIII). You have gained an understanding of how to create alchemical items! 10+n% chance to create 'Common' ranked alchemic items such as potions, where n = skill level! Each rank higher than 'Common' lowers chances of creation by a factor of ten! Example: chance to create uncommon alchemical items: ((10+n)/10)%. Rare: ((10+n)/100)%

Alchemical Lore (Novice VI). Many are satisfied with the end result of their potions, and simply follow the recipes to the letter time and again. You have started to dive deeply into the why *of alchemy. +1n% to creation of alchemical items, where n = skill level.*

It was extremely telling that, even with learning from someone that Joe *suspected* was at or above the Master rank in alchemy, Joe was only able to reach Novice eight in the skill. He pushed upward, frustrated at the slow progression. If any alchemist would have known his thoughts on that matter, they would have happily tossed a 'Flask of Bottled Explosions' at him. There was a reason alchemy was rare. It required high intelligence, dexterity, and extreme perception to get *anything* correct. It also had one of the highest reclass rates of all Eternium base classes, even higher than enchanter.

"I have no idea why you're coming back here and doing this almost every day," the trainer stated while shoveling coal onto Joe. "You do *realize* that without staying the entire time, you are only torturing yourself, right?"

"What if I'm just trying to get used to uncomfortable situations? Or I'm planning to dive into a volcano?" Joe shot back, his frustration leaking through and onto the trainer. *Everyone* seemed to want to tell him how he should be progressing, and it was getting tedious. "This is helping me do what I want to do, that's all. *Okay*?"

"Chill, man. Just trying to *help*." The next coal that was tossed on was a *lot* hotter than the ones before it. "*Oops*."

Joe knew without checking that Hammerwords had activated again and he had lost reputation with this guy. *Great.* At least his training was just ending, and he gained a strength and constitution point. "Not cool, man. Not cool."

Joe tossed the shield to the side and walked away, pulling a glowing battery out of his codpiece. "*Knowledge.* Alchemical Lore."

Skill increase: Alchemical Lore (Novice VII).

Skill increase: Knowledge (Novice II).

He basked in the feeling of everything he had learned the previous day becoming just *that* much clearer. It wasn't a huge amount, but it helped him connect the dots on a few subjects. One thing was still just a *touch* out of focus, and Joe had a vague feeling that he needed to hold his hands in certain positions to maximize the potential of the ingredients… it was gone. Drat.

Alchemy seemed to be *illogical*. It was *supposed* to be a cross between cooking and chemistry, but that was thinking about it from a mundane perspective. Even though the magic of the process was coming from the ingredients that were added, it was still *magic*. Joe decided that he was going to go work on some simple, logical, geometric rituals to take his mind off the 'art' of Alchemy. He rubbed his face and felt some soot, frowning at how much slower his aura ability cleaned him compared to Cleanse.

"Pardon me… Mr. Joe, I believe?" The sweet voice calling his name made Joe frown and look around for the source. An *unbelievably* beautiful woman was walking toward him. She was wearing a professional outfit, and had her hair pulled back into a ponytail. She reached out and shook his hand, "I've been looking for you. I am here representing the Architect's Union, which is what the previous Guild has restructured into after the change of ownership and management. I have a proposition for you."

"You're here to proposition me?" Joe spoke without thinking. "That is… I didn't mean-"

"Please don't worry about it." She blinked a few times and got back on track. "My name is Daniella, and I have an offer from you from the Union. We would like to offer you the chance to study any buildings in the city that we own, or those we can pull in favors from. Otherwise, we can offer you a few blueprints that you may use at your leisure."

"I see… and what's the catch?" Joe narrowed his eyes and tried to gauge how high her charisma must be to impact him so significantly even despite his huge wisdom score. It had to be at *least* third tier, probably in the early one hundreds.

"I'll be frank." Daniella lowered her chin and locked eyes with him. "We've been watching what you are capable of, and management is concerned that you are going to put us out of business if you go out on the open market. By giving you free access, you will need to agree that you will only make buildings for yourself or your Guild."

Joe really liked her direct attitude, even though it seemed slightly artificial. That meant either that her 'Union' had *really* been studying him, that her charisma was filling in the gaps for her, or a little of both. "Hmm… I can get behind that. Slight change. Myself, my Guild, and my *family*. Also, that limitation applies only in this Zone. I plan to leave Midgard, and I don't want to be bound by the rules of an organization that is *here* when I am fighting to survive somewhere else."

"Done." Daniella shook his hand. "I'll get the contracts ready. Is there anything you need from me?"

"I need a fat stack of high-quality blueprint paper at cost." Joe pulled out a bank note for fifty gold and handed it over. "I'll need that *well* before we get started."

"I can have it delivered today…" Daniella looked at the

note and winced as she realized how much paper that could buy when it was sold at cost.

"Get it here by noon, and we can start tomorrow morning," Joe cheerfully informed her.

"I didn't expect you to be so... decisive. Done." Daniella nodded and walked away, calling back with, "I'll add the at-cost paper to the contract. If you don't sign, you'll need to pay current market value!"

"Then make sure not to put any stupid clauses in the contract!" Joe yelled after her vanishing form. "Hmm. Gonna have to read that contract carefully. Hopefully Tatum will help me find any *hidden* sections."

By lunch, a courier sprinted up to Joe and handed over a large, well-wrapped box full of blueprint paper. Joe tipped him ten copper and got straight to work. He rounded up his Coven members and assigned them a task, "Taka, Kirby, Rob, Big_Mo, Hannah... sorry about this, but I need us to sit down and just make an unholy amount of this ritual diagram."

The group looked at the diagram for Architect's Fury and discussed how they could separate out tasks. It was Big_Mo who came up with the real issue. "Joe, I want to do this, but it's a *Student* ranked ritual. I'm still a *Novice* with ritual magic. It'll just explode if I try to make it."

He had a point. Joe had them all sit together at a table and tried to figure out a plan. "Alright... here's what we're going to do. Hannah, with the highest rank after me, is a solid Beginner that is getting close to Apprentice. Teaching moment here: since this is a Student ranked ritual, there are still two circles that each of you can draw up with a high probability of success. We are all going to make a diagram with the highest circles we can, then divide the work up."

"Those with the lowest ranks will draw the first Novice circles, then the next group does the Beginner ones. When Hannah hits Apprentice rank, she'll do those as well. Whatever *can't* get done is something I'll do. Also, I'll come around and make sure things are looking correct as we get started. That should help boost your productivity, grant a boost to leveling up your skills, and even help me rank up my teaching skill. Oh… never mind, I added that skill to a skill combo. Shoot."

Joe grinned at the confused faces. "Are you all waiting for an *invitation*? Let's make the magic happen!"

CHAPTER TEN

Daniella arrived at the same time she had the day before, just after Joe finished his hot-coal training. The extra point of strength and constitution was just enough for him to fully ignore a sleepless night. He had taken a peek under his shirt, and was pleased to see the first hints of beautiful abdominal muscles.

"Joe, are you ready to begin the day?"

"Good morning, Daniella." Joe responded calmly, just as the last hints of sweat vanished thanks to his aura.

Skill increase: Neutrality Aura (Apprentice 0): Your constant usage of this skill has made it feel all warm and tingly toward you. Mana reserved from mana pool to keep this skill active has decreased from 8% to 7%.

"Have you decided whether to take some unique blueprints from us, or to make your own based on what we can find in the city?" Daniella continued her line of questioning even as the air around Joe seemed to grow just a single shade darker. Not that she didn't notice; her *duty* was to notice details. She simply didn't feel the need to comment.

"I will *certainly* study buildings, thank you." Joe replied coyly. Daniella squinted as though felt a headache coming on, but she simply nodded and turned to walk toward Ardania. He reached out a hand to forestall her. "Wait. Follow me for a moment? I'd prefer not to walk all the way back to the city."

"Oh, you have transport? That will make things easier." Daniella followed him past an enclosure of various beasts. "Do you have a two-person mount? A carriage…? Where are we going?"

"Just trust me." Joe snorted softly as he held in a laugh. Perhaps he shouldn't be showing her his ability to fast-travel, but this was going to be a show of strength that he could use to his advantage in the future. They walked into the Pathfinder's Hall, and Joe saw Daniella try to stop herself from gasping. She failed, much to his pleasure.

The building was *dark*, but the interior was entirely open, except for the central pillar and the small booths designated for plotting out classes and skills. There was enough light to see the entire space, reflected from the glossy surfaces and galaxy-style points of light interspersed throughout. It felt like walking through space, and Joe knew *exactly* how amazing it was to walk through the building. Even more, he knew that an architect would nearly be *forced* to drool when they saw it for the first time.

"Oh, I suppose you haven't been allowed in here before," Joe spoke nonchalantly, taking the *long* way around to the temple. "Have you been in many Artifact-rarity buildings, then? I know it doesn't look nearly as interesting from outside."

"Artifact…!" Daniella caught herself and took a deep breath. "I would *love* to know more about this building. For instance… I don't suppose that you have an extra copy of the blueprints?"

"I don't." Joe wasn't lying; he had given the blueprints to the Scholars. Seeing her disappointed look, he continued. "Though, I *can* remake the building after I get my skill into the Master ranks."

"Oh…" She shook her head at that and changed the subject. Not a great sign. How difficult was it to *actually* reach the Master ranks? "Normally we work with tier one, *common-*

ranked buildings. Seeing something like this is usually reserved for those at the palace or the Mage's College."

"About that, what's up with the distinction between 'tier one' and 'common'? I thought that was essentially the same thing?" Joe coughed and blushed, not that it could be seen in the dark. "At least, I've been *using* those terms interchangeably."

"Ah. Easy enough." Daniella tore her eyes off the ceiling that seemed to show the far reaches of space. "There are two terms because the blueprint may be of a higher tier than the actual workmanship. A tier-one building means that the blueprint will make a common-ranked building if everything is done to specification. However, if you give that to a carpenter and they mess it up, you might end up with a tier-one design, but a trash building."

"Conversely, give that same blueprint to a Master Carpenter, and they may improve upon it during the actual crafting. That's how you get variations, but the base design is *still* only a tier *one*. It might be an *Uncommon* tier one, but there is only so much you can do to a place and have it remain the same building. Now, if a new blueprint is made from *that* building, it would be an uncommon blueprint, or tier *two*."

Joe nodded along as they walked. "So, the tier is all about what it *should* be, and the rarity is about the final product. Makes sense to me. Here we are."

Daniella had thought that she was done being amazed by the building, but as her eyes drank in the river, trees, fires, and dark shadows that whispered about hidden secrets… she couldn't help but gaze around like a tourist. "How did you manage… this is *not*…"

Deciding to rescue her, Joe released a happy sigh and looked around the temple. "So, if I am correct, this building - the Pathfinder's Hall, going by your measurement - is a tier *six*, Artifact-rarity building. That means that the blueprints were Artifact, and the final result was Artifact, correct?"

"Yes… that would be correct." Daniella's voice was faint.

"Good... ready to go? Another function of this building is..."

Would you like to accept the teleportation request from Joe 'Tatum's Chosen Legend'? Destination: Ardania Town Square. Yes / No.

"...Yes." Daniella stated, just before the two of them vanished from Towny McTownface.

Joe blinked at the sudden bright morning light that washed over the two of them. "Ardania. Perfect. Shall we get to it?"

Mind reeling, Daniella started walking. Slowly at first, then faster and with more purpose, as she snapped out of her passion-for-new-buildings fugue. She was nothing if not a consummate professional, and the fact that Joe had been able to catch her off guard so fully made her fluctuate between flattered and embarrassed. "The... first option I have for you to take a look at is a specialty store. This store is focused on high-end products, and has agreed - however begrudgingly - to allow you entrance to try to make up your own blueprints."

"I see. Is this the *only* place I get to look into?" Joe was already reconsidering the deal. He hadn't signed anything yet, after all...

"No, of course not." Daniella pulled out a short contract and handed it over for Joe to examine. "You are allowed to go to any of the structures that we have had a hand in building, so long as it is not a restricted access area. Then, even *our* clout can't get you close. You simply need an architect with you, and section three-dot-two-dot-one stipulates that we have twenty hours to provide you with a person upon request."

"I see." Joe read over the contract, and found that some of it was a strange flat grey color. His ability to read the truth was being interfered with somehow. "This section... can you put that in more simple terms for me?"

"Ah, yes. Legalese." Daniella looked at the section, "This is what I had just told you: we have twenty hours to get you an architect upon request."

"No, here. The next line."

Daniella glanced at it and gave him a quizzical glance.

"This line clearly states that you agree to give us the needed twenty hours to provide you with an architect."

"*Clearly*?" Joe started to read the text in an aloof manner. "Upon signing, the signatories consent to the aforementioned plurality of allotted time for the provision of an attendant companion, whereupon the restrictions of section three-dot-one-dot-three are considered fulfilled."

He looked up at Daniella and shook his head. "Lot of recursive calls in there. You know… the document referencing itself. Makes it seem like you are trying to hide things in the text to 'get' me."

"Would you like to create a different contract for us to work with?" Daniella pulled out blank parchment and a quill. They stepped into a small cafe and she wrote out in clear language what they had been discussing. When it was finished to both of their satisfaction, the document was less than a single page long. "You know that a simple contract like this, while easy to understand, leaves *much* less to be interpreted. It will be *very* hard to find any workarounds."

"Well, at least that will work both ways." Joe signed the parchment after Daniella signed on behalf of her Union. "I'm sure your people *already* knew all the loopholes in that last one. I'm just surprised that you are so willing to make a new contract."

"To be frank, Mr. Joe, we are worried that if you are allowed to make buildings for anyone who wants them, we would go out of business." Daniella blew on the parchment and whisked it away to some hidden spatial storage device. "The Union cannot match your speed and precision, and it is clear from your reputation that attempting to swindle you only leads to the utter destruction of an organization."

"I'm actually very nice." Joe stood as she did and they started walking toward the shop. "Most of the time, my future was at stake, and I did what I felt was needed in order to survive and thrive."

"Oh, I'm sure you did everything for a good reason,"

Daniella placated him easily. "I'm not terribly upset about getting the position I have now either, and that couldn't have happened if the Architect's *Guild* didn't become the Architect's *Union*. Here we are. Let's meet the owner."

They stepped into a small boutique, and the proprietor perked up… until he saw Daniella. "Ugh… *you.* I suppose that you came here to show the miscreant around? How long must I suffer your 'attention' for?"

"Now, now." Daniella gave the man a dark look. "You agreed to this, so let's not scare off the man who will let you repay your debt…?"

Joe wasn't paying attention at all. He was browsing the shop, intensely interested in what he was seeing. The shop itself was shaped like a cylinder, instead of the standard box that he had been expecting. There were only thirty items for sale, and each of them was hovering in the air over a small plinth. Off to the side was a small refreshment stand, where bite-sized sandwiches were creating themselves even as he looked on.

"This… this was never meant to be a *shop.*" Joe muttered to himself, looking around the spacious, well-lit room. "This is straight-up a trophy hall."

Wisdom +2! Charisma +2! For being able to see to the heart of a long-dead architect's design, you have proven that you are both wise and able to form a connection with another person! Too bad they need to be dead, but perhaps as you gain more charisma, you can try to connect to living *people!*

"I'll start making a blueprint right now, if that is fine with you both." Joe already had an Architect's Fury ritual in hand. His words interrupted the two quietly bickering people, and Daniella came over at once.

"You know this is only the *first* option, right?" Daniella looked at the door, then him. "You can look at some others, then decide where you want to start. There's really no rush…?"

She trailed off as Joe patiently stared and waited for her to finish speaking. "Right, but you said that I can make blueprints of all of them, right?"

"Yes… but how high are your skills that you think that you can casually make blueprints in a hurry that *function* proper-"

"Activate." Joe interrupted her, slapping his pre-formed ritual to the ground. A halo of light shot out, growing until it encompassed the building. A ritual diagram appeared under Joe's feet as the ritual began, and details began to appear on the blueprint he held.

Daniella watched in shock as the blueprint filled out over the next few minutes. When the ritual completed, she inspected the document in Joe's hand and nearly fainted.

Blueprint: Trophy Hall (Rare). Having a Trophy Hall will allow groups such as Guilds to display various trophies. Potent enough trophies will offer a small boost to either stats or skills.

There was more to it, something she didn't understand about a ritual, but the blueprint alone was enough to make her swallow in an attempt to moisten her suddenly dry throat. "You can do that… with *any* building?"

"If I have enough time, and I'm not interrupted." Joe made the blueprint vanish into his storage ring. The door to the shop popped open, and a flood of people entered to see what the light show had been all about. Joe and Daniella left the *very* happy shop owner to his business and started toward the next building that Daniella intended to show him.

"How many of those… building scanners did you bring?" Daniella nervously questioned.

Joe showed her a stack of papers.

"*Fifty.*"

CHAPTER ELEVEN

"Are you still wondering why I said that I was worried that you would put us out of business?" Daniella sounded *exhausted.* "If you can make half of those buildings, you'll be able to do something that no one in the Union has been able to do for over a century."

Joe had only scanned twenty-eight buildings, but the results had been spectacular. Not only did he gain mostly Uncommon and Rare blueprints, but each building he left suddenly had an influx of tourists. When it was near a shop, sales *spiked.* It seemed that people had started to correlate the light show of the ritual with something 'special'.

It was true, because Joe didn't bother to scan common buildings. His ability was too costly, and even though he had an eighty-five percent reduction in component costs, he had still needed to use seven and a half Cores, which left him with only a few much more potent ones that he wasn't going to use on *building.* Not unless he needed to do so.

A glance at all the experience he had gained for his Rituarchitect class made him grin; two thousand, nine hundred and ninety-six. He had reached class level *four* just by scanning everything; he couldn't wait to *build* them. The level increase had given him a new ritual, Structural Repair, but it wasn't overly useful at the moment.

"I honestly think that you are thinking about this too much." Joe started walking back to the town square, and Daniella followed. "I have no *time* to go out and about setting up basic buildings for people. I don't-"

"You don't have time right *now*." Daniella shook her head. "You think I haven't heard people discussing how they are going to live for a *very* long time? That I haven't seen people come back to life after being reduced to *dust*? This contract protects us against the *far* away future."

"I'm starting to be happy that I put in the provision that the contract is voided if your group collapses. *I'll* still be young and healthy." Joe winced as he realized how dark that sounded. "Also, good call on making exceptions for the kingdom's use. I hadn't thought about that."

"I really don't want to anger the only person on Midgard that can void standard contracts, so that only makes sense to me." Daniella shook Joe's hand and started to turn away, but Joe cleared his throat and she paused.

"I'd like to learn architecture. I need to get skills in this field if I want to improve upon what I can do currently." Joe looked at her meaningfully. "Do you know any teachers that I could contact?"

Daniella paused and nodded slowly. "I'll send someone along. Until then, try to learn the theory. I'll expect you to know what I mean when I say 'strut your struts' by the time a tutor appears. Here."

She handed over a small book that appeared from seemingly nowhere, and Joe read the title. *Basics of Architecture*. Daniella stepped away, "That should get your architecture lore skill to at least Novice five if you read through and understand all the material. Good luck."

"It was... *very* nice to meet you, Daniella." Joe didn't wait for a response and appeared in the temple at the Pathfinder's Hall in the next instant.

Calculation drain has taken effect! Overthinking so much made you miss a great chance!

"What? What was *that* about?" Joe glared at the notification. Shrugging, he stepped away from the altar and walked toward his friends. He had been thinking about his team, and had resolved to spend time hunting and completing quests with them.

He caught up to the group just as they were leaving Towney. "Hey guys! Got room for one more?"

"Joe! Of course!" Jaxon skipped over and gave Joe a hug. "We were just discussing whether we should continue on with you or apply for a different team leader, so I am *very* glad to see you putting in the effort!"

"You *what*!" Joe looked around at the group, but they merely shrugged.

Alexis motioned that they should keep walking. "Joe, we aren't trying to get rid of you, we are just trying to have a full party when we go out every day."

"You're already the second-in-command. Should we assign an alternate that rotates in when I'm not able to make it? Then you go out, Alexis is in charge, and you have a full team when I'm not here." Joe's words made most of them slowly nod, and Poppy actually sighed in relief.

"Thank goodness." Poppy winked at Joe. "Wasn't sure how we were going to kick you from *your* party, and I gotta tell you… it's been getting really difficult to clear different areas with only four people. Well… three people and Jaxon."

"I *am* a person!" Jaxon insisted as he skipped along backwards next to them.

"Of *course* ya are, ya big goofball," Bard agreed before turning to Poppy and shaking his head 'no' with wide-open eyes.

"Why has it been getting so hard to clear areas?" Joe had to hurry to keep up with everyone, making him wonder how they had become so *fast*.

"Easy." Alexis waved at the area around them, which had been cleared of all trees and turned into fields. "We, humanity, are expanding *real* fast. A billion people dropped onto Midgard, and a small portion of them are *way* better at min-maxing than the established guilds or other players. The *vast* majority are not good at gaming, and are expanding and making this a safe zone. Hunting monsters is getting harder because only the ones that are *really* hard to kill, or can't be hunted for food, are surviving."

"To me, it sounds like non-combat professions are going to start being the norm again..." Joe trailed off, so Poppy nodded and filled in what Joe was missing.

"Just like Earth," Poppy stated grimly. "It is likely that combat professions are going to be pushed out, and will eventually stagnate. There is a *huge* rush for fighting classes to get to the next Zone, but so far as we know... no one has been able to get their second Specialization. Lots of high levels, though no one is taking that step."

"People have still tried to get to the next Zone, though, right?" Joe looked around, noting the wincing nods. "It was that bad?"

"If the forums can be trusted, then everyone who tried it died and had a *huge* debuff. They were stuck in respawn for days, and when they got out... everything they'd had with them had been destroyed. Gear, weapons, money, spatial bags, things that were supposed to be soulbound... everything." Alexis shook her head at that. "It seems to be the same for everyone that's tried it."

"Geez... all I've wanted to do since hearing about that Zone is *get* to it." Joe sighed as he realized that goal might be a little too far away at the moment.

"Think about when we were playing games on Earth and a new expansion came out," Poppy offered with much handwaving. "It was always announced early to build hype, and then there was usually a whole *host* of quests, items, and whatever else was needed in order to actually *get* there. Sure, we know it *exists*, and we *plan* to get there… it'll just be a while."

"We're *here*!" Jaxon clapped his hands excitedly. "Joe, we found out that clearing this dungeon gives characteristic points as a reward! We need to agree what points we want before we go in, and the challenge changes based on that!"

"Is that how you guys have been getting so *fast*?" The group nodded at Joe's question.

"Been selectin' dexterity every day." Bard chimed in. "Lower yer threshold, higher the reward."

"I've only gotten a single point for clearing it every day." Jaxon admitted sadly.

"Ahm gettin' five ah day, but I got ta fifty yesterday. Everyone else is gettin' three ah day, so that's what I'm expectin' today." Bard gave a thumbs-up.

This was exactly what Joe needed. He grinned at the others as they passed the high-powered Guild guards. Apparently, this was a place that outsiders were *not* allowed into; and for good reason. If this place became too overused, who could say if the rewards it gave out would stay so good?

"One more thing," Alexis told Joe. "No cost to get in, but the rule is that you need to donate all meat or food gained to the Guild. All other loot is free game."

"Works for me." Joe followed along, stepping into a seemingly *massive* space floating high in the sky. "This is a massive… puzzle? Maze? What...?"

You have entered the Dungeon 'Trial section 118b'. Please cast your vote for party challenge! Strength / Dexterity / Constitution / Intelligence / Wisdom / Charisma / Perception / Luck.

Joe selected 'dexterity', as they had agreed previously.

Average party dexterity… 72. Scaling difficulty to 50-100 dexterity range. Good luck!

"What sort of monsters are in here?" Joe quizzed as the huge cube… thing… space? Whatever it was that was suspended in the sky *twisted* until a door appeared in front of them. A platform formed in the empty space, and they took turns jumping to it and then to the door.

Jaxon did a backflip to get to the door, and grinned at Joe. "The monsters in here are Neigh-Bears. Basically a centaur, but a cross between a horse and a bear. A bison, maybe? Eh, either way, huge, *mean*, and their main attack is a straight charge that you need to dodge. Also… good eatin'. You've been eating Neigh-Bears if you've had any meat at the guild in the last week."

"The goal of this dungeon is…?" Joe stopped speaking when he saw a *massive* number of creatures in a pasture. They seemed to be standing on an enormous disk, and along the side… there was only darkness off the edge.

"You need to dodge a hundred charging Neigh-Bears, and get to the center area." Poppy explained succinctly. "You can usually make that happen just by getting to the center. *Plenty* of creatures to avoid."

"This is my favorite part." Jaxon exclaimed as he stepped into the grassland. "Come get some old-man meat!"

The collective bellow from the creatures almost made Joe pee a little. It was the roar of a bear coupled with the high-pitched scream of a horse. Every creature they could see rushed them at top speed.

"Come get some!" Jaxon screamed back at them as his hands morphed into hungry T-Rex heads. "The weak are meat, the strong get to eat!"

CHAPTER TWELVE

Charging attacks avoided: 36/100.

Joe was twisting in midair, having finally found an outlet for his jumping skill. "Bard, on your left!"

The stocky Skald was having the most trouble of anyone present, but he still managed to roll out of the way of the thundering hooves. "Son of a biscuit muncher!"

"I *told* you to join my yoga class and get that dexterity up!" Alexis called out.

"Ah've been doin' *this*!" Bard shouted back, though he was somewhat muffled by the grass he was attempting to spit out. "*Rah*!"

A Neigh-Bear hit him from the side, its thick claws tearing open a wide gash along Bard's side. His armor protected his chest from getting the same treatment, but he went tumbling away from the sheer physics of the strike. Bard rolled to his feet and charged the beast in return. "Imma *eat* ya, bear-brain!"

Joe landed with a spinning flourish that halted his momentum and made another beast miss him by inches.

Charging attacks avoided: 37/100.

"Dark Lightning *Strike*!" Joe called out; his words instantly punctuated by a strange, near-silent bolt of darkness; every enemy within roughly ten feet of him took damage. The closest creature took ten damage, while everything else including his nearby teammates took only five.

Skill increase: Dark Lightning Strike (Novice II).

"That did literally *nothing* to them!" Jaxon called as he used Joe's shoulders as a springboard and landed on the horse portion of a Neigh-Bear. His hands tore into the back of its neck, and the beast collapsed a moment later. "Store that for me? I think you have a large storage, right? Oh! Good! Since you're useless fighting against these without ruining the meat, you can be our loot wench!"

"Add that to the list of things to never say again, Jaxon!" Alexis called over. The Neigh-Bears around her were still, and as she passed them, they fell to the ground. "Get these ones too, Joe. The poison won't hurt the meat, it just melts their brain for a second or two."

"*Another* thing I can't say? I'm already over here having an existential crisis about the mechanisms of those vertebrae, and now I can't *say* things?" Jaxon whined as he slapped a fuzzy muzzle. "You youngsters sure are picky about verbiage."

"Words have power here, Jaxon, and people have enough power that making them mad can get you killed over and over," Alexis explained for what must have been the tenth time. "Joe, these are good for experience if you can manage to take them down. They are designed to be hard-countered by people with high dexterity, which means they are all strength and constitution; they hit hard and have a lot of health."

Joe nodded and got himself ready. His lightning had a six-minute cooldown, so that was out for now. He was okay with that, as he had plenty of options to work with. The shadows of the long grass started shifting as he gathered them, and after a nerve-wracking moment, he pushed them into the shape of an angled spear and solidified them. The Neigh-Bear that was charging hit the spear and impaled itself, its momentum halted as it hit the wide guard halfway down the shaft.

Damage dealt: 330 (300+10% Pierce the Darkest Night title bonus)

"These things are armored?" Joe muttered after taking an instant to read the message. "Must be their thick hide counting as natural armor? Acid Spray!"

As the acid ate into the whinnying creature, Joe once again saw the armor-piercing effect come into play. He wanted to test it more, but was trampled from the side as he stared at the first and forgot to pay attention to the remainder of the creatures.

Debuffs activated: Risk Assessment. Calculation drain. You have fully lost focus of combat and are held until acted upon by an outside force!

Damage taken: 228 (228 damage absorbed by Exquisite Shell).

Exquisite Shell: 482/1510.

Joe skidded across the blood-slick grass, somehow staying upright. He shook off the effects of his loss of focus, and managed to leap over the next attack. As he was coming down, another Neigh-Bear swiped at him, but Joe managed to twist around it in midair and land solidly on his feet.

Charging attacks avoided: 38/100.

Skill increase: Aerial Acrobatics (Beginner II).

"Dodging swiping attacks doesn't count?" Joe grumbled as he started working to get to the center of the area. The area from the start of the dungeon to the center covered about a mile, and dodging the entire way was destroying his stamina. He was down to a third, and it was only coming back *slowly*. But this was one of the reasons he was here: to increase his physical stats.

"It literally says 'charging attacks' in the quest." Poppy landed next to him and shoved, sending both of them out of the way of an oncoming wall of flesh.

Charging attacks avoided: 39/100.

"That counted!" Joe slyly made a plan to make his journey to the center of the area more efficient. First, he would get everyone in position, then they would literally bounce off each- "*Ow*!"

Risk Assessment has activated.

Sneak attack! 510 damage taken! (482 absorbed by Exquisite Shell.)

Health: 332/350

Joe's shield took a critical hit and shattered, leaving him unprotected against the remaining attacks coming his way. "Ahh! Why is that *activating* so much? It's supposed to be ten percent!"

He started jogging toward the escape area, dodging and flipping out of the straight-line assaults. Joe was particularly proud of dodging an attack by leaping at a passing Neigh-Bear and pushing off of it, causing two of the huge beasts to collide. "Ha!"

Jaxon's body seemed to materialize next to the two creatures, and in an instant he had sunk his hands into their necks. Sprays of blood came from both as the T-Rex heads were pulled back, and Jaxon laughed maniacally as he was coated in the hot liquid. Joe narrowed his eyes and aimed at the left one. "Corify!"

Skill increase: Corify (Novice II).

"*Yes*! That one must have worked!" Joe dashed over and thrust his hips at the beast, storing it in his codpiece.

"Really, Joe? Teabagging is so… toxic gamer." Jaxon **tsked** and shook his head.

"Not at *all* what I was doing, and you know it." Joe looked around, noticing that they had cleared the area and now had a few minutes before any other creatures would be near them. "Jaxon, how often does your threshold debuff go off?"

"My what?" Jaxon looked over from allowing his hands to devour the other Neigh-Bear to maintain their form. "Sorry, Joe, no idea what you're talking about."

"Open up your menu and look at the 'active effects' tab. What's the percentage for charisma failure?" Joe was starting to get impatient.

"Nothing here but title effects, a 'filthy' notification, and my hands." Jaxon shrugged and kept working his hands deeper into the flank of the downed beast. "I've never heard of a threshold debuff."

Joe frowned and thought through the implications. "Could

this be… an effect of Tatum? Is this a 'hidden' stat that I can somehow see?"

Wisdom +1! Wow, that one was a long time coming. You should open up better communication channels with your people. Ya know what? You did *just do that, so…*

Charisma +1!

"Ignoring the snark. Alright… I need to think… I have five debuffs that have a chance to activate with almost any action. So… I don't have a ten percent chance of things going wrong. I have an, um, ten plus five plus… I have a thirty-one percent chance of things going *really* wrong?" Joe waited for a characteristic upgrade, but shrugged when nothing appeared. "I need to test this. I need to *science* this. Hypothesis is formed; now comes various experimentation. Unlike other people, I can *see* when these activate, which means that I-"

Calculation drain!

"*Joe*!" Jaxon tackled Joe, and they rolled out of the way of a charge. Unfortunately, Lefty latched onto Joe and pulled off a chunk of his bicep. "I was *yelling* at you to move!"

Joe screamed as he grabbed at his arm. His health plummeted, reaching forty-one points remaining in only seconds. "*Lay on hands*!"

Health: 281/350. Bleeding debuff removed!

It was kinda trippy watching his muscle and skin regrow out of dark water, but Joe *forced* himself to focus. He glared at the Neigh-Bear and held out a hand. He grunted out of pure frustration and dropped his hand. "At this moment, I am realizing that I only have three ways of damaging that beast. Acid, which is out of range, shaping darkness over a few long seconds, or my dark lightning which is on cooldown. I need to get some more versatile spells."

"Here, I can bite it, if that'll make you feel better?" Jaxon kindly offered.

"You know, it *would* make me feel better?" With Joe's blessing, Jaxon ran at the beast as it was turning around, latched his hands into it, and chomped down on its ear with his own mouth. The Neigh-Bear roared, and Joe dropped his head into his hands. Then he started laughing and couldn't stop.

Jaxon came back over, and grinned at Joe with bloody teeth. "Glad you feel better, Joe."

"Let's finish up this dungeon." Joe healed Jaxon once just to be sure he didn't have any hidden injuries, and they resumed dodging and weaving. Their goal was in sight.

CHAPTER THIRTEEN

"I can't help but feel that we missed something," Joe muttered as they walked away from the dungeon. "Something was nagging at me there at the end…"

"So, go back tomorrow and look," Poppy grumped at him. "Don't just keep repeating yourself. Did you get the five points of dex or not?"

Joe blinked and looked at the rewards. "Yeah. Oh! I also got a point for characteristic training! Holy… nine hundred and ten experience, too!"

As the notification faded, Joe was lifted into the air and an explosion of golden light raced away from him. He landed, took a deep breath, and *whooped*, "Level sixteen!"

"Congrats!" Bard cheered for him.

"*What?*" Alexis gasped with unrepentant jealousy. "There is no *way* that you were training dexterity for a full, uninterrupted hour!"

Shrugging helplessly, Joe simply declined to answer. "If I can do this tomorrow, I'll clear the threshold for dexterity!"

"Atta boy!" Bard whacked him on the arm. "Good things happen with tha'. Ya get all sorts of, ah… *flexible.*"

Alexis blushed, popped open a bottle, and tossed it at the Skald. "What did I *tell* you about embarrassing me in front of the group! Enjoy *emptying* yourself!"

Bard's stomach groaned loudly enough that Joe took a hasty step away. "Joe! No! *Cleanse* me, quick!"

"Bard! I don't have that spell anymore!" Joe looked on with horrified eyes as Bard sprinted toward the tree line. The remaining party gaped at Alexis, who simply raised a brow at them.

"Let that be a warning to the *rest* of you!" Alexis threatened darkly. "If I'll do *that* to my *boyfriend*, think about what *you* would get."

Poppy and Joe stared at each other. Jaxon jumped after a butterfly that flew past. Poppy unsheathed his rapier just an inch and looked Alexis in the eye. "Your *boyfriend* might stand that, but do something like that to *me*, and we're done. Think on *that* before you start making power plays and tooting your own horn. You've been pushing all of us pretty hard recently, and you've been doing a fine job. Start attacking *me*, though… I'll make sure *you* go off to respawn faster than *I* can inhale your poison."

Alexis deflated. "Wow, take a joke and turn it into… just *wow*, Poppy."

"Don't turn this around on *me*-"

"Oh, look! Loot!" Joe loudly exclaimed, dropping all the Neigh-Bears out of his storage devices. "Let's get these processed. I'm betting that we'll find a few Cores, lots of materials that will *sell* nicely…"

The party members turned away from each other, avoiding eye contact as they all went through and chopped up the Neigh-Bears. As a benefit of being on Guild property, each time they pulled usable meat off of a carcass, it vanished into nothingness and a notification appeared.

Contribution points added!

"That's handy," Joe mused, pushing a carving knife through

a thick section on the beast's haunch. "Easy cleanup. Now where's… that… *Core*?"

Joe kept slicing for another few minutes, then sighed and sat back. "Forget this. Shadows… pull, push… *solidify*!"

The entire beast was pulled into ten large chunks, the meat and bones *tearing* rather than being cut. "Shoot… still don't have perfect control of this. That was supposed to be razor sharp."

"Joe, that hide is totally ruined now." Poppy sighed and sat down as well. "Whatever… they aren't worth much these days anyway. Here's the Core; found it when the skull was pulled apart."

"Thanks." Joe took the Core and grimaced. "Common Core. Ugh. What a wasteful joke of an item."

"Those were pretty common monsters; I'm actually surprised they gave a Core at all." Jaxon leaned in and looked at the Core. "Seems… almost different than the others that I've seen."

"Huh?" Joe looked at the notification from touching it.

Common-grade synthetic monster Core found! Would you like to convert this into experience points? Current worth: Five hundred experience points.

"Five hundred?" Joe looked again. "*Synthetic*? This is a Common grade Core, why is it worth the same amount as a low grade, or damaged Core?"

"If you hadn't noticed yet, this is also a perfect *cube* instead of a gemstone shape." Jaxon pointed out. Joe had *not* seen that, the soft yet penetrating light emanating from it deterred him from looking at it directly.

"As long as it works for what I need, then I don't care if it comes out as a smiley face." Joe sighed and stored the Core. "Must have been my new skill messing with things."

"Good to know that there is another way to get those Cores. Have you *seen* what they cost at the contribution shop?" Alexis rejoined the conversation, clearly trying to put the previous sore conversation behind them.

"Mike actually got that up and running?" Joe chuckled at

the thought. He was sure the man was going to rub it in the next time they met. "Good for him, I suppose?"

Bard came out of the woods, gave Alexis a dark look, and walked off toward the Guild town. She swallowed and looked at the ground as they all resumed their journey. Joe mulled over his recent realizations, and had to sigh at the sheer amount of work that he had in front of him. "Hmm… show skill details: Ritual Magic."

Ritual Magic (Expert II): Ability to create, maintain, and change rituals much more efficiently than usual. -.5% mana and component cost per skill level. Ritualist class exclusive: -50% mana and component cost. Current bonus maximized at 85% cost reduction.

"I haven't been able to *budge* this skill in weeks now." Joe looked at his Ritual Alchemy skill, and hoped that with the new information he had gained, his skills would at the *very* least stop stagnating.

Soul Forge completed! New skill acquired: Artisan Body.

Artisan Body (Novice IX): Everything that you do with your body is just a tiny bit easier. Mind, body, or something more ephemeral, all Characteristics are .1n times faster to train during a daily skill increase, where n = skill level.

Joe stared at the new skill, trying to figure out how the skills he had combined were able to make this. "This means that… if I needed to train for a full hour, I'd only need to train for… almost fifty-five minutes? That means that I need to train for… about thirteen and a half minutes? Useful, but not really. But what if I took that to rank fifty?"

He worked through the mental math for a long moment, *really* missing calculators for the thousandth time. "No, I'm wrong from the start. It says '*point* one N *times* faster'. That means that… why am I having so much trouble with this? My math was right. At fifty, this would cut the time to train characteristics in half."

"Sir!" Joe jumped and looked around. He found himself sitting alone at a picnic table, and realized that at least an hour had passed since his team had started walking home. Joe focused his confused glance on a messenger, who handed over a box. "Package for you, sir!"

"Abyssal calculation drain… thank you." Joe took the box and stood, making his way swiftly to the temple. "I don't like this. I'm *not* this scatterbrained. These debuffs are messing with me way too much."

He looked at the extraordinarily plain box, pulled on his Exquisite Shell to the maximum, and opened it. The plain outer shell fell away, revealing a box with the Royal Crest on it. "*This*… is not what I expected."

Opening it revealed a letter and a small golden circle. He read the letter first, not trusting that he would know what to do with the other item.

To Joe,
Please be aware that we
are fully aware of the acts that you
continue to perform. We see the benefits you have wrought,
and hope that this upgrade of Our gift to you
will be put to good use.
Queen Marie.
-P.S. In case that wasn't clear enough, this is Our thanks for the new arena you built.
Touch the circlet to the golden marker on your forehead.
-P.P.S. Do ***not*** *combine the result with other things.*

"I mean… not going to throw it away, so I might as well use it, right?" Joe picked up the glowing circle and placed it on his forehead. "What was that last part about combin-"

Skill gained: Essence Cycle (Novice I). One of the four magical senses that can be granted by the King or Queen of Ardania. By powering your eyes with mana, you will be able to see the energy in all things. Practice will be needed in order to be able to ignore the ambient power in the environment. Higher levels of this skill will allow for more detailed studying of the energies. Masters of this skill are rumored to be able to perfectly learn spells simply by seeing them a single time. Effect: 1n%

increased mana-visual sensation, where n = skill level. Cost: 40 mana per second.

"Don't combine these with each other…? The skills from the Royals, right? That's the only thing that makes sense." Joe looked into a mirror, grimacing as he saw that the mostly-clear but slightly-gold dot on his head had turned into an outline of an eye. It was small, but it glowed softly, and he was bald. It was *very* noticeable. "I just… fine. Try it out, don't think about how weird this is. Just makes me look like a classic Monk powering a chakra, or whatever that is supposed to be. It's *fine*."

Sitting in the lotus position, Joe looked straight ahead and activated his new ability. "*Essence Cycle*."

In retrospect, sitting in a massive magical building, in the portion of said building that was devoted to the divine, may have been a bad idea. *May* have been. Hours later, Joe was able to pull away from his inspection of the deepest darkness that he had ever seen. He had been staring at and inspecting pure dark-aligned power, and really felt that he had gained something from it.

You have stared into the void and walked away with a smile on your face! Characteristic training complete. +1 Charisma. Caution: gaining charisma in this fashion may lead to side effects. For being the first traveler to discover this new method of characteristic training: Charisma +5!

Skill increased: Essence Cycle (Novice V).

Joe wobbled to his feet, feeling sick and wrung-out. His head was pounding, and he felt that he was going to drop. "Wh-what's *happening*? Character sheet!"

Name: Joe '*Tatum's Chosen Legend*' Class: Mage (Actual: Rituarchitect)
Profession I: Tenured Scholar (Actual: Arcanologist)
Profession II: Ritualistic Alchemist
Character Level: 16 Exp: 136,123 Exp to next level: 16,877
Rituarchitect Level: 4 Exp: 8,936 Exp to next level: 1,064
Hit Points: 282/350
Mana: 60/1,650 (115 Reserved)

Mana regen: 33.89/sec (Base 30.81/sec increased by gear)
Stamina: 315/315
Stamina regen: 5.68/sec

Characteristic: Raw score (Modifier)

Strength: 33 (1.33)
Dexterity: 48 (1.48)
Constitution: 40 (1.4)
Intelligence: 110 (3.1)
Wisdom: 85 (2.35)
Charisma: 40 (1.4)
Perception: 63 (2.13)
Luck: 31 (1.31)
Karmic Luck: 0

"Ugh. That constant mana drain… it must have eaten into my health when I was running too low on mana." Joe took deep breaths, waiting for his mana to quickly refill. "Right… onward toward my goals."

CHAPTER FOURTEEN

"To *arms*! Towny McTownface is under attack!"

The klaxon sounding throughout the Guild made Joe spring upright, and he ran to the wall as he shook off his grogginess. Out of the corner of his eye, he saw someone *shadowy* leaping at him. "Dark Lightning Strike!"

The strange-sounding lightning hit him just as the would-be assassin did, but the thin daggers dealt far more damage than the spell. Still, as the daggers bounced off his Exquisite Shell, the unexpected pain made his attacker flinch. Joe used that time to coat them with a thick layer of acid, though he no longer had the ability to channel the spell. A shriek filled the air as the figure's skin started to melt.

"My gear!" Then again, the assailant might not care so much about a measly sixty-five points of damage. The armor durability-destroying effect, on the other hand… "I'm gonna *wreck* you!"

"No thanks!" Joe called out without looking back. While the assassin was distracted, Joe started running toward a clump of fighters. They saw what was happening, and sent the assassin to respawn after a swift battle. Since the guy's gear was ruined, his stealth was a joke and the fighters had no issue taking him down. "Thanks, guys."

"Mages shouldn't be alone during an attack; you get hunted first. Come with us 'til you find your party." Joe didn't recognize anyone in the group, but he stayed with them and committed their faces to memory. He'd find a way to thank them later.

In a strangely short amount of time, the fighting was over and the town was secured. Most of the attackers hadn't gotten into the town itself, content to assault the walls themselves. Joe was pulled into yet another emergency meeting, where the Guild explained that this was likely the result of the other Noble Guilds, and possibly other groups, testing their defenses.

After the quick meeting ended, Mike pulled Joe aside. "We have no answers for this, Joe. This was well-organized. As soon as we started to respond, they fell back. Clearly they were only testing us, but I think we failed. Is there anything that *you* can do to increase our defenses?"

"No, there's…" Joe hesitated as he thought over the various effects that he had recently discovered with his rituals. "*Maybe.* No promises, but I might be able to set up some rituals that can be activated if they *absolutely* need to be. Still, I need time, both to research and to *make* them. Again, no promises."

"We should have time." Mike sighed in relief. "Tell me what you need, and I'll see what can be done."

They discussed terms for a short while, and came to an agreement. Just before walking away, Joe remembered that the shop had opened. "Hey, are there any Cores for sale in the contribution shop?"

"I thought you'd never ask." A sly smile appeared on Mike's face, "They are one of the most expensive items, and can *only* be bought with contribution points. Some of the other stuff can be purchased with coin, but *those*… well, you'll be very happy when you see that our deals have been working in your favor."

After parting ways, Joe decided that he should check in and see if more building material had been collected. It had been happening more and more rarely, but he was glad to see that there was enough for a full building again. He knocked on a wooden post to get the workers in the area to look his way. "Hey guys, I know it's early, but since everyone is awake… any of you know where the town planner is?"

A rumpled man wearing pajamas arrived a few minutes later, and they went through the new plans that Joe had been able to collect. Upon seeing the Trophy Hall, the man almost shouted for joy. "This! This one! We needed a building that *only* gives an overall morale boost, and if we build this one, we should hit town rank two right away!"

"Then let's do it!" Joe high-fived the guy; his enthusiasm was *infectious*. "I'll get my people together, where do we need to meet?"

After getting everything in motion, Joe raced off and dragged his Coven out of the beds they had just re-crawled into. They hurried to the town center and found that a good chunk of the upper echelon had also been pulled out to see what would happen. The building was scheduled to be placed north-east of the Guild Hall, so everyone set out for an early morning walk. When they reached the designated area, Joe rustled around for a few long minutes, examining details, making the outline of the building appear with his tool, and moving people for a good half hour before he was finally satisfied with the layout.

Then it was time for the actual building to be put into place. With a quick chant and a few drops of blood, Joe and his Coven were pulled into the air. In under a minute, the building had been completed. He turned to the town planner and shrugged. "Well, that's my part completed. I don't know what else to expect, but if-"

Class experience gained: 120.

Guild alert! The Guild's base of operations, Towny McTownface-

Joe chuckled as he heard Aten groan as if he were being cut apart.

-has reached town level 2: Actual Town. All offensive and defensive actions taken on behalf of the Wanderer's Guild while in Towny McTown-

face are increased by 5%! All resources collected and items crafted on guild property have their quality increased by 1%!

Guild quest updated: The making of an Elder. Current town level: 2/5.

"*Man,* that's a long-term quest." Joe shuddered as he looked around and saw all that had gone into making *this* town level. Then again, a few of the buildings were *incredibly* rare, so perhaps those weren't so far away after all?

As an additional reward for being the first Noble Guild to increase their town level to two, The Guildhall will now be upgraded to an 'Uncommon' ranked Guildhall!

There were a few screams that drifted all the way to the group observing the construction of the trophy hall as people were chucked into the air. The Guildhall shuddered and blazed with light, coming back into view about twenty percent larger and an extra story higher. Four new additions were clearly visible: large ballistae on each corner.

"Oh look… a new building to scan." Amongst all the other hubbub, Joe's comment went unheard. The remainder of the day proceeded as normal, the major highlight for Joe being another completion of the test dungeon, which caused him to reach the threshold for dexterity. Just outside of the dungeon, he collapsed as his nervous system was upgraded. When he came around, he was faster, more accurate, and could *feel* the utter nimbleness of his body. The best part was when he checked his debuffs… and 'Risk Assessment' was gone, hopefully forever.

A week went by with Joe working with his team, practicing his spells, and raising buildings. Between the monster fights and buildings, he had gained eight thousand character experience and fourteen hundred class experience. In short, he had worked his butt off to raise his characteristics and skills. At the end of the week, Joe had raised all of his stats except for luck above fifty points. Each of these had a differing effect on his body, and after comparing with his team and a few others in the guild, Joe started to see a pattern for the development of threshold rewards.

Name: Joe '*Tatum's Chosen Legend*' Class: Mage (Actual: Rituarchitect)
Profession I: Tenured Scholar (Actual: Arcanologist)
Profession II: Ritualistic Alchemist
Character Level: 16 Exp: 144,123 Exp to next level: 8,877
Rituarchitect Level: 5 Exp: 10,456 Exp to next level: 4,544
Hit Points: 350/350 -> 534/534
Mana: 1,381/1,650 (115 Reserved)
Mana regen: 33.89/sec
Stamina: 485/485 -> 528.5/528.5
Stamina regen: 5.68/sec -> 5.84/sec

Characteristic: Raw score (Modifier)

Strength: 53 (2.03)
Dexterity: 54 (2.04)
Constitution: 54 (2.04)
Intelligence: 110 (3.1)
Wisdom: 85 (2.35)
Charisma: 52 (2.02)
Perception: 63 (2.13)
Luck: 38 (1.38)
Karmic Luck: 0

All of Joe's physical attributes had given him the exact same thing: a ten percent boost across the board to all things that were considered 'bodily resources'. Instead of a point of constitution giving him ten health, now it was worth eleven. Instead of five points, stamina, strength, and constitution were worth five-point-five. This had been a *wild* change from crossing the thresholds for intelligence and wisdom.

What he found was that both his class as well as *how* he gained the characteristic points played a role. If a player crossed the threshold for strength by *mostly* doing characteristic training each day, they got a flat bonus. If they were a fighter and gained their points by fighting and training, they got the option to play a kind of inner mini-game for higher rewards, like Joe had when increasing his wisdom.

Class had an impact *mainly* because players tended to do class-related things with greater regularity. For instance, Joe had asked several 'tank' classers what they got at the threshold for constitution, and most of them had *doubled* the amount of health they gained per point. Some had even tripled it, and further discussion revealed that they had managed to pull through really tough situations, keeping their party alive for the great majority. After learning this fact, it was almost too easy to point them out. As could be expected, they tended to have impressive dents in their armor.

Charisma had a different effect, and Joe wasn't sure if he liked what had happened. He had increased charisma fairly naturally, and only since receiving the new energy sight ability from the Queen had he begun actively training it.

Charisma has reached the fifty point threshold! New effect added: Dark Charisma.

Dark Charisma is a characteristic shift, neither a skill nor title. Looking into the deep dark has fundamentally changed how you look at the world, and how the world looks at you. All active effects now contain a hint of the deeper aspects of existence. Those who are looking to solve a mystery or find a dark companion will gravitate toward you, but there will always be some that cannot handle what your existence evokes in their own minds. Tall, dark, and… something like handsome; since you do *have solid charisma now. Still bald though.*

Caution! Pushing for darker or more emotional reactions from people may cause this shift to become more drastic.

Joe had also been working on his skills, managing to bring Acid Spray to Beginner five, Dark Lightning Strike and Knowledge to Novice nine, Architectural Lore to Novice three, Alchemical Lore and Ritualistic Alchemy to *Beginner* one, Exquisite Shell to Beginner four, Corify to Novice six, and—after one unlucky encounter where Poppy got crushed between two Neigh-Bears—Resurrection to Novice four.

He was exhausted. Between all the training, studying, mana

draining, and research into protective rituals for the town, he was barely sleeping at all. Nonetheless, all of his outstanding debuffs had been cleared, except for luck. He had been managing a few games of chance, but they certainly had not been enough to make up for the low stat. Also… the 'luck' trial in the test dungeon apparently had the highest mortality rate of all the tests, and he couldn't risk losing a bunch of experience at such a crucial time. Which… the lack of risk taking perhaps *explained* why his luck stat was so low.

Something needed to change, or Joe was going to be locked into a cycle of repetition until he started to lose his mind. Then… something *did* change. On the eighth day of his intense training cycle, a letter arrived.

CHAPTER FIFTEEN

The letter was from Boris, and it held the information he had promised Joe weeks ago. Joe ran his eyes over it again as his team walked along, pleased as punch that he had come this direction before; it would help him gain an edge over someone else that had caused trouble for Boris.

Joe,
It appears that there may be an item that will allow you to specialize your current class into a higher one. It may be a type of book, a stone tablet, or another similar item that holds knowledge. There is only one thing that I am certain of:
This item is single use.
If you don't get it first, there is a strong possibility that someone else will. I am sorry to say that after finding this information, I returned to my desk and found that someone had gone through my notes. I suspect a group called the 'Upright Men' or some such nonsense. They are a guild of thieves that have been a plague on this city for decades.
There is more. I think that I am being watched, and I don't know by whom, or for what reason. But the fact of the matter is that this information was found stolen too quickly for it to be a coincidence.

I have included a small map that should get you close to where this item has been hidden. It will be up to you from here on out.
Best of luck, Boris.

"Hmm. Hope Boris is doing alright..." Joe muttered with great concern.

"Ya know, Joe," Bard grunted around a slab of meat he had pulled out of a sack, "Ah think it's odd that tha Guild is givin' us quests and fat rewards for helpin' ya get yer class upgrade."

"I think they really want him gone!" Jaxon cheerfully stated, giving Joe a thumbs-up. "When he gets to the next Zone, he can be his usual workaholic self and he won't have to worry about stepping on the toes of the Guild's investors. *They* will never go to the next area, so they might as well be totally separate guilds!"

"You know what, Jaxon?" Joe grinned conspiratorially, "I think I like that idea a whole abyss of a lot. Oh *no*, they want me to go to a place that only competent people can even *get* into! Not that! Anything but being surrounded solely by the hard-working members of the guild...!"

"I think that I found what I need to do to get into my next class too, which means that we should be able to go together!" Jaxon continued after nodding along gravely. "I got a job in the palace learning from the Royal Masseuse and the Royal Tamer! If I can get all of those skills and find a good way to combine them, I'm *sure* that I'll be able to get my next Specialization."

"I have plans for my class as well." Poppy let a wicked smile spread across his face. "But you're just gonna need to wait and see."

"I'm totally stumped on how to proceed," Alexis admitted carefully. "I think Bard is, too. We've been looking for ways forward, but either there isn't someone on our same path, or they are hidden pretty deeply. I think that a likely progression for me is into an Assassin class, and they aren't showing up and making an offer."

"Ahm still banned from the Bardic College." Bard grumbled. "Apparently, I got the attention of the Deity of Bards, and since he likes me… ahm not allowed back into the place."

"That's some backward logic, isn't it?" Joe spread his arms in anger. "If the freaking *God of Music* likes you, you get *banned*?"

"Nah. It's the Deity of *Bards*." Bard explained, "Apparently the guy hates Bards. So, they use tha' knowledge as ah litmus test. He likes ya, yer out. He *hates* ya, you are clearly doin' sommat right."

"Weird." Jaxon chimed in.

"I heard that he didn't want to be the Deity of Bards, he was forced into the role." Alexis told them. "Apparently Hansel was some form of Assassin that got immortalized in song, and somehow gained a ton of power from that."

"Wait… is this the same one from the song I keep hearing in taverns?" Poppy furrowed his brow, then snapped his fingers, "*Dangerlicious*! Is that the one?"

"Yup." Bard sighed dramatically. "Cause o' that, ahm stuck in my spot with nowhere ta turn."

"Don't worry, Bard." Joe patted the man on the arm. "I'm sure we can get something with the Pathfinder's Hall. Eventually the Bardic College will come in range, and we'll get all the information on every current classer in there. Same deal with an assassin ring, Alexis. It's only a matter of time."

"Where are we going right now anyway?" Jaxon questioned Joe directly. "I know almost nothing about this trip."

"Ah. Let me gather my thoughts." Joe pulled up his status screen and ran over the information he had available. "Looks like we are going to the south-eastern coast, and we need to find a temple that held ancient secrets. Likely, that means we are running straight at a dungeon, but whatever. Right now, we are going to swing by the guild we rescued when we came to the forest of Chlorophyll Chaos, the… Golden Greens. Yeah, specifically, I want to see what Teddy is up to these days."

An hour later, they found signs of the land being worked, and there were some impressive fields that had been plowed and planted. The crops were growing at a pace that was noticeable, and Joe had to assume that there was magic involved. Par for the course in Eternium. They met with a few people guarding a small village, and after a few messages were sent back and forth, the group was given a place to stay and Joe went to talk with Teddy.

They discussed how things were going, and made plans to talk more in the future. The Guild hadn't seen anything odd in recent days, which gave Joe hope for getting ahead of whoever else had this information. Since they were already fairly close to the coast - so long as they went east to the water and not south to the forest - another point of interest came up.

"We found a small shrine just off the road, about halfway from here to the sea." Teddy leaned in and gave him a knowing look. "If we can guide you there, you think you could go ahead and convert it? It'd make a good respawn location, *way* closer than the other one where you saved a bunch of us the last time we met. Also, that would knock a huge amount of time off our trips to Ardania."

"Of course." Joe was surprised by her earnestness. "Is this such a huge issue for you?"

"Yup." Teddy sat back with obvious relief. "Most of our guild is composed of noncombatants, so that walk means that a death can lead to three more for them. Oh, I also have a slew of clerics that follow Tatum now, and they were hoping you could find a place for them?"

"*What*!" Joe almost jumped out of his seat in his excitement. "Where! I, oh, right. Yes, I have *huge* positions for them. I have a mid-sized temple that needs a permanent person, and a *Cathedral* that is sitting empty in the middle of nowhere that *really* needs people in it to run things."

"Perfect, because I have a few introverts that want to hang out in lonely buildings," Teddy informed him seriously. "They avoid people to such a degree that they are having trouble out *here*, in the farmlands. I'll have them guide you to the shrine, and then you can show them to their new stations? As long as they can come visit every once in a while, they'll maintain their position in the guild."

The night came to an end a short while later, and the two parted ways. Joe slept excellently, and in the morning, the party set off with a small contingent of people that were dressed in robes. Jaxon was distrustful of them, and kept making biting motions at them with his hands. Since none of the new people had any idea what that meant, they simply stayed away from the strange man.

Converting the shrine was easy with so many clerics, because it seemed that they could all pool their mana for the event. Even better, after doing it once, they all got a skill that allowed them to convert structures for Tatum on their own. Joe was almost jealous, as he only had a static ability to do so: no skill appeared that would make it easier over time. From there, Joe popped them to the Cathedral or the temple, based on their preference.

After finishing up at the Cathedral, Joe was about to leave when one man stopped him with a question. "My apologies, but I am wondering how I can get a sigil like the one you wear?"

Joe simply returned a confused glance, then followed the man's pointing finger. Above his heart was a small rotating hologram that was a combination of his guild icon and Tatum's symbology. "Oh. That was pointed out to me by Tatum, but I think any of us can equip sigils in our sigil tab."

"Sigil tab?" the man repeated. His eyes grew wide, and then he winked at Joe. "Got access to it! Nice and sneaky way of keeping people from knowing everything. I'll make sure the others know to keep it to ourselves."

"No, I'm not trying to hide information-"

"After all, double reputation with a deity is hard to get." The man was lost in his own world already, and Joe was suddenly glad this one was staying at the Cathedral. "We'll get *so* many more options for spells when we level up than other clerics will!"

"I... hadn't actually thought about that." Joe nodded slowly. "Perhaps that *is* a good call."

Contemplating the different buildings he had converted made Joe wonder about his quest to free Tatum. He brought up the quest tab and nodded. Solid progress.

Paying a Great Debt. Current progress: 1,080,550/13,000,000. Current sources of divine energy: Altars: 5. Shrines: 11. Temples (small): 0. Temples (mid-sized): 1. Temples (grand): 1. Champions defeated: 1. Followers: 182.

"Hmm. I wonder how I can speed that up?" Lost in thought, he selected to teleport away. In the next instant, Joe was back with his party in front of the newly converted shrine. "Looks like we have a nice way back home now."

"Sounds good to me." Poppy turned and led the way back to the road. To Joe's *great* concern, a new group of people was traveling along the dirt path. One man looked almost like a member of the Three Musketeers, with fancy clothing and a foppish feathered hat. The remainder was composed of an obvious mage, monk, assassin, and heavy close-range fighter.

There was something about this group that made Joe's senses tingle, and a primal part of him was screaming at him to kill these people before they got too close. Before he could make a choice on what to do next, the man in the foppish hat waved at them and called out. "Hello there! I'm Sam! Nice to officially meet you! You wouldn't have happened to see any temple ruins around here, would you?"

"Officially? Because we saw each other on the road?" Joe narrowed his eyes and looked the man over. Something about his smug face just seemed so... *punchable*, and Joe decided to test the waters. "Hello, Sam. I'm Joe. Can I say, you really look like a fine, *Upright Man*."

Sam's face shifted, and Joe knew that he had been correct. These were the people that had gone through Boris's papers... and a dark feeling in his heart told Joe that they would end up fighting to the death sooner or later.

CHAPTER SIXTEEN

"Joe, is it?" Sam greeted him in a feigned affable tone. "I've met so many people named 'Joe' in the last few days that I feel like it is going to get listed as the number one name in Eternium any day now!"

"Ah-ha… yeah." Joe nodded at the group and stiffly turned away. They started walking, but stopped short when Sam called out to them.

"By the way… *Joe*. Something tells me that we might be looking for the same thing, and I'm going to tell you this right now. I *will* be the one going home with it." Sam was staring at Joe with a small smile on his face. "Though I feel like I have another book that you would love as a replacement. Just like my plan to win the day here, the information inside it is… *explosive*."

Joe's stare turned to ice. So *this* was the guy that had sent a bomb home with him? Even *more* reason to destroy him. They got a good distance away before Joe turned to his group and explained what he knew about Sam. Really, there wasn't much to tell, as the man seemed to know about *him*, whereas this was the first time that Joe had directly met Sam.

Poppy turned and half-drew his rapier. "That fool sent a *bomb* along with you? Into a random populated area? He could have hurt *dozens* of people with that stunt! Let's put that rabid dog *down*!"

Bard held him back, shaking his head. "Poppy, yah can't jus' attack. You'll get a player killer aura, an' then everythin'll turn inta ah right mess."

"*He* attacked Joe without provocation! I say we return the favor!" Poppy snarled as he pulled against Bard.

Joe was touched that Poppy was ready to go to war for him, though still he shook his head. "We are here to collect an item, not to fight over being in the area. If it comes to that, I'm glad to see that you are ready to fight, but let's hope it *doesn't*. If we are able to get in, get out, and walk away with the prize, we win long-term."

"Sometimes, don't you think the correct thing to do is the one that is *not* logical?" Jaxon wondered thoughtfully. "If they die, they have a *long* way to go to get back here, which gives us time to search and prepare. So, let's *wreck* them!"

"I...!" Joe met the serious stare down that he was getting and reluctantly nodded. "I think that you both made a good point... I just... okay. Let's get ready and ambush them."

They crept around the area, keeping the road in sight. After about ten minutes of searching, they found that the other party had vanished entirely. Alexis looked around and groaned, "Ugh... I bet they had the same idea and went hunting for us. We're probably circling each other and don't even know it."

"At least *we* don't know where *they* are." Jaxon ominously uttered. The silent plains around them suddenly seemed much more ominous. "Since, you know, this grass is almost neck-high, we could be completely surrounded and not even know it. Nature is crazy like that."

"Let's get down closer to the coast," Joe ordered with a dry throat. "The vegetation is sparse there, and we should get on with the hunt."

"Good call," Bard readily agreed. The group moved as silently as possible to the waterline and pulled out the map Boris had included with his letter.

Joe opened it up so everyone could see it. "We're gonna need to account for hundreds of years, and it's also possible that this place doesn't even exist anymore. It is *entirely* likely that someone else has been here before us and walked away with whatever scraps remained. It's equally likely that this place is buried. Luckily, if it is hidden, I actually have a *better* chance of finding it and raiding it successfully."

The group offered their own ideas, finally deciding that they should start by figuring out *exactly* where they were on the map; then they could look for inconsistencies in the area based on the differences. They started walking, but Poppy came to an abrupt halt and peered back up at the top of the hill they had just descended to reach the waterline. He pulled out his weapon and pointed with it. "They posted one person to watch us. I bet the others are sitting and having a picnic while they wait for us to do all the legwork."

"Then all we need to do is figure *everything out* and get the goods before they can react to it." Joe was starting to get a little snippy from the constant concern the other party had created by their mere presence. "Does anyone see anything that we can use as a landmark? I can't get a read on this map at all."

"I think that this section is…" Alexis leaned in and they went over what they were seeing. "But I can't imagine that the coastline would have changed so drastically in the last couple hundred years."

"Could be anything!" Jaxon joined in happily. "Imagine a powerful earth or water Mage that came through and was angry, or just wanted to test out what they could do! I bet *Joe* could make some really area-altering effects if he wanted, right? He's only been doing this for a short while! Think about someone that had trained at this for their entire lives!"

"He has a point." Joe nodded along, getting an arched brow

in return from Alexis. "We ran into the same issue with the forest. It was *hundreds* of miles closer than it should have been."

"What do you think we should do, then?" Poppy looked to Joe for leadership, and Joe straightened up at the realization that his team still relied on him.

"I think... that we need someone who knows maps better than I do." Joe started walking along the dirt road back toward the shrine. "Let's go get Jess. It's time for her to earn her pay."

Even though the trip was mostly uphill, it was swift. On a positive note, it turned out that Jess was spoiling for a change of scenery. She came along without fuss, and by evening, they had their bearings with the map. Jess slapped Joe on the shoulder, *hard*, and smiled widely. "You were close, but it seems that the water has moved in closer over the last few decades. That's why you have such a steep hill to get down to the waterline; all the gradual sloping land is now underwater."

"If I'm correct, the temple should be right... *there*." A glowing orb erupted from the water and shined purple light down in a perfect circle on the water. "That's only visible to you guys, by the way! It's a new skill! I can 'ping' a location that I want you all to approach."

"We jus' gonna slog our way down ta it, then?" Bard tightened his chest plate and took a step into the surf.

"Better idea." Jess pulled out a sack full of dead snakes and animated them. "I'll send these out to make sure that we can get there without a boat, and that we'll be able to breathe and such in there."

"Good call." Joe and the others sat down with Jess as she pulled out a paper and began mapping the ground along the coast.

"Pretty shallow... *there's* a drop-off, but if we go a few feet to the left..." Joe left her to her muttering as a small map took shape. "Oh, *that's* not good. Evasive maneuvers, snakes! Go, go, *go*!"

"Found the building. Lots and *lots* of creatures in the area!"

Jess was frantically drawing out her map, and it was getting less detailed as a result. "They're all carnivorous, and they apparently don't mind if their food is fresh or not. Ah, down to one snake. Slithering around the building…"

"Yes! Got an entrance, looks like they expected this to go underwater… following inside… it goes all the way to the top of the building." Jess was back to sketching details on her map, but suddenly swapped the paper with a fresh one. "It's a dungeon, alright. A *big* one too, if the top floor is anything to go by. Found a monster… what is that?"

She sighed and handed the papers over to Joe. "They got my last snake. That's the best I could do."

"You did a great job, Jess." Joe looked at the maps and bound them to his own personal map. The paper in his hand crumbled into ash. "Any details you want to share?"

"Sure." Jess stood and brushed the sand off her legs. "You can walk almost all the way there, but there are a few drop-offs that have monsters living in them. You fall in, and at *best,* you have to fight a monster on its home turf. Otherwise, the ground is pretty even. If there's a strong tide, that will clear most of the way and leave dry-ish land to walk on."

"We were here all day and the tide didn't go very far out." Poppy denied after a moment's thought.

"The moon's gonna pass us pretty soon." Jaxon pointed up, drawing everyone's attention to the oddly empty sky. Poppy gained a soft smile as he gazed at the place where his daughter was growing up, "Maybe a close and full moon means that the tides will shift?"

"Good catch… Jaxon." Everyone was keeping an eye on Jaxon, who had been shockingly normal and helpful the last few days. Joe cleared his throat and looked up at the moon. "I think that the time the moon will be closest will be tomorrow, so that gives us only a day to prepare. Let's get back to the guild and get everything that we might need."

Poppy looked up the hill at the heavily-armored, giant

weapon-wielding woman that was currently watching them. "Alexis, I'm gonna need some potent poison."

Alexis followed his gaze and showed a sinister smile. "I think that I have exactly what you need, Poppy. *Exactly* what you will need."

CHAPTER SEVENTEEN

"I need anything you've all been working on that might be helpful in water." Joe explained to his Coven as he shifted the room around slightly. He was in the Grand Ritual Hall, inspecting rituals for flaws or to assist with issues that his Coven had been having.

Big_Mo handed over some loose-leaf parchment. "I've been working on an interesting concept, but I think that it's at a higher level than I can manage."

"What… *is* this?" Joe looked at the variables, his eyes growing larger as he went through it. "Modified containment, but on a micro level?"

"Exactly!" Big_Mo excitedly pointed out his math. "This was something that I remember being a big deal back on earth. What *should* happen is that all hydrogen and oxygen molecules are pulled away from each other for the duration of the effect. In essence, low cost hydrogen and oxygen separation!"

"Which is great in *theory*," Taka interjected in exasperation, "but in *practice*, unless you can figure out a way to hold those gasses in a container, all it takes is a single spark added to the system, and you just made a massive hydrogen bomb."

"Which is *why* I'm bringing it to Joe for help!" Big_Mo turned and grinned at Joe. "He's just a little salty because the first try on this killed both of us. But it *also* cleared an entire dungeon!"

"All it did was kill everything and destroy all the loot before we got a chance to grab it! *And* we got no experience!" Taka argued vehemently. "I told you we should learn a light spell, but *no~o~o*, torches are so much *cooler*."

"Celestial Feces, dude, you already made a working model of this? What happened to it being outside of your ability?" Joe looked at the ritual and saw a few small changes that could be made. "Alright... two options for ease, unless you wanna rework this into a better ritual. Either add a point of capture here and add some tanks that can handle the pressure... or add an air-pressure directional *here*, and make the world's largest flamethrower!"

Joe and Big_Mo high-fived, and the conversation started to devolve into various ritual aspects. Hannah got them back on track with a simple, "Didn't you need to do something?"

"Oh, right. Drat." Joe sighed and looked at the new-model flamethrower longingly. "I need to go underwater for an unknown amount of time, clear a dungeon down there, while staving off a hostile party that will likely be trying to clear the same dungeon at the same time. Any ideas?"

"Water isn't my specialty, but I've been wanting to get to the bottom of a lake recently, so I've been working on this for a while." Kirby pulled out a sheet and handed it over. "It's the Ritual of Leaden Boots from that book you loaned us on beginner rituals. It'll pull you down right to the ground and will make it feel like you are walking on normal ground. None of that overly buoyant nonsense like you're on the moon."

"Nice! You mind if I make a copy of this?" Joe's eyes scanned the document and he found a few small mistakes. Once more, he thanked the system that dumped knowledge into his head whenever he leveled up a skill. "Just so you know, your math is wrong here, here, and here. As it is currently… this would be a ritual of feet crushing. Anyone below, let's see… thirty-two constitution would be *very* unhappy with you."

"Thanks!" Kirby smiled brightly. "I'll take a copy of both the original and the new one, if possible. I know a few people that I want to nail to the ground!"

Joe winced as he remembered that Kirby wanted to be an evil overlord. To each their own, he supposed. "Alright, if anyone can come up with a solution for the other factors I mentioned, please let me know. We are going to leave tomorrow and hopefully get where we need to be by moonrise, so please work fast if you plan to help."

They nodded and got to work. Joe immediately set to ironing out the issues in the leaden feet ritual, then modified it to work on a group. It was still a minor ritual, fit for a Beginner, so the cost was almost negligible. Not *quite* free, but he had gained several Trash-ranked Synthetic Cores on his frequent forays into the test dungeon, so the Core cost was something that he could manage easily.

A few hours into his work, Hannah came over with a design for him. "This is an interesting anti-personnel concept I came up with. Unlike the standard targeting mechanism, I used the blood added as a kind of access list. Anyone that approaches that *isn't* allowed will get a series of molecule-thin wind blades sent at them. Thoughts?"

Joe looked it over and winced. It was the magical equivalent of a claymore. "*Potent* booby-trap. This is kind of a ruthless effect, though."

She didn't understand what he was trying to say, so Joe pushed further, "If you power this up a little more, you could hurt a *lot* of people unintentionally. Also, there are no safeties built into it. Once it sends a wind blade, even people on the access list could be hit. All in all, *great* trap to leave behind in a dungeon or other enclosed area, *terrible* idea to leave out in the open."

"Who cares if it is 'ruthless'? Think of the applications for guild defense!" Hannah countered, obviously having put thought into her argument before coming over.

"Would *you* want to be the one to activate this?" Joe leaned in to hold her gaze. "Because that's the same as a Mage attacking a crowd of people with a fireball. You get a non-hostile caught in this, you're an instant player killer. If you devoted enough mana to it, you could get *dozens* of people cut down, and then your murderer aura lasts for *days*. Even if you don't care about other people, make sure to care about yourself."

"I-I do care about other people..."

Hannah looked down, so Joe decided to lighten up. "Now, to be fair, in this situation, this is *exactly* what I need. The only people that'd be in the area of effect are going to be trying to grab what I'm after, and a few days with a red aura is the least of my worries if they get it first. Good work."

"What?" Hannah looked up in shock. "But you...!"

"I am just making sure you know the *dangers*. I had a talk with Big_Mo about that water-powered flamethrower, too." Joe shook his head, smiling the whole time. "You guys are going a *far* more lethal route than I took when I was first starting out, but I guess the average person is all sorts of strong compared to then. 'Suppression' doesn't work if someone can just *ignore* what you toss at them."

"Thanks, Joe." Hannah grimaced and admitted, "I thought you were gonna yell at me or something."

"Nah, all of this is useful." Joe shook his head and sat down on a chair that formed with a thought. He loved this room. "Y'all just need to be careful when and where you use it, and my job is to point out the danger before you create something that hurts people you don't want to target. Want some coffee?"

Mate swirled up Joe's arm and burbled happily as Joe pulled out some espresso cups. "Double shot please, little buddy."

"*Brrb*!" Mate poured itself into the cups, then formed murky brown eyes and looked at Hannah. "*Drink me! I'm delicious!*"

"You sure are, Mate!" Joe coated his hand with mana and

petted the elemental, who bubbled and preened. The dark mana was sucked into its fluid surface as it sighed happily, swirled, and vanished. All that was left was a large coffee stain on Joe's sleeve. "I have a theory that my mana will eventually make his coffee a permanent dark roast. We'll see what happens."

"Looks like it isn't housebroken." Hannah gestured at his sleeve and chuckled as she took the drink. She tossed it back and opened her eyes wide. "Holy moley, that *is* delicious."

"Right?" Joe waved at his arm, "That's not a mess, that's just where Mate lives when he isn't fully… um… summoned? Otherwise, the cleaning spell I have would wash that away."

Observing the odd look he was getting, Joe offered more in-context information. "Yes, my familiar is a coffee elemental that lives in a coffee stain on my sleeve. This place is magic, and *this* is what makes you doubt that? Please. How else can I help you?"

"We need crafting items." Hanna waved at the rest of the group, who all looked up from what they were doing to nod along. "There's just no way that we can get access to the items that we need, even though the guild recently devoted an entire wing of the greenhouse to magical herbs and stuff like that."

Joe was torn. On one hand, he needed most of the items for himself. On the other hand, giving the Coven access to some of his gear would allow them to make progress at a speed that he could have only *dreamt* about at their level. Reluctantly, Joe started pulling items out of his Codpiece and holding them in the air. The room swirled, and a new area formed; a storehouse for the items that could be kept in the open. He quickly parsed through anything that needed to stay with him to remain fresh.

Knowing that they had money, or they *should,* thanks to what he was paying them, Joe used one of his Guild abilities for the very first time: setting a price for the items. "Alright, to take these items out of here, you need to pay for them. Free ride is over, unless it is a ritual that is needed either by myself or the guild. You can pay with money, barter, or… ugh… contribution points. Since only you guys can get in here, this is officially a shop for Ritualists only. If I find that you've been reselling these to others, I'll ban you immediately."

"That's fair." Taka stated while coming to look at what was available. "You're… this is all at cost!"

"That's right; I'm not going to make a profit off of you, unless the item you're buying is something really rare that I earned. If I *bought* it, I'll sell it to you at the same cost I was able to get it for." Joe took a deep breath and pulled out an ornate jar that he had purchased from Jake the Alchemist. "Now. Everyone see this?"

He held up the crystal jar, letting it catch the light and cast red sparkles across the ground. "This holds the blood of a stupidly overpowered endgame-style boss monster. First off, I'm going to set just *unlocking* the door to this at the price of two million gold, or five million contribution points. Taking out the blood costs an additional million, so that there are two transactions. Kind of an 'are you sure' thing."

There were exclamations of shock and outrage at the proclamation. Joe flat didn't care. "The price is there because I *know* that no one can pay it. The *only* time this will be free is when you are taking this to use in a ritual that helps *contain* the creature. If it gets free, it will *permanently* delete anyone it kills. Actual death at that point, folks. This jar is a preserver that will keep the contents fresh pretty much indefinitely. Even so, I don't like having this available at all."

"What's the big deal?" Kirby questioned bluntly.

"It can be used to twist rituals into something really nasty. Come here and look. There are *massive* penalties for using this in a ritual." Joe grimaced as he held out the jar, uncomfortable with allowing them so close to it. They all took a look, their curiosity shifting to pale-faced horror as they backed away from the container. "You all understand that this is a weapon against the creature itself, and not to be used in anything except that, correct? Swear that you will abide by that, or I'll take my chances with keeping it to myself."

Each of them swore, and Joe felt better at the notifications that they would gain *hefty* warlock titles if they broke the oath. "Good. Thank you all, and good work today. I didn't get everything I needed, but I'm hoping that my team did. We'll be back in a few days. Use what you have here to train yourselves up, and have questions ready when I get back."

Joe placed the jar on a shelf, placing a paywall in front of it. No one he didn't trust could access it, and now a backup was in place if there was some reason that he couldn't be the one to fight off that monster in the event that it ever got free.

CHAPTER EIGHTEEN

"Let's do a quick inspection before we go." Joe regarded the others, unable to see anything different. "I was able to make a few anti-personnel rituals, and I figured out a way to get to the bottom of the lake, but I wasn't able to find a way for us to breathe down there."

"I got that!" Alexis pulled out a vial that seemed to contain a tiny storm. "This is called a Fish-Flop Flask. It's a pretty common poison that makes anyone breathing it only able to breathe water for about ten minutes. Normally, you use this in dry areas so that people suffocate, but it can also be used just like a water-breathing potion, while being far less expensive."

"The downside being…?" Bard motioned leadingly.

Alexis rolled her eyes, "Well, clearly you need to stay underwater until it wears off. Unlike a potion, it is one or the other. Also, if you aren't in water, your body will start drying out badly enough that all of your skin will crack and bleed. Oh, and it *is* technically a debuff, so Joe will need to cancel his aura."

Joe winced at that; he had wanted to keep his aura active at all times so that he could get another bonus when he ranked up the skill. He nodded once to show his willingness, and *only* once to show that he still didn't want to do it. Jess coughed lightly, and handed a paper to all of them. "I made a copy of the map for everyone, so if you get separated, you will still be able to find your way around."

"I got accepted as a disciple of the Royal Masseuse, so I can give all of you extra-relaxing massages at the Beginner ranks!" Jaxon offered his news cheerfully. No one replied, so he just quietly continued humming.

"Made ah new song," Bard muttered when everyone stared at him. "Modified Haste spell that makes it feel like time is moving at eighty percent while we move at regular speed. It *isn't* ah time spell, just boosts your speed, thoughts, an' reaction time. Only lasts ah minute, so don't go crazy."

"That's super useful, Bard." Joe's brow was furrowed, already deep in thought about how he could put it to best use. "How often can you use it? Once per-"

"Hour."

Joe nodded at Bard, "Got it. Clearly, reserving it for a Boss fight would be great, but you'll see when we are in trouble. Always feel free to go all out, guys."

"Shouldn't we hoard everything we get and only use it after we have defeated all challengers in our path?" Poppy smirked as he spouted game logic. Before anyone could comment, he held up his hands in mock surrender. "Joking, of course. As for me, I basically worked on my skills. Oh, and I got my first Specialization."

There was a round of congratulations, then Jaxon voiced everyone's curiosity. "What is it?"

"Honorable Duelist," Poppy proudly stated. "The class ability I gained with it allows me to begin a duel, and we are moved to a private space where nothing can interfere in our combat. It's called 'Instant Arena'."

"I think that happens when Champions of Deities fight each other," Joe mused. "That sounds really handy. Is death the only way out of there?"

"Death or surrender," Poppy affirmed. "If we surrender, we get sent to our respawn location and get a hefty debuff. Not as bad as dying, but if the person who surrenders goes after the other person again within a day… the debuff doubles, and the loser automatically loses a single item to the honorable winner of the first duel. Ya know, because they acted dishonorably."

"You need to defeat others in honorable duels to get your class rank up?" Alexis guessed.

Poppy touched his nose with one hand and pointed at her with the other. "Got it in one. Expect me to vanish all the time, because I plan to *blaze* through the levels."

"Well, let's hope that you can't get too far on this trip, just from sheer lack of things to fight." Joe nodded at the others and pulled up his status screen. "I think we have everything that we need in order to at least start this challenge, so I think that it's time we got to it."

They vanished in a flash, reappearing in the grasslands near the coast just as the sun was setting over the sea. They hurried to the coast, arriving just as the final rays of light seemed to turn the entire body of water into a sparkling pool of blood before shifting to black as the sun vanished, followed by the moon bathing the watery world in silver.

"That were practically song-worthy." Bard looked up and stuck his chin out to point. "Yup, full moon, just as Jess said it would be."

"Now all we need to know is if she was right about the water levels." Joe was moving along at a speed just shy of jogging, keeping his eye on the coastline. "There it goes! She was right! Keep an eye out for other groups!"

"Of course, I was right!" Jess announced, making Joe flinch and shy away. "I told you that the full moon should make the water recede *almost* far enough that we would be able to get to the underwater dungeon building thing."

"When did you get here?" Joe asked her after he recovered from his shock. "I thought that-"

"She was with us all the way back at the Guild, Joe. Pay attention!" Alexis barked at him.

"Well, it wasn't like I was trying to ignore her; I'm just focused on-" Joe cut off his words as Jaxon put a hand on his shoulder.

"Joe. Do you understand the issue here?" Jaxon waited a moment, but there was no reply. "Right now, you are a leader, but you might not be one for much longer if you can't figure this out. There is a dichotomy to leadership, and every choice has two extremes. If you cannot find a balance between the two, you will topple over and lose it all. Right now, the balance you need to find is between micromanagement and abdication.

"If you become too focused on controlling every little aspect, you leave no room for the others to step in and find their own niche. They simply become combat automatons. Too *little* oversight, and people begin to think that you don't care about them." Jaxon sighed, then smiled as he dropped his hand. "The other option you have is what *I* did! Become a follower in the party, and you can just cruise along, doing whatever you want while someone else makes the choices for you."

Joe tried to argue, "But isn't that what you just told me not-"

"Ah, but that's *my* choice. I'm not the party leader." Jaxon winked at him. "See the difference?"

"Why are you so good at this?" Joe looked at Jaxon, somewhat concerned at the shift he was seeing in Jaxon's mindset.

"Joe, I'm over ninety years old now. I think?" Jaxon replied with a pearly-white smile. "I've had a lot of positions in life, as a follower, as a leader, and now I finally get to just do whatever comes naturally!"

Jaxon skipped away, then laid down and rolled down the incline to where the waterline had been. Joe watched him stand up and promptly fall over again, too dizzy to stand straight. "And he says *I* need to find balance…

"Just another thing to work on." Joe added 'leadership training' to his constantly growing list of things to do. He had been in the military and in a leadership role there, but not *really*. As a medic, he had been attached to another platoon and had been given free reign whenever he needed to do his job. He was only the uncontested person-in-charge during life-saving crisis moments. Other than that, he mostly followed along with the person who was running the combat operations. In fact, he had been a follower just like Jaxon had been describing. This - being in charge for real - was harder than he had thought it would be.

"Follow the maps I gave you!" Jess called from the side of the hill as they waded over sucking sands. "There are going to be a bunch of drop-offs, and some of them will have monsters!"

She didn't follow them the rest of the way, opting to hang back and watch their progress via her increasing class experience gauge. Thanks to her giving each of them a map of the area, they had a small minimap that they could follow around some of the more treacherous zones. When the water was up to their chests, they were nearly a half mile away from dry land. Bard suddenly dropped underwater, only to come sputtering back up a moment later. "Looks like that's the end of the easy part."

"Alright, I have our lead boots ready to go." Joe spit out a mouthful of salt water as a wave splashed over his face. "*Activate*."

Ritual of Leaden Boots activated! Time remaining: 3:59:57.

Instantly, the group stopped bobbing along with the water, standing still even as heavy waves smashed into them. Alexis coughed and yanked the cork off her bottle, managing to jump high enough to suck in some of her poisonous concoction. She was the shortest, so she went underwater as soon as she came back down.

I really don't want to turn my aura off." Joe grumbled lightly as everyone else took a deep inhale of the oddly pink cloud, and ducked underwater. He joined them a moment later.

You have been poisoned! Air is now impossible to breathe! Time remaining: 38:48.

Joe dismissed the information and started walking along the bottom of the sea. He got to the edge of the land, and hopped off. That was also when he took his first breath of water. His eyes bulged out as water rushed into his lungs, and he tried to cough it out, only to find more rushing in to take its place.

He was also falling much faster than he had thought he would. Joe had jumped off the equivalent of a cliff, and was falling almost as fast as if he had jumped off a real one. He hit the ground at the bottom *hard*, but he managed to mitigate the damage fairly easily, thanks to his Master ranks in jumping. Still, there was blood in the water from all the bones that were poking through the skin of his teammate's legs. Joe tried to heal them, but the spell didn't pass through the water.

Struggling to walk over to each of them individually, Joe cast Lay on Hands and managed to get all of them fixed up. None of them could speak with their lungs full of water, so they motioned toward the murky depths and began walking across the silty ocean floor. Luckily, their minimap didn't need actual light to operate, and Darkvision allowed Joe to see a decent distance; but seeing through the shifting water was a different story.

The briny liquid burned their eyes, and the group struggled to stay in a cohesive formation as they walked. Still, they got near to the underwater dungeon and looked up. With the moon now shining from above, they were able to see what looked like a school of fish swimming around a small mountain. If this area hadn't been highlighted by Jess's maps, they wouldn't have known that those weren't fish; they were a combination of monstrous eels and sharp-fanged predators.

It was time for the next part of the plan. As an overly-curious monster fish got close, Poppy's blade flashed out and sliced it in half. Blood flowed outward into a cloud, and the group dashed toward the hidden entrance as quickly as they could. If they were too slow, they would be caught in the chum and the incoming feeding frenzy.

Just before he ducked into the relative safety of the entrance, Joe looked up at the shining moon once more. The silver disk was now coming through a sanguine filter, and chunks of monster flesh were beginning to rain down. A sign of things to come, or an auspicious start?

CHAPTER NINETEEN

They were standing at the bottom of a huge tube. Staring up its length, the only thing Joe could think of was the similarity to missile silos. Jess had already searched this for any way in, but going to the top was the only way to progress. Joe looked at the others and nodded, then mentally commanded the ritual to stop.

End Ritual of Leaden Boots? Caution: this will end the ritual for all [5] of the people it is impacting! Yes / No.

Joe thought 'yes', and the group started to rise through the water swiftly. Once again, he was pleased by his forethought in making sure that all rituals he had a hand in designing would contain that mental shut-off feature. It might have been paranoia, but his rituals should never be able to be used against him unless *he* wanted them to be. They slowed about ten feet from the surface of the water, and Joe checked the timer for the poison. He frowned at the fact that there were still four full minutes left. On one hand, he was pleased that they had made good time trudging along the seabed. On the other, they would need to wait underwater for another handful of minutes.

He shrugged and activated his Aura of Neutrality. The timer on the poison started dropping by two seconds each second. They swam to the top of the water when there was about a minute left, and Alexis directed them all out onto the shore when there was twenty seconds remaining. She went first, and started heaving. Water poured out of her lungs, and everyone went wide-eyed as they realized what she was doing. Their lungs were full of water! In a few seconds, they wouldn't be able to breathe with that in their lungs anymore!

You have entered the Dungeon: Lessons of The Dark Age.

All of them worked to expel as much water as possible. Even so, when the timer ended, all of them began coughing furiously and painfully. They were shaking in fear, pain, and exhaustion by the end, and Joe couldn't stop the tears that leaked down his face. They mixed in with all the water on his face, but it was still a hard moment for him. "We were basically just waterboarded with salt water for ten minutes. That… that sucked so bad."

"Right…" Jaxon agreed.

"Getting poisoned sucks," Poppy grumbled.

Alexis sat up and glared at all of them. "We made it, didn't we? Yes, a potion of water breathing would have been great, but they are single-use and really hard to make or find!"

Joe held up a hand. "Alexis. You did an amazing job making this and getting everything ready. None of this is on you. It's my fault for not understanding what would happen when we used it. All of you, my bad. I'll try to find a way to make it up to you."

His words calmed the situation instantly, though it was the kind of awkward calm that comes when people wanted to yell and had the wind pulled out of their sails. They all stayed there for a few minutes longer, then stood in clean and dry clothes. Joe's aura had been working the entire time, so even their residual soreness from water-filled lungs had vanished a few minutes previously. Then they had simply needed the time to get their heads back into the game.

"What's *next*?" Bard grunted out. "Findin' ah pit of lava that we need ta squat over an' dip our b-"

"I *think*," Joe cut off Bard as quickly as possible, "that there are mainly just monsters and such."

Bard grumbled to himself, but led the way forward. When they got to the first turn in the tunnel, Joe asked everyone to halt as he activated the anti-personnel wind blade ritual that he had created with his Coven ahead of time. After he set it in place, they continued forward, moving at a snail's pace. "The annoying part of all this is that we need to go all the way down, pretty much to the same depth that we entered the place from. If we could have gone through the wall, we would have been there by now!"

"Too bad we don't have any sappers on our team." Poppy got the group to chuckle at that; they all knew that trying to blast their way into a dungeon was likely a good way for the system to slap them with penalties. "Where were the enemies supposed to be?"

"Oh, they're all over the place!" Jaxon pointed at the walls, making everyone's gaze over snap to stare at him. "You know, deeper in. Jess was excited because almost everything in here is mechanical instead of magical. Apparently we aren't going to see magically overgrown spiders, but we might see a *robotic* spider monstrosity!"

"Why doesn't that make me feel better?" Alexis spoke up, frantically going through her poisons to find something that might work on metal enemies. "Why is this the first I'm hearing about this?"

"It's on the map." Jaxon shrugged innocently. "She made a legend for us. Look at the silver triangles. 'Likely mechanical enemy'. She made all of these in record time and barely got time to hand them over. It isn't surprising that she didn't get a chance to explain every little thing."

"Oh." Joe examined his own map, and found exactly what Jaxon was referencing. "Yup, there it is. I guess her snakes didn't start any of them up? Either they won't do anything, or maybe they only get hostile when people get near them?"

There was silence for a long moment, then Bard cleared his throat and nodded at the walls. "Looks like Dwarves are ah thing in this world."

The party studied the walls as they walked, and realized that this was likely the Dwarven history in pictograph form. They walked past dozens of what appeared to be tribal-style Dwarves, then found a new style just before the room opened up. On the last image, a Dwarf was standing above the others with a crown on his head while the others kneeled. Then the pictures turned into a smear of red that seemed to bleed into the now-open room ahead of them.

"What do you think that all meant?" Joe's senses were tingling… this was important, he just *knew* it.

"Well, to me, the walls are letting us know that we are about to fight something." Poppy spoke in a too-friendly tone that they had started to associate with him being snarky. "Perhaps I am incorrect, and we are going to make some friends in the space ahead! I'm certain all the blood is just a misunderstanding."

"Oh, thank *goodness*." Jaxon sighed with relief. "I'm always looking for new friends!"

"He's being facetious, Jaxon," Joe stated wearily. They stepped into the room, and a door hidden in the hallway behind them corkscrewed closed with a long hiss of steam. Words started emitting from the room in front of them, but the language was so archaic that it was nearly impossible to understand more than a single word.

Tu sequere et vestigia tua maiorum. Win. Probare te digna tua est.

"Pretty sure that whatever tha' was about, we need ta smash those shiny bois." Bard hefted his axes as mechanical Dwarves entered the room through doors that had been hidden in the walls. Doors opened behind them as well, and more Dwarves began to pour into the room.

"How are we supposed to…?" Joe trailed off, looking at the

dozens of Dwarves that had surrounded them. One detail seemed to *jump* out at him; Joe stared at the sigils that they all wore, noting that there were five different ones, and all the Dwarves were separated by the sigil they wore. "There! Go stand with that group!"

Joe ran to stand in front of the group that had been wearing the same symbol as the 'King' of the pictograph. His team followed, and the room devolved into an all-out brawl. The Dwarves they had sided with didn't attack them, and Joe was glad that he hadn't stayed with the ones that entered behind them; they were wiped out in under a minute.

They found that most of their attacks dealt damage, but were overall fairly ineffective against the mechanical Dwarves. They seemed to ignore direct magical effects like Dark Lightning from Joe, though he could bind them pretty easily with his solidified shadows. Jaxon could be seen punching a metal Dwarf, and a moment later, Lefty and Terror were trying to chew through them.

Bard managed to bust them up with his axes, and Alexis's crossbow was armor-piercing, so her bolts penetrated through the plating easily. Poppy was having a *great* time, his rapier designed to be extra-effective against armored enemies. Though they were mechanical, they still dropped as a real Dwarf would be expected to do when stabbed in the eye. Soon, the four other tribes had lost seventy percent of their forces, and the rest kneeled.

Crude Dwarven Tribesman (Autonomoton) X22 defeated! Experience gained: 220.

'Their' Dwarves hoisted their axes and hammers into the air to show victory, and all 'defeated' Dwarves were dragged away as Joe's group was escorted down the tunnel. They came to a fork in the path. Bard rumbled, "Ah've been readin' the pictures we're goin' by. If ah have it right, this whole place is a repeat of history, ah lesson or summat. Ah think that a turn in tha tunnel means a choice that we are supposed to already know."

"Alright…" Joe looked at the steely Dwarves around them. "What have you figured out so far?"

Bard launched right into it, pointing at the trail of pictographs. "This was ah time o' peace after different Dwarven clans came together under a single King. Then there was a bloody war, and only the King had the majority of his clan at the end. Because of the early infightin', he ruled with an iron fist. Here… this turn shows us starting to trust and work with the other clans after maybe ah century? This other path is more warlike, stayin' in charge by military power."

"The choice I would make is to work together and grow as a single entity." Joe said without hesitation. "But is that the choice that we need to make here?"

The group dithered back and forth for a few minutes before finally agreeing to take the route of military might. That was what they decided a Dwarf would do. Taking a left, they walked along the path and carefully watched the pictures and mechanical beings that walked with them. "Bard, would you try to keep us up to date with what's happening? The map shows that all these routes go to the same place, but new doors keep opening up. I'm pretty sure we'll be going off-map soon."

Bard nodded and began a monologue. "The King kept his power, and consolidated everythin'. The clans grew more skilled, more specialized in the crafts that they chose for themselves. Their weapons became more potent, their cities became more beautiful an' advanced. But… uh-oh."

"What?" Poppy nervously questioned.

Pointing at the walls, Bard brought their attention to the fact that the pictures were starting to dissolve into red blood again. "They had no one ta' admire their cities. There were no one ta' use their powerful weapons against. The talented warriors that had fought for their King began ta' resent him. The people that he had conquered began ta' plot against him… and finally… coup d'etat?"

The wall in front of them spun open just as the wall behind them closed. They were standing at the base of a set of stairs that went up and up… revealing a massive Dwarf in Royal Regalia sitting on a throne. Joe's team tried to backtrack, but the Dwarves actively blocked their path. Steam started to hiss, and metal creaked.

The glowing eyes of the King opened.

CHAPTER TWENTY

"You would. Turn against. Your King?" The mechanical voice of the Dwarven King was slightly stilted, as it came from the actual automaton and not some kind of recording. It stood and pulled two warhammers off the ground, then started to glow in odd patterns across its armor.

"Oh, sugar snap peas…!" Alexis spat, "It's got enchanted gear."

"What did you expect from a King that took the best of everything from his people?" Poppy settled into a stance and waited for the King to close in on them. Still, even *his* eyes widened as the Dwarf flashed down the stairs and pancaked one of their mechanical allies with its dual-wielded war hammers.

"Go all out!" Joe ordered, setting the standard by casting Acid Spray with both hands.

Damage dealt: 252 (480 acid damage reduced by half; +5% spell penetration due to title. Target designated as 'gear'.)

"Hey!" Joe was shocked by the amount of damage he had done, even though a good chunk of it was brushed off. "The entire construct is considered an item! If you have anything that damages gear-!"

Current health: 64/534 (2,170 damage taken. 1,700 damage absorbed by Exquisite Shell. 450 blunt damage taken. 20 terrain damage taken.)

Joe coughed out a mouthful of blood as he slid down the wall to the ground. He had seen the hammers coming but hadn't managed to do anything about them. He was just too slow. A swift Mend reshaped his chest cavity and pulled him up to two hundred and twenty-nine health, and a follow-up Lay on Hands pulled the stat to four sixty-nine. "Heh. Nice."

His Exquisite Shell was gone for this fight; there was no way for him to remain combat effective as well as dump his mana into it to restart it. Once more, he was upset that he couldn't add more mana into his shield while it was active to repair it. A sound of tearing metal brought his attention back to the fight just in time to see Poppy's rapier sliding smoothly out of the King's shoulder joint. Jaxon managed to use the distraction to force the King to drop its left hammer, but the slender Chiropractor was sent tumbling from a backhand that he didn't manage to entirely avoid.

The metal Dwarves that had come with them were beating on the King with all they had, making the room sound like a forge. A **tink** sound came once a second as bolts lodged into the armor, somehow bypassing the enchantments and embedding in the armor itself. Alexis was frustrated; she couldn't hit any weak points. "I *gotta* get my crossbow skill above Beginner!"

Bard spit out blood when he heard that, both from a busted tooth as well as from anger. He was chopping at the King like an overly stubborn block of wood that needed to be split. "You're damaging *that* with only Beginner ranks in your skills? How!"

"It's because you all have that title that adds penetration to every attack." Poppy calmly replied, putting fresh holes into the King every chance he got. "I *told* you that was overpowered."

"It's only five percent, Poppy!" Jaxon had the King's attention, so his focus was entirely on dodging instead of attacking. "How overpowered can that be?"

"You. Are." Poppy grunted between attacks, "Adding true damage onto your attacks! No matter how much damage you do, at least five percent of the *maximum* damage gets through!"

The King didn't seem to like this reveal, or perhaps Poppy had just gathered too much aggro. It flashed gold again, as it had at the start of combat, and Poppy was slammed against the back wall from the first hit... then his face caved in from the second.

Party member 'Poppy' has died! Checking... brave death! Respawn set at four hours!

"That hurts." Joe had been staring at the King, and his Intrusive Scan finally gave him what he needed.

Name: King Drogren. Class: Warrior Automaton. Title: What Might Have Been.

Highest stat: Strength.

Ongoing effects: Runic Automaton. Mode enabled: 75% to death. Blocked. Blocked.

The weak points of the King lit up for his team, all of them in odd spots. Instead of the helmet being a striking point, the center of its chest cavity was shown as the best place to land a blow. "Right, *robot*! This thing probably has a central unit to power it!"

"*Speed of the body meets speed of the mind, Overhaste*!" Bard chanted. A pink glow enveloped the team, and suddenly the King was moving at a reasonable speed.

Alexis fired bolt after bolt, having four in the air as the first hit. "They're so slow!"

"Acid Spray!" Joe twisted as he cast the spell, making the acid spin a small amount as well. This turned it into more of a stream, which gave Joe an idea. He gathered shadows around the end of his Mystic Theurge staff and solidified a giant straw at the end of it. "*Acid Spray*!"

This time, the acid was forced from a cone into a high-pressure stream. It carved into the armor to deadly effect, opening a hole on the front chest plate. The King turned its shining eyes on Joe, and steam began to whistle as it built up the power for another charging attack. Bard stepped in at the last second, hooking his axes around the King's left leg and yanking backward.

Instead of charging at Joe, the King flashed with golden light and slammed into the ground. Bard barked out a 'Ha!' and started slamming the back of the King like a drummer playing a particularly angry solo. Joe couldn't risk more acid with his team and the Dwarves on his side attacking, and was at a loss for a moment… then he saw Poppy's body. "Yes!"

He ran over and started the process of resurrecting his fallen teammate, his mana flowing out of him like water from a burst dam. Joe had learned some new things about himself at this point. One, since his mana had stopped being contained and was now seemingly free-flowing through his body at all times, losing all of it at once left him feeling incredibly weak and drained. Two, there were benefits to doing new things.

Mid-combat Resurrection! Skill level increased directly to Novice VI! You either don't care about your enemies, or you fully trust your teammates to do the work without you!

Poppy stepped out of a portal that appeared just as his previous body crumbled to ash. "You won already? That's-"

Joe managed to pull him to the floor just in time to avoid a flying crumpled heap that had been a Dwarven comrade. "Still… in combat, Poppy."

His mana was coming back swiftly, but Joe still needed a few more seconds before he would be useful. Poppy glanced to the side and winced. "Need a heal, Joe. Came back below thirty percent."

"That's expected." Joe rolled to his feet and checked his mana. At thirty-three per second, he had plenty to heal Poppy, so he did. Lay on Hands cost one-twenty mana, so it took another four agonizing seconds to top him off. Then Poppy ran forward and got back into the fight.

Joe went back into full support mode, casting Mend at a

distance whenever his teammates took a hit. Alexis stood far enough away that all she had to do was occasionally dodge a Dwarf that had become a flying garbage pile. Bard was able to tank two subsequent hits, so long as they weren't critical or made when the King flashed gold, but after that, he would drop if someone sneezed too hard in his general direction.

"Jaxon, pull some aggro, then go full dodge mode! Bard, pull back and let me get you to max health! Poppy, hold back until Jaxon needs help. Alexis, you're lovely, keep at it!" Joe was barking orders at maximum speed while trying to use his abilities as well as possible. While he was thinking, he realized that he was lacking in combat rituals that could impact non-living enemies. Yet another thing to work on. "Lay on Hands!"

While Bard was being healed, it seemed that the King reached another milestone. Its gold became tinged with red, and Jaxon wasn't prepared. Just as Bard's haste spell ended, the King gained a speed boost and landed a solid punch with its off hand. Jaxon went spinning through the air until he hit a wall, then the outstretched fist lifted into the air and flashed royal purple. The King's dropped warhammer zipped through the air to return to its hand, and the Dwarf started moving toward Jaxon again.

"Target the hole in its chest!" Joe saw Poppy running at it, and yelled just before Poppy got close enough to target it with an ability.

The King lifted its hammers and brought them down at tremendous speed to finish Jaxon off, just as Poppy shouted, "*Challenge*!"

Both the King and Poppy vanished, but there were glowing orbs remaining that seemed to signify their position. The metallic one was the King, and the green one was Poppy. Jaxon jumped to his feet, staggering toward Joe. Healing was done apace, and the team waited for the outcome.

In under ten seconds, the challenge had concluded. Both the King and Poppy returned. The automaton turned and faced the group. It took a single step and fell with a massive **clang**.

Poppy staggered to the side and collapsed as well; his right leg bent like a banana. Joe immediately recognized the signs of a compound fracture.

"Poppy!" Joe ran over and focused his Mend spell. The leg slowly straightened, and soon the group simply lay on the ground in exhaustion instead of pain.

You have defeated the King that Might Have Been! Experience gained: 1,500!

"That's good, at least." Joe spoke to the roof, not looking around at all. "Seems low for the challenge rating."

"I don't think we were ever supposed to fight it." Jaxon pointed at the wall. There was no way to go further, only the way back had opened. "I think that was a punishment for going the wrong way."

Joe rolled over and thrust his hips at the fallen King.

Dwarven Automaton 'The King that Might have Been'. Item type: Crafting material.

"We'll hopefully get *something* out of this." Joe told the group as they all got ready to backtrack.

"Right, now we should just-" Bard's words stopped as the ground shook under them, and all the light in the dungeon shifted to a deep red.

Quest offered: Destroy them!

CHAPTER TWENTY-ONE

"Destroy them? Who is 'them'? Joe opened the details of the quest, blinking in surprise as he read.

Quest: Destroy Them. A team of adventurers have blasted their way into the final layer of this dungeon. They are disregarding the sacred traditions of the Royal Dwarven choosing site, and are damaging or stealing ancient artifacts stored within. Slay these adventurers and return all stolen items recovered to the dungeon. Reward: based on number of items recovered and targets slain. Accept? Yes / No.

Accepting the quest, Joe turned to the others and made sure that they had gained the quest as well. Upon confirmation, the team started moving toward the entrance of the dungeon. There was no point in trying to go down further; already, they could hear the sounds of water rushing inward from below. Joe had a guess as to who the invaders were, but he had no idea how they would have been able to get out to the area. He *especially* had no idea how they would find powerful enough explosives that they could break through a dungeon's walls. He knew from experience *exactly* how durable a single wall would be, not to mention however many layers this place could have.

"Joe, I really want to learn more of this history." Bard was looking at the walls wistfully as they ran away from the steadily increasing noise of water. "Something tells me that this will be not just important information in the future, it will be-"

Poppy interrupted Bard before Joe could get a word in edgewise, "Only way we are going to get lower is if we leave the dungeon and it is able to repair itself. Otherwise, we are going to need some kind of water breathing potion, and I don't think any of us want to go through Alexis's poison again."

Jaxon spoke up with a questioning tone. "*Did* we in fact have a plan to get back to the surface? I did not particularly enjoy the first-"

"There was a hatch right near the entrance that was locked from the inside," Alexis snapped. "I'm betting that will at least let us out near the top, and we can all swim to the surface from there. If you drown, well at *least* you don't have to go through 'my poison' again."

Joe simply kept his mouth shut and continued running with his group. When they got to the hatch that Alexis had mentioned, they opened it and stepped inside. They were surrounded by glass on all sides, but before any of them could question why, the glass enclosure shot upward. As they moved through the water, they were able to see all of the wildlife in the area. They were agitated, furious, and incredibly reckless. Several times, a fish or an eel bounced off of the glass, and the humans could only hold their breath and hope that the strange elevator they were in would not shatter.

After breaking the surface of the water, the glass unfolded and turned into a platform that raced across the surface of the water. When it got close to dry land, the elevator stayed in place, gently bobbing with the waves. They took a few more steps onto the sandy tidal shelf, looking for the people that had so abruptly interrupted their plans. At first, they were concerned that they had missed them entirely, but when a series of faces popped up in the water and made their way closer, Joe and his team could only smile as they readied their weapons.

"How? *How* in the *world* did you beat us here?" Sam, the leader of the other party, took his hat off and shook it. Somehow, this simple action was enough to remove all the water not only from his hat, but his clothes as well. He tossed his head to the side, and his luscious hair swept out as if he were shooting a shampoo commercial.

Trying his hardest not to hate the man simply because he apparently had everything Joe did not; Joe took a deep breath, gently let it out, and offered his ultimatum. "We were offered a quest to return the items that you stole from the dungeon. If you hand them over without a fight, we will put all of this behind us and work hard to never see you again. If you want to fight, well... I am fine with that, too."

His team had a large advantage. They were on dry, fairly stable ground, while Sam's team was still waist-high in the water. They were prepared, had their weapons out and ready, and had just been given a comfortable ride back to shore. Sam's team had needed to fight with other monsters the entire way back, while swimming and carrying the items they had pilfered from the dungeon. Though Joe really wanted to know why they had not stored them in storage devices or bags, he wasn't about to give the other team time to relax and prepare by asking drawn-out questions.

When the other group did not surrender, Joe understood that they had a fight on their hands. He lifted his Mystic Theurge staff and started casting Acid Spray at the group as quickly as he could manage. As that was clearly the signal to fight, the rest of his group began in earnest. Crossbow bolts thudded into a heavily-armored, hammer-wielding woman, knocking her back and causing her to slip in the water. A man dressed in a Judo Gi raced forward on top of the water as if he was ice-skating and sent a punch flying at Alexis. He was intercepted by Jaxon, who gasped when he saw how the other was traversing the water.

"You... you have *fish feet*!" Indeed, the Monk's feet from the ankle down had transformed into extremely large koi fish.

"Bro, you need to not worry about that right now." The monk shook his head as he used his forearm to push Jaxon's fist to the side. "Y'all messed up when you attacked us next to a body of water. There is no way that you can match my mobility."

"Your fish feet are no match for my T-Rex Head Hands!" Jaxon declared indignantly, sending a flurry of blows at the obviously confused monk.

Most of the group had paired off and were fighting battles one on one; Alexis had switched her targets to a lady dressed in dark leathers, clearly an assassin. It was a game of cat-and-mouse; the assassin would dive underwater as a crossbow bolt came her way, but she was also working to close the distance between them so she could put her blades to work. Alexis was having none of that, and was very carefully timing her attacks to coincide with the other woman's attempts to dash her way.

Joe had planned on being the one to fight against Sam, but a chunk of ice flying at his head made Joe focus on a man who was clearly a Mage. Bard stepped forward and engaged Sam in Joe's stead, using his double axes to fend off the flashing blade that Sam was using, and using his Skaldic chants to boost his resistance to the odd spells the man would intermittently send flying from books that floated around him.

Poppy had set himself up to fight the heavily armored woman, and his attacks were already creating fountains of blood that erupted from the joints of her armor. The woman was strong; even so, Poppy was able to hold her off with minimal effort. Each time she had a chance to step out of the waves, Poppy was there with a fresh wound for her. Finally, it seemed that she had enough, "*Devastating blow*!"

As the head of the hammer came toward him, Poppy calmly sidestepped and drew his weapon backward until his right hand was level with his right shoulder, his left hand was a flat Palm pointing at his target, and he lunged with a shout of, "*Hard Counter*!"

Eyes wide with shock, the woman tried to swallow the cold, wet feeling in her throat. She choked, and the muscles refused to obey her until Poppy had finished pulling his Rapier out of her trachea. She collapsed into the water, and Poppy moved to help Alexis with the Assassin.

Targets slain: 1/5.

"Solidified Shadows!" Joe finished his spell, and a dark ball and chain wrapped around the ankles of the Mage he was fighting. Already off balance, his opponent stumbled as a wave hit him from behind. The spell on his lips fizzled away to nothing and the congregated shadows began pulling him down into one of the tidal pools. The Mage was doing everything he could to pull himself out of the water, but Joe felt it clearly when something latched onto the chain and helped pull the man downward.

"Sam!" the Mage shouted in fear. Something in his voice made Joe pause. He had never seen someone react so violently to a little player-versus-player.

Bard went flying across the surface of the sand, tumbling and picking up muck as he went. Joe was uncertain what he had been hit with; as far as he could tell, it was some form of pure concussive force. Sam started running to the struggling Mage that was being pulled into the depths. When he realized what was happening, Sam turned to Joe and held his hands in the air. "Stop! You win! Let him go! *Please*!"

Fearing a trick or a trap, Joe blurted out the first thing that came to his mind. "Swear to me that you will give us all of the stolen items and leave without trying to harm us, and I will let him go."

"Fine! I swear it! Let him go *now*!" The sword in Sam's hand was shaking, and Joe knew he was about to get stabbed if he did not follow through immediately. The shadows wrapped around the ankles of the Mage vanished, and he crawled his way onto dry land as fast as possible. "Everybody, stop! We lost this one. You, why didn't you get a player killer aura? *You* attacked *us*."

"Prolly because we have a quest to kill you all." The other fighters slowly and carefully disengaged with each other. A double scream of primal reptilian joy made some of them flinch, and everyone looked over to see Jaxon's hands trumpeting to the sky before lunging downward to feast on the fallen Monk. Joe's face clouded, and he shouted at Jaxon, "Enough! You beat him, and they surrendered! Stop!"

Targets slain: 2/5.

Jaxon nodded, looked down at his fallen foe, and scoffed, "Fish feet *indeed.*"

Joe did a head count, and found that Bard and Poppy had both fallen in the last few moments of combat. He turned and eyed the heaving Mage. "That's a non-player character, isn't it? Why? Why would you endanger the only life he has?"

"If you try to use this against us in the future, I will devote everything I have into hunting you down," Sam coldly stated as he pulled his friend up into a standing position.

"Listen here, you *jerk.*" Joe coldly stared at the overly-ostentatious swordsman. "It took the slowest, *weakest,* single-target spell that I have to put that guy in a position where you had to surrender or lose him forever. Almost everything that I use has a massive area-of-effect and is deadly to everyone within seconds. If you come after us again, and he is with you, I *cannot* guarantee that he will survive... but I promise that *you* won't. Hand over the stolen goods, and get out of here."

The Mage coughed and looked at his leader frantically, "Sam! You can't give him the-!"

"Enough! We made a deal, and these aren't worth your life." Sam declared, getting a snort from Joe in return. He handed over two items; a stone tablet and a platinum ring. Both were glowing with a faint red Aura, and as Joe accepted them, he understood why.

Cursed Quest item. Cannot be stored in any container until the curse is removed.

There was no other information available, and there was no update from his quest, so Joe could only nod and stand aside as the defeated team walked away. He planned on returning to the dungeon immediately with the surviving members of his team, but just before they got on the glowing glass platform, a notification appeared in Joe's vision. "Son of a…!"

Sam_King has broken an oath sworn to you and gained a title of Warlock II!

CHAPTER TWENTY-TWO

"He broke his oath?" Joe's bald head furrowed as he worked to understand what that message meant. His eyes flew open, then narrowed in rage as it became clear. "That overly hair-conditioned peacock took one of the dungeon items with him! Come on, everyone; use whatever you have to utterly destroy him as soon as we find him!"

"Calm down, Joe." Jess walked into the area with a smile on her face. She winked at him teasingly. "I think I have what you are looking for."

Moonlight was reflecting from the top of Joe's head, seeming to match the light of his eyes as he debated whether or not to hunt down Sam anyway. Before he could give the order to set out, a snake slithered up, its tail coiled around a crystal orb that was glowing a soft red.

Cursed Quest item. Cannot be stored in any container until the curse is removed.

"You used your thievery skill?" Joe sighed as he tossed the crystal in the air a few times. He came to a decision; if he were to set out now, there was a high likelihood that he could end up losing the fight that he would race into. Joe was going to have to let this go… for now.

"Sure did!" Jess cheerfully admitted. "I saw your entire fight, and I figured I would be more useful to you by stealing this item back from him than by joining into a fight that it looked like you were winning. Apparently, it is pretty difficult to notice a snake swimming through the water toward you when you are swinging around a sword and chucking spells at people."

"Thank you, Jess. Please let me know if there is a suitable reward that I can give you for this." Joe turned back to the other two surviving members of his party and motioned at the glowing platform. "Are you guys ready to go and turn this quest in?"

"We are just going to go back there without the rest of our team?" Alexis shook her head. "That seems like a pretty terrible thing to do to Bard."

"He should get the quest completion rewards!" Joe defensively rebutted. "Besides, there is no way for us to put these things somewhere safe. If we have to wait a long time for Bard to come back to life and travel to us, there is a good chance that someone else will come along, or that other group will come back and try to take these. We need to go *now*."

With clear reluctance from Alexis, and only excitement about getting back on the glowing platform from Jaxon, they were soon sailing across the sea at speed. The platform started to descend, and soon they were back in a watertight cube. A few moments later they were sinking into the water, passing through the swarms of monsters, and approaching the underwater dungeon. As the glass elevator settled into place and the door opened, a small platform rose from the ground. On the platform were three outlines, one for a sphere, one for a rectangular block, and one for a ring.

Beyond being happy that he would be completing the quest, Joe was cheerful about denying any of the items back from the other team. He slotted the items in their spaces, and watched as the plinth sunk back into the floor.

Quest complete: Destroy Them. Objects retrieved: 3/3. Enemies slain: 2/5. Objectives completed: 5/8. Calculating... the objects retrieved were of far greater importance than slaying the thieves who stole them in the first place. Rewards shall be granted based on performance and suitability. Due to the circumstances of the quest, and damage to the dungeon, this dungeon will be considered 100% completed.

Experience gained: 6,000. Item received: Enhanced Class Advancement Tablet (Can be used by anyone with the base class of Energetic Bibliophile, Bibliomancer, Ritualist, or Urban Druid.) The standard class advancement tablet offers three choices, the enhanced version will offer a fourth option upon use.

Seeing all of the different classes that could use his newly-acquired tablet, Joe decided to waste no time and activated it on the spot.

Scanning... Base Class found: Ritualist. First prerequisite for usage met.

Scanning... Specialized class found: Rituarchitect. Second prerequisite for usage met.

Generating class selection options one through four... generated.

Scanning... Caution! Third prerequisite for usage not met. Base class 'Ritualist' requires that Characteristics 'intelligence' and 'wisdom' be at the Mortal characteristic limit before second Specialization can be applied. please try again after you have raised at a minimum these two characteristics to the Mortal limit of one hundred and fifty.

Enhanced Class Advancement Tablet (Soulbound). This tablet has been bound to you! You may now safely store it with the full knowledge that it will work for no one but you!

Joe stared at the message, full of conflicting emotions. On one hand, he now knew that he could safely work to achieve the new goal that had been set for him. It was good to have a set goal. On the other hand... he had a long way to go. He pulled up his character sheet and looked at it despairingly.

Name: Joe 'Tatum's Chosen Legend' Class: Mage (Actual: Rituarchitect)

Profession I: Tenured Scholar (Actual: Arcanologist)

Profession II: Ritualistic Alchemist
Character Level: 16 Exp: 150,343 Exp to next level: 2,657
Rituarchitect Level: 5 Exp: 10,456 Exp to next level: 4,544
Hit Points: 534/534
Mana: 1,381/1,650 (115 Reserved)
Mana regen: 33.89/sec
Stamina: 528.5/528.5
Stamina regen: 5.84/sec

Characteristic: Raw score (Modifier)

Strength: 53 (2.03)
Dexterity: 54 (2.04)
Constitution: 54 (2.04)
Intelligence: 110 (3.1)
Wisdom: 85 (2.35)
Charisma: 52 (2.02)
Perception: 63 (2.13)
Luck: 38 (1.38)
Karmic Luck: +6

His stats had not changed during his time in the dungeon, but that was not unexpected. What *was* unexpected… was that he would need nearly another seventy points of wisdom in order to reach the next class advancement. Also, a lesser but still difficult challenge was going to be getting forty points in his intelligence. Remembering the Injection he had swallowed that had given him a full fifteen points in his intelligence characteristic, Joe now *really* understood why items such as that were so highly sought-after and expensive. He had understood *intellectually* that they were going to be hard to get, but when information on getting to the second Specialization got out, it was going to be absolutely impossible to get his hands on anything similar.

"The dungeon is considered as complete, should we just… head home?" Joe wanted to go curl into a corner and fall asleep for a week, but he knew that was an impossible dream at this point.

Between the probing attacks on the guild and the deep-seated need to improve enough to get to the next area, Joe knew that he would be spending every waking moment on becoming more powerful or knowledgeable. As they rode in the glass elevator for the third time, Joe asked, "Would anyone like some coffee?"

He solidified a few small espresso cups out of the Shadows in the area as Mate appeared in his hand. The elemental bubbled and whistled cheerfully, putting a smile on Alexis's face and widening the ever-present grin on Jaxon's. They took turns giving Mate a gentle petting on his surprisingly dry - if somewhat squishy - head. Just as they returned to land, Joe got a notification he hadn't expected.

Your care and attention to your pet has increased its loyalty and affection toward you! 'Mate' has taken on some of the characteristics of the mana you have been feeding it with. Abilities removed: light roast blend. Abilities enhanced: medium roast blend, dark roast blend, espresso blend. Ability gained: Over-caffeinate.

Over-caffeinate: Similar to a traditional Haste spell, Over-caffeinate increases all effects of physical and mental characteristics by 10% for 10 minutes. After the spell ends, all physical and mental characteristics are reduced by 30% for 5 minutes and the user will suffer the effects of debuff 'Hammerwords' for 2 minutes or until the resultant headache debuff has cleared.

"That is some *excellent* coffee, Mate," Joe crooned to the small Elemental as he allowed it to return to his sleeve as a large stain. He was already thinking about how he could use this buff to its maximum effect, and he hoped that the effects of his Neutrality Aura would mitigate the detriments of using it.

In just a few minutes, the small party rejoined Jess and began walking toward the shrine that would bring them home. Contrary to Joe's expectations, the group began a lively debate. They were talking about the best ways to increase their characteristics, and Joe was pleased to be able to offer the knowledge he had acquired about the impact of future growth based on the effect of the method used to gain characteristics.

When they heard that there were tanks that had trained their constitution purely by taking damage, and realized that it gave double or more of a bonus to the total health pool, each of them revised their training plans at least a little. Joe was completely fine with the flat bonuses he would get for training his body with the daily characteristic allotment, but he needed to find the most effective ways to train his mind if he wanted to unlock powerful options in the future.

Jess interrupted his thoughts by clearing her throat and shyly looking at the three surviving members of the party. "I just wanted to say thank you for whatever you did in there. For some reason, after you went back out, I was able to get a class level up. I also got a new ability, and it is all because you were able to explore the dungeon to one hundred percent with my map. I know that my map was not *actually* that good, so there must be something else at play, but still. I know it sucked to lose Bard, so thank you for trusting me."

"It wasn't the intent, but I am glad you got something out of it. Your skills are lacking, and you have no decent combat skills to speak of." Jaxon nodded knowingly, folding his arms behind his back like a mysterious elderly master. "I know that you took the path of an assassin because you do not like to hear things beg for their life, and you did not want to give them the option. I think the path of a cartographer was a good choice for you, and-"

Jaxon dodged two throwing knives and a chucked snake, shaking his head sadly. "Meager skills, indeed. I already know this, Jess! You don't need to embarrass yourself by showcasing them!"

"First off, that is *not* why I became an assassin!" Jess retorted heatedly. They stepped into the shrine, and Joe activated the fast travel option. The distance that they needed to travel was so great, and the cost in mana and stamina so high, that all of them collapsed to the floor of the Temple in Towny McTown-face upon arrival. Jess wheezed as she attempted to finish her statement, "Secondly… I can… take you anytime, old man! You have no idea who I am-"

"I am sorry to break up this lively debate… but I do need to speak with you, young man." Joe had heard the voice before, but it had been a very long time. He craned his head up to face the wizened old man wearing white robes with black arcane symbols stitched all along the hems.

Joe forced himself into a seated position, and closed his eyes as the world spun. "What in the world could I have done to bring the Mage College's most powerful Master Enchanter all this way?"

CHAPTER TWENTY-THREE

Joe and the Master enchanter walked out of the temple and over to a small restaurant that had recently started up. They opened the door, but when Joe saw who was sitting at a table waiting for them, he stopped cold and started to turn around. The old man at his side gripped his arm firmly. "Please allow me to have a chance to explain my actions."

"You are going to tell me that you are the one who ordered her to spy on me. I understand that." Joe's mouth was a firm line, and he gripped the weathered hand on his arm for a moment before throwing it off. "I am not particularly interested in letting *you* explain this away. Friends do not spy on their friends; usually, that is reserved for people they see as enemies. As for you, Terra, why didn't you just come to me directly and discuss this? Why did you bring him along? Am I so frightening that you need a third person just to have a conversation with me? I don't deserve this kind of treatment."

The Enchanter held up a hand to stop him. "Joe, you have to understand; you know how oaths work. Not only was she risking a title, she would have automatically lost her apprenticeship with me. The reason I am here now is that there are still things she cannot reveal, and I needed to offer the explanation for her. Now, here is the truth of what was happening. I was attempting to scout out an extremely talented individual without alerting my own enemies to my interest."

"That ship has sailed, and now I am risking you being drawn into my fights because I messed up and didn't place enough trust in my chosen apprentice." The old man waved at the table, where Terra was staring down at the wood. "It was my fault that she lost a friend. I just want a chance to explain myself and make the offer I originally had planned."

"If this is about the Mana batteries, I'm sorry to have to tell you that I really want to keep that design to myself for now. Beyond that, the item I used to craft them was destroyed when my guild was attacked by a different group that only had their own interests in mind. I don't see myself recreating such an expensive process, especially not to hand it over to another person who will not tell me the *full* truth. If you planned to tell me the actual, *full* truth, only Terra would be here." Joe was pleased to see the enchanter wince.

"I feel that very little would change your mind on this, so I will get right into what I have to say, and you can decide for yourself." The elderly man collected himself. "Terra has explained to me that you have an incredible affinity for enchantment. You have been able to craft not just standard things; you have been able to generate and refine recipes for enchantment that others have given up on. Your Mana Batteries were not the only thing I was interested in, but that did play a large part in grabbing my attention. Now, there are interesting things that you have created, but I also see the glaring holes in your ability to progress."

"Joe, there is a reason the College exists. There is a reason that we have teachers that are able to help students along the path they choose. Without the wisdom of those who came before you, you are treading your own path through the wilderness while marching alongside a paved road that already leads to your destination." The elderly man sighed at the hesitance he still saw in Joe's eyes.

"Everything has a cost," Joe simply replied. "I would prefer the cost to be decided by me, and not by what someone decides is best for me."

"The College is *different* now," The Enchanter promised him with a serious tone. "I will not ask that you give me anything right now, not even an answer, but please think about the things I have said."

He paused to gesture at Terra, who had flushed a brilliant scarlet and still had not looked up from the table. "I simply wanted a chance to explain myself and attempt to make reparations. She was never meant to be *spying* on you, per se. I didn't even actually *send* her. Terra was there because she wanted to be, and I simply asked her about your potential and such. Then I asked her to keep my interest private, and that is where I went wrong."

"For now, I offer to bring your knowledge of enchantment to an acceptable level so that you would not destroy yourself or others. I will take you to the Beginner rank in whichever enchanting discipline you desire as recompense. From there, you will need to register as my student to go further. What I will *not* do… is go easy on you! Be prepared to hate me for entirely different reasons if you come for tutelage!"

"With that said, please enjoy lunch on me." The old wizard strolled out of the room after flipping a few coins onto the table. Joe focused on Terra, who had still declined to move. He maintained his gaze for a moment longer, but when she didn't react at all… Joe turned toward the door.

"Please wait," Terra quietly requested. Joe paused, but did not look back at her. "I am sorry that I so thoroughly ruined my friendship with you, but please take my Master's offer. The things that you can already do… I can only imagine what you would be *able* to do."

"I have never really had many friends, Terra. I find it really hard to trust people, or forgive when I feel that my concerns are ignored." Joe remained in place, then reached up and grabbed the beam alongside the door and leaned on it. He was struggling with himself; self-reflection was hard. "I am an independent and inventive person… I know that I can be preoccupied with my thoughts, I can become detached and isolate myself. In spite of all that… I want to be capable, and competent. I want to possess knowledge and understand my environment. Most of all, I fear becoming useless or trapped."

"I didn't know what to think, back when you walked away after I joked about calling you a spy. It was clear that *something* had happened, and I could only assume the worst." He turned to face her directly. "In the future, if we are going to have an issue, please come talk to me yourself. Even now, I feel oddly paranoid and want to lash out. I don't know what to think… so I am going to fight myself, and take your word that there was no ill intent. Until I see something different, that is how I'll *try* to act, as well."

Terra's eyes widened at his words, but still she swallowed hard and nodded. "I really did not think that what I was doing was wrong. Honestly, I agree that the fact that I couldn't explain myself and had to simply leave made things a hundred times worse. I understand… it won't happen again."

Joe nodded, "Thank you. I'll also try not to be so quick to anger. I tend to *jump* to conclusions, but right now I could also… really use a friend. Shall we try to catch up?"

"I already ordered some food. Please sit and eat." Terra pushed his chair out with her foot, and he sat down. They talked for a little over an hour, awkwardly at first, but getting warmer as time went on. Apparently, she was still dating Tsnake, and the relationship was going very well. He told her about some of the issues that he had been having recently, and they exchanged information about interesting items that they had seen circulating.

Too soon, Joe needed to leave and get back to his normal duties. "Thank you for this, and thank you for the explanation."

"Thanks for letting me give one." Terra smiled brilliantly at him, and Joe rolled his eyes at her overacting. Feeling happier than he had in a week, Joe emerged into the Guild area and looked around. There was plenty of work for him to do, and now seemed like the right time to do it, so he decided to sit down and think about what he should prioritize. He broke it down into a few broad categories.

His current quests, his duties for the guild, his personal characteristics, and his overall skills. Upon recalling his overall skills, Joe remembered to use his lore increase for the day. Architectural Lore was to Novice nine by simply focusing on it and activating, "*Knowledge*!"

Joe needed to return Daniella's book to her. It had helped him get up to Novice five, and he had been diligently working to maximize his level in the novice ranks before he saw her again... Joe blinked and worked to refocus. He had been finding it harder and harder to remain on one subject recently, and he was uncertain as to why. Perhaps the fact that there was just so *much* to do made him want to ignore it all and go lay down in bed? That sounded pretty normal to him.

He decided that since he was thinking about his skills anyway, he would start there. Joe knew that he needed to increase his combat proficiency; he was becoming nearly useless in fights beyond being a support character. Even there, his non-combat abilities had been stagnating. Now, he knew there was nothing wrong with being a support, but he wanted to be able to have a greater impact in fights if possible. Whether that meant finding new skills or improving his current ones, only time could tell.

Joe pulled up his Ritual Magic skill and sighed as he realized that it was still at Expert two. For some reason, no matter how innovative he had been with his rituals, no matter the complexity he created, this skill had barely increased since he had become a Rituarchitect. Before, he had assumed that he just was not using enough of them or challenging himself.

With a fresh attitude and a new outlook, he contemplated the book he pulled out of his storage ring: Alchemically

Enhanced Components. "You hold the key, don't you? A cook could never become a Master Chef simply by having the ability to chop his ingredients really well, by having the best pots and pans, the best ingredients, or the best recipes. It is a combination of *all* of that, and why would Ritual Magic be any different?"

As soon as he voiced his thoughts, he had an epiphany. Joe staggered as his heart pounded and a strange energy seemed to well up within him. Black energy started to seep from his pores, and the sclera of his eyes flashed with spinning ritual circles. His eyes closed, then reopened, completely clear of whatever had affected them.

You have reached a deeper understanding of not only your skills, but your class and the inherent benefits and limitations it holds. Your base class has been upgraded from Ritualist to Ritualist+. You have gained at minimum a Novice understanding of the five component skills that comprise Ritual Magic as a whole. Form a deeper understanding of not only who, but what you are, to increase your base class further. New Prestige classes have opened further along your path.

Ritual Magic (Expert II): Ability to create, maintain, and change rituals much more efficiently than usual. This is a category of magic that advances based upon the understanding of the subskills within it. Only when one is a master of all the portions of this category can they be true Masters of Rituals. (Bonuses currently maximized at -85% mana and component cost.)

Alchemical Rituals (Novice III) (Passive): this governs the ability to use alchemically enhanced components in rituals to alter, further Specialize, or broaden the effects of a ritual upon activation. This is a subskill of the Ritual Magic category. +1n% to use Alchemically enhanced components in a correct manner. This may include choosing which component to use, where to place it, or how to refine it. This bonus is applied to skill checks when creating alchemical components for rituals, where n = skill level.

Enchanted Ritual Circles (Novice I) (Passive): Whether it is the storage of Enchanted gear, the usage of Enchanted inks, or the linking of multiple ritual circles, this skill governs the ability to use those enchantments in the creation of ritual circles. This is a subskill of the Ritual Magic cate-

gory. +1n% to use enchantments correctly in the creation of ritual circles, where n = skill level.

Ritual Circles (Expert II) (Passive): The creation of ritual circles is a meticulous and tedious process that few have the patience or prowess to pursue. Simple mistakes lead to catastrophic results, but correct usage may lead to unfathomable power. This is a subskill of the Ritual Magic category. +1n% to use, create, destroy, or alter ritual circles, where n = skill level.

Ritualistic Forging (Novice I) (Passive): There are a plethora of components that can be created to change rituals. However, each alteration will increase the inherent instability of the ritual itself, possibly leading to catastrophic failure. However, with Ritualistic Forging, you are able to create helpful items, totems, and eventually pylons that will aid in creating a stable environment for your rituals! Use rituals to make items that help use rituals! Recursion is fun! This is a subskill of the Ritual Magic category. +1n% to the chance of creation and effect of ritual stabilizing items, where n = skill level!

Magical Matrices (Beginner IX) (Passive): Math, the bane of adventurers. Knowledge of how things are, how they should be, and the ability to prove them is the true path to mastery. This is a subskill of the Ritual Magic category. +1n% to use math and lore skill correctly in the creation of spell diagrams when applying the skill to the creation of magical diagrams when a form of higher math is required, where n = skill level.

Joe swallowed as he looked over the new additions to his skills. "That is a lot of information to take in... I feel like I should be a little offended that my entire class just became a giant passive ability? That doesn't seem like it should be right, and this! What does it mean that new 'Prestige' classes will be available? What is a 'Prestige' class and how do I get one?"

CHAPTER TWENTY-FOUR

After spending the better part of an hour working to parse and understand the information that had filled his head with the addition of the new skills, Joe was feeling very pleased with the transition. The skills themselves seemed to support each other in a way that he had not been expecting. The ability to create ritual circles was actually only the most basic portion of what he could do.

With the Alchemical Rituals skill, he could almost completely alter the final effects of a ritual activation, though he would need to experiment to get a better understanding of what that meant. He had gained a few levels in the skill already, likely from fiddling around by adding potions and such to his rituals haphazardly. It seemed that the Ritualistic Forging portion was designed around gaining the things needed for adding a stabilizing portion, and Joe had an inkling that it could support the hard-to-control enchantment area of rituals.

It was the magical matrices that truly opened his eyes. Anyone could carve a circle and place a pentagram in it without understanding anything about rituals. He knew this for a fact, as that was the diagram for the very first ritual he ever performed, 'little sister's cleaning service'. But it was within the clinical facts of mathematics that true understanding could be formed. Luckily for him, his understanding of mathematics had allowed him to reach the Beginner ranks as soon as he had gained the skill; almost stepping into the Student ranks, in fact.

So far, he had been working from a flawed understanding of the ritual diagrams themselves. Using 'Little Sister's Cleaning Service' as an example, he now understood that he could have achieved the effect of some of his basic diagrams by implementing a simple sine wave instead of using both the pentagram and circle. This change would not only save him time in creation, it would reduce the amount of mana required to power the ritual before his class bonus was ever taken into account.

One of Joe's biggest impediments in the creation of rituals had just been solved. It was going to take a lot of work, but he could now custom-design ritual diagrams without the need to search to the ends of the earth to find and adapt a ritual that someone else had left behind. It was a freeing feeling, and he was itching to go and create something completely random just because he knew that he *could*.

"I still need to think about other skills, particularly combat skills." As excited as he was about his new class development, he reigned himself in and tried to refocus on his current goal. "Combat skills… I'm looking at you, Effortless Shaping of Shadows. You are supposed to be a Legendary skill, but I have so much trouble getting you to work correctly that I can only use you on the slowest and weakest of enemies."

Joe took a deep breath, knowing that what he was about to do was probably stupid. He took his Legendary-ranked Effortless Shaping ability and placed it in the soul forge with his only Mythical skill, Solidified Shadows. "I can't use this properly right now, and I am going to have to go and learn some new spells anyway…"

Right before he pressed the button to combine them, he paused as 'Query' activated on its own. Another skill caught his eye; Dual Casting. He supposed that wouldn't hurt. Now that he was using a two-handed staff to channel his spells, there were very few times that he was using both hands to cast either the same or separate spells. He added that to the mix, took a deep breath, and hit the button.

Time until skills have combined: 18 hours.

Joe was trying to keep his hands from shaking as his most potent active skills vanished into the ether, the knowledge of how to use them pulled directly out of his brain. In terms of attack spells, he now only had Acid Spray and a Dark Lightning Strike to rely on. He could only hope that he had made a wise decision for his future growth.

At the thought of future growth, he looked at his characteristics scores and decided to take a run at increasing his luck. Joe started walking toward the testing dungeon, deciding not to go with his team this time - he was planning on taking the test with the highest mortality rate. As he moved along the packed dirt road, he pondered his current quests and decided that there was nothing pressing for him to follow up on. Most of them were high difficulty, nearly impossible to complete at this time. One of his quests had expired: the daily hunt for Wolfmen had been greyed out, and now had an 'inactive' tag that he had never seen before.

He could go over to Ardania and heal up some prisoners or guards, but he decided that could wait for now. Not wanting to neglect them entirely, he would make a point of swinging by the guard Barracks the next time he went into town. Now Joe smiled, feeling much more at peace with himself. Something about organizing the massive, sprawling individual list of things that needed to be accomplished into such broad categories allowed him to look at things with greater clarity. Perhaps he had simply been struck with choice paralysis? Joe felt his angst and worry draining away, and by the time he reached the dungeon, he was feeling positively chipper.

After entering the dungeon, he selected 'luck' as the trial he wanted to attempt and waited while it configured itself. Unlike the dexterity trial, there was no jumping or leaping across platforms to get into the dungeon space. There was simply a door, which he opened and stepped through. After taking two steps through endless darkness that even his eyes couldn't penetrate…

Bad Luck! You have died! Calculating… You have lost 3,200 Experience! You will respawn in two hours!

He stood in his white death room with a look of shock and horror on his face. There had been nothing behind the door. Joe had simply stepped through, step, step, dead. This had to be a monumental joke. The test of luck was literally 'you either die or not'? There was no skill? There were no chances to do anything different, he just died on the spot?

"*Ahh*!" Joe screamed into the air. He rubbed the center of his forehead with one hand, right on the glowing eye, and decided to go sit down and wait. After a few minutes of thinking about it, he started to chuckle. Joe knew that if he told anyone else about this, they would laugh at him. Therefore, he decided to keep it to himself… but use it as a lesson going forward.

He stopped to consider this trial. Was it going to be worth gambling thirty-two hundred experience for five points of luck? His experience gains had slowed significantly now that he was not engaging in active combat as much, so the loss definitely hurt. Pulling up his stat sheet, he decided that yes, it was worth the risk. Joe had been planning to do more fighting, more often, either way. This would be a good motivator, and would save him five days' worth of characteristic point training each time the gamble succeeded.

While he had another few quiet moments, Joe's eyes lit up as he remembered that he had eight unused free skill points. He plotted out the skills that would be getting a sudden boost in efficiency… then paused. He remembered that when he had gained the Rituarchitect class, he had been informed that he could not put any more skill points into his Ritual Magic skill. But now that he had subskills… would he be able to place the skill points in those? He was excited to give it a try, and as soon as he respawned and stepped back into the temple, then made sure no one was around, he opened his skill sheet and placed a single point into Magical Matrices.

Skill increase: Magical Matrices (Apprentice 0). Your understanding of the higher mathematics behind spell theory would make you the envy of any comic book convention you attended! Unfortunately, it would not stop the other attendees from arguing with you over the nuances. Bonus: basic calculus formulas are as simple for you to solve as standard addition and subtraction!

"Nice!" Joe was excited to test that out, since he had never gotten a bonus quite like it before, and was looking forward to seeing how it worked. Next came the real test. He placed a skill point into Ritual Circles, and it increased to Expert three! His Ritual Magic category did not increase, oddly enough, but still Joe pumped his fist into the air and whooped. "We are *back* in business, baby!"

He had six more free skill points to spend, but decided to hold off for now. No, wait. After scanning his skill list again, Joe realized that there was one skill that could use the boost. Knowledge. Right now, all of his lore skills would stagnate without dedication. If he didn't rank up the skill, he would need to learn more lore skills so that he could use it on them.

Skill increase: Knowledge (Beginner 0). This skill can now be used on lore skills at the Beginner tier. If used on lore skills at the novice tier, the cooldown is reduced by 20%.

"Only have five free skill points remaining, but it was totally worth it!" Most of Joe's other skills were low enough that he should have no issue training them up, but Ritual Circles was still far enough from the next tier that he did not want to devote his points there right at that moment. Still, the information that he had just gained had given him an idea that he wanted to test out. Staying within the building, he walked down to the Grand Ritual Hall and started sketching out his thoughts.

"If I can take two of the ritual circles and combine them into a single, smaller one… will it still count as a beginner Circle, or will it be a novice Circle again?" He selected a simple ritual diagram that he had been working on recently, his attempt at creating long distance communication. "If I take this circle out… I can replace both the inner and the first of the outer rings with a combination of 'y equals cosecant x', 'y equals secant x', and 'y equals cotangent x'."

When he was done, he no longer had a circle in front of him. He had what looked like a fancy, triple repeating and connecting, curvy 'X' that had the top left and bottom right legs connected with an 'S'. Joe had linked them, so it was *kind of* a circle. Did that still count? As far as he could tell, it should. He had a thought, and had to voice it aloud, "You know, this almost looks like a radio antenna fractal. Funny!"

Joe poured mana into the small ritual, and was pleased when it lit up and a notification appeared.

You have activated Ritual of Communication (Basic)! Range of communication: 50-mile radius centered on the ritual. This ritual is toggleable. By pausing it, the amount of active time remaining will not decrease. When this is activated, it will automatically activate the linked ritual of communication. Caution: this ritual is not linked with another. Active time remaining: 11:59.

If he had not understood that he needed to enchant the ritual circles to work together, he may have tried to simply activate two of them at the same time and hope for the best. Still, he did not yet know how to do that. It seems that he would be taking the offer from Terra's Master after all. The other good part was that the activation did not require a double ring's worth of mana like a Beginner ring would have. For the first time in his life, Joe was exceptionally grateful for higher mathematics.

He left the Grand Ritual Hall and walked outside to let his team know where he was going to be for the next few days. He sniffed at the air. What was that? Joe's eyes narrowed when he realized that he was smelling smoke. That was not campfire smoke; it was the greasy, meaty smell of a building on fire. He sped up, running toward the sound of raised voices and shouted orders.

CHAPTER TWENTY-FIVE

"Welcome to the party, Joe!" a guard shouted at him. It took a moment for Joe to place the man's name; he was completely coated in blood and soot, making him almost unrecognizable.

"Uh… Jay! What's happening?" Joe looked around and saw that there were various Mages blasting water at the burning barracks, and even more people were running toward the walls.

"Under attack from, I don't know, some kinda collabor-" Jay coughed in pain as a blade erupted through his chest. Joe's eyes shot wide-open as an assassin resolved out of the shadows for only an instant before vanishing again. For the first time, Joe started having serious doubts about losing his ability to see and interact with the shadows. Before, he had been able to somewhat see the rogues. With the loss of his shadowmancer skills, that extra defense was apparently gone.

Almost before thinking of it consciously, Joe used Mend on Jay and brought his health back from the brink. He wasn't able to fully heal the critical backstab, but Jay didn't die instantly. "Dark Lightning Strike!"

There was a clap of thunder as his skill impacted his shield and traveled across the ground. Two previously stealthed attackers appeared, and he pointed his staff at the one that was dripping blood from his blade. The man flinched back, but a moment passed and nothing happened. Joe cursed as he remembered that he had no idea how to call the shadows anymore. "Wither… Plant!"

The spell fired off and hit the assassin, who looked at himself and found no wound; then started running at Joe with his daggers out and poised to strike. Joe turned and ran, cursing himself repeatedly. "I literally only have Acid Spray right now!"

On the plus side, that was a spell that could be blind fired. He cast over his shoulder, using his staff so that it wasn't too awkward to keep running. He was aiming his sprint for the open doors of the Pathfinder's Hall, and while running he promised, "I'm getting a weapon skill as soon as this is over!"

Critical strike! You have been backstabbed! Exquisite Shell absorbs 822 damage! 42 damage taken due to defense penetration! Bleeding heavily due to damage being focused on kidneys! -15 health per second. Poisoned! -20 health and -50 mana per second! Mana regeneration halted. Poisoned: Mage Murder: 00:01:29

Exquisite Shell: 878/1,700

Health: 457/534

"I hunt Mages like you for fun!" The assassin called at him, clearly furious about the face full of acid. "You're already dead, you just don't know it!"

Joe put his full strength into a leap, shooting forward like a rocket and covering dozens of yards in an instant. The assassin called out in shock, but remained focused on ending him. He made the mistake Joe had been hoping for, following him into the building. "Juggernauts! Enemy attack, defend the building!"

"*Acknowledged.*" Purple and silver raced up the suit of armor as it activated, and the assassin was cut in half by the third step he took. "*Warning blow given. All future attacks will be instantly fatal. Enacting defensive protocols.*"

Joe healed himself, stopping the bleeding, but keeping an eye on the poison that was coursing through his body. His aura made it last forty-five seconds instead of the ninety it was supposed to, but the poison was draining him of mana at a huge rate. At the last second, he healed himself one more time, bringing his mana to zero. He gasped as his aura collapsed and the poison started vanishing at its normal rate.

He did the math as quickly as possible, and sighed in relief as he saw that the poison would end in twenty-three seconds. That would take four hundred and sixty health, but leave him with roughly forty. Joe was going to survive. "If I couldn't heal myself, that single attack - one I mostly blocked - would have killed me..."

"Hold up." Joe looked at the Juggernaut. "Did you say that was a warning attack? The one where you sliced him in half?"

"*Affirmative. Deterrent protocols. First offenders are given a warning.*"

"But you cut him in half."

"*He survived long enough to receive the warning.*"

Joe gulped, once again *very* pleased that these things were on his side. It did make him consider and discard his idle thoughts about stealing active temples from others; they would certainly have their own ability to defend themselves. "How in the world did I get into this building? I was running, and I jumped, but..."

Since Joe could barely move, and didn't really want to crawl to the exit, he pulled up the information for his Jump skill; trying to determine if there was any information it could give him. After a moment, he closed it and sighed. He would need to search for answers elsewhere.

Poison: 'Mage Murder' has worn off!

After another ten seconds, Joe used Lay on Hands, then again until he was at full health. He waited for his mana to reach full, then activated his Exquisite Shell and Neutrality Aura once more, and waited longer to recover full mana. "That took... like three minutes. That's pretty rough... I would have been nothing but a liability if I would have stayed in combat."

Now determined to help, Joe raced toward the fighting. He healed everyone along the way that didn't have a player killer aura, and avoided anyone who did. After searching through the chaos for a short while, he heard Bard's voice chanting something and followed the sound to the source. He stepped through the choking black smoke and found Bard and Poppy with their backs to the burning barracks as they faced off with three attackers in hot pink armor.

Since they were facing away from him, Joe felt comfortable with his next action. "Acid Spray!"

The attackers screeched as their gear started melting, giving off a toxic odor. His teammates used the opportunity to take down two of them, then Poppy vanished with the third before coming back a moment later, standing over a corpse. "Whew, that skill is sure seeing a lot of use today!"

Joe sent a heal to Poppy, who was bleeding freely from a cut that ran from his nose to his temple. "They catch you with your pants down?"

"Basically." Bard coughed as he pulled in too much smoke. "Ya see Alexis anywhere?"

"No, I almost got killed by a mage-hunting assassin." Joe's aura finished off their smoke-inhalation debuff just as he asked, "Do you have any idea what's going on?"

Poppy replied, too calm for the situation at hand. "It appears that we are under attack from the other three Noble Guilds. As far as I can tell, they are targeting buildings and attempting to sabotage our progress."

Quest update: The making of an Elder. Town rank has fallen to Rank One! Current progress: 1/5.

"Oh, Celestial Feces! That's not gonna fly! We need to put an end to this right now!" Joe's entire bald head went red as fury coursed through him. He turned and ran toward the gate, trying to think through options to fend off three guilds' worth of attackers, but honestly couldn't think of… Joe winced as one thing came to mind. He still had one more anti-personnel ritual ready to be activated, but if he just dropped it somewhere, it would impact his guild mates as well.

"Bard, can you watch my back and help me get to the main gate?" Joe didn't wait for an answer, jogging toward the place where the smoke was most prevalent. It seemed that there was a huge amount of fire mages or something similar attacking over there, and he was never more pleased that the walls themselves were a combination of metal and stone; those wouldn't be burning anytime soon.

"Want me to come too?" Poppy's voice was so serious that it was clearly sarcasm.

"Of course! I need someone to clear the way!" Joe kept his eyes forward, so he missed the smirk on Poppy's face. The town was pretty small and compact, so it only took a few minutes to push through the smoke and devastation. The main gate had been forced open, and the Wanderer's Guild was fighting in the chokepoint and trying to push the people back. There were clearly heavy losses on both sides, but there were so many more people attacking than defending that the tide was shifting drastically.

"Aten! Mike!" Joe's voice was barely heard over the din of battle, but between one moment and the next, Aten was in front of Joe.

"What, Joe? I know this is important, because otherwise you wouldn't be interrupting me in the middle of a siege!" Aten barked, his eyes glowing almost as brightly as his armor and weapon.

"Guild Commander!" Joe returned with as much military discipline as he could muster. "I need to get to the gate, then I need all our people to move back! Area of effect coming. Friendly fire is a concern, but it should give us a serious reprieve!"

"I'll make it happen." Aten didn't ask for any more specifics, simply turning and barreling into the cluster at the gate. Joe and his current teammates followed as closely as possible, but Aten was *fast*. His sword was dancing through the air with flashes of light that seemed to capture too much attention. At one point, Joe was almost positive that he saw Aten punch people with both his hands while his sword cut down another foe at the same time.

Joe blinked, and Aten's sword was in his hands. That had been a… mirage? With Aten leading with such momentum, they were able to shove the fighting back a few feet. That was enough. Joe took the metal plate the ritual was inscribed on, slapped it on the ground, covered it with bloody dirt to hide it as much as possible, then brought up the activation option.

"Full retreat!" Joe bellowed, his odd dark charisma making people around him flinch. Aten echoed his order, and the Wanderer's Guild fell back, losing all the ground they had just managed to take. Enemies started pouring through the breach, and Joe let loose a deep breath.

Activate Ritual of Proximity (Wind Blades)? Yes / No.

"Yes."

Defensive charges used: 0/500.

Joe opened his eyes as the ritual powered up. Wind blades started sweeping through the area, faster and faster as the ritual realized that there was a plethora of targets. The screams of battle turned to pain and outrage as the gate area was turned into a charnel house. Only the people without defensive abilities or high constitution were killed or heavily damaged outright, which turned out to be a surprisingly small number of the players that were attacking them. Most were able to tank several hits before they took critical damage; but there was a secondary effect.

Joe noticed another weakness: the ritual seemed to have no tracking ability. As soon as the target was determined, a blade flew out. Here, it didn't matter too much. There were so many people packed together that even if someone dodged, the blade still hit *someone*. On the plus side, the blades hit *hard*, which meant knockback came into effect. Thanks to that, enemies were sent onto the waiting blades of the Wanderer's Guild or slapped back into the enemy lines.

"Poppy, Bard!" Joe bellowed, over not only the combat, but also the rushing wind. "We are the only ones it won't outright attack, we need to get over there and close the gate!"

Joe and Poppy ran into the open space and started pulling

the left gate door closed. This left them open to spells and archers, but most of them were at the back of the enemy lines and didn't have a clear shot. The attacks that got close were tanked by Bard, and he also worked to shove bodies out of the way as the gates were pulled.

"Gah! Need ah heal, Joe!" Bard painfully called over as he pulled an arrow out of his clavicle. Joe wasted no time, slapping a hand on the Skald and pumping him full of healing energy. When the left gate was closed, they moved to the right one and started repeating the process.

Defensive charges used: 431/500.

"Aten!" Joe shouted into the town, "Five more seconds, and we could use a hand!"

"Charge! Close the gates!" Aten bellowed, charging forward. He took a wind blade, then two, and the ritual collapsed. More people grabbed onto the gate, while those that had been slightly slower cleared the fallen. The gate slammed closed, and a few bars were loaded onto the rungs.

"Reinforce this!" Aten moved from fighter to Commander in an instant. "I need everyone in the first and second division working together to sweep the town! For anyone that doesn't know what I mean, that's all rangers and people that can spot stealthed players, paired up with a fighter to hold them off! Move, move, move!"

Joe collapsed against the wall and heaved in a few breaths, his stamina hovering near empty. He watched Aten run to the top of the wall and shout at the people now trapped outside. He couldn't hear what was being said, but Aten came down with furious eyes almost ten minutes later. "Joe, top level meeting, right now. Come with me."

CHAPTER TWENTY-SIX

"They're threatening to wipe out our base." Aten began the meeting as soon as the last person had filtered in. "We've been number one for too long, and it's clearly attracted the notice of some unsavory people."

"They banded together to attack us? This was just a *warning*?" A sharply-dressed man that Joe hadn't seen in a long time cleared his throat and lazily spoke from the relaxed position of his chair. "So what do they want? I'm sure they demanded to be paid off or some such nonsense."

"Mr. Banks, they wanted only that we stop progressing until they have had a chance to 'catch up'." Aten's eyes flashed. "They said that we had an 'unfair advantage', and that we were somehow cheating. They said that if we get back to town level two in the next six months, they are going to come after us with all of their allies and everyone they can think of that would participate in our destruction."

"I think I can speak for everyone in the guild when I say that is not an option." Aten stopped speaking when another hand went up and waved slightly to get his attention. "*Yes*, Mr. Johnson?"

Joe inspected the speaking man with his Intrusive Scan, and his name popped up after a long moment, followed by his highest stat. Joe almost couldn't stop himself from speaking aloud, so he muttered too softly for anyone that mattered to hear, "His name is literally 'Mr. Johnson'? Highest stat… charisma. Oh, this isn't gonna be good."

"*I* say… why *not* give them what they want?" Mr. Johnson smiled at the others in the room. "We have plenty of other projects, so why worry about getting the town as high as possible right now? Perhaps we skew toward more *luxurious* pursuits for a while? We just made a delightful new wine blend, and even the press wine had a lovely body and bouquet! Why risk losing all of our hard work because we haven't settled into our lifestyle properly?"

There were murmurs of agreement from about half of the table, while the other half looked on with faint disgust. Aten swallowed and took a deep breath. "Mr. Johnson, I think that you may be disregarding some of the potential benefits of the buildings that we are bringing in. Even the grapes for the wine you are describing came from the greenhouse, which is one of the buildings that helped bring us to our current town level! Beyond that, you are talking about a business venture that could take *years* to mature. If we do not expand our Guild's military might to acceptable levels, there's a good chance that we lose everything to someone who simply has the power to take it."

"Nonsense!" Mr. Johnson sputtered. "Who would do that? We would bring the Kingdom into-"

"Mr. *Johnson*." Aten had steel in his tone. "You ask that question while smoke is still rising from the buildings burning around us. Who would *do* that? These same people who are threatening us now, even though we have more military might than all of them individually! *They* would take it, and send us to respawn as thanks for all of our hard work!"

"That is *enough*, Mr. Aten." Mr. Banks stated coldly. "I appreciate your fervor, but I will take this opportunity to remind you that you serve at the convenience of the board of directors. You will not speak to-"

"I am *Guild Commander Aten*." The bass in Aten's voice shook the room, and several wine glasses shattered with the reverberations of his low snarl. "*You* would do well to remember that your companies from earth no longer *exist*. You are acting with an outdated view of the world, and-"

"I think that it may be high time for a change in leadership." Mr. Banks darkly announced. "In fact, in light of recent events, I am hereby *removing* you from your position. I will negotiate with these Guilds myself."

"I was hoping you would say that." Aten smirked just as a pop-up window appeared in front of Joe.

The council of the Wanderer's Guild has started a 'No-confidence' vote to remove Guild Commander Aten from his position! Should he be removed? All Guild members currently waiting on respawn automatically vote 'abstain'. Yes / No / Abstain.

Joe pressed 'no' without hesitation, barely taking the time to finish reading the prompt. Three bars appeared in the box; a red, green, and a gray bar all started moving. In just under a minute, the vote had ended. The result was clear, Aten was here to stay.

"Now that this farce has ended," Aten told the sputtering board members, "we will be working hard to boost our defensive capabilities to the maximum before bringing the town back to town level two and beyond. As per the no-confidence clause, I am implementing a new Guild policy. No one under level ten is allowed to call for the removal of Guild members in positions of power. They will also *not* sit on the council. Guards, remove these hangers-on from the war room."

It was clear that the board members did not know how to react to the sudden change, as not a single one of them was able to muster a defense before they had been whisked from the room. Just like that, the only people remaining were those who had a vested interest in increasing their Guild's - and their own -

power. Aten looked around at the silent people that remained and smiled.

"I am sorry you needed to see that unpleasantness, but I think this will make for a much more successful future." Aten motioned for some documents to be prepared, and sealed what he had just ordered. "Now, I would like to discuss my plans for the near future with all of you."

When Joe was finally able to leave the command tent, his head was spinning but he was beaming proudly. Following a strong leader had always given him a powerful surge of motivation. His role was clear: Joe was to salvage what he could of the damaged buildings, work with the guild and his Coven to design and implement defensive measures, and once that was all ready... bring the power of the guild to new heights.

"I am *so* ready for this! Let's fix up those bad boys!" Joe gathered up his Coven and filled them in over the next hour or so, after which they worked to assist Joe in creating a ritual of Structural Repair. Joe explained the steps that he was using to make everything, and it seemed to boost their spirits. Joe was pleased. As much as he loved learning, he also loved teaching. In fact, if things had gone differently for him, he would have loved to be a teacher.

"What can you see from the diagram *here*?" Joe pointed at a small double helix that encircled everything else on the ritual, then looked around at the others.

"Journeyman ranked ritual, since that's the fourth circle. Boom!" Kirby gave a thumbs up and waited for confirmation.

Joe blinked at the instant response, and looked at the ritual, then her again. "Well. Yes, that is technically correct, but I meant-"

"Technically correct is the best kind of correct!" Kirby held up her other hand as well, displaying a double thumbs-up. After letting Joe sputter for a moment, she snorted and dropped her hands. "I'm totally kidding. Seriously though, that's the only thing I can get off of this ritual diagram. Way too advanced for me."

"Right. Um. Anyone else?" Joe tried not to laugh, since it would only encourage further ridiculousness. Wait. That was a good thing! He let a soft chuckle slip out, and Kirby brightened right away.

Hannah leaned in and made an educated guess. "Well… we already know what this ritual *does*, right? It repairs damaged buildings. So I'm guessing that this part of the ritual actually makes that happen?"

"Correct! *Fully* correct, this time." Joe winked at Kirby. "Look here. This section checks the building for damage. This one holds any resources or components needed, the third circle pulls off anything too damaged to salvage, and the DNA-looking part takes those resources and binds them - hopefully - flawlessly with the building materials already in place."

"I heard that you can just drop a building, regain everything used to make it, then put it together again flawlessly." As Big_Mo paused, Joe nodded for him to continue. "It takes only a few minutes to do that after the ritual diagram is all drawn up, so why not do that instead?"

"Great question! Mate, a coffee for him, please." Joe gestured with his arm, and a significantly darker coffee elemental appeared, bubbled happily, and vanished after filling the cup Joe was holding out. Big_Mo took the drink gingerly, not sure what to say. "There are two issues with this plan, and one thing you don't know. Any guesses?"

"Time investment?" Taka grunted from his chair. He was the only one not standing and looking at the new plans.

"That's one." Joe nodded at the seated Warrior-Ritualist. "Each ritual needs a blueprint, and each ritual itself is slightly different because of that. Mass-production is not possible, in other words, unless we are making a lot of the same building."

"I'm guessing… cost?" Robert asked after a moment of silence had passed.

"Yes!" Joe pointed at the new ritual diagram. "Both Structural Repair, as well as Architect's Fury, are Journeyman-ranked rituals. Just getting the blueprint of the building so that we *can* go to the next step costs as much as repairing the building directly. Now, here is the part you don't know. This ritual needs to go onto an item that is at least four hundred pounds. I'm not sure why, but I've been seeing more restrictions like that recently."

"The other part is that it needs a constant mana supply, and all the materials need to be in a storage device that the ritual can pull from. In return, we can work on multiple buildings at the same time, and target new ones when each is fixed up." Joe paused and nodded deeply, "So long as we have the materials required for the building, we can fix it."

The group left the Grand Ritual Hall and convinced some guards to bring a large slab of marble from the guild storehouse over to standing stone number three, which were a stand-in for street names. No one had been able to agree on them yet, as the common offerings were 'Streety SuperPath' or 'Mr. GravelLine Road'. While the Coven were waiting for the guards to show up, they inspected the worst-damaged buildings and tried to decide what they would need most.

"It's an Uncommon-ranked barracks." Hannah was pointing out, "It shouldn't have any unique requirements! Wood, nails. Done."

"Don't forget shingles." Joe quipped, though none of them understood the joke.

"Doors!" Taka called.

Hannah grimaced. "That's still *wood*, Taka. Joe, does this need to be processed materials, or can it be just the raw material? Can we chuck a couple trees in a storage bag and have that fix things?"

Joe considered that, "You know, I have no idea? It won't hurt to try, though."

When the guards arrived and dropped the marble slab on the ground, Joe waved away the dust and asked them to bring raw wood and metal in a storage device. They looked a little miffed, but walked off to do as he asked. Nearly an hour later, Mike showed up with a bag.

"You know that spatial storage devices are restricted items, correct? We can't just give them out to a guard because he says you need it," Mike grumped at Joe as he tossed the bag at him. "I'll need that back when you are done here."

"So you're staying to watch?" Joe looked into the bag and smirked when he saw that this clearly high-quality bag still only had a fraction of the storage space his codpiece did.

"No real choice." Mike sat on a bench and watched them as they worked to put the finishing touches on the marble.

When they had finished, the previously pure white marble block was covered in black formulaic etchings. Joe had them gather around it, and started pouring mana into it. With six people powering it, the ritual was soon ready for use. "This is a strange ritual, in that it only takes very basic activation components. A core, then a pound of iron, water, wood, and coal. Why would that be the case… Kirby?"

"I'm guessing because it will take components and resources to use, not just to activate?" Kirby replied easily.

"I think that's accurate." Joe nodded at the fire damaged buildings in front of him. "Should we give it a try?"

Activate Ritual of Structural Repair? Yes / No.

"Yup."

Select target damaged structure.

Joe pointed at the building in front of him. It was enough.

Checking…

A ring of light swept over the building for a long thirty seconds. Joe felt a pull at his mana and grunted, as did the others.

Unable to repair structure. Structural integrity is under 50%. Please select a new target.

Joe shared the news with the others and selected a new building. "Well… looks like we *will* need to take a few of them down, after all."

CHAPTER TWENTY-SEVEN

It took a while to make their way through the damaged buildings, but Joe was pleased to see that those that didn't need to be torn down looked shiny and new at the end. The main reason this process had taken so long was that the materials seemed to be torn apart and replaced into the structure bit by bit; so much so that it looked like the building was growing instead of being built.

"Looks like non-processed materials are fine," Joe nodded at Hannah, "but they need to be *ready* for processing. The green wood didn't get touched, and iron ore that hadn't been purified wasn't used either. Good call on testing that."

The next portion went much faster, since the building that had been the main target of fire was razed in under a minute. The recollected materials went into the sack, which went to Mike. Mike took the bag reverently and thanked the Coven. "If we had needed to do that manually, it would have taken days. Here's a bonus from me."

You have gained 1,000 contribution points.

Hannah looked at the message they had all gained, then

back at Mike. "How many points do you have that you can give them out like this?"

"I'm the vice guild leader." Mike explained, seeing the understanding in her eyes, "I can give out whatever is needed for a job well done. Within reason, of course. I have to account for all of it with the guild, but the paperwork is pretty minimal. You all did a great thing for us, and I look forward to seeing what you can do in the days to come!"

The group broke up, and Joe looked over the gains that he had gained for working on the buildings.

Class experience gained: 420 (100 for razing a building, 320 for repairing 8 buildings).

He was making good progress with his class, and was *nearly* halfway to level five. Deciding that he needed to work on more physical things, he went to train his strength and constitution. Joe walked to the training ground, got into position, and the hot coals started being shoveled onto the shield he held in the air.

Ten minutes in, his arms were burning. Literally *and* figuratively. Twenty, and he was getting ready to move on with his day. Thirty, and the coals were getting *much* hotter. At forty-five, he almost tossed the shield to the side and moved on. His willpower refused to let that happen, which meant that he lasted for the entire time required, just about fifty-five minutes.

Characteristic training completed! Strength and constitution +1! These cannot be increased through training for 24 hours!

Skill increase: Artisan Body (Beginner 0). You have taken a solid step upon the path of refining your body and mind! Bonus: From this point forward, threshold bonuses for characteristics will give you a small percentage bonus to earned rewards.

Joe sat on the grass, panting as he looked over his notifications. The trainer was glaring at him; Joe had earned a reputation as a quitter, and none of them liked to work with him on his training. "You had *five* more minutes before you were halfway there, man! Why are you doing double training if you can't handle it? Go pump some iron or settle into a vat of water over fire if you need to do one at a time!"

Joe ignored the grumbling, though it was nice to know the options. Why had the training taken so long? Normally he was done in half that… right. He had gotten to the next threshold for both of those! The time required to train them had doubled! If he didn't have his four times boost, the training would have taken two hours apiece. With that bonus, coupled with his Artisan Body, each characteristic took… twenty-seven minutes? Obviously, since he was training two at a time, fifty-four minutes.

Joe looked over his skill and was *really* tempted to start dumping skill points into it, but forced himself not to do so. Not yet, at least. He got dressed and walked away, pondering what he should be doing. His team had split up temporarily in the wake of the attack, each of them feeling the need to focus on their individual abilities and boost skill levels. Joe hadn't fought it in the slightest; he was feeling the same as they were.

"You there!" A voice shook Joe from his thoughts. A dark-haired man confronted him with a serious face. He was wearing leathers and had an odd array of weapons with him. "You look like someone that could use some extra training! How would you like to join me, Weaponmaster Everard, for some demonstrations?"

"No, that's okay. Thanks, though." Joe walked past the man, who clearly hadn't been expecting to be ignored.

"What's the matter? All I need is someone to use as an example, and all you need to do is learn!" The man, likely 'Weaponmaster Everard', calmly called after him. "I need a chance to showcase my teaching ability. First lesson, no charge?"

"Please find someone else to use as a punching bag." Joe looked at Everard sourly. The man was walking with him now. "Oh, how exciting. I see that you seem to have decided upon me. Why?"

"You are a well-known figure in this guild." Everard told him without hesitation. "Not only are you known as a Mage, but no one that I have asked has seen you use a weapon as more than a spellcasting medium. You have access to the highest members of the guild and could help me start my own Training Stalle here. And…"

"So you were looking for me specifically." Joe stopped and faced the man. "Go on, what's the last bit?"

"Frankly, people are kinda excited to see you get beaten into submission." Everard shrugged at the expression on Joe's face. "I asked who they respected but wanted to see get whooped. Seventy percent of the time, that's you."

"Oh, lovely. Let's go and show my blood to the crowd."

"Excellent."

"*No*. I'm more likely to ban you from the town than join you right now." Joe was exasperated by this conversation.

"*Five* free lessons? Half price from there on?" Everard raised a brow. "I also heard you were a miser, so I have prepared various tempting discounts."

"Have you ever been hit by lightning?"

Everard shook his head, still unsmiling. "Look. Have you ever needed to use a weapon, but didn't know how? Mana isn't endless, and fights can go a long time. Why don't you let me try to train you? If we do it publicly, it'll even be free."

Everard's words echoed what Joe's thoughts had been not too long ago. Still, he was feeling like resisting the temptation. He pulled out his Mystic Theurge staff, and handed it to the Weaponmaster. "Could you teach me to use this in combat?"

"Huh." Everard flipped the staff a few times, then started swinging and swiping with it. Joe winced when it cracked against the ground, and took it back possibly faster than needed. "Sure can, but how specific do you want that training? That's only gonna be good for a few more levels. The rarity is high, but the materials themselves are only… meh. If you do any dungeons, or go to any higher-scale custom shops, you could replace this with a snap. So… my recommendation would be 'polearm' training."

"That would cover you for spears, staves, and halberds." Everard cracked a small smile for the first time since Joe had met him. "Whaddaya think? Staff Mastery would be better for that *specific* weapon, but I stand by my words. I also think it would appease some of your people to take a few hits in front of them. Ya know. Let them release steam without attacking you by themselves."

"You think that this would be *that* useful?" Joe knew that he was letting himself be convinced. It wasn't for the discounts. Totally not. He went along with the Weaponmaster when the man gave a somber nod. Joe was led to the square, where a large group of people were already waiting. A few cheered, and some even passed coins around.

"Are you ready to see him *bleed*?" Everard bellowed into the crowd, who all seemed to be ready to reply instantly.

"*Yes*!" came the reply, sending some soot flying.

"*Yeesh*." Joe muttered as he looked at all the people that wanted to see him in pain. He straight-up had no idea who most of them were. "I'm starting to think that this-"

"Raise your staff, position yourself like this... left foot back a little further, there you go." Everard was speaking in a calm voice that only Joe could hear over the jeering crowd. "I'm gonna hit you now, so try to block over your head."

Everard moved, and Joe swung to block an attack from above, only for the weighted wooden sword Everard was using to crack against his ribs. Joe took no damage, since his Exquisite Shell was active, but he turned cold eyes on Everard, who shrugged. "Lesson one, don't trust your opponent to let you know what they are about to do. Turn off your shield, or this will mean nothing."

Joe really didn't want to do that, as the ring of people around him looked like they were about to rush over and beat him themselves. Still, he had come this far, and there was literally nothing that he couldn't recover from. Exquisite Shell came off, dissolving into motes of light. "Good. Left hand higher on the staff. You aren't using it to channel anything right now; you are using this for attack and defense. Keep your hands apart so I can't break them both with a single hit."

Then the sword started swinging. With a crunch, it slammed into Joe's left pinky finger. If he hadn't crossed into the new tier of constitution, the bone would have been paste. As it was, Joe got a notification that it had broken. He yelped, and the crowd roared approvingly. Everard swept his sword low, and Joe found himself looking up at the sky. "Watch that footwork."

Blow after blow rained down, not intended to do too much damage, but in a fight every one of the strikes would have made him vulnerable to a finishing blow. Here, it was simply humiliating. Joe focused on the sword coming at him, and saw something… different. There was the faintest of lines in the air behind the sword, and as the wood flashed out and hit him again, he saw that the sword sunk into him before rebounding.

"Illusion?" Joe muttered.

"Oh, saw that, did you?" Everard evenly replied. "Good. Just another trick. Good luck on this one."

The faint line was in front of the sword this time, and Joe realized that Everard was changing his tactics just slightly enough that it was almost impossible to adjust for. Still, Joe managed, thanks to his higher-than-Everard-expected dexterity.

**Crack*.*

Joe blocked the attack, surprising both of them. He didn't block the next hit, this time to his wrist. Still, he felt somewhat satisfied at what he saw.

You are training under the tutelage of an Expert! Skill gain modifiers: Expert teacher, Ritualist skill increase bonus, Pathfinder's Hall skill increase bonus.

Skill gained: Polearm Mastery (Novice VI). This skill gives a small boost to use of all polearms in melee combat, both attack and defense. Impacts Halberds, Spears, Staves, and any other weapons that fall under the broad 'polearms' category. +1n% accuracy, damage dealt, and damage blocked when using polearms, where n = skill level.

Joe got back to his feet, adjusting his stance and the way he held his weapon slightly. Everard nodded slightly and addressed the crowd, "Just like that, I can take a Mage that carries a stick… into a warrior who specializes in staff combat! Come train any weapon you want to learn at Weaponmaster Everard's Stalle, hopefully opening soon!"

There was a smattering of applause, but it cut off quickly. The crowd didn't disperse, much to Everard's confusion. "Oi, keep goin'! He's barely bruised!"

Everard shook his head and opened his mouth, but the others shouted agreement for the first voice. He shrugged and turned back to Joe. "I won't kill you, or let them do it, but I need public opinion on my side, and this seems like the way to make it happen."

"Dude." Joe weakly replied as the sword came at him *much* faster than before.

**Crack*, *crack*, *crack*.*

You have taken 43 blunt damage! Stunned!

Joe stumbled as the world seemed to turn dark. Wrist, knee, temple. Joe dropped, head swimming. Wanting to protect himself, he thought of using Acid Spray, but decided that using something like that in a spar like this would be seen as far too ruthless. Everard had been correct. People seemed to have some serious animosity for him; no need to pile onto that.

He slapped a hand to his chest and healed up, then sprang to his feet. Everard chuckled, "Looks like he can take more damage than we expected!"

The group cheered at that, and Joe swallowed deeply. He narrowed his eyes, and set his sights on getting stronger. If he had to fight, he would learn as much as he could. Joe took strike after strike, but almost every time he managed to block one, his skill level increased. Each time his health started to drop too far, he healed. Soon Everard was frowning. "If you don't go down, I'll need to *make* you go down."

"Don't wanna waste my first free training session." Joe had blood pouring out of a busted lip. "I'm a *miser*, remember?"

The next hits were *much* harder and faster, and Joe was forced to focus on healing himself until Everard backed off. "Seriously, Joe. Just stop."

"Can't do it at this point," Joe replied after he heard people calling for Everard to bash his face in.

"Sorry about this, then."

Soul Forge is complete!

The message blocked Joe's vision, and he went tumbling one way as a tooth went another. The crowd gasped as Joe heard a sound from Everard that he had wanted to hear since the public lesson had started:

"*Ow*!"

CHAPTER TWENTY-EIGHT

Soul Forge complete! Skill gained: Retaliation of Shadows.

Retaliation of Shadows (Apprentice I) (Legendary): You have forgone the active usage of the Shadows around you for the ability to use the Shadows at a more... instinctual level. When you are attacked, your mind automatically reacts. Whether it be from a physical blow, or a magical attack, the shadows will lash out on your behalf. Effect: upon taking damage, an instant retaliation will strike your attacker for 1n% of the standard potential damage of the attack, up to 10n damage, where n = skill level. As the retaliation moves at the speed of Darkness, only the most agile of foes will be able to dodge. Toggleable. Cost: Reserves 15% of total mana pool while active.

Joe sat up, healing himself in the same motion. He saw Everard standing and looking at him with a question in his eyes and blood rolling down his face. "Did you *slap* me?"

"What? No." Joe took an unsteady ready stance as Everard flew at him. His sword went point-first into Joe's hand, and he could feel the bones breaking. At the same time, for a bare instant, he saw a perfect copy of himself appear in front of Everard and slap him soundly across the face.

"Ow! You did it again!" Everard snarled. Joe was too busy

fixing his ruined hand to care what this man had to say for himself. Another strike came in, but Joe managed to get his defense up in time, and cleanly blocked it.

"Guards are here! Scatter!" The crowd thinned rapidly, but Everard remained standing in place, glaring at Joe as a few confused guards walked past. They didn't even bother to stop and check on anything, as they had literally only been passing through.

"So, where should we meet up for the next lessons? Five free ones, yeah?" Joe had a faint smile on his face, and Everard slowly nodded.

"Somewhere *private*, so that we don't have a mess like this." Everard's training sword went into his belt, and he reached out a hand. They shook, and Joe used Lay on Hands at the same time. "Gah! Why is your hand so slimy…! Oh, I feel better."

"You should; I'm a Cleric. I heal people." Joe made his staff vanish into his ring.

"Cleric? I was told that you were a Mage." Everard offered plans to train soon before departing, and Joe checked his skill notices.

Polearm Mastery (Beginner III).

No bonus, but he was using his staff at the end like a person who had trained for months, rather than only a few minutes. That man was *talented*, and Joe was going to make sure the guild knew to snap him up as soon as possible. Now, Joe wanted to look deeper into his new skill. Since there was no one else to talk to, he summoned Mate and spoke to the coffee elemental.

"Think through this with me. Retaliation of Shadows… let's see… at Apprentice three, looks like you return up to twenty-one percent of damage taken, up to a maximum of two hundred and ten total damage." Joe thought the percentages over and nodded thoughtfully, "Interesting. I can do more damage directly to armor with Acid Spray, but there is one thing missing from this that makes it extra powerful."

Mate bubbled inquisitively, and received a pat for being a good listener. Joe gleefully rubbed his hands together, "Just think, Mate! It's missing a limit on *simultaneous targets*! Hopefully I never have hundreds of people hitting me at the same time, but if I do… I'll… oh… slightly inconvenience them. Before dying. Right… I'd need to tank all that damage. I can see the drawbacks. I guess that's why it dropped to Legendary instead of taking the higher Mythical rank. Thanks for helping me work this out. Let's see…"

Mate nodded sagely, swirling in place.

"I have to give up fifteen percent of my total mana, but then it doesn't take any mana to function. That's… three hundred forty-six mana for unlimited retaliations. Good trade. Should I work on boosting my defenses now, or figure out a better fighting style that incorporates this?" It only took Joe a moment to decide. "Best way to survive is not to get hit. New spells are the way to go, maybe more polearm training later. Good. Now…"

"Oh, I know!" Joe snapped his fingers and made his way to the Temple, deciding to pop over to Ardania. It was time to start his journey with enchanting.

As the sun started setting, Joe reappeared in the temple and collapsed to the ground with a groan. The Enchanter had not been kind, and had demanded that Joe demonstrate all his current ability in enchanting. Then, he had taken the majority of their time together to show Joe why his methods were dangerous, inefficient, or both. Joe had even broken down and shown the man his enchantment for creating Mana Batteries in an attempt to gain *some* respect.

Instead, the Enchanter had become so furious about the wasted potential of the Cores that he had kicked Joe out of the building. Joe was told by Terra to come back after a day to give the old man a chance to calm down. Currently, Joe laid in a pile, trying to figure out why he was so despondent. "All of that… and not a single skill rank in Enchanting."

There *had* been a gain, and Joe was almost embarrassed by how accurate the feedback must have been to get his skill all the way from non-existence, to…

Skill gained: Enchanting Lore (Beginner II). Allows you to fine tune Enchantments that you find or create. Can increase potency of enchantments and/or decrease cost of creating enchantments.

"Why do I hate that I only got a Lore skill so much?" Joe sat upright and rubbed his eyes.

"*Finally, something I can work with.*" The voice boomed through the room, and Joe felt a huge amount of fury welling up within him. Just before he shot to his feet to attack the intruder, he caught himself and realized that the emotion was certainly not natural.

"Who-"

"I am Tommulus, deity of fire and wrath." The voice was coming from that altar, where a blood-red flame was burning without flickering. It had gotten quieter as well, and roiling emotions were no longer impacting Joe. "I have an offer for you."

"Interesting." Joe smoothed his robe and stood tall. "Why now? You have been here since I built this temple, and have never spoken before. What changed?"

"*You*, of course. When have you been here before, full of fury and shame?" The deity didn't seem coy, instead listing apparent facts. In fact, the voice was honorable; something he would expect from a noble paladin. "You lay on the floor of my temple, enraged over your lack of knowledge, and full of anger over being beaten like a rug publicly. If you didn't come here today, and had instead acknowledged your feelings and moved past them like an adult, who knows when we may have spoken?"

"First, ouch." Joe's cheeks were flushed, and he was filled with embarrassment over his flaws being so clearly shown. "Second, good to know that there were requirements to speak with the deities."

"Of course there are. Even you were originally contacted only because you gained access to a hidden class. Occultatum took the first person that met his minimum standard." Tommulus stated clearly.

"Are you the god of wrath because you make people angry, or…?"

"The truth often enrages those who cannot handle it." Tommulus's words made Joe deflate like a popped balloon. "Will you hear my task, or no?"

"Please, feel free." Joe sighed and waved for the flame to continue speaking, only realizing afterwards that he was expecting a fire to read his motions. Magic was weird.

"Good. I need you to help my cleric, Crimson Flame of Wrath."

"Crimson…? Is that Crim's full name?" Joe held back his laughter, but only barely. He was going to need to re-estimate Crim's age when they met again.

"Yes." Tommulus solemnly intoned. "There is an opportunity for Crim to gain a specialization that would also benefit you greatly, but I think that you already have plans for your own advancement. There is another group that is seeking the same holy relic, the Golden Tome of Divine Favor. You have bested them once before, and I hope that you will be able to do so once again."

"I see… and in return?" Joe knew that there needed to be a reward for a quest like this, so he didn't feel too bad being blatant about it.

Quest offered: The Golden Tome of Divine Favor. Retrieve the Tome for Crim, the cleric of Tommulus. Reward: Tommulus has offered you a chance to gain favor from him! Accept? Yes / No.

"Nope, try again." Joe shook his head, hearing a slight chuckle in reply.

"Had to try. I will do one of three things." Tommulus stopped speaking, and a quest appeared in front of Joe.

Quest offered: The Golden Tome of Divine Favor. Retrieve the Tome for Crim, the cleric of Tommulus. Reward: 500 gold for each participating party member. 5,000 experience. Joe only, choose one: Cleric spell on the path of Wrath. +5 in all characteristics. Divine Infusion x1. Accept? Yes / No.

"What is a Divine Infusion?" Joe questioned Tommulus.

Everything else was pretty straightforward, but that had no other information.

"It is a short term buff that imbues you with the power of the deity you follow. For ten minutes, all of your stats reach the peak of the tier that your highest stat resides within, and there may be other effects. Some good, some... not as good, depending on the deity." Tommulus stated the last bit only after a moment of hesitation. "There is a week before anyone will be able to enter this holy site, and I guarantee that others will be after it as well."

Joe swallowed the mouthful of saliva that had built up. That sounded amazing. If he got his intelligence to one hundred and fifty-one, then used Divine Infusion, suddenly *all* his stats would be at two hundred for ten whole minutes. He was sure that he would *really* feel like a demi-god for that time period. "What if I fail to return with the Tome?"

There was silence for a long moment. "That will depend on you, I suppose."

"Then I accept the quest."

Reputation increase: +100 reputation with Tommulus.

CHAPTER TWENTY-NINE

The week passed in a blur of training, studying, and practicing. Making rituals had been put to the side in favor of gaining the skills needed to improve rituals to a higher degree than fancy circles would allow for. Since Joe had devoted *all* his time in Eternium until now into ritual circles, it was understandable - if frustrating - that the other skills would take as long or longer to reach the same heights.

He had also been able to bring his Architectural Lore to Beginner I, Alchemical Lore to Beginner V, and Enchanting Lore to Beginner III. All the increases were gained by using his Knowledge skill, which had been raised to Beginner II from all the usage being near the Pathfinder's Hall. All in all, Joe was pleased with his growth during the week.

Name: Joe 'Tatum's Chosen Legend' Class: Mage (Actual: Rituarchitect)
Profession I: Tenured Scholar (Actual: Arcanologist)
Profession II: Ritualistic Alchemist
Character Level: 16 Exp: 152,143 Exp to next level: 857
Rituarchitect Level: 5 Exp: 14,176 Exp to next level: 824

Hit Points: 622/622
Mana: 1,137/1,755 (491 Reserved)
Mana regen: 36.68/sec
Stamina: 585/616.5
Stamina regen: 5.88/sec

Characteristic: Raw score (Modifier)

Strength: 61 (2.11)
Dexterity: 70 (2.20)
Constitution: 62 (2.12)
Intelligence: 117 (3.17)
Wisdom: 92 (2.42)
Charisma: 59 (2.09)
Perception: 70 (2.20)
Luck: 45 (1.45)
Karmic Luck: +16

Even his Karmic Luck had reached new heights, though he wasn't sure why, or what that changed for him. Joe was struck by a thought; why not ask Tatum about that characteristic? It would need to wait, as his team was currently on their way to the 'holy site' indicated by Tommulus. It just so happened to be the main Temple area in Ardania.

"So, this is just right in the center of Ardania?" Alexis sighed as she pushed someone out her way in the road. "It is something that everyone knows about? How is this something *rare*, then?"

"It's in the main Temple of the city," Joe distractedly repeated for the third time. "There is an event that happens every once in a while, and the tome we are after is apparently one of the rewards this time around."

"You're starting to sound like an NPC, Joe," Alexis teased him.

Joe was distracted due to consolidating the gains he had made during the previous week. All of his time in the testing dungeon had been devoted to Dexterity, which explained such a large gain compared to the others, but nearly every other waking moment had been devoted to alchemy, enchanting, and finding better ways to use his staff in close combat. He had only gained a small amount of experience, less than two thousand in total, but with all the buildings he had repaired or built, Joe was getting close to both a class and character level.

Alchemical Rituals (Novice VII).

Enchanted Ritual Circles (Novice III).

Skill gained: Enchanting (General) (Novice IV) Enchanting is the domain of higher-order beings, and is the process of writing down a portion of the laws of the universe and using them to your advantage. This seems like a good fit for you: lots of chances to blow yourself up or catch the attention of something you really don't want watching you. Effect: +1n% power of created enchantments that you have a role in creating or modifying. +1n% chance to successfully disable enchantments without catastrophic failure, where n = skill level.

Magical Matrices (Apprentice II).

Polearm Mastery (Beginner IX).

Profession experience gained (Ritualistic Alchemist): 1337

Ritualistic Alchemist reaches profession level 2!

He was pleased with most of his progress, most of all Magical Matrices. It seemed that it impacted almost all magical crafting attempts, and that it was considered one of the most difficult skills to raise. Joe's teachers had showered praise on him for increasing it to this level, and Joe didn't have the heart to tell them that he had basically only just officially gained the skill.

Joe's enjoyment was cut short as Alexis sharply jabbed him to regain his attention. "Joe! How *dare* you just ignore me like that after I *specifically*-"

"That's *enough* of that. It's time for me to find out what's going on here." Joe cut Alexis off sharply as he focused his gaze on her. "Intrusive Scan."

"*Excuse* me?" Alexis started reaching for her crossbow, only to be unexpectedly stopped by Bard. She fought against him for a moment, but by then Joe had seen everything he needed to see.

Alexis the Miasma.
Highest stat: Perception.
Ongoing effects: Sight Unseen. Blurred confusion. Cursed (item based). Well-hydrated. Well-adjusted.

Cool title aside, Joe recognized two positive effects. One from himself, one from Jaxon. The other three negative effects… Joe focused on them, and a helpful information bar appeared.

Blurred confusion (Perception two tiers above intelligence): Solve the Problem? I can't figure out which part is *the problem. I can't compartmentalize, I see it all. Effect: Constant low-grade migraine from sheer sensory overload. +5% chance to take no action that involves movement. Refreshes every .001 seconds.*

Sight Unseen (Perception two tiers above luck): Yes. I know that dragon was polymorphed and didn't want to be seen, but I saw it anyway, and that's why we're running. Effect: 1% to notice truth that nobody will believe.

Cursed (Ring of -cursed- courage): This ordinary-looking ring is guaranteed to improve confidence, helping the wearer to overcome whatever their previous fears may have been. Hidden effect: Cursed. This ring will achieve all previously promised goals by making the wearer aggressive and paranoid.

"I have good news and bad news." Joe started.

"The bad news is that you are about to die from poison." Alexis fired a bolt at him that bounced off his Shell. She was slapped to the ground by his shadow in the same instant, and Joe dove away from the small cloud of poison that erupted from the point of impact.

"You have a curse on you!" Joe shouted at Alexis as she was rolling to get into a better firing position. This made her pause a moment, and Joe took the time to explain about her ring.

"So what?" Alexis decided after a long moment of thinking. "It's better this way! I can have full conversations without panicking, and everyone likes me better now that I make them know what I want!"

Bard had a huge smile on his face as he walked toward her. He put his arms out and swept her into a giant hug. "Ah *told* ya ah liked ya jus' how ya were! Ah was wonderin' where we went so wrong that ya stopped likin' me. Ya *do* still like me, yeah?"

"I… of course I do!" Alexis demanded impatiently. "That's why I got this ring of courage in the first place! I needed to be able to show affection and speak in public!"

"Nah." Bard shook his head. "That's not sommat that ya can just skip inta. That's long months or years of work, 'Lexis. Public speakin' is hard, and scary. Beyond tha', why would you think that I want you to do somethin' ya don't wanna do? If ya don't wanna be touchy-feely in public, ah respect that! If it's somethin' ya *do* want, we can work on it at ah comfortable pace."

"I…" Alexis flushed angrily. "It doesn't matter, the ring doesn't come off."

"That'd be the *curse*," Joe muttered very quietly; she was still pointing her crossbow at him, after all. "Alexis, I think that you've also been having a low-level migraine for a while? That's a debuff from having your perception two thresholds above intelligence, just like Jaxon has a charisma debuff."

"Hello!" Jaxon called cheerfully. "What's happening now? Joe was practicing acrobatics? Can he *tumble*?"

Joe looked at Poppy as well, but the man jumped and rolled behind Bard. "Keep your eyes to yourself! Some of us don't want to share all our flaws and secrets!"

"Fair enough. I'm just trying to help. You've been really paranoid and grumpy, and I was hoping to help!" Joe shrugged and started walking after dusting himself off. "We'll figure out a way to get rid of that curse, Alexis. If that's what you want."

Alexis looked at Bard, who was smiling happily at her for the first time in almost a week. "I think that would be for the best. I should work on myself if I want to be a better person, rather than relying on something 'giving' me what I want."

"So mature!" Jaxon's voice rang out. "Back to the present moment, then. Joe, how do we get around the blockade? Do we just let them know that we have a quest, or what?"

"Blockade?" Joe noticed what Jaxon was talking about right away. A wall of city guardsmen were redirecting people down other roads, away from the Temple. Joe walked up to the first of them and offered a salute. "Good morning, gentlemen! Might I ask why this road is closed?"

"Joe? Joe! So good to see you!" The guard shook Joe's hand enthusiastically. "I never got a chance to thank you in person for bringing me back from the brink, and on your first day in this world, at that! Meant a lot to me, and my wife has been poking at me to go looking for you for weeks!"

"Then… you must be Bobby?" Joe thanked his huge intelligence score profusely, as it allowed him to remember things that he should have forgotten long ago.

"You…! Yes! I am, and I can't… I can't thank you enough." Bobby the city guard was gripping Joe's hand far too hard, and his eyes were getting rimmed with red. "If you ever need *anything* from me that's inside my power…"

"Well, I'm trying to get to the Temple to complete a quest…" Joe stated leadingly.

"Ah…" Bobby smiled ruefully. "By order of the Royal High Cleric, the routes to the temple are to be fully inaccessible unless someone has a writ of passage."

"I see." Joe looked up and around. "But is it illegal to get past you, or to go to the Temple?"

Bobby raised an eyebrow, then looked at the glowing golden eye on Joe's forehead. "Interesting thought… let me tell you our exact orders. We are to make a barricade and stop anyone we see from passing us. Now, we are all facing *this* way, and none of us are looking behind us. There are archers on top of the buildings, and if we see someone trying to get past us we are to stop them. But let's say that we see someone *already* in the area. Why, we would just have to assume that they are supposed to be there, as we collect the writs of passage as people come through."

"Got it. Well, that's too bad. I guess we will just have to give up on this! I'm glad you are doing well, Bobby." Joe nodded and winked at the guard.

"Better than I ever had hoped for. By the way, legally speaking, no one can deny another access to the Temple. Only the path there may be closed; never the Temple itself." The guard nodded deeply. "Good luck in your future endeavors, and I look forward to our next meeting."

"Same, so long as it isn't like our first." Joe turned as they were both chuckling, walking to his team with a serious face. "It seems that someone pretty high up is trying to make sure that they are able to claim all the prizes within the upcoming event. We need to find a way past all these people."

"I have a plan for that." Jaxon called. The rest of the team looked over to see him squeezing a small wooden barrel.

Alexis slapped at her hip, then looked at the barrel with more concern than Joe was hoping for. "Jaxon! No! That's-"

"-a smokescreen, you already told me! It blocks vision!" Smoke started to leak out between Jaxon's fingers, and he threw the barrel to the ground, where it detonated into a huge cloud with a **whump**.

"It's a concentrated poison of blindness, not a *smokescreen*!"

CHAPTER THIRTY

"*Gas, gas, gas!*" Bobby the guard shouted as a wave of charcoal smoke washed toward them. They knew what was coming, since they had been close enough to hear the entire conversation. The street filled with panic as everyone nearby tried to avoid the poison that was billowing around. After only two seconds, the guards were swallowed up and trapped in darkness. Only a few seconds after that… the smoke cleared.

"Everyone okay? What happened to the poison?" Bobby looked around frantically. He glanced behind himself, and *almost* called out as he saw Joe's team hurrying away. Snorting through his nose, he realized they had been hoodwinked, misled, and possibly bamboozled. "So that *was* only a smokescreen? Sneaky little…"

Joe was laughing so hard that he had to work to maintain his balance as they moved. "How did you guys come up with something like that in the few seconds I was talking to him?"

"It was easy when I realized that I wanted them to not be able to see us!" Jaxon explained earnestly.

"That was a huge batch of smokescreen that was ripening,"

Alexis grumbled. "If it had matured fully, we could have gotten triple the effect for a quarter of the amount."

"Why have something if you aren't going to use it?" Jaxon queried as they raced toward the looming temple grounds. "Seems like a waste. 'Oh, I invested in a rare wine. No! Don't you even *think* of opening that bottle!' See what I mean? Waste of money to have something and not use it."

"Right, but this was *ripening* so that we *could*-"

"Stop right there!" Three men in red robes appeared in front of them with a flash of fire. "The Temple is closed, and you may not enter!"

"Who are you to stop us?" Joe demanded.

The man in the middle responded proudly, "We are the Inquisition!"

Joe nodded, "Ah. I didn't expect you..."

"No one ever does!"

"...to flout the law and bar entry, as it is a crime against the kingdom." Joe finished his sentence.

"Pah! So what? By the time some random people find a way to complain, there will be-"

Joe pointed at his forehead, where the glowing eye signifying his 'Extended Royal Family' status was imprinted. "If I am able to enter the Temple, there will be no reason for me to bring the full might of internal affairs against the Inquisition, will there?"

There was a pregnant pause, where the three men clearly debated rebuffing or outright killing them. "Fine. But know that you have gained unfavorable attention from Elemental Fire."

Reputation decrease: -200 reputation with Deity 'Elemental Fire'. New reputation rank: Cautious.

"Well, that seems arbitrary." Joe glared at the three of them. "*You* were the ones breaking the law. Shouldn't followers of Elemental Fire be *neutral*, not tending towards evil? If you ask me, I think that you are straying from neutrality."

As Occultatum's Chosen Champion, you have decreased the reputation of the three followers of Elemental Fire by -800. Their new rank with Occultatum: Cautious.

Their eyes bugged out, but Joe was too invested in the fact that he could decrease reputation to listen to any more of their drivel. His party entered the Temple, and a message appeared.

Quest update: The Golden Tome of Divine Favor. You have passed the first bars to entry, getting to the Temple by hook or crook! Now that you have stepped in, your party will automatically have the option to teleport to the Hallowed Lands when it opens!

"How *dare* you enter this place!" A voice bellowed, shaking Joe and his team to their core. There was a massive amount of power in that voice, and... something else. Something that *really* resonated with Joe. The most graceful man Joe had ever seen stalked toward them, his every motion flowing into the next. There was only one word for this person:

Deadly.

"I, Aaron Slender, Champion of Elemental Water and High Cleric to the Kingdom, have given orders that this day would be the one day a year the temple was barred to all!" Aaron's voice, despite *hissing* at them, was loud enough to make them tremble and nearly fall to the ground. Joe glanced up, and saw *several* parties using this distraction to dash into and out of the temple with grins on their faces. "I hereby cast judgement upon you for breaking this holy order! *Cavitation Prison*!"

The area was suddenly filled by a tidal wave that converged on their location. Joe's party was wrapped in a bubble of air, which explosively decompressed.

Damage taken: 0 (3,000 backlashed)

The water vanished, and Aaron dropped to his knees and vomited blood. His eardrums had burst, and his nose and eyes were bleeding. There was even fluid dripping out from beneath his fingernails. Before anyone could speak, a message appeared to all of them.

The Temple of Ardania has long been neutral ground for all Champions. When access to the Hallowed Lands opens, this law is enforced by the entire pantheon. There will be no attacking each other within these walls.

Aaron collapsed to the ground fully, foam mingling with the

blood that poured from his mouth. Joe rushed over and slapped a hand onto the fallen Cleric. "Lay on Hands! *Mend*!"

"Joe, what are you doing?" Poppy was shocked at Joe's instant move to save someone that had tried to kill them.

"This guy isn't a player! If he dies, he's gone! The kingdom will lose a powerful ally, and he will have died for no good reason!" Joe's eyes were hard as he used his healing spells as quickly as possible. Aaron's condition stabilized, and soon he was merely sleeping on the hard stone floor. Joe flopped onto the ground, even as the blood in the area dried and flaked away thanks to his aura. "I think he's okay, but that was a *nasty* spell backlash. I wonder how much damage he took."

"Almost seven thousand, spread over five seconds." Aaron answered for himself as his eyes snapped open. "I thank you for your assistance. I would have certainly died here without you. Though I would not have been in the situation if you were not here. Still… I may have been too hasty in my judgement."

"*Clearly*." Poppy called dryly.

"A dozen parties, at *least*, entered the temple while you were… *waving*… at us." Jaxon quipped at the stricken Cleric. "If Joe weren't the one to be attacked, you would likely have died to one of them from backlash, and I doubt they would have cared."

"I knew that this was a bad idea. We've never limited the Hallowed Lands before. Why did I let them talk me into this?" Aaron closed his eyes, thinking deeply. Then they snapped open, and locked onto Joe. "What you did for me, after what I tried to do to you, demands compensation. What can I offer you?"

"I'm after the Golden Tome of Divine Favor in the hallowed lands, but I assume you can't do anything about that?" Joe wanted to say that there was no need, but that part of him had slowly been dying in this dangerous world. He gestured at Alexis, "My party member is wearing a cursed ring, and we were hoping that we could find-"

"Done. *Cursebreaker.*" Aaron waved at Alexis. Nothing happened, so he frowned and tried again. "*Greater Cursebreaker.*"

The ring on Alexis' hand screamed as the metal tore and shattered. *She* screeched as the shrapnel tore her hand up, but Joe was there in a moment to fix the damage. Aaron shook his head, "How odd; that must have been in place for a long time for such a small curse to grow into a greater curse. Still, that small favor does not nearly reconcile our debt."

"Can we perhaps put that off until after we return from the Hallowed Lands?" Joe asked hopefully. "I have no idea what to ask for, but perhaps I will find something fitting?"

"Hmm. That should be fine." Aaron sighed and stood. "What a *waste* of resources… I'm going to go call off those guards. Doesn't matter at this point."

"That was an odd encounter." Bard released a huge breath, relaxing as the strange man vanished from the temple. "Joe, while we're here, why don' ya scan this buildin'?"

"Oh!" Joe's eyes lit up, and he pulled out a copy of Architect's Fury. Just before he could use it, a huge red light washed over him. He looked at the message that had appeared, the only time that he had ever seen a message where the text was colored red, and put the ritual away as quickly as he could.

If you use that here, your reputation with all deities not associated with your own will decrease by 5000.

"Whoa." Poppy clapped a hand on Joe's shoulder. "We could all see that. Scary. Not great to have a few hundred gods ready to light you up, huh? Straight to 'Loathed'. Yikes. Good call not using that thing."

"Look at *you*!" The voice that called out made Joe's ears perk up and set a fire inside of his heart. Sam continued speaking, "You're like a bad penny, always showing up when I want you gone!"

"Oh, great, the musketeer is back," Joe scathingly retorted. "Didn't you learn your lesson last time?"

"Oh, I sure *did* learn my lesson." Sam replied coldly, inspecting a rapier that had suddenly appeared in his hands.

"Don't trust someone not to attack you when you are at your weakest and have spent everything you have on just keeping your team alive. Also, expect that they will rob you at the first opportunity just to take what little you could scavenge from a miserable outing."

"You were the one that broke their word." Joe's voice was cold and quiet, no matter how much he wanted to shout.

"A promise given under threat of my friend being murdered was no promise at all. It took all of an *hour* for me to get that title removed." Sam hissed at Joe. "You got shipped to and from the dungeon, while we *fought* for our right to be there! We created a unique situation to tackle the dungeon instead of just acting like all of this is a game! That was *our* prize, and you stole it out from under us!"

The Hallowed Land calls for Champions! Would you like your party to be teleported? Yes / No.

"Yes." Both Joe and Sam said at the same time, glaring at each other until they were whisked away. Joe blinked rapidly to clear the spots from his eyes, then looked around at his surroundings. He and his party were seated on couches, and for a moment, Joe thought they were in a respawn room. Then torches began to light themselves, starting close to them and rushing into the distance.

Welcome to the Event Dungeon: Hallowed Lands. This dungeon is filled with artifacts that will be of use to anyone with a class relating to the divine. The only exit is death. Though no experience will be lost, this dungeon will be closed to current participants until its reopening in one year. All experience and skill gains will be calculated upon leaving the dungeon. You are only allowed to tackle this area with what you have now. Monster Level will increase by one every hour, on the hour. Better start praying!

CHAPTER THIRTY-ONE

Poppy was the first to point out the obvious. "We need to start moving! Even if everything in here starts at level one, we'll only have half a day before they start catching up to us in levels. Somehow, I doubt anything worth keeping will only be guarded by something at level one, so that means we need to move even faster!"

Please name your party.

"What?" Joe stated without thinking.

There are 27 parties attempting to use party name 'What'. Please choose a new name.

"Extra-friendly wholesome clerics of happy happy joy joy." Joe sing-sang firmly.

Gatherer Ladder ranking for Party Extra-friendly: 40/40.

Hunter Ladder ranking for Party Extra-friendly: 40/40.

"That's not what I said!"

Every five hours, all parties under the top ten in the hunter rankings will be forced to fight one other party. Gain hunter rankings by destroying monsters or members of other parties! If you defeat a party, you may take any one item they gained while in the Hallowed Land! Use the gatherer ranking to choose parties that have found good items!

"They're giving incentives for fighting each other?" Alexis shook her head. "That's... um... that's really not cool."

"Alexis! I missed you!" Bard swept her up in a huge hug and twirled the beet-red-faced woman around.

"Bard!" Alexis pouted at him as she looked at the others frantically, "We need to move!"

"I don't care! The curse is gone!" Bard squeezed her, still holding her in the air. Alexis gave up and just seemed to be trying to enjoy the affection.

"Alright, lovebirds." Jaxon poked Bard three times, then pulled his needles out of the areas he had struck a moment later. "There you go! That should be enough to slow your blood flow! Good for reducing bleed damage, and keeping your mind in the moment."

"Jaxon, ah think ah might kill ya." Bard growled, slipping back into his accent now that his elation was dissipating. The group seemed to relax as they got into formation, which was odd for a dangerous location such as this. Perhaps it was the difference in feel between them, the compatibility that seemed to be back in place. They chose one of the six paths and started walking.

The relaxation didn't last long. Before they had gone thirty feet into the tunnel, they heard flapping wings. Oddly round balls with wings swooped at them, and the group was forced to dodge by diving out of the way. Jaxon ended up driving his fist into one, and screamed as his hand started to smoke. "They're flying *slimes*!"

Joe decided to take out the group of creatures all at once, "Acid Spray!"

Damage dealt: 0. Angelic Slimes are immune to acid damage!

"Oh, that's really bad." Joe swatted one onto the ground with his staff as it zipped at him, and the round slime splattered into a puddle before quickly reforming. Joe's staff sizzled where it had touched the slime, and he noticed the durability drop. "And now I have no abilities that can damage these things. Guess I'm going full support!"

"My axes are doing nothing!" Bard complained loudly, his point proven by slicing an Angelic Slime in half, only for it to reform as soon as his axe was out.

"Slimes are resistant to physical damage unless there is a core for you to target!" Poppy informed them while he punched a hole through a flying creature with his rapier. That seemed to be effective, and he quickly told them why. "Using skills that require mana make your weapons hurt them!"

Jaxon let a dozen silver needles fly, and the slimes that were struck were yanked to the ground as if ten-pound weights had been dropped on them. "Joe! Shock them!"

Joe *jumped* toward the fallen slimes, "Dark Lightning Strike!"

Crack!

Lightning struck him, washing over his shell and dissipating into the slimes on the ground. A shadowy copy of himself appeared, stared at him for a moment, then vanished. Joe swallowed deeply as he made a realization. Had his passive retaliation almost hit *him*? It seemed like it! The dark lightning dealt forty-five damage to the pinned slimes, which finished them off when the damage was combined with the needles. However, more were coming and Joe didn't know what he could do to help; Dark Lightning Strike had a six-minute cooldown.

Then he remembered what Poppy had said, that they were resistant to physical damage *unless* there was a core to aim for! He targeted the first one and barked, "*Corify*!"

The slime sank a few feet as a portion of its innards were pulled into a cube. Joe slapped the slime with his staff and the forming core was torn out of the creature, killing it instantly and making the synthetic core solidify fully. Joe pumped his fist in the air and tried again. This time no core formed, and Joe had to face the fact that at Novice six... there was a good chance that the skill was going to work very infrequently. Still, it gave them options.

Joe moved back in the formation, focusing on healing his team when needed. Over the next hour, they plowed through an unceasing trickle of slimes. The tunnel looped and twisted, but there was never a time where an offshoot or branch appeared. Finally, they found the end of the tunnel and a floating conglomeration of slimes. Joe used Intrusive Scan, only getting to see the creature's name before it started launching magical attacks at them.

Laura, the Angelic Slime Hive Queen.

"Boss monster!" Joe called as the others retaliated or dodged acidic icicles. There were a few grunts of acknowledgement, but no more words were spoken. The battle was very straightforward: don't let the slime engulf you, dodge the attacks, hit back with the most powerful attacks you can.

"Dehydration powder! Don't breathe this in!" Alexis called as she whipped a canister at the slime. It entered the body, then the powerful corrosive effect of the slime came into play and destroyed the canister, releasing a burst of pressurized powder. The powder foamed, absorbing liquid from all angles before it became too heavy and fell out of the floating slime.

The next few attacks hit semi-solid surfaces, and a huge amount of damage was dealt to the queen. It roiled and condensed; dropping portions that were badly dehydrated onto the ground. It was still over six feet in diameter, but progress was being made! It flew into the air, paused, then *zipped* toward the ground. When it hit, it turned into a giant puddle that washed over their feet before sucking back into a giant ball. This inflicted acid damage on all of them, and pulled the lighter members to the ground.

A dark mirror of Joe slapped the hive, and Bard used the distraction to bellow a chant, then dove at the creature as it reformed. His axes were glowing, and he managed to split a large chunk off of the main body. The chunk seemed to have no will, and splashed against the ground like regular water; deforming completely. The queen seemed upset by this, and retaliated by engulfing Bard entirely. In no time at all, the group could see him start to dissolve along with his equipment.

Joe targeted the queen in a panic, "Corify!"

Failure. The team started attacking with all their might, but they could see the area around Bard filling with blood. Five seconds passed, and Joe tried again. "Corify!"

This time, there was a clear disturbance. Joe targeted the center of the movement, then used everything he had to *jump* at that spot. He dove *into* the queen, emerging on the other side with a large cube in his hands; which he swiftly stored in his codpiece. The slime queen stopped flying and splashed onto the ground like a water balloon. Even so, Bard didn't move.

"Mend! Lay on Hands!" Joe saw Bard's skin reforming where the Mend had landed, so he knew that at the minimum, the man was still alive. It took some coaxing and plenty of healing, but Bard was soon back on his feet. After he could stand again, the group searched the room and found several items that they couldn't identify. Almost all of them seemed to be accessories of some kind: rings, necklaces, bracelets, and bangles. There was sure to be a use for them, but right now... they had no idea what that could be.

Zone cleared! For party 'Extra-friendly', current Hunter ladder ranking: 12/38. Gatherer ladder ranking: 8/38. Time elapsed: 1:38:56. Returning to safe zone in three... two...

In a moment, the team was back on the couch in the starting area. The lights on the path that they had finished started winking out, leaving the hall in murky darkness. Joe nodded excitedly as the group got off the couch and started down another hall. Over the next two and a half hours, they cleared another path. This one had many small rooms that branched off the tunnel, which held either treasure or monsters. These monsters were mainly sanctified skeletons, which sent Jaxon into fits of joy. The final boss barely required any help from the other team members to fall, but Jaxon did claim most of the loot.

As the loot was holy bones, the team didn't fight against him very hard. They were back on the couch, and only had a short while before they would find out if they would be forced to fight another group. At the end of the tunnel, their group managed to take number ten on the hunter list, but stayed at number eight on the gatherer list. While they recuperated, their hunter rank dropped to eleven. They rushed down the third hall and started crushing small pixies that zapped them with holy light and lightning.

The group didn't bother to collect any remains, focusing entirely on destroying monsters as fast as possible. Their rank went back to ten, then down to eleven, over and over again. As the final seconds ticked away, they held onto position number ten.

Hunter / Gatherer results at the end of five hours: 10/34, 15/34. Keep working hard to stay ahead! All groups below position ten on the hunter ladder will now be forced to battle another group!

"Take a breather!" Joe gave a *very* welcome order. Thanks to stamina and mana regen, they were able to keep going. Still, Joe could see that small debuffs were starting to appear due to the strain and required endurance. They could easily be cleared with a long break or nap, but until then they were slowly decreasing the very regeneration that was keeping them going. "We need to start collecting stuff again, or this will turn into a giant waste."

Their pace slowed, and the group felt much better after a short while, thanks to Joe's Neutrality Aura. About twenty minutes later, a new message appeared that made their hearts sink.

Battles concluded! Current Hunter / Gatherer rank for party 'Extra-friendly': 23/23, 22/23.

Jaxon succinctly summed up everyone's thoughts. "Well *that* plan backfired."

CHAPTER THIRTY-TWO

There was nothing to do but keep fighting. Eventually, the group got to the boss of the area, or where the boss *should* have been. The room was covered in battle scars, and clearly a serious battle had taken place. However, it seemed that the group must have died right as they finished off the boss, as it was an empty room with a non-looted treasure at the other end. Joe looked at the item with excitement: it was a book! Not only that, the cover was a deep, burnished gold.

Joe had found what he was looking for! Cautiously moving through the room, they watched for traps or sudden boss encounters. But there was nothing.

Zone cleared! For party 'Extra-friendly', current Hunter ladder ranking: 23/23. Gatherer ladder ranking: 22/23. Time elapsed: 5:38:56. Returning to safe zone in three… two…

Joe darted forward and grabbed the golden book, which felt warm to the touch. A moment later, they appeared in the safe area. He held up the book and shouted, "*Yes*! We got it!"

He opened the cover to read the title, and a strange note caught his eye.

Thanks for clearly stating your goal when you fought that priest. Gave me a clear target that you wouldn't expect. -Sam

Joe blinked, then realized that he was on the ground with Alexis waving something under his nose. "Wake up! We've lost almost two hours to whatever knocked us out! Joe! Get *up*!"

As soon as he was awake, his Aura of Neutrality kicked on and it became *far* easier to awaken the others. Joe wasn't sure *how* his aura had been turned off, but once it was on, the 'unconscious' debuff started flashing and draining away from his team, helped by the smelling salts that Alexis had pulled out.

"Whatever that was, it got through my poison resistance… but only a little," Alexis told Joe. "I think that it should have held us down for three to four hours, but…"

"Thank you, Alexis. Now we're behind, but at least we aren't getting dropped into a fight with other parties while knocked out." Joe's sincerity made Alexis blush and shut down, and she simply nodded in reply.

"Well, that's it for us then, isn't it?" Poppy flopped onto the couch and laid down. "Might as well just wait and get ready for the fights in a few hours. At least we'll be rested."

"No, remember that we only get to take a single item from another party if we beat them." Joe motioned at a different hall, "Let's get going. We can still figure out a way to get some good gear and such. This is a treasure hunt! Let's go hunt some treasure!"

Everyone was on board except Poppy. "Joe, think about this logically. Everything in there is going to be at least, what, eight levels higher than it started? We've already cleared a hall just to find a defeated boss and a trap, what's to say we won't get stuck battling, only to not find a reward?"

"Poppy, it's better than just giving up." Joe looked at the Duelist, and a hint of a smile appeared on his face. "You know… are you just having trouble waking up?"

"I am not known as a morning person." Poppy unrepentantly snuggled into the couch. "Feel free to motivate me, bossman, but I'm feeling pretty cozy. Pretty sure this couch is the entire reason that this area is considered 'hallowed'. It's *heavenly*."

"Feel free to motivate you? Can do." Joe nodded sagely as he summoned Mate from his sleeve. "I have a cure for what ails you, friend. Mate, use hyper-caffeinate!"

Nothing happened, and it took Joe a moment to realize why: he got the ability wrong. "Shoot. Mate, use *over*-caffeinate on Poppy!"

This time, streams of scintillating liquid lanced out of Mate. The rainbow effect looked nothing like coffee, and Joe realized that he was seeing distilled and purified caffeine being injected into Poppy. With a yell, Poppy suddenly shot out off the couch and started vibrating. "What in the…! Joe! I don't feel energized! All that happened is that my heart is pounding!"

"Tone it down a notch next time," Joe muttered to Mate, who bobbed in place happily before wrapping around Joe's arm, giving it a squeeze-hug, then seeming to evaporate onto Joe's sleeve again. "Right! Let's go!"

"I'm gonna vote to boot you the next time Alexis brings it up." Poppy grumbled at Joe as he grabbed at his rapier and missed due to his jitters.

Alexis looked stricken. "I… I won't do that!"

Bard laughed as Poppy grumbled. The Duelist was moving *fast*, and his rapier seemed to be everywhere at once, practically doing sonic damage from how much he was vibrating. "If I die from this 'buff', Joe, you're going down next."

They were speeding through the tunnel, though the monsters were all level eleven. The most numerous creatures by far were the fairy-like creatures. Each of them seemed to use a basic element of magic imbued with holy power, making their damage output terrifying. Yet, they were fragile. With Poppy's speed and accuracy, combined with his critical hit range, the fairies dropped like common flies.

Alexis and Joe were both happily tossing the fairies' remains into their bags. Each of the fallen monsters left behind a small bag of fairy powder; something Joe recognized as a rare but often required component in several alchemical recipes. As time passed, they reached the end of the hallway… and heard the sound of battle from the boss room.

Joe peeked around the corner and confirmed that there was a team engaged in combat with an extra-large Fairy Queen. Just within the few moments that he observed, the boss used every basic element, each of them clearly imbued with holy power. The magical damage the team must be taking should be massive. Joe focused in on the Fairy and used Intrusive Scan before committing to any actions.

Ursula, Seelie Queen of the Fairies.

Highest stat: Wisdom.

Before he could get any more information, the Fairy glanced his way and flitted to the other side of the room, breaking his line-of-sight. This helped the team that was in combat, but concerned Joe. Since the queen was in combat, someone observing her shouldn't have even registered. Though the highest stat shown was wisdom, her perception couldn't be far behind.

"Two options, guys." Joe looked at the others, laying out his plan. "We either join combat now, and have to deal with the two groups ourselves. Or… we wait until one side falls and attack the other right away."

"I say we snatch the reward," Poppy instantly stated. "Let them duke it out, then we kill off the weakened party. They got here first, let them fight."

"Nah, hit 'em both while they're distracted." Bard disagreed with the fighter. "Never know what sorta out-of-combat recovery they have."

"We should…" Alexis looked around, counting faces. "Where's Jaxon?"

"*Craw*!"

"*Nyah*!"

The battle cries of Jaxon's hands joined in on the cacophony of spell effects and crashing metal. Joe cursed and stalked into the room. "Looks like we're fighting."

Jaxon had somehow gotten onto the back of the Fairy Queen, and his hands were chewing into her wings, greatly reducing her mobility. "No one should have wings! If you want to fly, you should be a bird or build an airplane! These should be artificial! No, even then! Are you a bird? No? Then stop *acting* like one, you overgrown cockroach!"

It appeared as though the other group of people had been inflicted with a confusion spell. The main tank of the party glanced at the leader, a Mage, for orders. The Mage shrugged and launched a neutral magic spell: Concussive Blast. "Not our people, fire at will!"

The Fairy and Jaxon were both slapped into the wall. Jaxon fell off her back, but managed to take a wing with him. He came running to Joe with the Queen sprinting after him screaming bloody murder. "Joe, toss this into a bag!"

Joe did so, and as soon as the wing was gone… Queen Ursula paused and turned crimson with rage. A holy-flame nova exploded from her, knocking back anyone that had been getting close. When Joe turned his eyes onto her once again, he felt sick. Her skin was boiling, the flesh moving as though snakes were slithering under the surface. Her size increased by almost double, the loose clothing she had worn now straining not to tear. Ursula's hair, previously gold, turned black. The golden eyes flipped to red, and her straight teeth elongated into something an angler fish would wince at.

Joe managed a scan for only long enough to get her name before she attacked again, moving in a flash.

Sabine, One-winged Unseelie Queen of the Fairies.

Swooping in front of Jaxon, Sabine swept deep gouges into his chest with her three-fingered hands, sending Jaxon tumbling in a spray of blood. Joe reacted instantly, a Mend spell reaching the Monk before he even rolled back to his feet.

Cursetouch I has inhibited healing! Healing spells and items have their effect reduced by 50%!

"Well, feces." Joe managed to get out just before a straight snap-kick caught him in the face and sent him into the wall a half-dozen feet away. A shadowy image of himself appeared and slapped the Queen, interrupting her follow-up assault on the now-prone party leader.

Damage taken: 0 (233 absorbed by Exquisite Shell.)

Cursetouch resisted! (50% resistance to Dark Magic.)

While Sabine started laying into Joe's team, the other group had taken the initiative to back off and heal up. They watched Joe's team with angry eyes, though they were clearly mocking them as well. A ranger sent an arrow at Alexis, but his barbed words had more impact. "Should have minded your own business! Now *we* get to clean up after that thing wipes *your* group!"

"Abyssal *Jaxon*!" Bard roared, using both his axes to block the black claws that were aimed for his eyes. Even though he was successful, Bard skidded back a few feet and black mist seemed to drift into him. "This curse stacks! Watch out!"

Alexis was in front of Bard suddenly, and the massive crossbow on her back swung into position. The Queen's red eyes narrowed as a huge bolt flew at her, and she managed to catch the bolt just behind the barbed head. Still, the force sent the Fairy backward and put her in striking range of the other party.

Joe realized then that the Fairy must be very light, though her body was almost the same size as a normal human at this point. He applauded Alexis' perception, and was about to compliment her when he heard her soft mutterings. She was glaring at Sabine, "Petite double zero, you better stay away from my… *emulsify*!"

A small glass barrier inside the bolt that the Queen was still holding shattered, and the two liquids stored in the shaft mixed together and erupted into a cloud of sparkling pink smoke. The other team and the Fairy screamed as welts appeared on their skin, and Alexis winced. "I'm so sorry about that!"

"What just happened?" Joe asked as his team got back into a formation.

"Yeah... that's a really nasty itching poison." Alexis grabbed Jaxon and pulled him as he tried to rush forward. "Wait! I don't have an antidote for that, and if you try to itch yourself, you're gonna get bitten! Three seconds before it doesn't make new welts!"

Sabine screeched, alternating between mauling the other party and tearing at her own skin. The lines that her claws left behind oozed a dark light, and Joe realized that she wasn't immune to her own abilities. Each of the people impacted by the poison were screaming, both in pain and fury. It seemed that the melee fighters had gone berserk, ignoring defense in an attempt to deal as much damage as possible.

The spellcasters and ranged fighters kept interrupting their own actions by scratching at themselves, and Joe decided to help the battle along by getting close enough to spray their opponents with acid. The open wounds combined with the itching welts, and the other team became desperate. One strike, two, and some kind of bash brought Sabine to the ground. The fighter raised his sword for a coup de grace, but as his sword reached Sabine's heart, she vanished into a ball of light.

Another ball of light zipped toward Sabine's position, and in a moment both Poppy and Sabine appeared. The Queen was no longer moving, Poppy's rapier having pinned her to the ground and bottomed out her health bar. "Not totally honorable, but still counts toward my level."

Jaxon launched himself among the furious team, his hands tearing into the unprotected flesh of the healer and mage. They fell in seconds; their melee teammates having been forced into combat with the remainder of Joe's team. In under thirty seconds, the other team had vanished into motes of light, and Joe was shown a listing of the items they had collected. There were a few interesting items, and he was even able to see a description of what they did.

Everything they had collected so far had its description

hidden, and they could only go off of context and hope that they had collected something good. As Joe was pondering what the difference was, a notification appeared.

Hunter position updated! Assigning random item in ten seconds. Make sure to choose an item before this if something specific is desired. 9…

Joe quickly chose a cauldron from the list, since nothing else had stuck out to him. He remembered something from his alchemy book about cauldrons, and he knew that Jake the Alchemist took care of his own cauldron as if it were a fragile flower instead of a five-hundred-pound, magic-imbued metal that couldn't be damaged by a level fifteen berserker using a warhammer. The item appeared in his codpiece of holding, and they worked to collect everything not bolted down. Soon the room was bare, and a familiar notification appeared.

Zone cleared! For party 'Extra-friendly', current Hunter ladder ranking: 17/22. Gatherer ladder ranking: 18/22. Time elapsed: 9:38:56. Returning to safe zone in three… two…

A meaty **thunk** caught his attention, and the teleportation message vanished. Joe turned to the side to find Jaxon pinned to the ground by a familiar Monk who was sending continuous attacks into his side, and Poppy had taken a warhammer to the side of his head. Alexis fell with two arrows in her neck, and Bard charged into combat with a roar.

Fluid sprang from Joe's hands, but the abomination that was Sam_King threw a paper into the air, and Joe's acid fell to the ground as it encountered an arctic wind that froze it solid. Joe saw the air surrounding a floating book shake like the aftereffects of an explosion, and Sam nodded like he had just heard something important. "He has a retaliatory effect, everyone. No big hits, death by a thousand slices for that one."

After his party was slain, Joe was slowly and carefully beat to death. Somehow, the other team had access to lots of health-restoring potions; so even though Joe's shadow appeared and slapped them around, and a Dark Lightning Strike caused them to wince in pain, it only took a few moments for Joe to lose his

Exquisite Shell. From there, it was only two seconds before he fell.

You have died! Calculating… no experience lost. You have been barred from the Hallowed Grounds for one year.

Calculating… item snatched by party 'Wolf Pack': Golden Tome of Divine Favor.

Quest failed: The Golden Tome of Divine Favor. You have failed to return with the quest item! Return to an altar of Tommulus to gain pro-rated rewards.

CHAPTER THIRTY-THREE

Joe pounded his fist into the wall as he appeared in the Grand Temple of Ardania. "That slimy son of a-"

Reward calculations granted! Item descriptions available! You now have a choice: you may forfeit any of the items collected. You may keep any of the items collected. Each item will be assigned a point value, and all items turned in will grant each party member an equal share of points. If there is a dispute, party members may use their points to purchase an item. The spent points will be shared to the other team members. All leftover points can be traded for experience or coins.

What followed next was a huge listing of all the items that had been collected through the course of their time in the Hallowed Land. The five party members went down the list quickly, and most of the items were converted into points and shared out. Everyone took a few trinkets or things that they wanted, and there were a few surprises.

"Seriously, Poppy?" Joe's voice was strained from pure exasperation. "You stole the couches?"

"And I would like to keep them, thank you very much." Poppy grinned as he considered how well he had slept on the plush, golden, overstuffed cushions.

"Challenge," Jaxon demanded instantly. They started a bidding war with their points, and soon Poppy was wearing a pleased smile.

"Thank *you*," Poppy lightly stated. "Joe, would you be so kind as to keep those stored for me till we get back?"

"...Sure." Joe and the others kept moving through the listings. Joe claimed the cauldron, but it cost most of his points, since Alexis also had a use for it. She got most of the crafting materials, and Bard saved his points in case he saw something he really wanted. At the end of the bidding war, Jaxon had taken a small Unique necklace named 'Attention'. There was no other information on it, but Jaxon wanted Attention so badly that he got it pretty easily.

"There's a list where we can spend points on things we didn't find." Bard happily informed them as his fingers moved a screen only visible to him. "Expensive as all get-out, though."

Each extra point could be taken as ten experience points or one silver. After the sale of all the other items in their possession, Bard had collected thirteen thousand points in total. He had enough to bring a level zero character directly to level fifteen if he cashed out, but he only had eyes for one option. He made his choice, and golden light bubbled up in his hands. It formed into a two-handed axe; the weight of which made him grunt.

"Now we are talkin'." Bard shifted the weapon, letting one of the sharp edges rest on the ground.

"What did you get, Hon?" Alexis carefully inquired.

"It's ah *triple axe*!" Bard told her excitedly. The blank expressions around him made the Skald snort, so he decided to show them. With the handle pointed into the air, he brushed his hands against the golden handle and a mellow chord rang out. "Not only is it an axe that ah can use ta slice an' dice, it's an *axe*. An electric guitar! Well... mana guitar?"

You are under the effects of Power Chord. All damage dealt increased by 5%.

"Ha! That's naw even ah *song*! That's just an idle strum!"

Bard crowed excitedly. "Jus' wait till I figure out how to use Beast to his best effect! That's a Special Unique weapon for ya!"

Joe was blown away by the utility of what Bard had gained, but as he looked at his own point balance under a thousand, he knew that there was nothing he would be able to gain beyond regret if he looked at the listing of purchase options. He swallowed and exited out of the purchase options.

Points remaining: 861. Convert to experience or coin?

"Experience." Joe stated firmly. The next question that popped up made his eyes bulge, and he shouted for everyone to wait before choosing to buy anything else.

Where would you like your experience points to go? Character level, class level, or skill level?

"We can convert the points into experience for class or skill levels!" Joe explained when he gained odd looks.

Class level selected. Active class: Rituarchitect.

"Wait! Back! I was just telling them that…" Joe trailed off as he watched his point values drain away into nothing. Then, silver light poured off of him, and he was filled with euphoria.

You have reached level 7 as a Rituarchitect! 5,214 experience remains until level 8!

Rituals used to build structures now have a fixed 10% chance to absorb a portion of the mana invested in the ritual, gaining an additional effect. The effect will be random unless you learn how to stabilize the mana draw from the materials.

"Well that's pretty neat." Joe was utterly elated. He had gained two class levels just from-

*Now quantifying growth from event 'The Hallowed Lands'. Calculating… 5,355 experience gained! See full listing of monsters defeated by clicking *here*.*

Joe skipped clicking the listing, and a golden aura lifted him off the ground and exploded around him as he was lifted to level seventeen. His party members were undergoing similar effects, and the combined energy scoured the surrounding area clean. He landed on his feet, and the notifications continued. There were so many that he simply stared. Every ability he used had increased by at least one skill level, even if he had only used it a single time.

The bounty of the Hallowed lands has boosted the energy you are able to maintain. Boost has been compounded by Ritualist class bonus! Skills increased:

Mend (Student VII).
Lay on hands (Apprentice IX).
Neutrality Aura (Apprentice VIII).
Corify (Beginner I). Created Cores now have a uniform size, regardless of the amount of experience they contain! Caution, powerful Cores may cause blindness if you play with them too much!
Hidden Sense (Apprentice I). Items that were lost or hidden by amateurs hold no mystery for you! They will practically whisper to you, and you will need to intentionally ignore them if you don't want to bother finding them.
Retaliation of Shadows (Apprentice VI). Getting a little slap happy, aren't you? You know you need to get hit in order to rank this up… right? Or are the concussions getting to you?
Polearm Mastery (Apprentice I). You want to use your silly stick to hit other people that have actual weapons… okay. Yeah. Let's see where this goes. While using a polearm, you now have a flat 1% chance to disarm an opponent that is using a one-handed weapon.
Mana Manipulation (Student IV). More mana!
Coalescence (Student VII). Denser mana!
Acid Spray (Apprentice II).
Dark Lightning Strike (Beginner VII). You are *attractive. To lightning. Still, it's a start.*

The gains were, in a word, unbelievable. Especially in the case of Dark Lightning Strike, which had directly doubled in skill level. Sure, he had *used* all of these, but… this was too much! The others also started muttering about their increases in an excited tone. Joe's pupils shrank to dots as he had a disturbing thought. "We need to leave. If this is what we got for being in the *middle* of the pack, what is the first place team going to come back with? I think we may have made some enemies…"

The general consensus was that *yeah*, it was time to go. Joe promised himself that he would come back soon to talk to the powerful cleric of Elemental Water, but for now he contented himself with looking at his status as they fled to the safety of Towny McTownface.

Name: Joe '*Tatum's Chosen Legend*' Class: Mage (Actual: Rituarchitect)
Profession I: Tenured Scholar (Actual: Arcanologist)
Profession II: Ritualistic Alchemist
Character Level: 17 Exp: 157,498 Exp to next level: 13,502
Rituarchitect Level: 7 Exp: 22,786 Exp to next level: 5,214
Hit Points: 622/622
Mana: 1,129/1,872 (617 Reserved)
Mana regen: 39.44/sec
Stamina: 610/616.5
Stamina regen: 5.88/sec

Characteristic: Raw score (Modifier)

Strength: 61 (2.11)
Dexterity: 70 (2.20)
Constitution: 62 (2.12)
Intelligence: 120 (3.2)
Wisdom: 95 (2.45)
Charisma: 59 (2.09)
Perception: 72 (2.22)
Luck: 45 (1.45)
Karmic Luck: +20

Joe was having a good time going through everything while they leisurely walked toward the main square. Now he had nine unassigned skill points, his stats were looking good, he had apparently done something right if his Karmic Luck were anything to go by, and-

"-that's why we need everyone we can possibly get if we are going to launch an offensive against a Noble Guild!" The person speaking had drawn a huge crowd, and was standing on top of a statue. "We know for a fact that they have an endless food supply! They have housing, clothes, weapons, and have been funnelling resources into *beautification* projects while *we* are starving to death again and again!"

Joe's party had all stopped to stare at the man. Was he trying to infuriate a mob? Though the densely packed city had thinned as people got used to this reality, it didn't change the fact that over a *billion* people had entered Eternium. Though… that thought felt… fuzzy. Joe narrowed his eyes as he realized that he hadn't thought about earth or the destruction there in days, possibly weeks. This place had a way of making you forget your past troubles in order to focus on the future, and the present. For most people, that was only helpful… but here, it was being used against the Wanderer's Guild to paint *them* as the true monsters.

"Three days from now, we will march against this repository of 'elite players' that are making it impossible for us to better our own lives! Join us now, and we'll work with you to get ready! Three days, and you will be powerful enough to take everything you need! Once we have seized the means of production, we will *all-*"

"Let's go, guys." Joe started pushing at the crowd. "I think we need to talk to someone about this."

CHAPTER THIRTY-FOUR

"Seriously," Joe complained as he worked to fine-tune a ritual diagram. "I warn them about an incoming attack on our town, and they shrug it off like it doesn't matter that a huge amount of people are coming here to claim the greenhouse and smash up our town. They're too worried about the Noble Guilds? Who do they think is riling up the masses?"

"They obviously don't know that the time investment on food production is absurd," Hannah grumbled along with him. "Did you know that a couple deer got in there somehow and totally destroyed the apple trees? The gardener in that area was so mad about it that he killed them as soon as he found them, and now we have deer-men spawning in that wing. Now there is a strict no-killing-new-things rule in there. It's already starting to act like a dungeon, even though they've been careful to cut down all the 'weeds' that have been popping up."

Joe nodded along at what she was saying. "This entire world is designed to get the best out of people. You work hard, and you get rewarded in a tangible way for it. Can you imagine how that would have changed our lives back on earth?"

"That would have been interesting to see." Hannah looked

at Joe, opened her mouth, then closed it before she said what she had planned to say. Joe saw, and simply waited quietly. If she had something to say… "I just want to *make* them see! Seriously, if people would just work as hard as we do, they would have their own ways to become powerful! Abyss, have you seen what that level twelve Janitor was able to do? He can walk into an area, and everything starts to clean *itself.* He still gets experience for it, too!"

"Wait, really? Does that mean… hold on." Joe took a step back mentally; Hannah had just said some *dangerous* things. "It really isn't our place to tell people how to live their lives, Hannah. If we force people to have our same viewpoints, that becomes a bad day for everyone. I recently had to fight a cult that had the actual same mindset on everything, and they were only used for someone else's gain. Imagine if a king or something had that kind of power? That's not a leader anymore, that's a tyrant that people will fight with everything they have."

"Huh." Hannah's non-answer made Joe sigh. It seemed that she had her own viewpoint on this, and had been hoping for a simple agreement, not a conversation. It had been difficult to find a good conversationalist recently. Joe chuckled at that thought: 'Conversationalist' sounded like an upgraded Bard class. In fact, he was almost sure that existed somewhere.

But, Joe had found that once someone had formed their own opinion, they needed to experience something that let them change their mindset. Talking it out or being presented with data had almost no bearing. He connected the final symbol on his ritual and gently blew on the ink to dry it. As far as he could see… perfect. "There we go. Now, here's the fun part."

He took out a small ingot of gold, placing it in the center of the ritual diagram. Since he was making a Novice rank enchanted ritual, his personal mana was more than enough to fill the diagram. The diagram lit up and wavered on the paper as it sought an acceptable item to merge with. The gold was detected, and lines started flowing from the paper to the ingot. There were a few more moments where the gold buzzed, but the high purity and density of the material allowed the magical matrix to settle.

Ritual of Remote Activation complete! Select up to four rituals to modify.

"It worked!" Joe lifted the world's most expensive remote into the air excitedly. The difficulty of this ritual was simply the high barrier to entry: clearly shown by the cost of the materials. He looked closely at the 'remote', seeing that it contained a large central button and four smaller ones next to it. After pulling over a ritual diagram and holding the remote next to it, a message appeared.

Rituals selected to be used in the Ritual of Remote Activation must be primed.

"Okay..." Joe searched for a primed version of the flamethrower ritual, one that had already had the mana and activation components stored within it. He only had a single one, but he added it cheerfully. This time, as he moved the ingot close, one of the smaller circles slid off the ingot and added itself to the activation portion of the flamethrower ritual.

Chances of accidental activation, mitigated by spell stability: 8%. Stabilizing... stabilized.

Joe blanched at the line that flew through his vision. There had been a chance that adding the remote activation would have activated the flamethrower while he was *standing over* it? Not only that, but his spell stability was... Joe checked. "Fifty-eight percent? So there was originally a *two-thirds* chance that this would have activated by adding in the... abyss!"

He looked at everything that was neatly stacked and organized in the room, and decided that they would no longer be adding effects to primed rituals while surrounded by expensive consumables on all sides. It would be a good chance to play outside. "What if I added a Ritual of Remote Activation to *another* Ritual of Remote Activation? Would that check against all the spell stabilities that the first one was connected to?"

It had been his plan at the outset to connect four of the remote activation rituals together so that he could activate sixteen flamethrowers at the same time. He wasn't going to give up on that dream, but perhaps the *Novice ranked ritual* that he was currently using wasn't the best choice to make that happen. It was like connecting a power strip to the wall: one was fine, but if you connected a power strip to another and another; you only created a nasty fire hazard. Actually, in this case it was *exactly* like that.

Joe got a few members of his Coven together and empowered three more flamethrower rituals, then hooked up the Ritual of Remote Activation. Eight percent chance to have it go off was a risk worth taking, and the remaining circles all settled into place without issue. Joe stored everything into his ring and waved as he walked to a strategy meeting. His concerns had been *mostly* ignored, but that didn't change the fact that they had to get ready for an attack.

As he walked into the war room, Mike looked up, nodded, and waved him over. "Good, you're here. I want you to take a look at this map and tell me if there is anything that you can do to help us get ready."

After getting close, Joe raised an eyebrow as he saw the quality of the map on the table. It looked almost like a satellite image, certainly not something hand-drawn. Still, it *must* have been hand-drawn. Mike pointed out the trouble areas right away. "Here, at the center of the town, we have the Guild Hall. Connected to the hall is a barracks, one at each cardinal direction. In the north-east section, we have the greenhouse. South-east holds the mess areas, also known as the general courtyard. South-west holds the wells where we draw our water when there are no water mages to fill up the cistern in the same area."

Mike took a sip of water, likely reminded of his thirst as he discussed the wells. "Now, here in the north-west section, we have built nothing yet. Nothing permanent, at least; though there are a few merchants that have set up a small shopping area. They might protest, but they need to move out so that we know that this area is secure. Thoughts?"

"Yes." Joe waved at the rest of the map of the town. "What about everything else?"

"We'll get to that," Mike promised, waving away Joe's concerns. "Right now, I am looking at the worst-case; if we need all of our guild to be brought in behind the secondary defensive wall."

"You think you might need to sacrifice the rest of this?" Joe pointed at all the other buildings on the map, lingering over the Pathfinder's Hall.

"Again… worst-case," Mike nodded and continued. "Thanks to your magic and our resources, we have an outer wall around the entirety of the town, as well as this core area. What I would like to see in this section to be emptied is either a defensive structure or something that can give us a large-scale defensive boon. Is there anything you can do about that?"

"Mmm," Joe muttered, closing his eyes. The first thing that came to mind was some kind of altar or the cathedral, but the Pathfinder's Hall had an attached Temple that gave out no area buffs. Was that only because he didn't know how to make it happen…? Either way, "I can't think of anything that I can add in there right now. Perhaps after I spend some time learning about all the options from my architect instructor?"

"Nothing in the short-term, got it." Mike turned back, "Keep your eyes open for something. We need to find a way to defend our area without losing people."

"I can make a ritual that makes people sick if they aren't supposed to be there." Joe offered with a shrug. "It won't hurt them, beyond some embarrassing accidents if they press on, but you can activate it every once in a while to flush people out?"

"Can you make one that hits anyone that comes within, say, fifty meters of our walls?" Mike asked hopefully.

"I… could do one that will do that for *one* of the walls, but…"Joe's eyes trailed off, and he thought about his new remote activation ritual. "Yeah, I could do that. It'll be expensive though, because it is four large, fine-tuned rituals that will be linked by yet *another* ritual that activates them all at the same time."

"Make it happen. We'll cover the costs." Mike signed a requisition order and handed it over. "Feel free to delegate some of this, as well. I know you have been teaching some people your class abilities. I don't need *you* to do it, I just need it done."

"Fair enough." Joe grinned at the blank requisition order and waggled his eyebrows at Mike, "It's a *lot* more expensive when someone else does it, though. I maxed out my bonuses already."

"We'll cover it." Mike pointed at another few areas. "Here is another section that we need to defend, and the unfortunate part is that the wall that we have will make it hard to hit attackers here, here, and here."

"I am really glad that you are so invested in all of this. I was originally worried that you were just going to blow off my warning." With a dark chuckle, Joe pulled out a paper. "Let me ask you something. Would having four massive flamethrowers for those trouble areas interest you?"

Mike took the paper and read it, his face contorting in confusion. "Why are they labeled as 'Flammenwerfer'?"

CHAPTER THIRTY-FIVE

Directly after the meeting with Mike, Joe went to the temple area of the Pathfinder's Hall to inform Tommulus that he had failed his quest. He was sure that the deity already knew, but it was better to be forthright about it. Joe felt that it was a Bad Idea, with intentional capital letters, to ignore a god of *wrath.*

Joe walked into the odd interior of the temple, moving around the mid-sized Tree Ents that were growing along the edge of the river. Walking directly up to the flaming altar, Joe sighed and spoke. "I'm sorry, Tommulus. I failed to return with the book."

There was no reply. Joe waited a moment longer, then turned and walked away.

Quest complete: The Golden Tome of Divine Favor. Though you failed to return with the requested item, Tommulus has seen the fire in your heart. You failed, but offered no excuses. You accepted your loss and returned to face a possible punishment. Rewards are halved, but you have not lost reputation with Tommulus. Reward: 250 Gold per participant, 2,500 experience. No bonus rewards are granted.

Even as he blew out a sigh of relief, Joe couldn't help but feel disappointed. He had hoped to find out if the divine buff could be used to trick his way into his next specialization. Still, perhaps it was for the best that he didn't look for a way around the rules. Perhaps there was a reason the prerequisites were that high, and who knew what would happen if he got the specialization and then lost the requirements to keep it?

For now, the best course of action would be to focus on his personal arsenal and the town's defense. In reality, every time he was able to positively impact the guild by raising a building, he was also increasing his own personal level. In his opinion, having a quest to help boost their power was only a bonus, yet very welcome, addition. Joe pulled open the new town map from Mike and tried to decide what to do next.

In the core guild area, behind the inner wall, there were only seven official buildings. There were a few watersheds in the south-east corner, but while people still used them, they had become redundant thanks to the water purification properties of the greenhouse. Since that building acted both as a sewage system, food source, and a wellspring of clean water, the final choice for the south-east courtyard was to turn it into something more usable.

As for the north-east courtyard, there were currently grumpy merchants being removed from the area and put outside the inner wall. It wouldn't do to have untrustworthy people in the most protected guild area. Not when an attack could come at any time. Still, the question remained about what to do for these freshly vacated areas. Until that was decided, there was still plenty that Joe could work on.

Just by looking at his map, he could see that twenty-three buildings had been built within the walls of Towny McTownface, and eighteen of those had been built by him. Well, if the walls counted, then Joe had built twenty of twenty-five. The other five buildings had been put together by twenty-five-man teams that had been working tirelessly. Joe almost felt bad when he realized that two of the buildings that had needed to be torn down after the attack had not been built by him.

Joe paused just before his gaze slid past those points. "Did…

I never explained to most people why we had to tear those down and build new ones. Is that why such a large group was egging on that weaponmaster so he would beat me up?

"Eh... something to look into." Joe perused the mapped-out sections. There was a fifteen-meter empty space around the entire inside of the wall that was supposed to stay clear for purposes of defense and rapid movement; as well as to provide a clear line-of-sight if any enemies did manage to break through. Even with that requirement, there was enough room in the town to accommodate another fifty standard-sized buildings.

There would have been room for another seventy-five, but the Artifact-ranked, egg-shaped Pathfinder's hall took the space of a full twenty-five buildings; it was just that massive. Still, it did contain a medium-sized Temple, so that was another concern alleviated. Though it seemed like there was a massive amount of room for growth, the fact of the matter was that the guild now had close to twenty thousand members, and was still growing daily. Unless they started building Rare or—even better—*Unique* buildings, they were going to fill the area with structures that would need to be torn down in short order.

While they could expand, and had plans to do so, it was better to take the time to do things correctly. Mike had asked him to start working on a new blueprint that they had purchased: a set of apartment buildings that could be rented with contribution points. Right now, anyone in the guild could either sleep in the barracks or the single tavern in the town, but there was little privacy and no real personal space at all. The apartments were a quality-of-life upgrade, and the boost to morale might be the difference between a powerhouse staying in the guild or abandoning it when a better opportunity came along.

Naturally, team leaders and upper-members of the guild would get first dibs on these rooms as they became available. In other words, being slightly self-serving, Joe wasn't about to put off getting these into place. They had the materials for five of the buildings, but each of them would take three building spaces. That would still leave room for thirty-five more buildings, but would be a significant drain on the available space. Mike had left the placement to Joe, and Joe was currently debating whether to put them side-by-side, or to space them out around the town.

In the end, he chose the second option. While it might be nice to have all the housing clustered together, it would make an enticing target for anyone attacking the town, and slow down deployment of adventuring parties to the remainder of the town. On another note, putting them in one spot would mean that many people would have a much longer commute through the town if they had a job at one of the other buildings. This way, people could live close to their business if they wanted to do so.

Joe laid the buildings out in his mind as a hexagon that surrounded the inner walled-off area. They would be halfway between the inner and outer wall, and should be good places to live while being protected from anything coming in over the walls; such as combat mages' artillery spells. "Hmm… I wonder if there is such a thing as a force field that I could build? Or a stationary mana shield? It *has* to exist, right?"

Joe moved over to the Pathfinder's Hall and accessed the secret path down into the Grand Ritual Hall. Most of his Coven members were present and working on their own projects, including Big_Mo, who was once again coated in dried blood for no reason that Joe could discern. Joe walked over and allowed his Neutrality Aura to clean the man up as they all discussed various matters.

As the talk wound down, Joe waved Hannah over and gave her a guild quest. "I need you to design four large rituals that I made a long time ago, called 'Quarantine Area'. The four rituals will need to be modified into arcs that connect to make a large circle facing out of the town, and we'll use a remote activation so that they can all be activated at the same time."

"Nice! This will drive off attackers, then? How deadly are

the results?" Hannah took the ritual diagram and started looking at it intently.

"Not deadly, unless they're pretty dehydrated, I suppose." Joe shook his head. "This is a deterrent. It'll make people feel ill, and people don't like to climb a wall with, um, messy pants. Try to make it as effective as possible, but remember that we need to power everything. Again, this is going to be something that helps us push people back, so the worst they feel, the better for our defenders."

"Got it." Hannah didn't hide her disappointment, looking over longingly at the flamethrower that a couple of the others were working to perfect. She looked pleadingly at Joe, who chuckled and shook his head.

"This is going to be *way* more effective in the long run than those are. Trust me. People see fire and avoid it, but it is really hard to avoid a magical field that makes you sicker the closer you come to the epicenter of the effect. This is more important." Joe looked over at the other project, then tossed them a diagram as well. "Guys, try to find a way to get those two to line up with each other. What I just gave you was a chunk of another ritual called 'Ghostly Army'. I used that to create a fog bank that was thousands of feet wide. The chunk I tore out of it should create a simplified ritual that absorbs the same amount of water, then releases it as a continuous high-powered stream."

Big_Mo considered the new ritual. "So… this is going to turn into the ammo for *Ze Flammenwerfer*? Is that what you are trying to get at?"

"If you can make it happen." Joe paused as he registered what had just been said. "Hey, that was what you put on the forms you had given me to request items, too. Caught me off guard when Mike brought it up; why are you calling it-"

"Ze Flammenwerfer?" Big_Mo chuckled at that. "It's a thing from the internet. When someone was doing something really stupid, you would call someone to bring 'Ze Flammenwerfer'. Just go with it."

"Um. Fair enough." Joe had no idea what they were talking

about. "Any improvements? I need to get these in place near the walls soon. We don't know exactly when we will be under attack."

"So many improvements!" Kirby chirped, her excitement getting away from her. "Not only did we find a way to make stable ritual traps, Big_Mo found a way to collect blood from-"

"Hey!" Big_Mo glared at her, and she sheepishly covered her mouth with her hand. "Let me try that again! Based on the wind blade ritual, and using our research on the flamethrowers, we are able to make ritual circles that create either wind, frost, or fire novae centered on a single point. So, if we put them on large rocks or something, we can start using the terrain to our advantage."

"What's the downside?" Joe's question caused Kirby to shrug.

"The area-of-effect is pretty small, and once they know that the trap is there, it won't be hard to avoid it. Using it in the open means that people are only going to be impacted by the damage a single time. Then, it'll be pretty obvious that the giant rocks are traps." Kirby helplessly explained.

"No, wait." Joe's bald brow furrowed. "We *can* use that to our advantage. If we scatter rocks all over out there, people will be really cautious about moving near them. We can either funnel enemies where we want them to go, or trick them into thinking that they are safe. Good, I want fifty of those on my desk by tomorrow."

"Yeah, no." Big_Mo shook his head instantly. "Too high of a skill level required, we can do *twenty* at best, especially if Hannah is working on something else."

"Fair enough." Joe nodded easily. He had been joking about getting fifty anyway. Mostly. Partly. "Since all of you are getting pretty busy here, let me offer an additional incentive. When you hit Journeyman in ritual magic, I'm going to have all of you build your own Covens and be in charge of them. You'll get squad leader pay, and essentially become salaried. Also, I'm going up top to build apartment buildings that squad leaders get first dibs on. Work hard, y'all. There's a light at the end of the tunnel, and the rewards are in sight."

With that, Joe walked over to another part of the huge room and started creating a ritual around the blueprints Mike had entrusted him with.

CHAPTER THIRTY-SIX

Sunset was approaching by the time Joe completed his diagrams. He looked over the shifting surface of the diagram, pleased that he was finally going to have a room to sleep in where he wouldn't be awoken by a drunk barfly shouting from the common room. It had taken so long to formulate the diagrams only because these buildings were Uncommon ranked, *right* at the edge of Rare buildings. Luckily, his Architectural Lore skill had helped him fix a few of the issues on the blueprint, but that had also added to the time requirement.

"Oh… I can even furnish my room by myself if I grab a few beds out of storage." With rosy thoughts leading him, Joe left the Pathfinder's Hall with the intent of finding all the people in the guild that were construction workers. He got some names from the guild, and started his search. At this time of the day, they were either eating a late dinner or on their way to the tavern, so Joe tried the dining area first. He had a plan to start getting the workers onto his side, but he knew that the initial effort was going to suck.

"Excuse me, are you Emjay?" Joe vaguely recognized her, as he had watched the construction workers to try to build up his lore skill. It hadn't worked, but it had made them look at him less favorably, as he had simply stood there watching while they worked.

"I am. You're... Joe." Emjay turned back to her meal without another word. Joe winced, wondering what his reputation score would be with this lady. Probably pretty low.

Joe sat next to the woman at the long table, and the atmosphere turned tense. All the people eating here were part of the same crew. "I am. I think there have been some issues between us because we haven't had a chance to communicate. I'd like to take all of you over to the location where I am going to be building a new apartment building, and we can discuss any issues that I've caused for all of you. Would *all* of your team mind joining me for a short explanation?"

Emjay's jaw was clenched, though Joe knew she didn't have anything in her mouth. The last bite she had taken had been before Joe had arrived. "You taking us over there to show off, then? Teach us all how little we are needed here? That's already pretty clear."

"Exactly the *opposite*." Joe's sincere words made Emjay look at him in confusion. "Please? It'll all make sense soon."

"You have interesting timing." Emjay stood up, and Joe realized that the bench designed to hold ten people shifted upward significantly when she did so. This lady was *solid*. "C'mon, boys. We're gonna go learn how to put up a building the *right* way."

The knuckles cracking around the table did not make Joe any less concerned. He really hoped that he hadn't made a huge mistake, but there was nothing to do but follow through. The group of around twenty people followed Joe to the southern location and looked on as he instructed various guild members to arrange the pallets of material in the correct order. When everything was situated, Joe started talking to Emjay directly, as he didn't know the names of the other people.

"I'm here to show you all exactly *why* what you are doing is so important to the guild. The fact of the matter is that what *I* am doing is only going to be available for a short time. I'll be leaving on the bifrost as soon as possible." Joe pulled out the three Mana Batteries that he still had and arranged them in a balanced formation around him. "Even so, for as long as I am here, there is a reason I can't do this sort of thing alone."

"*Oh*, now it all makes sense. You're *leaving*, so we'll suddenly have job security." Emjay spat out the caustic words and turned to speak to her people.

"Please just watch. You'll understand soon." Joe softly implored. With that, he injected mana into the ritual and activated it. In the twilight, the glowing ritual circles that expanded were incredibly eye-catching. Joe and his batteries were lifted into the air, and soon the building materials started floating into position.

As much as Emjay didn't want to admit it, this was an impressive sight. The entire process, aside from Joe chanting, was almost entirely soundless. The boards and beams came together, the nails and screws sank into them. It was like watching a movie of a house being built on fast-forward. Something splattered on Emjay's face, interrupting her show. She wiped the liquid off with a hint of disgust. "Wha…? *Blood*? Where…"

She turned her attention to Joe, who was spasming every few seconds. Now that Emjay looked closely, she could see that the shining orbs that Joe had put on the ground were dark now. What did that mean? Ten seconds later, the building finished and Joe was set back on the ground. As soon as his feet were on soil, he collapsed into a heap, gasping for air and bleeding from his eyes, nose, and mouth.

The construction crew ran over to help him up, recoiling in horror at the bloody mess they found. Joe was bleeding from every orifice, his eyes were shut, and every breath created a short-lived dark-red bubble. Emjay, as the foreman on the crew, had one of the highest-level inspection abilities in the group. She looked at Joe with the skill active, wincing at the blinking health bar that appeared. "*Celestial*, kid! You practically kill yourself getting one of these things up?"

They all knew what happened when you got injured. Returning to full health couldn't happen without magical healing or coming back to life, so there was a chance that Joe would be out of commision for a few days… or he might die right here. He *had* lost a lot of blood. Emjay was trying to figure out how to help when Joe's hand weakly reached up to his own face. "Lay on Hands."

Joe's health bar soared upward in an instant, and the accumulated blood somehow started vanishing shortly after that. If she hadn't been there to see it herself, Emjay wouldn't have believed it. She swallowed at what she saw, and spoke. "Kid… you go through that every time you get a building up? Even if you can bring your health back, that's… you're torturing yourself. Losing so much health… that kinda pain… this isn't right. Is the guild *making* you do this, somehow? We can get you outta here."

"No." Joe sat up and steadied himself. He hurt all over, though it was fading fast. "Normally, I have a team of six that helps me, and we are able to share that pain across all of us. If we do things right, we usually don't get hurt, either. But even beyond all of that, every time we build a house, we need to use one of these."

Joe tossed over a Core, which was something that Emjay had never seen before. She caught it, and her face went white. "This… this is worth twenty-five hundred experience! We only get a thousand total for *building* a building!"

"Right." Joe took the Core back. "Now you can see why what I am doing is unsustainable. If we didn't *need* to build everything like crazy people, we would never be so incredibly wasteful with our resources. But the fact of the matter is… the other guilds have started a war with us. We are going to be attacked in the near future, and we need every advantage we can get. I just wanted to explain everything to you guys."

"Well…" Emjay looked at the others, then turned to face Joe once more. "I told you earlier that you had interesting timing. Reason for that is, we were going to leave the guild in the morning. Already voted on it. But… now that we know this… we'll just suck it up and keep working. I'm not afraid to admit that I'm jealous of your ability to make buildings, but there's no chance of me putting my crew through *that* to make it happen. Now this at least makes sense."

Joe took Emjay's hand and was pulled to his feet. "I do hope you stay. There are great things coming for the guild, I know it. I'll also see what I can do to help you guys out every once in a while, if you want that."

"Same to you, kid. No, sorry. *Joe.*" Emjay shook Joe's hand, then turned to her crew and nodded. They started moving off toward the tavern, all of them pretty quiet. They had a lot to think about.

Joe stayed where he was, looking at the building. It was a nice-looking apartment building, but that wasn't the reason he remained. He looked over his notifications again, just to be sure that he hadn't misread the information. This was a classic good news, bad news situation; it seemed that the bonus he gained for advancing his Rituarchitect class to level seven had come into effect.

Structure 'Uncommon Apartment Building' has transformed into 'Hungry Apartment Building (Rare)', and absorbed a portion of the mana invested in the ritual, combining with the lifeblood of the builder to impart an additional effect! Upon sleeping in an apartment for at least five hours, experience gain will increase by 50% for 18 hours. Every five nights, there is a 5% chance that one of the occupants will suddenly die, whereupon the walls will bleed lightly for thirty minutes. All traces of blood will vanish after that thirty minutes have passed. Each day that the effect does not trigger, the chances increase by three percent.

Class experience gained: 1000. You succeeded in upgrading an Uncommon-ranked building into a Rare building, experience gains for a Rare-ranked building have been doubled as a bonus.

"Now… do I tear it down, or just go to bed?" Joe shrugged and went in, taking a room on the ground floor for himself.

"I'll let Mike figure that out… tomorrow."

CHAPTER THIRTY-SEVEN

"No *way* am I letting you tear it down!" Mike told Joe as he looked at the hungry new building with shining eyes. "Our guild members would eat you alive!"

"I don't understand," Joe admitted after staring at Mike long enough to make both of them uncomfortable. "Did I *not* just tell you that once every five days or so… someone will die in there?"

"Exactly!" Mike's eyes were practically releasing a light of their own. "*Only* once a week or so, and *only* one person! You know how often people die out there? How many party wipes? It's constant. Everyone will *fight* to stay in here for that experience bonus, and they'll train their luck to *not* be the person that dies! Can I name the building?"

"Technically, it is called 'Hungry Apartment Building'." Joe was shaking his head at all of this; the situation seemed odd.

"I'm gonna market it as 'Gamble Hall'." Mike was rubbing his hands together. "When people see the blood coming out of the walls, they won't be freaked out or scared… no. They'll *cheer*, knowing that *they* survived!"

Joe started to reluctantly nod. "Alright… I can see the appeal."

"Can you make more of these?" Mike bluntly wondered. "I want ten."

"I can't right now, and I personally think it is more important that people can sleep safely?" Joe didn't want to have to scan and figure out how to make the newly Rarified building. The scouts estimated the battle to be a day away, if the enemy continued their slow progression down the road. This meant that only a single day remained before the blatant attack, and there were still many things that required his attention. "Do you agree?"

"I mean… yes, of course." Mike coughed into his hand and had the good grace to look slightly embarrassed. *Only* slightly. "Anyway, if you can get the other four set up as planned, our teams should be in high spirits for the battle tomorrow. Other than that… any updates?"

"Not particularly." Joe thought for a long moment. "I've had a few members of my Coven doing research at the library, as well as the Mage's College. They might be able to come back with something interesting. Oh, and I completed five scrolls for the guild this morning, though I'm gonna need payment for them."

"Oh? What are the spells?" Mike took the scrolls that Joe handed over, his eyes going wide when he saw them. "Cone of Cold, Dale's Shattered Earth? The first one is understandable, but what is the second?"

"First off, what do you know about scrolls?" Joe prodded him.

"Lets you cast a spell from it even if you don't know the spell, correct?" Mike raised an eyebrow at the question. This was gaming one-oh-one.

"Yes, you can cast the spell directly. If you cast these as-is, they will be as powerful as an upper-Apprentice casting it. But… you *also* could use these as study material. If someone manages to do it, they will learn the spell somewhere between

Novice one and Novice nine; if they are both intelligent and lucky." Joe's words made Mike look at the scrolls in a new light. Even with the discount they got at the Mage's College, learning a spell from them took a large chunk of gold. But the spell would usually start in the Beginner ranks, so there was still some trade-off. "I'd also trade directly for some Cores."

Mike waved off the issue of payment; that would be handled by acquisitions. He had stopped making those deals himself after he got in trouble for being too generous; a fact that would have made Joe scoff at him. "You'll get paid. Fair market value, I guarantee it. What do the spells do?"

"Cone of Cold sets out a blast of cold air… more like a spray of liquid nitrogen, actually. It does frost damage, and it also inflicts the 'brittle' debuff. That makes rigid things take more damage, and increases the damage done to the durability of armor and such. It should do between… three to five hundred cold damage to anyone in a cone, if the scroll is used as a spell." Joe had done some quick math on that one. Hopefully he wouldn't need to show his work.

"Interesting." Mike held up the other one. "And this?"

"I think it is something like a siege weapon." Joe answered after a short pause. "Really quick, do you know how depth charges work to destroy submarines?"

"Joe. Of course I do." Mike chuckled at the question. "The explosion creates a cavitation bubble, and the actual damage is from the weight of the submarine settling into that and getting shaken really hard. It's called hydraulic shock."

"Right, same concept here." Joe motioned at the scroll. "Unlike an 'earthquake' spell, this creates a targeted sinkhole. The ground literally shatters, and that can cause damage as well. This was filed away into the 'useless' archives a long time ago, because it is really hard to level up the spell. Using it on monsters doesn't offer any increase, and there are only so many buildings that you can build and destroy. Outside of war… yeah, not really so useful."

"So why make it?" Mike asked the easy question.

Joe grinned darkly. "*Huge* casting range. Let's say someone brings siege machines, you can drop those into a sinkhole that should be... twenty feet deep and wide? Or, if we counter against an aggressor, this should be enough to destroy a large section of wall or an important building."

Mike gulped at the intense look on Joe's face. "Put a lot of thought into this, have you?"

"I'm trying to think of a way to counter it, actually." Joe admitted ruefully, realizing that he was getting too intense for Mike. "If someone uses that against us, we would need to rebuild whatever building was hit. Also, only Uncommon and higher buildings can resist an under-Journeyman ranked earthquake spell. Found out about that in a lore book on architecture."

"When do you have time to read *lore* books?" Mike scoffed, but Joe only shrugged.

"I don't sleep all that much." Joe summoned Mate, as well as two coffee cups from his ring. "Want a cup of me?"

"What?"

"Want a cup of *Joe*?" Joe chuckled at the pun as he downed his fifth cup of the day. It was already nine in the morning, after all.

"No thanks, I don't want your *sleeve coffee*." Mike shook his head with his eyes closed, causing him to miss Mate making a rude gesture. "Besides, what makes you think that they will have siege equipment? This is gonna be a bunch of low-level people trying to zerg rush us."

"Mmm." Joe held up a finger as he drained his cup. Mate bubbled happily before sinking into Joe's sleeve. "Ahh. Probably, but there's no way that this isn't an attack sponsored by other groups, right? I'm betting that there will be a lot of really high-levels hidden among all the lowbies. That would just make sense, right? *Right*?"

"That is a possibility that we considered." Mike admitted easily, stepping away from the highly-caffeinated man. "The fact remains that we will have the full, concentrated might of the guild in a defended location. I feel confident that we will easily be able to turn them away if needed."

"Got it. I'll be back at one, so try and have the materials for the other buildings ready to go!" Joe nodded and started to walk away. He paused. "Mike, one last thing. If you know that we can push them back, and *they* know that we can push them back… what will be the *actual* point of them attacking?"

Mike froze, and nodded slowly as Joe walked off. "Good question… we'll need to look into that."

Joe continued walking, his plan for the morning already set. He was on his way to the testing dungeon, and he was going to be trying to solo the dexterity area. While the increase at the end would be nice, Joe was actually after the Neigh-Bears. There were very few places with such a high concentration of monsters, and even though there was a low success rate, Joe was planning to grind his skill levels for Corify and his newly learned spell: Cone Of Cold.

The reason he had been willing to trade the scrolls for Cores was pretty simple: he was out. He hadn't given too much thought to the matter before, but beyond two powerful Cores that he had stored in his codpiece, Joe was flat *out.* He tried to think about everything he had been pouring the Cores into, but in truth, he just had no idea where they had all gone. Hopefully the investment into his growth would pay off in the future. He started trying to psych himself up.

"It's *fine*, Joe! It's all~l~l goose." Joe sputtered as his attention returned to the present. He stopped in place, then started laughing at tripping over his words; this was going to be a new saying for him. "It's all goose! I can only flap my wings and honk angrily at the injustice in the world!"

CHAPTER THIRTY-EIGHT

You have entered the Dungeon 'Trial section 118b'. Please cast your vote for party challenge! Strength / Dexterity / Constitution / Intelligence / Wisdom / Charisma / Perception / Luck.

Joe selected the dexterity option. The odd cube-shaped world rearranged itself and settled. He jumped to the platform, then to the door, and stepped inside.

Average party dexterity… 70. Scaling difficulty to 50-100 dexterity range. Good luck!

"Not so much about luck here, is it?" Joe was still salty about the luck-based trial being decided practically instantly. A roar shook the surroundings, and Joe immediately focused on the incoming battle. The great part about this area was that it contained a high concentration of monsters to combat. The terrible part was that they would happily destroy him if he messed up. This area was designed for people with anywhere from fifty to a hundred dexterity, so there was a good chance that there would be Neigh-Bears present that were more than a match for his abilities.

Joe readied his mind, and threw himself into combat after taking a look at his newest spell.

Cone of Cold (Novice VIII). Ever wanted to look at a group of people arranged in a cone within thirty feet of you, and tell all of them to chill at the same time? Looks like you found the right spell! Effect: Release super-chilled air from your hands, dealing 15n damage on all enemies within thirty feet in a cone-shaped area-of-effect, where n = skill level. Inflicts the 'Brittle' debuff. Cost: 20n mana. Cooldown: 30 seconds. Requires both hands to use, or channeling through a two-handed weapon which allows spellcasting.

Brittle: doubles durability damage against rigid objects. This is only accounted for when the object is struck. No, you can't boost the damage your acid does, nice try. Ignore 20% armor rating for any metal armor where 'Brittle' is applied.

Joe was crossing his fingers that, as he leveled this spell up, he would be able to slow the movement speed of enemies as well. It seemed that it was more of an actual *ice* spell, and Cone of Cold was, in truth, an 'air affinity' spell. Still, while it wasn't as effective as it could have been, it would get the job done. "Cone of Cold!"

In an instant, one hundred and sixty mana left him, and the three charging Neigh-Bears took one hundred and twenty damage. Beyond the addition of shivering, there was no change in their pace toward him. At the last moment, Joe jumped into the air and angled to the left. He thought he had made a clean getaway, but his fluttering robe was hooked by a sharp claw. In the next instant, Joe was slammed against the ground, completely winded.

Damage: 0 (120 terrain damage absorbed by Exquisite Shell).

A shadow of himself appeared and slapped the bear in the face. Taking the chance his skill had given him, he rolled back to his feet in a flash. Joe found himself surrounded by charging monsters. "Perfect. I can attack in any direction!"

As the paws struck down at him, Joe called down a Dark Lightning Strike, then dove under the attacks as the Neigh-Bears flinched back from the unexpected pain and odd snapping sound that the lightning produced.

Charging attacks avoided: 5/100.

"Thank you, system, for the timely updates." Joe started jogging away as the bears awkwardly turned to face him once more. He lifted his staff into the air, twirling it while he prepared Acid Spray, then abruptly angled it behind him. The pained scream of the bears made him smile. The Polearm Mastery skill was coming in handy in unexpected ways. He had never been able to maneuver his weapon so easily, always just carefully pointing and shooting like he was using a flamethrower or rifle instead of a staff.

"Let's see if I can write my name in the air as I spray acid." Joe *jumped*, whirled around, and managed to draw a 'J' and about half of an 'O' before the acid ran out. He had been trying to regain his ability to channel, but for some reason couldn't get a handle on it like he had the first time. "This reminds me of making yellow snow."

Charging attacks avoided: 8/100.

Joe landed lightly, preparing another attack that would strike the backs of his assailants. Instead, his head snapped forward as a clawed paw smashed into him. Joe flipped and bounced twice on the ground before friction forced him to a stop. He got up, slightly disoriented but ready to fight. His heart sank at the sight before him.

Sneak attack! Damage: 0 (511 damage absorbed by Exquisite Shell).

Exquisite Shell: 1,297/1,928.

There were another six Neigh-Bears coming for him, and the one that had hit him was clearly an elite version, being a full head taller than the others. His horse body also seemed to be on par with a draft horse in terms of size, though admittedly Joe didn't know his horse breeds very well. Joe looked up at the face of the bear, which seemed especially furious now that it was sporting a handprint on its fur that seemed to be *just* about the size of Joe's hand. "Well, you're a big boy, aren'tcha."

A bellow came out of the bear head at such a high decibel that Joe's shell took a single point of sonic damage; just enough to get another slap to the face from Joe's Retribution of Shadows. Joe twirled his staff and pointed it at the bear, his eyes narrowing in focus. "It's gonna be like that, huh? I hope you're prepared for my specialty, then!"

The Neigh-Bears charged at him in formation, and Joe took a deep, steadying breath… before turning and running away like a scared little forest elf. "Nope, nope, nope! Don't gotta fight, just need to dodge!"

The speed of a magical horse hybrid was clearly higher than what Joe could manage. He started gathering his mana, preparing to use Cone of Cold again as soon as the thirty-second cooldown had completed. Sadly, thirty seconds during combat was a terribly long time, and the Neigh-Bears were never going to allow him that respite. Now that there were nine total beasts after him, Joe started to think that he may have made a terrible mistake.

"Can't let… random monsters kill me!" Joe puffed out as he ran frantically. The thundering hoofbeats behind him were coming closer and closer, and Joe desperately worked to think of *anything* he could do. As the claws of the elite reached for him, and Joe could practically feel the rough horse hair, he *jumped* as hard as he could.

His body exploded upward and forward, his physical limits being tested by his Master-ranked skill. As Joe soared up, and up, and up, he could only reflect on his choices. "Something seems different this time around."

That was an understatement, as he still had yet to start falling downward. His eyes flashed to his mana, and widened as he saw what was remaining.

Mana: 526/1,872 (617 reserved)

Whatever had just happened had pulled away effectively half of Joe's usable mana. He tried to figure it out as he started falling back toward the ground and awaiting Neigh-Bears. "What was different? I was running, I started jumping… I shot off like a bottle-rocket. I…! I had gathered a bunch of mana in preparation to cast a spell! Wait! I've used mana in jumping before, but only for skipping along so that I didn't need to use stamina! Can I *empower* my jumps with mana at the Master rank?"

Skill increase: Jump (Master I). Your understanding of this skill has reached a new level! Even though you had used this ability in the past... you know what? Just enjoy the increase. Go, go, rocket boots!

Information flooded into Joe's mind about how to use his mana within his body to further supplement his jumping abilities. Just before he hit the ground, the only thing that Joe could think was, "I bet thieves would *love* this skill."

Then he was rolling through the long grass, bouncing off rocks, before finally coming to a halt at the rear feet of a Neigh-Bear. It started to turn, so Joe tried to force himself to get moving. He struggled to his feet, and glanced at the waiting flash of notifications.

Charging attacks avoided: 21/100.

Exquisite Shell: 832/1928.

He had taken four hundred damage from falling from that height? Didn't he have fifty percent falling damage reduction? Yes; yes, he did. Joe started running toward the center of the testing area as the herd found him and came running. Joe prepared his spell, then jumped forward and spun around to cast Cone of Cold. The elite merely shivered, but the others started faltering. The first three that Joe had fought were clearly weakened, so Joe cast Corify on one, then sent acid at the entire group.

With the second casting of Acid Spray, the Neigh-Bears were on him once more, so Joe stored his staff in his ring and jumped to the side, pushing off and returning to his original position as soon as the elite thundered past him. Because of this, Joe was able to avoid every attack from the 'V' formation of monsters.

Charging attacks avoided: 30/100.

He lashed out with the staff as it reappeared in his hand, smashing the blunt endcap into the rear-right kneecap of the bear that he had targeted with Corify. With one more spray of acid at its face, the bear died. Joe turned to the others, already weary but fortified by the excitement burning within him. Acid started to drip from his staff, and he whirled it in a circle to create a field of pain around himself.

"Alright, you overstuffed teddies. Let's play."

CHAPTER THIRTY-NINE

Joe looked at the six Cores he had managed to obtain, then down at his tattered clothing. "I… I think that was worth it?"

Each of the Cores held thirty-five hundred experience, putting them right in the center of the Common ranks. Meanwhile, Joe's equipment had dropped in durability from the beating he had taken at the paws of the herd, as well as his own attempts to regulate mana flow to his jumping skill. "Ugh… if only that elite would have dropped a Core when it died!"

Durability of Wise Man's Wardrobe: 8/100.

Charging attacks avoided: 100/100. Leave the dungeon to collect your reward!

"Mm. I don't think the 'minor self-repair' function on my wardrobe is going to cut it with this. I should really keep a closer eye on my gear." Joe sighed as he moved toward the exit. He had killed three dozen Neigh-Bears; increasing Corify to Beginner III, Acid Spray to *Apprentice* III, Dark Lightning Strike to Beginner IX, and Cone of Cold to Beginner 0.

He was a little grumpy that he didn't get a bonus for that spell, but when he thought about it; Joe hadn't ever used the spell in a unique or interesting way, simply casting it as soon as it came off cooldown. Even so, the gains had been really good, and he realized that in order to grow rapidly, he might need to start taking more risks. He couldn't even remember the last time that he had gone to do solo adventuring.

“There’s always more to learn in this world.” Joe chuckled ruefully. He hadn't seen much of a bonus for increasing his skills in a while, and he was starting to think that he was missing something. Even so, he couldn’t think of what it could be. Stubbornly refusing to look at the gains he had made in experience, since his goal had been grinding skills and collecting Cores, Joe reached out a hand to select the option to leave the dungeon.

**eeee*.*

Joe paused as his ears started ringing softly. “I thought coming into Eternium fixed my tinnitus? Wait, that’s not… oh! That’s my Hidden Sense! Ugh… I always forget to use Query… I should do that more often. Sorry, Tatum! Just not used to asking for help on things!”

He had forgotten that he had faintly sensed something when he had cleared the dungeon the first time, but hadn't bothered to find what it was. Now, since he had some free time and his Hidden Sense had reached the Apprentice ranks, he was *far* more aware that something was calling out to him. Joe started slowly circling the area to find where the noise was the strongest. Bizarrely, he kept returning to the plinth that led to the outside world.

“What *is* it about you that’s special?” Joe wondered quietly. He started running his hands over the stone, but no matter what he did, he could find nothing. In fact, it was really annoying, because every time he touched the plinth, the same question would appear. Finally, he growled, “No, I *don’t* want to leave right now!”

“Last try, then I use Query.” After searching the plinth, Joe decided that it might not be the object itself: perhaps it was on top of something? He started shoving the stone, but couldn't manage to make it budge. Trying different angles did nothing, so he tried climbing up and jumping on it. As soon as he did, a sound of grinding stone filled the area. The entire stone platform that Joe was standing on started to swivel, and Joe would have fallen if he hadn't hopped off the plinth.

You have followed the instincts that have been granted to you!

Skill increased: Hidden Sense (Apprentice II).

"The skill went up?" Joe stared at the hole in the ground. A ramp appeared under the plinth that descended into the depths, certainly too far to see the end. "But that skill *just* went up recently? How would it have increased again so…?"

System response: As this is a deity-granted skill, more information is available. Skill 'Hidden Sense' increases in skill proficiency via usage that allows you to find hidden things. There is a skill proficiency multiplier that increases skill gain when something hidden has been investigated by others, and yet remains not found. The more people that do not find the hidden person/place/thing, the higher the skill multiplier increases.

"Oh. Handy." Joe resolved to use the skill more often for searching ruins or something that thousands of people had been able to access before him. In the short term, he decided to cautiously walk down the ramp and follow along the path. As he was on the lookout for traps and monsters, Joe moved slowly and inspected everything. As the ramp widened out into a large room, he was slightly surprised to realize that there hadn't been anything that suggested danger.

Joe stepped into the room, a massive sphere of a room that held a small waterfall, and looked around. It was dark, but that was no issue at all, thanks to his Darkvision. "This room is empty?"

A small hill near the waterfall suddenly *moved*, and Joe found himself looking into a pair of enormous orbs. No, they had just blinked at him. Those were eyes. The 'hill' stood up, and resolved into the single largest Neigh-Bear that Joe had had the misfortune to meet. The creature spoke slowly, carefully. "Room. Not. Empty."

Staff pointed at the creature, Joe swallowed and barely held off from casting Cone of Cold. "What… *who* are you?"

"I am Arthur. Warchief of Neigh-Bears." The huge beast

took a few steps closer to Joe, his voice starting to smooth into a more natural cadence. Had he simply not spoken in a long time? "Have you come to help?"

"Help?" Joe was surprised; was he about to get a quest from this behemoth? "What do you need help with?"

"You… it is not known?" Arthur hesitated, then seemed to shrink into himself a small amount. "Rage has clouded the minds of my people; they have become lesser. It was the war between the Centaurs and the Neigh-Bears. Once, we were two sides of a coin. We were the melee fighters, berserkers, and true warriors. They were the fleet-of-foot mages, the archers, and scouts. At some point, they named themselves our betters, and attempted to make us into nothing more than beasts of war."

Arthur paused for a long moment, coughing deeply. Joe took a step forward, wanting to hear more of the story. "Are you ill? I can heal you."

"No, it is fine; I'm just partly horse." Arthur didn't give Joe a chance to respond, launching back into his tale. "We devolved into war. They have range and superior firepower, but we had thousands; neigh, *tens* of thousands more warriors than they. The battle was decided in an instant, though the Centaur race refused to back down. As we surrounded them and demanded that they stop this madness, their most powerful Warlock sacrificed himself and the remainder of his race to curse us."

"Are you hoping that I can break this curse?" Joe offered, somewhat unsure how he could go about doing that.

"Are you a fourth-tier Oathmaster, that you would offer to break a curse of this scale so lightly?" Arthur snorted loudly. "I can only ask that you go and relieve my brethren of their lives, that they may have at least some form of peace. Also, please, do not tell others of this great shame. If you do this for me, I will give you a token that can be used to summon me to your side. I promise you; I am a powerful combatant."

Quest alert: Centaur of a Grizzly War. Kill 100 Neigh-Bears without any teammates present. Reward: summoning token. Failure: none. Accept? Yes / No.

"I will happily accept this quest, though I do have a few questions for you." Joe took a deep breath and edged closer to the massive beast. "First, if your race was cursed, how are you still sane? Second, do you mind if I inspect you? I can't be responsible for accidentally unleashing something on the world that is going to harm others."

"I will certainly harm others, but only the people you send me after." Arthur waved at the water flowing behind him. "This water is the only thing that allows me to retain my mind, and I can only be without it for a small time before I fall under the same effects my brothers and sisters have succumbed to. This means that when the allotted time of the summoning ends, I will not just return here happily; I will *flee* here to regain my thoughts and wisdom. Feel free to inspect me, for it will only reveal the truth of my words."

Joe nodded, then studied Arthur with Intrusive Scan. In the next few seconds, information began to appear.

Name: Arthur G. Bearnard
Highest Characteristic: Strength
Active Effects: Force for Good. Cursed (Tier III Insanity, Shifting Alignment). Massive. Thundering Physique. Summonable. Holy Water (03:23:22).

Skill increase: Intrusive Scan (Beginner 0). Sometimes all you need is a willing target! Skill usage time requirements -.5 seconds!

Joe cut off the skill; not only had he seen everything he needed, he was shocked by the massive jump of *six* skill levels and the bonus for the skill. "I... yes, I will do what I can to help you, Arthur. Is the holy water what keeps you safe?"

"It is."

"With alignment shift, does that mean that all other Neigh-Bears are evil at this point?" Joe was nearly done with his questioning, but this detail was important to him.

"Yes. Currently, all others are evil."

"Almost finished." Joe took a deep breath. "That token is to be used in a time of great need, which means you are essentially telling me that by completing this quest, you are offering me an insurance plan. So, my last question…"

"Insurance plan?"

"You know, because, like a good Neigh-Bear, you'll be there." Joe grinned at the huge, confused creature. "Are you wearing Khakis?"

CHAPTER FORTY

Joe left the dungeon six hours later, having finally defeated the full one hundred Neigh-Bears required by Arthur's quest. In total, he had slain one hundred and thirty-six of the creatures on this trip, and he had gained good rewards for doing so. After confirming that he had only gained four dexterity - three for the challenge, and one for the uninterrupted twenty-seven minutes of training - Joe counted all the Cores he had gained, pleased with the amount.

"Twenty-two common Cores, a summoning token that I can regain every five days so long as I kill a hundred Neigh-bears after each use..." Joe skimmed his notifications for the pertinent information, nodding as he continued muttering to himself. "Between the quest and the kills, seven thousand two hundred and twenty-two experience. That's not bad at all for a night of fighting. Less than four thousand to level eighteen!"

Joe started on his way back to the guild, cheerfully skipping along as he thought over the *other* gains. His highest increase was Retaliation of Shadows, which had risen three skill levels. Sure it meant he had taken dozens of hits, but... worth it? Fighting against another hundred opponents had allowed him to raise most of his combat skills twice: Cone of Cold, Polearm Mastery, Acid Spray, Corify, and even Exquisite Shell. His Dark Lightning Strike had only increased to Beginner IX, but Joe was sure that it was getting close to the threshold. Even his Jump skill had undergone serious refinement, though he was certain that it wasn't about to rank up.

He was now casually feeding mana into every small jump and skip that he made, causing every step to propel him about three meters before he touched the ground again. While this helped him cross distance quickly, Joe knew that it also made it really hard to change course. This was for travel or fast escape, certainly not for close combat. At least… not yet. He had plans to change that if it ever became a viable option. There were all sorts of things he could do with this skill if he could get creative enough, and creativity was one of his stronger points.

Joe was moving *fast* as he sprang along the road, easily double his previous movement speed. Even so, when Towny McTownface appeared in the distance, he sped up to the maximum that his body and mind could handle. The reason was simple enough: the attack had arrived early. Way too early. It was currently dark out, making Joe recalculate the amount of time that he had spent in the dungeon. He had been having a really good time of it; which made him think that he had been in there for over half a day. Whoops. He had thought it had been six to eight hours, tops.

However, as Joe approached the town, he noticed that the intermittent flashing lights and explosions were coming from traps and the rituals that had been attached to rocks. The only sign of an attack were all the bodies strewn around, and none of them were wearing the Wanderer's Guild insignia. To be fair, Joe didn't wear it either, but most of the guild displayed their sigil proudly. It helped with reputation quests and granted access to certain NPC-run areas. The sigil was a winged shoe that was marked on the side with a triple triangle. It made sense in the context of 'Wanderer', but Joe much preferred the holographic book sigil that showed his ties to Tatum; which was what he chose to display.

"What happened here?" Joe called up to the gate guard. "Wait, Jay, is that you?"

"Son of a... Joe? You don't have Jaxon with you, do ya? I'm not opening the gate if you do!" Jay called back playfully.

"Let me in, or I'll tell him that you lifted a dungeon boss with your back only, while twisting your torso harshly!" Joe shouted with a laugh. If Jay was making jokes, then the situation probably wasn't too bad.

"Gonna be about twenty minutes, Joe." Jay was serious this time. "Guild is on lockdown; something's got their tighty-whities in a bunch."

Joe looked at the wall, then up at Jay. "Any issue if I come in without you opening the gate?"

"Please don't knock the wall down, Joe. I know you built it and all, but-"

"What sort of reputation do I have with you, Jay?" Joe wasn't sure if Jay was joking, but it sure didn't sound like it. "Just watch out!"

Joe retreated about fifty meters, then started running at the wall. With every step, he poured more mana into the bottoms of his feet, and each footfall became faster and moved him farther. When he was ten meters from the wall, he released a huge burst of mana and *jumped*. Joe soared up, and up, and... not quite high enough. The metalic-black wall loomed closer and closer. "Jay, help!"

Jay tossed a rock straight down off the wall. The projectile had been placed there to throw at attackers. It was a good throw, falling down directly in front of Joe. He managed to get his feet in position, and another burst of mana later... Joe reached up and grabbed Jay's extended hand. Jay wasn't at *all* happy. "Two leaps, and you are suddenly almost forty feet in the air? How the *abyss* are we supposed to defend these walls if people can just... pop to the top of them?"

"Pull me up first, please!" Joe was still dangling, but with a heave and a grunt, Jay yanked him over the edge of the wall. "Whew! Thanks, man. Also, I have a Master-ranked jump skill, so that exact thing isn't something you really need to worry about someone else having. But I'm sure there are going to be a ton of different ways to invade towns and cities. The walls are really only ever going to keep out land-based monsters and low-leveled people."

Jay grunted, still clearly unsatisfied with that answer. "You should get over to the Guild Hall. Big meeting going on; I know they like you there for those."

"Can do, but first, what happened?" Joe gestured at the blood-soaked field outside the wall.

"Exactly what we were warned about." Jay waved a spear at the mess. "Just a huge mob of new players. Most of them didn't even get in shouting range before our rangers and mages cut them down. But it was classified as an invasion, so we all got rewards for defending our guild."

"Gotcha." Joe excused himself and went to find a ladder. He got off the wall and hurried to the Guild Hall, which seemed almost deserted. Joe made it to the outside of the war room, only to find two guards blocking his path. When they recognized him, they let him through. Joe opened the door and was hit by a wall of noise. Literally hit by it? No. Still, the damage to his eardrums was enough that Retaliation of Shadows triggered. Suddenly, every person that was screaming got smacked in the face by a shadow-Joe. They didn't take damage, but it was confusing enough that the room went quiet.

"What is *happening* in here?" Deciding not to waste the opportunity, Joe stepped into the silence and pitched his voice as he often had to do back in his military days. "Have you all lost your abyssal *minds*? Do I need to remind you that the people in this room are responsible for the lives and livelihoods of *thousands* of people? Get your act together!"

"Now, you listen to me, *Joe*." One of the people at the huge table stood up and released an imposing aura. It didn't seem to be a skill, more a combination of charisma, anger, and strength.

"You're not gonna get away with treating us like *children*. We're powerful team leaders as well as-"

"Stop." Joe demanded in return, the area around him darkening enough to be seen by the naked eye. "I could only *hope* that if I were acting like a child, I would be called out on it. *Especially* when I was in a public place, even *more* so when it was in front of my fellow leaders, whom I need to respect; and who I need to respect *me*. So, I say again, stop screaming, and have a civil discourse. What has everyone so riled up?"

"Tch." The man sat down heavily, his plate armor making the chair creak in protest. "All of that, and you don't even know what's happening?"

Aten smoothly joined the conversation from the head of the table. "Joe, thank you for joining us. Your group was instrumental in fending off the invasion, so thank-"

"That's part of the *issue*, though, isn't it!" Another person slammed their hand on the table, and several other voices joined into the conversation.

"*Enough*... please and thank you." Aten's voice was sharper than Joe's Taglock needle. Joe winced and reminded himself to put that back on his staff; he had taken it off to train with the polearm. "Joe, the issue is simple. We fended off an invasion perfectly, but almost everyone that attacked was under level five. Because we defended ourselves so... *vigorously*, there is a huge public outrage. Not a single one of the people that attacked us survived, and most of them were hit by attacks that would have killed them a dozen times over."

"They are calling us war criminals." Aten finished grimly. "We even have a new guild title, which I'm not exactly happy about. Though, frankly, it does offer a really nice bonus. Take a look."

Joe pulled up his 'Guild' tab to see what Aten was talking about.

New guild title gained! As it is the only title your guild has gained, this is automatically displayed!

'The Wanderer's Guild: Ruthless Defenders.'

CHAPTER FORTY-ONE

Ruthless Defenders: this is a guild-wide title. You have stood against an invasion of at least a thousand strong, protecting what is yours and not leaving a single invader alive. To upgrade this title, destroy an invading force of at least ten thousand without letting a single invader escape! Effect: While defending the territory of the Wanderer's Guild, reduce damage from invaders by 5%, and increase damage dealt by 5%. Enemies slain on the guild's land have a 20% chance to drop an equipped item.

"I see it; that's a really solid increase." Joe looked around at the group as they shook their heads. "What's the issue here?"

"Joe, this is a public relations nightmare." Mike took the initiative to speak, and his words turned the atmosphere gloomy. "This was a trap the entire time. Because we thought that there would be expert players hidden in their ranks, we threw everything and the kitchen sink at them. Now, not only did scouts from various factions see what we were capable of, they are using the fact that we went all-out against low-level people as a way to incite a large-scale operation against us. This was just the beginning, and it was a trap from the start."

Joe listened quietly, as did the entire room. They were

suddenly in a bad position, and they all knew it. Still, Joe had one thing to say:

"So what?"

"What?" Mike and Aten spoke together, startled at Joe's words.

"I said, 'so what'." Joe stood tall and swept his gaze around the room. "Were we trying to recruit people, or show them that we wouldn't let our guild be robbed? Were we trying to feel them out? Hope that people coming here to steal our gear and burn the rest to the ground… would suddenly be friendly to us?"

A long moment passed, then Joe stepped forward and slapped the table. "No! We were showing everyone watching, and everyone that would attack us, that we will be serious against *every* threat, no matter how small! Yes, there will be people that hate us for not letting them *take* what we *earned*, but who cares! As for everyone else, don't you think our guild is celebrating right now? Don't you all *realize* that security at this level is what people have been *dreaming* of ever since Earth was ripped away from us? When I see this title that our guild has gained, all I want…"

"I want…" Joe took a deep breath, and tried to meet the eyes of all the people around the table. "*All* I want… is to *upgrade* this title to the next rank! If we need to be Ruthless to protect ourselves, then I know that *I* will be at the front lines, casting the biggest spells I can. If people die because they are attacking us… it is *their. Own. Fault!*"

There was a roar of approval, and everyone started talking again. This time, it was about how to improve the defenses further, how they should take a stand, or what preparations should happen next. Aten nodded at Joe appreciatively, then frowned. In an instant, he was next to Joe, catching him just before he hit the floor. Even though the room was full of people, almost no one noticed; they were too engrossed in the conversation.

As for Joe himself, he had collapsed only after receiving a concerning message.

All prerequisites for full characteristic shift of Dark Charisma have been met! Before, you had managed to feel a hint of this shift, and it had been meant as a warning or an opportunity. Similar to an alignment shift, you have used this characteristic in a specific way so many times that it has centralized around the core concept of your usage!

Effect: Convincing others to take dark, violent, or passionate actions now have a fixed 10% increased chance to succeed! All actions that lead to peaceful, non-violent, or purely logical actions have a fixed 10% increased chance to fail! Your methods of gaining charisma in the future have been altered.

As one of the first five hundred players to achieve a characteristic shift: Charisma +10.

Changing a main characteristic has dangerous repercussions to the body and mind. While this update is taking effect, you shall be rendered unconscious. Starting in 3… 2…

Joe's eyes flew open, making Aten shout in surprise and jump away from him. Aten had been putting Joe into a bed in the Guild Hall. The space was usually reserved for people that had worked too many hours and would be starting their next shift shortly after sleeping. Joe sat up, raising a brow at the large warrior. "Aten, I know we're close, but I don't think that we're *that* close."

"I thought you were *dead*, Joe." Aten glared in an attempt to hide his shock and embarrassment.

"Hmm. If you were thinking I was dead, and you were getting that close to my face, what does that say about *you*?" Joe teased the flustered man.

"That's not funny! I was checking to see if you were breathing!" Aten shook his head, puffing up to defend his own honor, when Joe started chuckling. "You think you're *so~o~o* funny, but you're not!"

"Sorry, sorry; I was just testing out the new function of my charisma." Joe waved off Aten's retaliatory snort. "Seriously! I just had a characteristic shift. Apparently, it is now a lot easier for me to rile people up, to make them give in when logic is taken out of the equation."

"You became a politician?" Aten took a step away from the bed. "Joe, that's such a downgrade from what you had."

"No, no." Joe hesitated as he swung his feet over the edge of the bed. "It's... really hard to describe. I can just *feel* what buttons to press when I want an emotional response from you. It's... hmm. Interesting, for certain."

Aten considered the man in front of him for a long moment. "I will say, your words feel smoother. As in, when you were speaking... I don't know, you just seemed to really *mean* what you were saying in a way that I haven't seen from you before. You seemed more... sincere?"

"Probably because my charisma jumped by ten points right before I dropped." Joe shrugged at the flabbergasted look Aten sent his way. "Apparently you need to use your characteristics in a specific way for a long period of time. I have no other information to share about this right now; if I find some, I'll let you know. What was decided in the meeting?"

"The meet...? Right." Aten shook himself out of his dreams of sudden stat increases. "We are going to push into getting the town to tier three. I have some people that have managed to get some building plans for three rare buildings, and one 'Special' building. These by themselves will probably be enough to get us to the next town rank."

"You found a *Special* ranked building?" Joe's eyebrows flew up, making it look like agitated caterpillars were skittering across his bald head. "What does it-"

"Don't get too excited. The Rare buildings are more useful than the Special." Aten shook his head. "It's a luxury building. No strategic value, it's just a quality-of-life thing. It'll help with morale and such, give a few non-combat players a job."

"What actually *is* it? I need details, Aten! Do we have the needed materials to make it?" Joe was practically salivating over the thought of all that juicy class experience.

"I think we do. It's an open-air bathhouse, Japanese-style. It looks pretty cool, and it apparently gives a bonus to durability and characteristic training after using it. Minor things in the short term, *really* important in the long run." Aten shrugged as he described the structure. "Honestly, I'd be really excited about it if we weren't caught up in a propaganda war right now."

"I'm still pretty excited about it." Joe admitted after thinking through the benefits. "We only know for sure that the other guilds *are* going to come after us; we don't know *when*. If there is a chance for us to raise our base characteristics by a large amount, we could take the others completely by surprise. Something that has been really drilled into my head during my time here: only intelligent planning and preparation are a match for absolute strength. If we have *both* strength and craftiness, we are going to be too hard of a nut to crack. Eventually, they will have to give up."

"Interesting. You know, we won't even be trapped in here during a siege, thanks to the fast-travel system in the temple." Aten scratched his chin and contemplated the ceiling. "I know that we have a lot to do, you especially, but please keep an eye toward the development of our town. We're frantically bringing in as many supplies as we can so that we can get the buildings all set up, mainly because we think that there will be a huge reward when we get the town to the third rank."

"What makes you think that?" Joe didn't want to miss out on whatever rewards might be offered, but he didn't want to get his hopes up. He had found that when he worked, and did his best, that had to be reward enough. Then, if there *was* a big reward, it was amazing. Otherwise, when he expected huge rewards, the best thing that could happen was that he would meet his own expectations. Most of the time, he *wouldn't* meet his own expectations, and that was crushing over time.

Aten knew what Joe was really asking, "Data. Pure data. There are records of the kingdom's establishment and all of the outlying towns that it developed. Beyond that, our spies are keeping tabs on anyone else that is building up a town. All of them are also *frantically* building up their towns in an attempt to get to town level three, and they attacked us and demanded that we stop progressing. All of this matches up with our own research into the subject. With all of this combined, our guild is *certain* that something will happen at that town level three."

"Another thing: there is a reason we want you to build up our town as fast as possible. The threats came only after we reached town level two and we were showing no signs of slowing down. Our intelligence says that if we sprint at the next town level, they are certain we can force our enemies to play their hand before they are ready." Aten was staring into the distance, and he heaved a great sigh before turning back to Joe. "The longer we wait, the more time they will have to prepare for us. If there is anything. *Anything*… that we can do in order to make you more productive, know that you have the full might of the guild behind you."

Joe knew that Aten was being extremely serious, but he still couldn't help himself. "Aten, I already told you, I know we're close, but I don't think that we're *that* close."

Aten started tapping his foot impatiently. "Joe, I will put you through that wall, then make *you* repair it."

"Oh, look at all the work I need to do." Joe planted his feet on the floor and rushed out of the room, pretending to be afraid. When he reached the hallway, he started sprinting, shouting over his shoulder, "Aten, I don't *like* you like that! You're just going to have to find someone else!"

"*Joe*! Get back here!" Aten barreled out of the room, playing right into Joe's trap, but Joe was already sending mana to his feet with every step; he was *long* gone.

CHAPTER FORTY-TWO

With public opinion turning against them, the Wanderer's Guild started having a rough time. At four in the morning the day after the battle, hunting parties were sent to respawn in the woods near Towny McTownface. By seven in the morning, it was discovered that player-run shops in and around Ardania had started increasing their prices for guild members, and the cost of living for most members of The Wanderer's Guild started to climb.

These changes forced the guild members to begin frequenting non-player-character shops more frequently, which sold a much smaller variety of items, and at a lower quality. In retaliation, the guild instantly announced that they had plans to create their own general goods trading firm. The decisive reaction shocked the collective guild, but it also lit a flame in their hearts to know that their guild leaders had their long-term success in mind.

Just as Joe was finishing his morning coffee and puzzle cube training session, Mike appeared at his table. "Good morning, Joe!"

"Hello, Mike," Joe muttered as he stared at the puzzle cube.

He had been working on this for weeks, and it looked… it *looked* as though he had nearly completed it. There were just a few more…

Mike cheerfully handed over a large tube. "Here is the first of the blueprints that we were able to secure. This is a Rare building; a three-story trading house with a deep basement. The basement serves as a warehouse, the ground floor is for general goods, the second floor is hard-to-obtain items, and the third floor is an auction house!"

Joe looked at the silvery blueprint in awe. "I don't think I've actually seen a blueprint where each level serves a different purpose like this! I mean, I've built large buildings and such, but there is almost always a uniform purpose to them. This should be interesting… do we have everything we are going to need to build this guy? Ouch; I just realized that we need at least a Rare Core to make this…"

"Ah." Mike's face fell at Joe's words. "That could be an issue. I thought you could make things cheaper when you built them?"

Joe shook his head at Mike's hopeful tone. "Yes, but not to the extent you are thinking. I've tried that before. Though I won't need an entire Core to *build* the building, it needs to be the correct rarity. Core rarity determines the density of the power they hold."

Pulling out the perfectly square Uncommon Core he had taken from the elite Neigh-Bear, he set it next to a Common one. They were the same size, thanks to the new benefit of his spell, but the Uncommon one was so bright that it left retinal afterimages if they stared too long. "Think of them like batteries: no matter how many watch batteries you use, you could never start a car. Conversely, if you have a car battery, even if it has a low charge, it can get the engine running."

"Oh. Well, that actually made it pretty clear." Mike rubbed at his bristly chin. Clearly, he had not had a chance to shave this morning. Joe realized that was an unexpected benefit of his Baldy title: it was easy to get going in the morning. "I'll see what

I can do, but it might be a while before we can make that happen. I don't know if you heard, but we just found out that our guild members are getting overcharged at shops. The backlash for wiping out all those players has already started."

"Ah, that's the reason for the shop, then?"

"Exactly." Mike sunk a little closer to Joe as he spoke. "We were going to do this eventually anyway, since we need a proper place where people can buy things with guild contribution points. The Guild Hall really isn't set up for it, though this was intended as more of a… long term plan than anything else. However, if our hand is going to be forced, we are ready to make that move."

"Gotcha. I'll get this made into a ritual, but it'll be a side project until you tell me that we are getting close to having everything we need. Also, if we need a merchant or anything, go to the Odds and Ends shop. My mother runs it." Joe knew that the conversation was over, so he didn't mind when Mike started walking away without saying another word. The next task he wanted to complete was his strength and constitution training, so Joe spent the next fifty-four minutes on the training field as vindictive trainers dumped coals on him.

When that was done, Joe returned to the mess area, already sparklingly clean thanks to his Neutrality Aura, and drank a cup of coffee provided by Mate. Joe got the attention of one of the food vendors, and asked him to make sure that Joe moved after half an hour had passed. Seeing as Joe was sitting in a prime area to access the roasted venison, the vendor was only too happy to have an excuse to tell him to leave in a certain timeframe.

"Okay… gotta get a handle on this ability." Joe took a deep breath and centered himself. "Essence Cycle!"

The world shifted into grayscale, then darkened further and further. Soon, Joe was once more mesmerized by the titanic currents of power that invisibly surrounded all of them. His goal had been learning how to break out of the cycle on his own, but the fact of the matter was… it was too easy to get trapped. Half an hour passed in the blink of an eye for Joe, and he was soon being shaken by a man smelling of woodsmoke and meat. "'Scuse me, sir. Ya asked me to tell you to leave?"

"Ah, sure did." Joe stood on unsteady legs, having a difficult time adjusting back to reality. It was now about nine-thirty in the morning, and Joe was absolutely *starving,* even though he had eaten breakfast only three hours previously. "Can I say, you smell amazing? Please tell me that is from the food you serve, because I really don't want to believe anyone naturally smells like this."

"Ha!" The man chuckled as he switched to sales mode. "Come on over and try for yourself! Best breakfast is one that started out wild!"

Joe bought a large plate of meat, then looked at his stat sheet as he munched.

<u>Name: Joe '*Tatum's Chosen Legend*'</u> <u>Class: Mage (Actual: Rituarchitect)</u>
<u>Profession I: Tenured Scholar (Actual: Arcanologist)</u>
<u>Profession II: Ritualistic Alchemist</u>
Character Level: 17 Exp: 167,220 Exp to next level: 3,780
Rituarchitect Level: 7 Exp: 25,286 Exp to next level: 2,714
Hit Points: 633/633
Mana: 1,087/1,887 (679 Reserved)
Mana regen: 39.86/sec
Stamina: 627/627
Stamina regen: 5.89/sec

<u>Characteristic: Raw score (Modifier)</u>

Strength: 62 (2.12)
Dexterity: 75 (2.25)
Constitution: 63 (2.13)
Intelligence: 121 (3.21)
Wisdom: 95 (2.46)
Charisma (Dark): 70 (2.2)

Perception: 73 (2.23)
Luck: 45 (1.45)
Karmic Luck: +27

Joe saw some serious improvements, but had to pause a moment when he saw the increase to his class experience. “Where did that extra fifteen hundred…? Oh! The other apartment buildings. Right… I can't build anything right now. I haven't seen Daniella in days, and the Master Enchanter is busy until next week. Jake the Alchemist?”

Leaving the mess area behind, Joe soon arrived in Ardania, thanks to his fast-travel options. He walked over to the alchemist’s shop and waited for a short while as the customers browsed. When Jake was finally free, Joe struck up a conversation. “Hi, Jake! How are you?”

“Oh, fine. Just fine. Lots of people buying poisons for their weapons these days.” Jake looked Joe up and down. “Pretty sure that’s all thanks to you; they all seemed to have a grudge against the ‘tyrant guild’. Good money in it, if you are interested in helping me make poisons that they can use against you. Thoughts?”

“I’d… rather not?” Joe held up his hand as if to say ‘duh’. “I don’t want to be responsible for members of my guild dying?”

“Hmm. Shame. I suppose you are here for your next training session? It's been long enough that you should have absorbed the lessons from last time, so shall we have a test before we get started?” A puff of red powder rose from a tube that had been hidden in the wall and settled across Joe’s face. “What was the first rule of working with poisons and powders?”

Joe screamed as his health started to plummet. His face felt like it was on fire. He had been sprayed with mace back in his army days so that he could experience it for himself, but this was a dozen times worse. His hands slapped at his face, and he just *barely* managed to keep from touching his skin. “Gah…

pah… don't! Don't touch your face when working with components!"

"Close enough." Jake sprayed something on Joe's face, and it foamed into a bubble around Joe's head before vanishing entirely, along with the pain. "Always remember, you are going to get *something* on your hands or gloves. If you touch your face, it'll get into your system, and you *will* die. This will happen to you at some point, I can almost guarantee it, since you have not trained for this profession since you were a child. Still, at least you can come back after you mess up. It might even raise your skill level. Actually, let's give it a-"

"I was here for something *specific*." Joe spat out a mouthful of blood as he healed himself. "How did that get through my Exquisite Shell?"

"How does air get through it? Same concept." Jake waved his hand nonchalantly. "When you have been in the alchemy business as long as I have, you have to develop a few methods for killing grumpy Mages. If you do it in a spectacular enough fashion, the others tend to leave you alone."

"*Abyss*, that's dark, Jake." Joe swallowed at the careless way Jake talked about permanently murdering someone. "I was here today because I was hoping that you could help me with something. I found a cauldron, and I can't identify it."

"You *found* a cauldron?" Jake smiled faintly. "How cute. Let's see the overexaggerated cooking pot someone tricked you into taking, then."

Joe pulled the waist-height cauldron that he had gained in the Hallowed Lands out of his codpiece, smiling at the burnished-gold glow it let off. Jake's own smile vanished, and he leapt over the counter to look it over more closely. The silence stretched, and Joe was starting to think that Jake didn't know what it was. "Anything?"

Jake looked over at Joe, and it was clear that he was slowly putting away various bottles that he had pulled from the insides of his robes. "Joe, the only reason I haven't killed you so that I could claim this as mine is that I know you would only come back and take revenge when I was less prepared. So… instead, I'll buy this from you for one hundred and thirty thousand gold."

"What?"

"Fine, fine. Two hundred thousand."

"*What*?"

CHAPTER FORTY-THREE

"Come now, you admitted that you didn't know what this was. You have no way to use it to its full capacity. Sell it to me," Jake demanded calmly.

"Jake, tell me what it is, or I'm going to take it somewhere else and get it appraised." Joe replied quickly, reaching out to grab the cauldron.

"All that would achieve is you dying and this vanishing forever into the black market." Jake slapped Joe's hand away from the surface of the oversized metal bucket. "Fine. Listen, this is an authentic Morovian-metal cauldron. This… this is a true *Artifact.* I mean that both in terms of its quality, as well as its historical significance. It provides three functions. First, it cleans and neutralizes itself. Second, it can be used to prepare potions, powders, and pills at any rarity. Third, every *millimeter* can be set to reach only a specific temperature. This part could be a thousand degrees, and still freeze whatever touches it *here.*"

"An Artifact?" Joe's smile lit up the room. Even his most powerful book of rituals was only Artifact-ranked, and it contained war rituals that could starve a nation or reshape the terrain of a huge area. "Those functions seem nice, but they don't seem enough to make something an Artifact…?"

Jake stared at Joe with a flat expression, then let out a slow breath. "This is why you should give this item to me. You having this and wasting time making Novice and Beginner potions would be like a child finding a Radiant Core and using it to reach level ten ahead of their friends."

"I will explain the functions again, but *slower*." Jake held up a single scarred finger. "It cleans and neutralizes itself. *Perfectly*. I know that you have never seen the sludge that is created when a high-tier potion-making attempt fails, but the setback means days, or weeks, of cleaning. It neutralizes itself. That means that the only things in the cauldron are what you *want* in there. No *dust*. No *air*. *Nothing* beyond what is needed for the recipe. This *alone* makes it worthy of being an Artifact. But it still does *more*. It can prepare *any* rarity of alchemical goods. Most cauldrons can make potions within a difference of a single tier, meaning that there could *never* be a possibility of a critical success."

"Lastly, the perfect temperature control means that the *only* variables are our own motions and the quality of the goods we put into the cauldron. Knowing *exactly* what the temperature will be will increase the chances of success for a *Concoction* by thirty percent." Jake cocked his head to the side. "Do you know what that means for me? Any idea at all? What do you think my chances of creating a Concoction are, if *I* use this item to make them?"

"I… I have no idea."

"That's right; thirty point five percent." Jake slowly nodded as if Joe had been the one to speak. "I have a half of a percent chance to create a Concoction naturally. For *you*, this would bring your chances all the way up to negative twenty-nine percent, since you are at Beginner rank one."

Joe lunged forward, touched the cauldron, and stored it in his ring. Jake, who had been leaning on it and hugging it protectively, fell to the ground. "It seems that we need a different deal, if we are going to move forward. I'm not opposed to you having this cauldron. *But…*"

Jake was practically nose-to-nose with Joe as he waited for him to finish his statement. Joe nodded as he thought over the deal he wanted to make. "But… I would need you to become a crafter for my… no. For me directly. I have a land token, and I plan to use it to claim my own lands when we go to the next Zone. We already have a deal that I will bring you along when we create an area for our guild at the next Zone, and we can expand on that."

"I'll offer you at-cost for all items I can produce, and half market value for your guild," Jake offered instantly.

"For at least ten years," Joe sternly demanded. "Also, I will remain the owner of this cauldron, but you will have exclusive rights to use it so long as you train me *properly*. I understand that me using it would be wasteful, so I'll use something else. At the end of that time, we can renegotiate. Deal?"

"Almost." Jake stared greedily at the ring on Joe's hand where the cauldron had vanished. "A cauldron like that needs a proper home. You will need to build or buy a Unique or higher alchemy shop. So long as I have that, I am fine with the rest. My goal has always been to become the Alchemical Sage, and this cauldron may be the key to that. Really, it's too bad that you didn't have this before selecting your new profession. I would have recommended taking something else."

"No; even ten years is only a small portion of time. I need to know how to support myself fully, though I will happily rely on you when I can."

"Fair enough." Jake put out his hand, and they shook on the deal.

Quest updated: Homebrew. Jake the Alchemist has made a new deal with you! Make him a new workshop of at least Unique rarity in the next Zone where you make an outpost, and give him exclusive rights to use your cauldron for ten years. Time limit: 364:23:59:59 Reward: Profession (complete), 'at cost' alchemical goods, and first pick on produced goods, for ten years. Failure: Full hatred with Jake and other organizations, and you will be added to a 'Rob and kill on sight' list.

Joe blinked as he saw the changes in the quest. He had a year until it failed? He hadn't put that stipulation in! Jake cleared the criteria up hastily. "Now that I know that you have this cauldron, I can only hope that you will work quickly to ensure that I am able to *use* it. Otherwise, my desire to grow might overgrow my fear of retaliation."

"I see… in that case, shall we get to work? I'd love to do some training while I'm here." They did get to work, and Joe winced when he saw how roughly Jake was now treating his cauldron. Before, he had always treated it like a favored child, yet now he was carelessly whacking his whisk against the edges of it like it was a pan he had gotten in a garage sale. "Jake, easy! There is a long time between now and when you get an upgrade; treat your equipment correctly!"

"Hmm?" Jake realized what he was doing and yelped, patting his gigantic green cauldron sheepishly. "Indeed. Well. Let's get to work."

Over the next few hours, the two of them created various Trash-tier potions for Joe's rituals. Only once was Joe able to make a Common-ranked Ritual Strengthening potion.

Ritual Strengthening Potion (Elixir). Adds 1% effect to the main target of a completed ritual.

"Wait, it says that my potion is an Elixir?" Joe looked at the small amount of fluid he had been able to scoop out of the bottom of Jake's cauldron. "I don't understand."

"Oh, you made an Elixir already? You're progressing exceedingly quickly." Jake looked at the bottle, and held it up to the light. "Yes, that's an Elixir, alright."

"But it's a potion?" Joe tossed the small bottle into his ring storage space.

"Correct." Jake pulled out a list titled 'Alchemy for Dummies' at the top of the page, and handed it over. "Here is a reference guide. There are three different types of alchemical goods. Potions, powders, and pills. A 'potion' is actually a Trash-tier ranking, but it is so common that it became the name for all liquid alchemical goods."

"In terms of rarity, the rankings go: Potion, Elixir, Draught, Vial, Philter, Tonic, Brew, Ichor, Injection, and finally Concoction. These rankings are used on all alchemical goods. But..." Jake cracked his neck, sharply yanking his head to the side, "A *powder* is made by taking a potion, distilling and reducing it until all that is left is a powder. The failure rate for this is *astronomical*, as even a single degree difference can turn a success into a failure. Also, a powder can only be created by reducing a potion *two* ranks higher than the outcome of the powder."

Joe listened attentively, then waved at his list. "Then how could you ever make an Injection-rarity powder? That's not possible?"

"It is, but only by combining powders that have the same potency and composition." Jake gave Joe points for realizing that issue out of the gates. "Now, if you have a powder and a potion of the same ranking, which do you prefer?"

"The powder, clearly." Joe's words made Jake nod again. "Even though they are the same rarity, the powder will be as effective as a potion two ranks higher, yes?"

"Correct. Now, as for *pills*..." Jake shook his head. "The difficulty rises to an entirely new level. You need to combine powders of variable strength and effect in order to make a pill. I have never seen a recipe for a pill that reaches above the 'Vial' rank. In fact, I only know for certain that higher pills *exist*, because the King once gave a Philter-ranked - or 'Rare' rarity, if you go off the general rarity rankings - pill to a war hero, once upon a time. Part of the reason I want to go to a higher Zone is that there will be a higher chance of finding recipes that will allow me to increase my abilities."

Their conversation lapsed, and Joe focused on increasing his alchemical abilities once more. By the time he left the shop, he had increased his Ritualistic Alchemy skill to Beginner three. Even though it was only two ranks for over six hours of work, Joe's eyes were shining. He had even been able to make a Basic

Ritual Strengthening Elixir that increased the effects of a ritual by five percent! That was a five hundred percent increase over his first success! They had even accidentally added too much liquid silverleaf to an attempt and made an Elixir called 'Ritual Draught'.

The draught, when added to a ritual, would make the entire ritual into a *liquid*. The ritual, though fully prepared, would pause activation until the liquid was swallowed by someone. The best part? The target was set by drinking the ritual, so it was a perfect way of making food-related traps or things of a similar nature. They had spent over an hour attempting to replicate the potion, and now had a working recipe.

Of course, there was a trade-off for these Elixirs; they would only work on rituals at the same rank. That meant that these were only compatible with Beginner-ranked rituals, but… Joe sighed happily as he arrived home and placed the potions for sale in the Grand Ritual Hall. "It's a start."

CHAPTER FORTY-FOUR

Joe had started getting into a good routine again, and there had been no signs of an incoming attack. He and his team had managed a few more quests and test dungeon runs, and now that the curse on Alexis had been broken, team cohesion was moving slowly but surely higher. Three days had already passed, and Joe had managed to pull in another eight thousand experience, reaching level eighteen. During this time, the guild had been working to gather building materials and everything else that was needed to create a shop, while the public opinion of the Wanderer's Guild had continued to drop steadily.

This made it harder to purchase goods, of course, and it had subsequently slowed down many other aspects of their plan to rapidly base-build. For Joe, though, it had been a golden time for skill progression. He had been able to meet with the Master Enchanter early, had pushed his understanding of enchanting to Novice nine, and was *just* shy of being able to break into a new tier. Joe's teacher had informed him that bottlenecks were common, and the best way to push through them was to succeed at making something at the tier he was striving for.

Joe sighed deeply as he forced himself off the floor. His last try at his current ritual attempt had destroyed half of his Exquisite Shell and had embedded him in the wall of the salt mine where he practiced. There was a good chance that if he made them in the Grand Ritual Hall, he would succeed. There was an equal chance that he would damage a *lot* of other research that was in progress, and he didn't want to take that risk. Not when the results had continued to be so interesting.

Big_Mo was certainly running down the path of a Blood Ritualist; Joe had no doubt that the class existed. The man seemed to be fascinated by discovering the myriad uses of blood, and had even started conducting research into Ritualistic Alchemy on his own. His ritual designs were secret, to anyone except Joe, who helped him to refine them. Joe also guided them away from anything *truly* dark; so the rituals tended to be more in line with buffs and healing effects.

Hannah seemed to be following the path of a Macro Ritualist, with her focus being on terrain shaping and terraforming. Joe wasn't able to offer much in the way of designing the rituals, but he was able to smooth out some errors. Taka was going the opposite route, attempting to find the smallest things that could be changed. He had been fascinated by the ritual that transformed water into fire, and he seemed to be following his original plan of being a magical gunslinger. He had shared that he was planning to use rituals to densely enchant projectiles, which was the main reason that firearms were useless currently. There simply wasn't enough space on bullets to embed enchantments that could pass through magical defenses.

As for Kirby… she still wanted to be an evil overlord. Joe shook his head as he remembered her most recent ritual design, which was supposed to be a defensive ritual that blinded people with constant light. His head was swimming from the recent impact with the wall, so he sat on the salty floor and recalled their conversation.

"Kirby, you realize that you incorporated sections of the water conversion ritual here, right?"

"Yes!" Kirby had excitedly exclaimed. "With the refractive

quality, no matter *where* people look, the light will be right in their face!"

"Oh, Kirby." Joe had chuckled at her falling expression. "This is an effective, well-made ritual… which makes rainbows. Just rainbows. If it helps, they would be rainbows that you could see at night, or use to light up an area. If there are things like sporting events or concerts, this is something they would love to have. But, this is a lifestyle ritual, a tool of beautification. It is certainly not going to be effective in battle."

"There's no way to… I don't know, make it into a laser?" Kirby pleaded even as Joe shook his head 'no', and she sighed deeply. "Next time, for sure!"

That memory brought a smile to his face, and reminded him that sometimes his own failures would achieve unexpected results: such as the Ritual Draught. He hadn't been *trying* to make it, but he was glad he had. Joe even had a term for this sort of success: 'Failing Upward'. Joe pulled himself out of his thoughts and stood up, salt running off of his Exquisite Shell as he did so. "Time to be like Kirby! I have a goal, and I didn't get there. Next time… I will!"

After saying his words out loud and only getting an echo in reply, Joe approached the smoking crater that remained from his previous attempt and inspected the mess as well as his notifications.

Accessing ritual 'Featherfall'… accessed. Attempting to implement combined enchantment 'Proximity Activation' and 'isFalling'… variables are outside safe parameters.

Caution! Spell instability at 127.69 percent, mitigated by 58% personal spell stability to 69.69%. Heh. Spell instability has taken hold. System recommendation: run.

Joe groaned as he looked over the notifications. The time from the appearance of the first letter to the magic going out of control had been under a single second. "How the *abyss* am I supposed to fix a non-stable ritual if I don't get a chance to move? I-"

He stopped and closed his eyes. When he opened them, Joe

pulled up his skill sheet and read a line out loud that he had forgotten about. "'However, with Ritualistic Forging, you are able to create helpful items, totems, and eventually pylons that will aid in creating a stable environment for your rituals'. Of *course* I am able to do that. And, oh *look*, the skill is at Novice *one*."

If he had been in his room, and not in the bottom of a salt mine, he would have given up and flopped into bed. Instead, Joe pulled out his ritual design and went over it once again. His eyes flew back and forth, and after a few minutes, he still hadn't found a single mistake with the design. "If the design is correct, then the problem must be with the execution. It looks like I only have a thirty percent chance of making this ritual work right now… so. What can I do? Why am I talking to myself? Mate, come here, please."

His coffee elemental bubbled up and roiled around on Joe's arm for a moment, then seemed to focus on Joe. It was hard to tell for sure, since Mate's eyes were coffee beans, but it seemed to be starting at Joe and waiting. "Alright, Mate. I have two choices. Figure out how to increase spell stability, or get to a higher level in enchanting and brute-force it."

Mate didn't speak, though Joe *swore* that he had heard the creature speak before. Still, his beans seemed to be full of admiration; not only for Joe, but also for the idea that Joe should look into forging if he were going to go after his current pursuit. Joe smiled at Mate in reply, and soon the elemental vanished once more. Joe shook his head and felt like he was waking up. "Did I figure out how to read the emotions of coffee? Is that a thing?"

He didn't set out right away, instead taking the time to recreate his ritual, as well as spending a half hour carving out the Runes and geometric patterns necessary for the two Novice-ranked enchantments that he was trying to use in the ritual. Those were interesting to see, as they went *between* the ritual circles. Standard ritual circles contained everything *on* the lines of the circles themselves, and in comparison… Joe thought that ritual circles combined with the enchantments just looked cooler. He was glad that he was learning and gaining new abilities, even if the time and resource cost was high.

After everything was perfect *except* for the spell stability, Joe started skipping out of the cave system. If anyone came across the ritual, they would likely leave it alone. If not, it would explode and kill them. Almost a guarantee. If it *didn't* explode… Joe would thank them profusely. All in all, a safe bet. For him.

Joe had high hopes for his Ritualistic Forging skill, for multiple reasons. One, there were *many* more people that he could get to teach him. There were Expert-ranked smiths practically all over the place, especially in comparison to alchemists and enchanters. Two, he knew that there were going to be smiths that could train him within the area-of-effect of the Pathfinder's Hall. This meant that he would be able to benefit from the increased skill gain in the area, so this should be one of his fastest-growing Ritualist skills; at least at the start.

Third and finally, Joe was highly motivated and focused. If he were able to use his subskill of Ritualistic Forging and ignore having to work on something like nails or horseshoes, all the better. Since he didn't need to focus broadly, he could aim for deep and narrow skill growth. His eyes glowed as he thought about the ritual that he had just left on the ground behind him. Joe finally had a short-term, achievable goal: he was going to stabilize that ritual to at least fifty percent within three days.

CHAPTER FORTY-FIVE

Joe grumbled as he pounded on a bar of iron so that he could get it soft enough to pull into nails. "This is stupid and I'm going to fix this entire broken business model and its dumb face and-"

"Hey! The metal knows when you're treating it badly." The smith was a player that had worked with metal his entire life before coming to Eternium, and his skill level was already near the mid-Expert rank. It would be higher, but there was so much *more* to metalworking at the high levels. Things such as adding in magical materials, powdered Cores, and various flames all had an impact on the final result, so knowledge and experience was king. "I already took you in under protest, so you'd better not torture my metal."

The smith watched as Joe turned the metal and placed it back in the fire. "Hmm. Better, but your attitude sucks. This is why I have no interest in apprentices… ugh. You know, you could always just quit."

"Can't do it; then you get a spot in the guild for free, and I miss out on valuable training." Joe 'cheerfully' shot down the man's hopes. The guild had promised the smith a forge of his own in the town, so long as he was able to prove his ability; which included getting an apprentice all the way to the Journeyman Ranks. That was the highest that an Expert could train someone; they needed to be a Master in order to train someone into the Expert ranks.

"Whatever, kid. All I need to do is either get you to quit or reach a high enough skill level, and I think that I choose 'make you quit'." The man smirked and turned to leave.

Joe pulled the iron ingot out of the fire and nonchalantly made a comment that made the smith stop cold. "You *do* realize, I hope, that it is *very* likely that I am going to be the one that builds the forge you are going to use? An *interesting* part of the deal is that you were only promised a forge. Not a forge *above* Trash quality…"

As Joe walked out of the guild-only temporary forge six hours later, he was carrying eleven iron triangles that each increased the stability of a Novice-ranked ritual by two percent, so long as a prime-number amount was used. "These are so interesting! I mean, they don't help me right now, since I need at least a Beginner set, but I'm sure that someone in the Coven can use them!"

Under the effects of both the four times skill gain multiplier of his class, as well as the Pathfinder's Hall passive effect, on top of an Expert teaching him directly, Joe had been able to drop right into the middle of the Beginner ranks of Ritualistic Forging during his session.

Ritualistic Forging (Beginner V).

Joe was now *able* to create the items that he needed, but he needed to find a design that he could follow. He couldn't just make random shapes and hope for the best. He either needed to find or create a lore skill for his forging, or he needed to find someone that could help him locate existing designs. After storing the stabilizers into the Grand Ritual Hall for any of his Coven to use, Joe was caught by Bard before he could leave the building overall.

"Joe, yah gotta help me." Bard was panting, covered in blood, and clearly had been put through the ringer.

"Lay on Hands!" After casting the spell, Joe pulled Bard deeper into the building so that they wouldn't run into any surprises. "Bard… what's happening?"

"Ya know how ah've been stuck, been lookin for ah specialization that fit?" Bard wiped some blood off his face, pleased that he was no longer wincing when he did so. "Ah found one, but… there's ah requirement, and I made ah lotta people angry."

"What do you need from me?" Joe was ready to jump into the action, a fact not lost on Bard.

"This is… *ahem.* I need yah to give me permission to add Hansel to the rudimentary pantheon that yah got goin." Bard looked at his party leader pleadingly, knowing that it was a big ask. "I'll owe yah for ah long, long time, ah know. Still, please? There's nowhere else ah can set up an altar that the Bardic College can't find and destroy."

"*That's* who's after you?" Joe winced; the guild would *not* be happy if he turned the largest propaganda center in the Zone against them. "I don't know if that's a good idea, Bard. The repercussions against the guild as a whole could be devastating."

Bard had clearly known that the plea had been a long shot. "Ah'll… think of somethin' else…"

Joe watched as his teammate turned away from him, and Joe felt that the turning was going to be more symbolic than literal if he turned his friend away now. "No. Bard, to the abyss with it. What's one more enemy? They can just get in line, right?"

"Yah… yah *mean* it?" Bard whirled around and slammed his hand onto Joe's chest hard enough that he got a shadowy slap in return.

Skill increase: Retaliation of Shadows (Student 0). Slapping a friend to gain the next tier, nice. Really shows your character. You have found that there are things that matter more than waiting around to get hit! Now, you are going to be able to use this skill as a preemptive *retaliation! Bonus effect: When you are targeted by an attack of any kind, there is a 10+n% chance that Retaliation of Shadows will trigger for maximum skill damage against the attacker! They will still be hit by a regular retaliation if their attack lands!*

"Of *course* I mean it!" Joe read his notification and could barely breathe. *Now* the skill was starting to live up to its Legendary ranking! "How soon do you need the spot?"

"I have everythin' I need." Bard was deadly serious and highly focused. "If we get to the Temple, I can take ah spot right away."

"If?"

"Yeah, I had ah *ton* of assassins and the like after me." Bard sighed deeply in relief that Joe was going to help. "I lost 'em for ah bit, so... they're prolly at the Temple waitin' for me?"

"I assume that you were intentionally waiting to tell me this so that you had a higher chance of getting me to agree?" Joe gave Bard a piercing glare, to which the powerful Skald simply chuckled and admitted that Joe was onto him. "What do you need to do?"

"I have a small golden idol; just gotta drop it on an empty altar and it'll do the rest." Bard started hustling toward the Temple area, and Joe hurried to catch up to him. "Jus' so yah know, these guys sent Alexis ta respawn."

"*What*?"

"Yap. They told me tha' I either hand over the golden lute, or they'd kill 'er. They had captured her and a bunch of 'em had a sword to her neck." Bard growled at his memory. "She tol' me that I better finish the quest no matter what, then pressed one o' her mystery buttons and vanished behind a wall of poison. I saw her go grey on my party setup, but I know she took a bunch with her."

"Juggernauts, clear the temple area. If anyone refuses to go, cut them down." Joe called loudly. He knew that he didn't need to shout, but he did want to give fair warning to anyone that was listening. There was always a Juggernaut in the Temple area, and he had no issue with waiting a few minutes while any issues were dealt with. "No one attacks *my* team and gets away with it."

"*That was a warning blow. You will not get another.*" Hearing the inorganic voice of the Juggernaut, Joe pulled Bard to the side of the door just before it blasted open and chunks of dead person were tossed through. Bard looked at the mess, then looked at Joe with wide eyes as the sound of a blender came from the next room over.

"Yeah, it considers an attack where they don't die instantly to be a 'warning blow'." Joe shrugged as he explained. "I'm not a huge fan of that, but what am I going to do when *that* tells me it won't change?"

Joe waved at a Juggernaut that stepped heavily out of the Temple area and scanned the room. Its helmet locked on Bard, but Joe gave an order to let him through. After a brief pause, the Juggernaut nodded and spoke. "*Twenty-two hidden presences are approaching at high speed. While these people are fools for assuming that anything can be hidden from the sight of Occultatum, they are spread out and may enter the area through various means to circumvent the rules.*"

"What... what is it sayin'?" Bard swallowed nervously as the purple-glowing Runic Juggernaut loomed over them.

"As in, you can't understand the words, or what he is getting at?" Joe wondered idly.

"The meanin'. The words are... *very* clear." Bard shuffled along the wall to avoid becoming trapped by the huge figure.

Joe started walking normally, pulling Bard along with him. "He said that there were people in stealth coming through the Pathfinder's Hall, and that they were too spread out to deal with easily."

As soon as they were in the Temple proper, they rushed to one of the two remaining open altars, and Bard pulled a golden lute out of his bag. "Thank goodness. This sucker is *heavy*, and the blasted thing can't be put in a spatial bag!"

"Bard, is it *stolen*?" Joe stepped away in case the lute started to scream or something. "I've only seen quest items gained in unsavory ways not be able to be stored in spatial gear..."

"Only *technically* stolen," Bard grumbled as he slammed the lute onto the altar. "It's the artifact of a *deity*, I had a quest *from* him ta move it. People's 'property rules' can eat a giant turd."

The altar started shining a dark red, then brown. A deep, bone-chilling sensation emanated from the altar. Both Joe and Bard were forced to take a step back as the chill suddenly changed: a raging pillar of strange brown fire exploded from the altar. A deep, sonorous laughter erupted from the flame as a wave of fire rolled off the altar and swept through the Temple and into the Pathfinder's Hall, only parting to pass by Joe and Bard. Both remained locked in place, watching the fire with concerned expressions.

Screams echoed into the Temple as people caught in the flame were reduced to ashes; only staying alive long enough to feel as though they were purified in the most literal sense. Joe swallowed deeply, and glanced sidelong at Bard. "Are you *sure* this was a quest from the deity of *bards*? Not an evil god that tricked you into getting into our pantheon?"

"Joe, if I were tricked… how in the world would I know?" Bard managed to get out as the flame started collecting on top of the altar.

"Brown flames, sudden murder of a bunch of people?" Joe turned his attention to the fire once more. "Any of that making alarm bells go off?"

Bard didn't get a chance to answer as words shook the air around them, clearly originating from the altar that had just been activated.

"*Freedom! Hundreds of years of being stifled, and now I! Am! Free!*"

CHAPTER FORTY-SIX

"Now that ya mention it, Joe, I am getting ah vibe that somethin' mighta gone wrong," Bard mumbled as the flame finally finished transforming. A person now stood on the altar, and he danced around the surface without leaving the confines of the superheated stone. Hearing Bard's words, the being turned and stared down at them with a cold expression.

Upon seeing who had spoken, the man did a backflip off the altar and alighted in front of them; somehow landing facing them directly. "You! Bard! Oh, such an unfortunate name, but such a virtuous person! You've freed me from the forced seclusion and terrible offerings of the Bardic College! Quest complete in the most *spectacular* of fashions! Here, have a class upgrade! Specialization, whatever!"

Bard's eyes rolled up into his head and he slumped to the floor before Joe could catch him. Joe turned his attention to the deity that was now considering *him*, and gulped. "You're the owner of this building, huh? Let's see... pantheon... Oh? Occultatum is The Master of this pantheon? Bet he loves that, the old windbag. Oh! Tom's here! Hi, Tom!"

"*Tommulus*," came the grumpy reply from the red flame on Tommulus's altar.

"Millenia, and you still have that stick up your butt." The brown-flame deity smiled kindly all the while as he said this. There was no reply. "Hmm, hmm, haa. Ritualist, Rituarchitect, oh, a Scholar-slash-occultist? Interesting, not unexpected. Moving into blacksmithing and alchemy recently? You mean professions that rely heavily on earth, wind, and fire? That's gonna be hard with your affinities so heavily skewed toward infer… that is, *darkness* and water. Well, you deserve a reward too; perhaps I can help with that?"

"I'm sorry, so sorry to interrupt; who are you?" Joe managed to get out after his Neutrality Aura moistened his mouth enough for him to speak again.

"What? I'm Hans! The deity Hansel? Lord of Bards?" Hansel shook his head and muttered about education standards slipping. "Oh, wait! This is *good*! The College kept me so hidden that there isn't a great record of my abilities! I can rebrand myself! Thanks, little spellweaver!"

A new Deity has joined your pantheon: Hansel, Greater Deity of Bards, Teachers, and Political Assassins. There is a great synergy between Hansel and Tommulus, resulting in a 20% bonus to a student's skill gain when being taught by a teacher in the area of effect of Pathfinder's Hall (Temple).

You have gained +2,222.22 reputation with Hansel! New reputation rank: Friendly.

"Alright, here is a little reward for you, Joe! Sorry about the pain, but it'll be worth it. Opening affinity channels is *always* worth it when you survive the process!"

"Wait, I-" Joe couldn't get any other words out before brown fire surrounded him and started burrowing into him. His clothes seemed to scream, and Hansel winced.

"Oh, sorry about that. You'll need new clothes, but it's still worth it!" Then, either Hans vanished or Joe passed out, because Joe was suddenly looking up at the ceiling and blinking.

Class restrictions on fire usage removed! No longer will you have -50% to skill gain and usage when using fire-based skills!

Perfect Fire Affinity gained! You now have a bonus 100% skill gain and usage when using fire-based skills!

Durability limit reached! Set equipment Wise Man's Wardrobe has been totally destroyed!

Durability limit reached! Mystic Theurge Staff destroyed!

Joe sat up and realized that he was naked except for his Spatial Codpiece. *That* wouldn't do. Sending his thoughts into his storage, he pulled out the only clothing he had; wrapping himself in the Cloak of Liquid Darkness. "Been a while since I wore you, hasn't it? Well… better to look wet than to be walking around like gladiator Tarzan."

"Bardbarian?" Bard sat bolt upright. "I'm a Bardbarian! I finally unlocked a specialization! Joe! I have a clear path to my second specialization as well! I'll eventually be able to be a *Lore Keeper*!"

"That's-"

"Even better than I had hoped!" Bard was on his feet now, and he slapped a hand on Hansel's altar. "You're a good man, Hansel! Abyss *right*, I'll be taking that path to the next tier with you. No worries; I'll make sure to spread around the story we came up with!"

A brown flame, more like a spark, appeared and stabilized above the altar. It was similar to Tommulus's altar in appearance now, though the coloration was different. Joe also realized that soft music was now playing in the Temple, shifting the still and silent nearly-forested area into a relaxing and peaceful area for seclusion and self-reflection. A good upgrade overall, even without all the other bonuses they had gained.

Joe was *thrilled* with the bonus that adding Hansel to the pantheon had provided. With a twenty percent boost to teacher-student skill gains, Towny McTownface would eventually become the center of learning for every craft, trade, and profession in the entire Zone.

The Rituarchitect was shaken from his internal dialogue as

Bard slapped a binder into his hands. "Here ya go, Joe! Present from Hans, as recompense for 'leaving you more naked than the day you came into this world'. Apparently he really overstepped his bounds in his excitement? Is that why you're dressed differently? What, ah… did I miss while unconscious? Know what…? Nevermind. Hansel says to wait on using it for another twenty-seven fourteen? He didn't tell me what that meant."

"I don't know either - wait." Joe pulled open his character sheet and looked at the information, his eyes going wide. "That's the exact amount of experience I need to get my class to level eight. Let me inspect this…"

Item gained: Golden Path Advancement. Increase either character or class level by two levels.

"Celestial snapdragons," Joe sputtered as he realized what the bonus meant. "What is he even talking about, saving it only 'til my next class level? He's outta his mind. I'm saving this until I'm level forty-eight! It says two levels, it says nothing about restrictions! Wait, there's more to the description…"

All experience gained for the selection will need to be repaid, and will be absorbed as it is gained.

"Ah." Joe shrugged at that. "Okay, I'll need to repay the experience, so what?"

Bard spoke up as they were walking out of the Temple together. "Well, isn't it harder to gain experience at higher levels? You'll be getting less experience for doing anything, unless you are doing things that are challenging for higher level stuff. Sounds like that actually has *quite* the drawback."

"Well, I'm gonna…" Joe tossed his hands in the air in frustration. "Whatever! We'll see what happens. Also, what's wrong with your voice?"

"I am uncertain what you mean, Joe." Bard replied clearly.

"That! You still have your accent, but you're speaking with a coherent accent now!" Joe had nothing else to get angry about right now, Bard was shooting down his plans too easily.

A wide grin spread across Bard's face. "Why, I am certain that I have no idea what you mean! Unless you are talking about the Silver Tongue ability I gained as a Bardbarian that makes my words smooth? I mean, I only got a bonus of ten charisma and dexterity!"

"Does dexterity help with speaking?" Joe rolled his eyes as the obvious question popped out of his mouth. "Never mind; I have no interest in hearing about how nimble your tongue is now."

Bard's grin smoothly transitioned to smug, and Joe snorted at the fact that he had caught on to what Bard was about to say. "Okay, I still have a lot of work to do, Bard. I need to get going, and you should go find out when Alexis will come back."

"Sounds good. I have to figure out what my new responsibilities are as the Champion of Hansel, anyway!" Bard waved and jogged off while chanting a movement speed enhancing spell.

"Interesting." Joe watched Bard run off. "Two Champions in a party… that'll be a tasty target for anyone needing to grind Divine Energy. Makes me wonder if-"

"Joe! There you are!" Aten himself was jogging over this time; he hadn't sent Mike as he usually did. "The Bardic College has launched an attack against us, and-"

"It's already taken care of, Aten." Joe waved at the massive building behind him. "We killed off like twenty assassins and such. They should be all cleared out."

"No, Joe." Aten shook his head gravely. "Whatever else you had to deal with, this is different. The Bardic College has openly stated its support for the assault against us, and even now they are ordering all their members to start singing against us in all taverns and public areas. Now that a major power has publicly announced their support, half a dozen other powers have joined in as well. A huge mob is turning into a huge, well-funded, well-trained army."

"What does this mean? Why is this happening?" Joe was stunned by this turn of events. He never expected that the Bardic College would act so swiftly; they wouldn't be so petty as to go to war over this, right? Surely there had to be more to it than Bard getting away with an idol of Hansel?

"Something about one of their greatest treasures and secrets being stolen." Aten lifted his hands in confusion, and Joe maintained a flat expression. Welp. Guess the College *could* be that petty. "At the rate people are joining up, and given their lack of resources - especially food - the next time we are attacked is going to be tomorrow; the day after at the latest. Is there *any* way that you might be able to help us get ready for this attack, or for the seige?"

Joe contemplated the path advancement and closed his eyes. Hansel had *known* that this would happen; there was no way he had been given that item just because his clothes got destroyed. Ugh... gods and their games... Joe locked eyes with Aten, and nodded sharply.

"Maybe."

CHAPTER FORTY-SEVEN

"So is there a *reason* that Aten made me come with you?" Mike grumpily demanded as Joe and several other people with extremely high carrying capacity walked deep into Ardania. "I know that you said you needed help, but why should the Vice Guild Leader have to be the one that helps you with a secret task?"

Joe stopped dead in his tracks and turned to Mike. "Listen. Do you remember when I talked to the guild about buying up all the items and materials that they could? How I really *pressed* the issue, and the board of directors vetoed it until they saw that prices were starting to climb? How the guild *missed out* because they didn't listen to a basic economics lesson?"

"I do, and I was the one who went in and forced that decision through, lest you forget." Mike raised a hand to calm Joe. "We missed the best opportunities, but we came in and walked away with a large profit. I've been on your side for all of that."

"Yeah, well." Joe ran a hand over his bald head. "I'm the reason that the guild missed out on all the really good stuff. When I first got to Ardania, I had a hundred thousand gold with me. Since then, I've spent *most* of that on goods. Through proxies, of course. My mother was able to get merchant discounts, Jess was able to put together lists of everything she could think of that I'd need, and I gave both of them access to my accounts. In fact, I'm just about broke right now, to the point that I can't even buy replacements for the gear I lost today."

"What? Really?" Mike's face lit up. "We'd be *happy* to help you out by buying what I assume is building materials?"

"And you just found out why you're here." Joe handed over a parchment with Aten's signature on it. "I'm selling everything we need, at double what I bought it for, to the guild."

"What? What about all the discounts you were talking about?" Mike's left eye twitched as he looked at the authorization order from Aten. "*Double* what you paid for them? I *highly* doubt-"

"Here is the expense report, and everything you can expect for cost." Joe handed over a full scroll full of numbers and items. "On the left is what I'm willing to sell to the guild, followed by the *price*. The column after that is current market value, and the final one is our estimate on what it would cost the *guild* to buy these things with our reputation as it is."

Mike scanned the document, his face paling. "Has the price on these cured oak beams *really* quintupled?"

"You are free to run to the market and confirm it for yourself." Joe told him directly. "Remember, Mike. A *billion people* were dropped into an area that was previously barely supporting a *quarter* of that. A single loaf of fresh bread is getting close to a silver right now."

They kept walking as Mike kept reading. "Do you really have all of these things?"

"What you have in your hand is the list of all things in my warehouse that are for sale, given to me by my mother. She is also the one that listed out the market value on each item. If there is a more accurate list in all of Ardania, the only place you would find it would be her shop." Joe smiled as he thought of his mother, and her relationship with Blas. He had never seen her happier than she was now, and it blew him away how well she had settled into a life in Eternium. "We're here, so let's put these guys to work. Make sure to keep a proper accounting of everything they carry, because if we don't use it and it goes missing, you're still on the hook for paying for it."

"Won't be an issue, Joe." Mike nodded at the people with them. "These are some of the guild's most trustworthy people. Besides that, none of them would want to lose their position, benefits, free food, and affordable housing over *building* supplies!"

Joe decided not to comment on the fact that Mike was being louder than conversational volume. 'Trustworthy' members *indeed*. The shadows in the area were deep enough that Mike couldn't see their expressions, but Joe clearly saw them grimace. He hoped that it was only because they were having their honor called out so blatantly, but either way, they simply and silently got to work. Mike supervised the men as wood, cut stone, crates of nails, fashioned doors, and pallets of shingles were loaded into storage devices. Mike looked sidelong at Joe when they got to the shingles, but Joe was innocently looking away.

Joe's eyes suddenly widened and his head snapped around to focus on Mike. "Wait a second… we get *benefits*?"

"*They* get benefits."

The talking ended, and everyone set to work. Thanks to the spatial bags, rings, packs, or other storage devices being used, the entire process took under an hour to complete. In fact, it would have gone much faster if they hadn't needed to check every item and write it down. Eventually, and reluctantly, Mike had to call everyone to a halt. "That should be enough for our purposes… as much as I want it *all*, this is a shop and we need to pay for whatever we take. We *do* still have to pay for it, right?"

Joe rolled his eyes at the hopeful question. "*Yes*, Mike. Unless I can just walk into the guild treasury and clean it out for free as a 'reward' after an extra large raid?"

"Fine, I see your point." Mike sighed and the group started walking out of the building. Realizing that Joe wasn't joining them, Mike gave him a questioning look.

"I have some things I need to get while I'm here. I'll see you all back at the guild." Joe closed the warehouse doors, and turned to look at the huge stacks of *stuff*. Even with all the things that the guild had just bought, the room was still three-quarters full. Not everything was building supplies; about one-twentieth of it was components, rare materials, and various objects of interest. Even so, at the time of purchase, those articles had cost as much or more than the significantly larger portion of building supplies that filled the warehouse.

Joe started walking through the structure; awkwardly pushing his hips forward and letting the stacks be swallowed into his Codpiece of Holding. Since he was starting near the bottom of each pile, everything fell straight down and was pulled in directly. There were a few times when a corner came down awkwardly and landed on him, but all in all, it was a *very* efficient method of grabbing everything. Besides, he was able to restore any pulverized bones after a little screaming and a quick spell. After that, he pumped mana into his recently-shattered Exquisite Shell and kept going.

In about an hour, he was able to clear the entire warehouse simply by walking through it and directing his codpiece accordingly. Joe scanned the empty space and nodded sadly. This was the first place he had really done research on rituals. Right over there, Joe had captured Cel and kept him in a ritual of containment while testing healing spells on him. Still, it was time to let go of this place. "I'll miss our times together, Potato."

Joe hadn't been joking when he told Mike that he couldn't currently afford to replace his gear. Jess had run up to him while he had been talking to Aten, handed him a foreclosure notice, then took him aside to let him know that she and his mother had spent every single gold he had put in the bank. At first, Joe wasn't sure how to react, but everything had worked out pretty well. By selling five buildings' worth of raw material, he should have enough to get by until he and his team were adventuring heavily again.

Either way, he only had until midnight to clear out the building before the owner of the Odds and Ends shop would be forced to confiscate all his goods. His mother, the owner, had tried to figure a way around it, but the kingdom used royal authority to purchase all the land in this area. Though Joe had a lease, it was annulled and he had made a bit of money back. Joe looked down at his spatial storage device and grinned while shaking his head. "I have made a warehouse out of my junk."

He left the building behind and traveled back through Ardania to the town square. At this time of the night, at least there was no one recruiting for the destruction of his guild. No one was singing about their black hearts or lack of 'charity' either. Joe snorted at that; his guild gave out more free food than any other. He pulled open his quest list and reviewed the task his guild had given him.

Quest completed: Feed the People! The greenhouse that you have created is now able to support the nutrition requirements of ten thousand people! Good thing they can eat vegetables, right? Reward: 10,000 guild contribution points!

Quest gained: Feed the People II. Figure out a way to stretch resources enough to support 25,000 people! Reward: Guild contribution points, reputation increase with the people being fed! Failure: reputation decrease with the guild. Time limit: 30:18:23:33.

"Thirty days to figure out how to feed twenty-five thousand people? Guess I'm gonna take a hit to my reputation unless I flood the greenhouse with monsters and make it a food dungeon. Forget *this.*" Joe realized that he was getting grumpy from sleep deprivation, so he went back to the guild to get some shuteye.

Most pressing, Joe needed to get rolling on making some buildings. Still, even though he had *so* much to do the next day, he ignored his spinning thoughts and fell asleep as soon as his head hit the pillow. All too soon, *far* too soon, he was awakened by the rising sun streaming onto his face. Joe grumpily covered his eyes and shook a fist at the window.

"I need to figure out who in this world makes curtains, and then put them on retainer."

CHAPTER FORTY-EIGHT

"That's the last of the spare buildings." Joe wiped his face with a towel as he landed on the ground with the rest of the members of his Coven. "All that we have to do now is wait until we have a higher-grade Core, and we can get the main bathhouse up and running."

"Can I say, that sounds super out of place?" Hannah offered seriously. "You said that it's an open air Japanese-style bathhouse, right? That makes no sense with the rest of our architecture being… I don't know, modern-medieval?"

"I don't think the guild cares about making everything look the same, Hannah," Kirby joined in. "Everyone that's at the top of the rankings was a gamer at some point, and all they care about is having the best stats and functionality. That's why you see people dressed in patchwork gear. It's the best that they have to offer at that point in time."

"There's a word for that, right?" Big_Mo seemed to be wracking his memory.

"Hobo?" Hannah scoffed at the thought. Joe hadn't realized until just then, but her outfit was perfectly coordinated in both function and form. Set equipment?

"That's it!" Big_Mo snapped his fingers and beamed. "Murderhobo! Because they show up looking like a hobo, but they are way stronger than anything they are killing because of it."

Mike interrupted their conversation by strutting over with a huge smile on his face. A stack of papers appeared in his hand, and they vanished into Joe's ring as soon as they were handed over. "Payment for goods. It's all there. But, that's not what I'm excited about!"

The influx of cash was what *Joe* was excited about; wearing only a cloak and codpiece was getting a little… drafty. Especially when he was floating in the air and being spun around by his rituals. He was *far* too pale to be showing off his thighs to the general population. 'Day glow Joe' wasn't his favorite nickname. Mike reached into a bag and handed over a small lockbox. "We got the Core. The bathhouse can go up."

"That'll push us over the edge, won't it?" Joe gulped and stared at the box in Mike's hand. There had to be at least a 'Special' Core in there, which would be worth at least ten thousand experience to absorb. He couldn't imagine how much it was worth in the city. Even though he could earn the same amount by grinding challenging monsters for a couple of days, there were *many* people who would rather purchase than fight; and *everyone* was trying to get a leg up on the competition.

"I think so." Mike took a deep breath and looked at the box. "The town will reach tier three, and there should be one abyss of a benefit waiting for us. Remember, tier five is all we can reach before we switch to a city, and we need permission from the Royal family to do so."

"I think I know someone who can get you the chance to ask permission." Joe winked at Mike, who returned a wan smile.

"Mmm. Sorry, I'm excited, but can we go and make this building? If it doesn't seem to be worth the wait and the money…" Mike swallowed deeply while nodding nervously, "then a *whole* lot of risks that I've taken are going to come back to bite me in the butt."

"You're really that concerned?" Joe waved to his Coven, and

they all started walking excitedly toward the center of town. Today was a *great* day for experience and skill gain.

Mike was quiet for a long minute. "I have made town development my main issue as Vice Leader. I have spent so much of our money, and slowed down the progress of *so* much else… if we don't see a good return, I'm almost guaranteed to be voted out."

"It's not that easy to vote someone out though, right? I know Aten was able to retain his position pretty easily." They had only another few minutes, so Joe tried to push for as much information as possible.

"His position is determined by the guild at large. Any living guild member in the game at the time of a vote gets their chance to speak up. Sorry, in the world; not a game." Mike stood straighter. "Until we make the transition to a Sect, and Aten has more power than this current model allows him, my position is at the leisure of the council and Guild… Commander Aten. They can try to fire me, and he can veto it, but they can overrule him if they vote unanimously. After we are a Sect, only Aten can give me the boot, and I've proven myself to be too indispensable for that to ever happen."

The picture was starting to become clear to Joe. "So, if this doesn't pay off in a big way, they are going to see all of your actions as self-serving to the extreme. They will think that you are just trying to solidify your position, and are willing to put the guild at risk to make it happen."

"Pretty much." Mike didn't sigh, but he *did* let out a long, low breath. The clear risk that this man was taking made Joe want to do something nice for him, but he had only managed to get his ritual subskills to the Beginner ranks. Even though he wanted to do something special for this building as it went up, it was going to be 'Unique' ranked. Joe had no potions, stabilizers, enchantments, or activateable effects that he could use to guarantee anything extra.

"Well, the ritual is ready." Joe didn't pull it out of his ring yet; that would be a waste of time. He retrieved his Rituarchitect Survey Grid and started inputting the measurements. Then he *did* pull out the ritual, because he remembered that he could just link the two and he would get an exact illusion of the building. Joe was glad he hadn't said anything out loud; he could have embarrassed himself there.

The illusion filled the southeast courtyard almost entirely, and there should have been plenty of room for it. Still, no matter how he twisted or refined the shape, it remained red. Joe looked at the ritual again, trying to locate the issue. "Hmm."

"What's the matter?" Mike questioned him anxiously.

"Ya know, I just don't know?" Joe walked away from the area, and the illusion went with him. When he was about twenty yards further south, but not yet at the wall, the illusion turned green, indicating that the building could be built there. "What's different about that spot?"

Taka called over just before Joe was about to ask for soil samples or something, "What about these water wells and stuff?"

Facepalming hard enough that his Exquisite Shell shimmered more than usual, Joe groaned. "That would do it. Rituals are designed to do a certain thing at a time: this can't raze and raise at the same time. "Yeah, good catch, Taka. Mike can we get those knocked down, please?"

Joe spent the next short while playing poker with the Coven members as a few strongmen were called over to knock down and carry away with the previous simple structures. Normally, it was considered bad form to gamble with people that worked for you, but all of them took the opportunity to work on their luck characteristic after Kirby pulled out the cards. By the time things were ready to progress, Robert had quietly won nearly a gold from the others.

Finally, they were ready to get the bathhouse in place. Joe checked his Rituarchitect Survey Grid once more, and this time, everything flashed green. "Excellent… now all we need is about thirty more people to participate."

"What?" Mike shook his head. "Joe, that's really short notice. I thought you said you had everything you needed."

"I do. I already know where we are going to get all the people that we need to fill this ritual." Joe pointed sharply at the Guildhall. "Most of the people in there are working with really high intelligence, which means big mana pools. You need to evacuate the building anyway, because the last time the town went up a level, it chucked everyone out of there. Pretty violently, too."

"You planned this?" Mike's eyes narrowed as it clicked in his head. "I see… you didn't remind us to evac, because then there wouldn't be a high enough number of people that stayed around. Since they are all so clustered, we can grab them and put them to work. Sneaky. I like it, but I'm sure the highly intelligent people that are working the guild's office jobs will not approve, and will figure out what you're up to."

"Not a problem, just have them come on out!" Joe enthusiastically promised Mike. The older man peered at Joe over the top of his glasses, but still did as he asked. Soon, people were flooding out of the main building and gathering in the courtyard. After ten minutes, no one else emerged. Joe lifted his hands and shouted to get their attention. "Hello, everyone! I'm Joe, in case we haven't met, and these are my… coworkers! Taka, Robert, Big_Mo, Hannah, and Kirby! We are going to be doing some work, and I need some volunteers."

There was no reply beyond scathing or confused looks, so Joe pressed on. "We are going to build a giant bathhouse right here, and it should take under ten minutes to finish. If you volunteer, here are the benefits: your mana resource will unlock, if it hasn't already. You may get an additional benefit for doing it this way, though it does hurt a little. Next, I'll make sure you get priority access to the bathhouse. It is going to be a combo of a giant pool, baths, and soaking areas. Very relaxing, and close to work for you!"

A few people stood forward right away, smiling at the offer.

Not enough. "Anyone else? I need twenty at least, no... twenty-three, I need a prime number and only have six right now."

No more people stepped out. Mike took over for Joe, "You will also get contribution points, as many as working a full day."

More people joined the group: an extra day's worth of pay was a good motivator. Mike sighed and waved his hand. "If you participate, and the Guildhall gets larger, you get to choose your new seat, within reason. After that, you get the day off with full pay, or extra contribution points. Everyone else goes back to work."

Joe couldn't allow all the people to join him now. Almost everyone had jumped at the chance to get a day off. He had to decline a large amount of people, but still ended up with a total of thirty-seven participants, including himself. Getting them all arranged was like herding cats, but soon everything was ready. The ritual unfurled, and Joe took a deep breath to begin the needed chanting.

"*Enemy sighted*!" The bellow rang through the area as Jay the guard ran into the area at top speed. "There's a *huge* army coming through the woods!"

Mike took charge. "How far out?"

"Thirty minutes... tops." Jay heaved the reply as he bent over to catch his breath.

"How did they get so close? Where are our scouts?" Mike demanded as his fists clenched.

"Dead, all dead. They have some *really* high-powered assassins with them." Jay coughed and stood tall as his stamina reached an acceptable level. "Only reason we have *this* much warning is because someone used a voice transmission spell. They said that the army was sneaking through the woods and avoiding the roads, then screamed something about clowns attacking them."

"Clowns?" Mike reeled backward with his hands in the air. "What kind of malarkey is... Joe?"

"Not clowns." Joe was as white as fresh snow. "*Jesters*. It must be. High-powered assassins that look like clowns? It's gotta be… but how?"

"There's no time for this." Mike started snapping orders, but Joe stopped him with a shout.

"Mike, we need to build this *now*. We need whatever the reward is before they get here." Joe locked eyes with Mike. "The only reason for them to be attacking us now is that they had someone watching the progress. It's too quiet otherwise; *someone* would have known about it."

There was silence as Mike thought over his words, before reaching a snap decision. "Do it."

Joe collected mana around his hand and slapped his palm on the ritual diagram before anyone could leave their position. "*Relinquo sordes*!"

CHAPTER FORTY-NINE

There was an almost unbroken circle of vomit around the sparkling new bathhouse. The office workers that had been on the outermost ring had been spun so quickly that a few had passed out from the g-forces that they had been subjected to; not to mention that most of them were the people that had their mana forcibly opened. Joe was watching and hoping… if his characteristic was going to be applied to the building it would be any second now.

Structure 'Bathhouse (Unique)' absorbed a portion of the mana and spare materials invested in the ritual and has transformed into 'Filthy Bathhouse (Unique)'. All accumulated filth in the bathhouse will be evenly applied to all water in the soaking and bathing areas. Without a powerful filtration system, keeping this building clean will be a monumental task.

Class experience gained: 3000.

The ritual diagram turned to ash in Joe's hands, and he cursed darkly. No second chances on this building, and any new scan of it would simply give him a copy of the 'filthy' version. He felt like his class 'bonus' had just critically failed him, and he was starting to resent that he couldn't turn it off. So far it only made things more dangerous or far worse. Still, he had achieved what he was after.

Rituarchitect has reached level 8! Congratulations, make sure to follow your chosen path until the end!

Joe didn't even get a chance to look over the *positive* bonuses the bathhouse gave before he was knocked off his feet by one small but powerful shockwave, followed by another, and again. Everyone within fifty yards of the Guild Hall was continuously toppled as a tremendous amount of power gathered above the Hall.

Zone alert! Towny McTownface, the town of the Noble Guild 'The Wanderer's' has reached town rank three! The guild has gained 1,000 reputation with Ardania for doing their part to take care of the land and the people in it!

Guild notification: Towny McTownface has reached town rank three! As this town has been built from scratch by the guild 'The Wanderer's', the town and guild have earned a symbiotic bonus. Calculating bonuses based upon the buildings that have been added into the town… Calculating… Cal… culating.

Buildings scanned. Current buildings: 1 Artifact. 3 Unique. 2 Special Rare. 5 Rare. 21 Uncommon. 4 Common. 0 Trash. Normalizing… analyzing weighted bell curve. Weighted bell curve results: Special Rare.

Towny McTownface has earned a Special Rare reward building for all of the hard work that has gone into making an exceptional town. Attempting to apply to the highest graded building… failed. Artifact too potent to apply substandard reward. Applying to a secondary target. Success. Interfacing with guild bonus 'Ruthless Defenders'. Guild Hall is gaining an additional bonus: Town Aegis.

Town Aegis: once a month, the owner of the town can activate a defensive formation that makes all buildings within town limits immune to damage for 24 hours.

Secondary effect: any damage dealt to members of the guild 'The Wanderer's' within town limits will not be applied, instead rebounding upon the attacker for double the damage dealt.

Joe alone was also shown another small message, and frankly it seemed overly passive-aggressive.

This effect is not part *of the Guild Hall, it is an added bonus that is not recreatable without significant knowledge of enchanting or related fields of work.*

Mike's eyes were roving across text that was invisible to Joe, though he assumed that it would be something similar to his own notification. "Well now, that is certainly going to make this place easier to defend during an attack. A siege will still hurt, but at a time of our choosing, we could all just go to bed and have a luxurious day off."

"Or we could launch a counter-offensive, knowing that even if it fails, we will come back to our home intact." Aten had joined them just in time to hear Mike's declaration. "Now that we have a trump card, we need to determine our next step. I think that I-"

Joe's attention slipped as Aten continued speaking. As much as he loved strategy and being a part of things, there was a reason that Joe had never gone the officer route during his military career. He pulled out the path advancement pamphlet and eyed it, then decided not to waste any time. Joe activated the booklet, and chose to bring his Rituarchitect class to level ten. Instantly, a shockwave similar to the Guild Hall originated from him and knocked down the people in his immediate vicinity.

Then his eyes rolled back in his head, and knowledge of a new ritual filled his brain. This one was a doozy: a Grandmaster-ranked ritual called 'Ritual of the Traveling Civilization'. Details filled every line. Every arc had meaning, every *blank* space acted like a barcode which provided spatial coordinates. The material cost was massive, and the mana requirements would make the previous daily absorption of The Accords seem paltry.

But the effects... the effects alone would make it worth creating. Joe's eyes snapped open, and for a bare moment... a library's worth of information could be seen spinning in his sclera and irises, like galaxies drifting through the night sky.

Ritual of the Traveling Civilization (Grandmaster). There are times where constructing a building, a town, or a city would take an inordinate amount of time, effort, or otherwise be an excruciating task. This ritual allows any building below the Mythical rank to be transported to another location, irrespective of said location. This ritual allows you to link up to one hundred buildings, either at once or over time. So long as the proper mana debt is paid, the building and all of its non-fauna contents will be scanned, atomized, and reconstituted at the new demarcated location. Time needed to transport buildings is variable, and based on structural rarity.

Note: does not allow dimensional transport without an established, permanent link. Yes, the bifrost counts.

The massive load of information seemed to shrink away from his surface thoughts, and fell behind a barrier in Joe's mind that kept it contained and neatly packaged in one location. That was good. The prerequisites to understand that information… Joe blinked away the involuntary tears that had been streaming down his face. It had been like staring into the face of a beautiful horror.

Joe had been unable, *unwilling*, to look away from the pure, mind-rending information. It had been equivalent to writing Java code for a dozen years without once looking up an answer online or pressing backspace, then having it compile and run perfectly on the first attempt: simply not possible with his current brainpower and understanding. Still lying on his back, Joe pulled up his status and looked himself over.

Name: Joe '*Tatum's Chosen Legend*' Class: Mage (Actual: Rituarchitect)
Profession I: Tenured Scholar (Actual: Arcanologist)
Profession II: Ritualistic Alchemist
Character Level: 18 Exp: 175,220 Exp to next level: 14,780
Rituarchitect Level: 10 Exp: 45,000 Exp debt: 14,714
Hit Points: 677/677
Mana: 1,167/2,059 (762 Reserved)
Mana regen: 40.39/sec
Stamina: 671.5/671.5
Stamina regen: 5.92/sec

Characteristic: Raw score

Strength: 66
Dexterity: 88
Constitution: 67
Intelligence: 132
Wisdom: 107
Charisma: 74
Perception: 82
Luck: 49
Karmic Luck: +30

Joe saw a few major differences on his sheet, and he tried to puzzle through them. His mind was moving so *slowly,* though. The… 'experience till next level' on his class had turned into 'exp debt', his Karmic Luck had jumped again and he *still* had no idea what it meant, and the 'modifier' after his characteristics had vanished. "My characteristic modifier is gone…?"

"He's awake! Give him some air!" Aten's shout literally forced people away from Joe, since he was using his ability as Guild Commander to make it happen. "Joe, you keep passing out when I'm around. Should I start wearing less revealing clothes or something?"

"He said something about his modifier?" Mike broke the silence as it began to stretch. "Didn't you turn that off?"

"I did; set that as the default for the guild, too. Maybe he hasn't looked at his stat sheet in a few days?" Aten helped Joe to a seated position and handed him a glass of water. "Joe, the modifier was only a way to look at your characterics and see where you had improved from the human baseline. People were trying to use their modifier as math, thinking that it impacted skills or success rates somehow. The fact is: it doesn't. It is *only* another way of looking at stats, so I set the default for the guild view as 'off'. You can turn yours back on if you want."

"Wait…" Joe blinked rapidly and got to his feet. "It means

nothing? I left it on because I figured it meant… *something*! It should do…"

Aten was shaking his head. "Does nothing. It's been proven. It was even a part of the tooltips that appeared when we first came to Eternium; we all just seemed to gloss over it. Listen, there is an attack coming, and we are unprepared. I need to know what just happened to you."

"I got my… specialization to level ten." Joe smiled as he realized what that meant. "I did it! *Yes*! I can get a second specialization now. I just need the raw stats to make it happen!"

Aten blinked, and looked over at Mike. "You could specialize right now?"

Joe slumped slightly. "Yes, and no. I have everything I need to make it happen, but my raw stats are still too far away for it to be possible anytime soon."

"Let me see your characteristics." Aten ordered, though he amended that into a polite request when he realized how rude and invasive the demand was. He perused all the stats, muttering half to himself. "Hmm. I see that your luck is right at forty-nine… too bad. What do you need in order to go for specialization?"

"One-fifty in intelligence, wisdom, and perception." Joe replied instantly.

Aten looked at the numbers again. "You're a whole tier below what you need for perception. What… I have an idea, but you need to get your luck up to at least fifty. My idea requires you to have a *lot* of luck."

"Sky Eye seven-three reporting, the army stopped moving!" A voice projection shouted in the area. "It appears that the Zone announcement bothered them. We believe they are waiting for orders."

The voice cut off, and Aten snapped his gaze to Joe. "Is there any way for you to get that last point in luck?"

"I already trained my luck today, so not until tomorrow." Joe's eyes widened. "Wait, no! How much time do I have?"

"Who knows?" Aten shrugged and turned. "Too bad. I need to go get the guild ready for the attack."

"I can get that luck, if I'm lucky enough!" Joe started running, and Aten had to jog to catch up to him. "I'll be back!"

"Where are you…? Joe! If you go out there, we might not be able to let you back in!" Aten grabbed at Joe and tried to stop him, but Joe pushed mana into his feet and shot forward faster than Aten was expecting. "Joe, I'm ordering the gates sealed!"

"I don't need the gates!" Joe's voice barely made it back to Aten. "Wish me luck!"

"Abyss it, Joe, that's what started this mess!" Aten shouted after the running, possibly skipping, man. "Joe! Joe! Son of… what if I need someone to get those rituals activated?"

Aten watched as Joe slipped out of town, just before all the gates were finished closing. A resounding **boom** filled the area as huge stones were rolled behind the gates to make it impossible to open from the outside. Unless Joe had a special way to get in that Aten didn't know about, he was going to be trapped outside with thousands of people that wanted to kill him. All Aten could do now was act as any good leader should. He went back to the Guild Hall and opened the door. There were commands to give, and people to protect.

"Son of a *gun*…" Just before he closed the door, Aten hesitated and looked off into the distance. "Good luck, buddy."

CHAPTER FIFTY

Joe sprinted up to the test dungeon, only to find that the guards were being attacked by a swarm of low-level people. In a real way, the guards were more annoyed than anything else. They were holding interlocking shields and thus blocking the entrance to the tunnel as solidly as if they were a steel door.

"Filthy enemies of humanity! Get out here!" One of the attackers shouted at the shields.

The guards were having none of it. "Oh, yeah, *sure.* How about I pop out so that you can attack me for no reason? Oh, even better, why don't I attack you so you can go crying to your swarm about how 'unfair' I was being toward you?"

Two people worked together to throw a large rock at the guards, but beyond ringing the shield like a gong, the rock did nothing but fall to the ground. Joe had seen more than enough. "Hey! You don't seem to *understand* your situation! You are trespassing during a war event and attacking guards. If we send you to respawn, the only people that are going to be hurting is you! Leave them alone."

Joe's commanding tone caused the people to turn, startled that someone could sneak up on such a large group. One of them glanced at Joe and snorted, "Shoo, freak. You don't even have clothes. We could wreck you."

"Hey! He said 'we'! He's one of *them*!" another shouted, getting the small mob riled up again.

"Don't. Unlike those overly kind guards, *I* won't hold back," Joe warned as the enraged people charged at him. Joe sighed and held out his hands. "Enjoy respawn. Cone of Cold!"

Even though he had known that they were at a low level, he wasn't prepared for the utter devastation his spell created. Most of the people were under level five and had never figured out how to train their characteristics independently of their level. In an instant, twenty people froze solid and died instantly.

Damage dealt: 140.25 cold damage x20. (Title effect of Tatum's Chosen Legend reduces damage to characters of a lower level than you by 15%.)

Even with the damage reduced by almost twenty-five points, Joe had dealt double their total health in damage. He assumed that most of them were between twelve and fifteen points of constitution; nowhere *near* enough to survive even a Beginner-ranked spell. They also had no magic resistance or life-saving items. Joe shook his head at their underpreparedness, and walked over to the now-relaxing guards. "Hey, guys, don't hold back. We are the Ruthless Defenders, and we need to act like it. A deterrent only works if people know you will use it."

"Is that a direct order?"

Joe paused. He wasn't going to do that to them. "No, I'm not going to demand that you kill people. Use your judgement, of course. But don't idly stand by while you are being attacked either. Pardon me; I need to get into the dungeon."

He walked down the tunnel, and soon stood in the 'choosing room'. Joe set the dungeon to 'luck' and walked over to the door. Tossing it open, he stepped inside… to total darkness. Joe took a second step, and found himself stepping out of the door into the dungeon area.

Success! You have gained +5 luck! Three Karmic Luck has been consumed.

Joe shook as though he had been hit by a lightning bolt. There was no vision, or passing out, or anything *noticeable* as he passed the threshold, but he felt *altered*. Joe reviewed his active effects and noticed that the final threshold debuff was gone, which was a happy extra bonus. He considered the trial, and once again felt that there should really be more to it.

Walking toward the entrance of the tunnel, he kept waiting for it to get brighter. As he stepped out into the open air, the guards yelped, and one even took a swing at him. Joe dodged it easily enough, but frowned at the two in confusion. "Guys, what the heck? I *just* went in there."

The guard only recognized him after a long moment of panic, "What…? Joe? You're alive? You were in there for practically the entire day!"

Checking the sky, it was easy to see that they were telling the truth. There were only a few hours until sunset - at best - and Joe had likely been missing the entire battle. Without another word, he turned and started sprinting toward the guild, kicking up a huge dust plume as he empowered his extra-bouncy run with mana.

"Wait! Are we getting any guys here for the next shift?"

Joe only heard the faintest part of the shout coming at him from behind, but he didn't bother to figure out what they were saying. He tried to think of a way to not only help when he arrived, but to explain his absence. It was likely that anyone who had seen him running away thought that he was a total coward, and that made his stomach churn.

Joe found himself in range of the sounds of combat not five minutes later, but the cataclysmic booming of artillery spells wasn't exactly a great indicator of proximity. "Where in the abyss did they get siege mages?"

He kept going, and soon the smoke-covered battlefield was in view. Joe was approaching the back line of a huge horde that must have been at *least* a million strong. The people were packed so closely together that there was no clear path forward. Scanning the ground, he could see that the terrain was completely demolished; likely from so many people tromping through the area. The fields that the guild had been attempting to cultivate were now nothing more than mud pits, any food that had been ready to eat was gone, likely already gnawed down to nothing.

Trees in proximity to the mob's passing had been stripped of bark all the way to about seven feet off the ground, and Joe could see people chewing on it while they waited for their turn to throw themselves against the defended town. Wanting to test the levels of his targets, as well as what help he could provide from his location, Joe got right up to the back line and cast Cone of Cold.

Damage dealt: 140.25 cold damage x41. (Title effect of Tatum's Chosen Legend reduces damage to characters of a lower level than you by 15%.)

Forty-one people dropped by the time the spell ended an instant later, and Joe jumped away as people started to realize what had happened. He heard someone scream, "Oh my gosh! They're *dead*! Why would someone attack *us*?"

"Which one of you sickos did that?"

"I think, oh man, oh man…" That voice devolved into hyperventilating a moment later.

Joe was completely thrown off by their reactions. They were attacking a town. Did they not think that the town would attack in return? The cries of outrage swelled, and soon people not involved were screaming and cursing at each other as they got shoved. Fists started to fly, and the mob surrounding the dead players turned into a brawl. The chaos lasted only a few minutes before the area took on a slight blue tinge, and everyone stopped cold. They got to their feet and stood patiently, otherwise not moving a muscle.

The phenomenon was explained a moment later, as a Jester walked out of the crowd and examined the people. He fiddled with something, and the blue tint in the air vanished. People started blinking, then looked around as if they had forgotten something. A few started crying suddenly as they nursed broken jaws or bruised body parts. Joe recognized that effect; it was an apathy… something. A field that muted emotions and made people forget to protect themselves. He tried to keep an eye on the Jester, but the assassin vanished back into the crowd a moment later.

"Dangerous." Joe muttered softly. It was time to act. He walked over and started making his way through the crowd, only making it a few dozen yards before he encountered something *very* unwelcome.

"Come along, make sure to set this as your bind point so that you come back if those jerks in there attack us! No one wants to have to walk all the way back here from Ardania!" There was a bard standing by some kind of a totem, and people were appearing next to it almost as a continuous stream. They all seemed cheerful, and Joe realized that it was because the bards were giving generous mugs of what he assumed was beer or ale to anyone that reappeared in the circle.

As much as he wanted to destroy that respawn point, he could see dozens more of them poking above the heads of the crowd off in the distance. All that attacking right now would do was put him at risk, and make all the other areas better-defended. Joe pressed forward, his winding path through the crowd giving him a good look at many of the active command structures.

"Don't forget, this is all vengeance for Master Reggie!" a purple-robed man was shouting at a crowd of mages that Joe recognized as specializing in silencing spells. "Death to those who harbor the destroyer of the Mage's College!"

There was a roar of approval from the mages, and Joe winced. Whoops. He had figured that cutting the head off the snake would kill it, but it seemed that this group was a cockroach: cut off the head, and the body would run around for a while. Or… was that a chicken? Okay, cutting the head off the snake would kill it, but the fangs were still filled with a deadly poison. There. Joe felt better with his thoughts sorted.

Shortly after that run-in, Joe passed what seemed to be a

group of engineers or… he paused to listen as one of them started speaking excitedly. "We finished the scan of the outer wall, I just sent off the specs of all weak points! Sappers are going to take it down, then we'll get to work on the inner wall right away! Take a breather, everyone. I laid out estimated town maps, so make sure to look them over."

"The walls of the Architect's Guild will rise again, stronger than before!" One of the younger members of the group shouted in glee. The others nodded appreciatively, and Joe decided that this group was too dangerous to simply walk away from. As the group started to cluster around a large round table that had clearly been pulled from a storage device, Joe steeled himself to act.

"I need to be ruthless now, if we are going to survive in the future." Joe swallowed, his throat feeling like it was full of gravel. He took a few slow, hesitant steps as he steeled himself for action. He *jumped*, landing on the wooden table with a **thump** that made everyone's eyes jerk up to look at him. All of those eyes were filled with confusion at first, and just as a few started to turn into recognition, Joe acted.

"Dark Lightning Strike."

Damage dealt: 165.75 dark damage x42.

Damage dealt: 80.75 dark damage x118.

(Title effect of Tatum's Chosen Legend reduces damage to characters of a lower level than you by 15%.)

The nearly silent strike spread across the ground in a twenty-foot circle around Joe, killing a hundred and sixty people instantly. Joe knew that those confused eyes that had been looking up at him would haunt him for many nights to come.

There was no respawn for the non-player characters in this world.

CHAPTER FIFTY-ONE

Joe was running as hard as he could. He had given up on the ground, and was now taking his chances with much less stable footing: people's heads. Even with all the death that Joe had just caused, there were simply too many people packed together to make a huge commotion. It might have been a different story if his lightning had been accompanied by thunder, but the near-silent kills only caused people to shout after a short while. Almost everyone was still facing the town, and his kills had been nearly unseen.

Nearly.

The reason Joe was now running was that several Jesters were bouncing along people's heads just behind him. They were shouting, trying to get people to see Joe and stop him, but the sheer amount of speaking, yelling, and detonations happening made that an unlikely possibility. As he was bounding along, Joe split his focus to cast Cone of Cold behind him; taking down a thirty-foot swath of people. The Jesters fell as their 'ground' gave way, and Joe was finally able to gain some distance.

Since his presence was known, Joe started alternating between Acid Spray, Cone of Cold, and Dark Lightning Strike every time they were off cooldown. As he rushed forward, he was able to single-handedly kill *thousands* of attackers. Joe was planning to get to the walls and jump up, but the constant stream of arrows and spells going both ways made that mostly impossible. Still, he resolved to do it, and began picking up speed. He dropped back down to the ground as he got close to the wall; the mob had begun thinning out onto a large killing ground where people weren't as densely packed.

Seeing Joe charging forward so recklessly, a huge wave of attackers cheered and madly followed his rush; mistakenly thinking that he was spearheading an assault. As Joe got closer to the walls, rain started pattering off his bald head, and he looked up in surprise. There were no clouds accompanying the water that was falling, only rising smoke. "Oh, no! Ze *Flammenwerfer*!"

Joe used someone ahead of him as a springboard, jumping back the way he had come and sending the person sprawling with an 'oof!'. He empowered his jump again as he landed, backflipping and sailing over the heads of a large group. They looked up in concern; why was he running? The water in the area suddenly vanished, and a torch was thrown over the wall. Joe jumped *one* more time, and *just* managed to get away as the huge flamethrower ritual roared to life; incinerating a circle of thousands of people surrounding the town and filling the air with the scent of burnt hair and roasting pork.

He dropped to the ground, gasping for air. His stamina and mana had taken a huge hit in the last few minutes, and Joe needed a full minute or two to get back up to maximum power. He felt a hand on his arm, and was pulled to his feet a moment later. Joe locked eyes with a purple-robed mage, who was grinning at him happily. "That was an epic escape! I could see so much mana coming off of you, I couldn't *believe* it! With reserves like that, you should talk about joining The Silence when this is all over!"

"Oh, ah... thanks." Joe muttered as the dust slid off his Exquisite Shell.

"One, um, thing." The mage made a 'mystical' motion with his hands, and a set of neatly folded purple clothing appeared. Clearly, he had pulled them from a spatial ring and didn't expect Joe to know what that was. "Feel free to get dressed. You can have the clothes as a sign of good faith. Look for me at the Slithering Eel back in Ardania, and you can get tested for the group."

"I'm sorry to say, I'm not sure what your group does…" Joe spoke without thinking as he pulled on the clothing. As much as the items were from a group he didn't want to be associated with, he was showing off only a little less than a true Scotsman, and he was jumping off people's heads with surprising frequency. That was a little *too* much trauma for them, by his standards. Soon Joe was all geared up in his new clothes, and they stood together and stared at the unending flames.

"Abyss, how long is this going to last?" the mage groaned.

"I'm guessing about three minutes and forty seconds longer," Joe answered truthfully. He was trying not to look the man in the eye; he didn't want to remember his face going forward. Especially considering what was going to happen next. Joe was counting down, and when there was only forty seconds remaining, he scooted back another ten yards and prepared himself to run.

The mage looked around, and caught sight of Joe. "Hey, why did you-"

**Whoohff*.*

Flames wrapped around the mage, and the entire group in front of Joe. He had almost misjudged the blast's reach; the flames came within five feet of him. Just like when a grill or stovetop was being put out, there was a brief moment when flames exploded outward. The burst was more dangerous than a small-scale stovetop, obviously, and the flames were at least twice as hot as they had been a short moment before. As the fire receded, Joe started running when there were only ten seconds remaining on the ritual.

A Dark Lightning Strike finished off the people around him

as he got moving, and soon Joe had already blown through a quarter of his mana. Ten feet… five… Joe *jumped*, blasting mana out of his feet and spinning uncontrollably through the air as the force sent his legs above his head. He was running on only the fumes of his mana at this point, but the wall was speeding past him. The top came closer, *closer*… then Joe was above it.

The downside was that he was tumbling uncontrollably, and there was no easy way to course correct in midair. Just as he was about to slip below the crenellations, he was clipped by a ballista bolt and slammed into the wall. Joe managed to secure a grip, and pulled himself up… only for the tip of a sword to slide off his Exquisite Shell. "Guys! It's Joe! I'm in the guild!"

Another sword clattered against his head, and his shell was finished off. Then a strong hand gripped him, and Emjay the construction worker yanked him over. "Kid, you're lucky I was bringing up some more bricks for them to throw. The abyss are you doing, *jumping* into the town in the middle of a war? Not a lick of sense in that shiny head of yours!"

"I'm doing something right, since you're still around and I made it up here." Joe smirked, then collapsed as resource deprivation hit him like a ton of bricks. "Ugh…"

"Well, come on then. You're useless up here." Emjay grabbed Joe by the arm and dragged him toward the stairs, forcing him to stand or bounce the whole way down.

Joe struggled to his feet and wobbled down the stairs, hurrying to the command area of the Guild Hall. The raised voice of an unknown person met Joe as he approached, "We are getting overrun out there! The defensive magical crud is all used up, and we're sitting ducks! Did you see how many of them there *are*?"

"Chauncey." Aten's voice was stern, and his eyes were hard. "They are on the other side of the wall right now. As far as we can see, they have no way over. Not a single attacker has made it in, so calm. *Down*."

"It's going to take some time before more defenses are ready, anyway." Mike joined in. Joe could finally see what was happening. The doors to the war room were wide open, and thanks to the recent upgrade, the room had excellent acoustics and stadium seating available. Joe slipped onto a bench, noticing that everyone present had a seat if they wanted it now. It seemed that the days of crowded meetings were over. "Activating the aegis now will only make it harder for us to hold out. It will give us a day, yes, but we need to use that when it is *needed.* Using it now is no different than wasting it!!"

Joe spoke up from his bench, as relaxed as if he had been present the entire time. "I think that it would be a good idea to have repair crews on standby at the outer wall. On my way back in here, I overheard a group that claimed to have found the weak points in our outer walls and passed them to sappers. If the magical defenses are down now, I think it is likely that there is about to be a breach."

The room quieted, and Aten did a double take as he recognized Joe's voice. "Joe, when did…? How did you get back in here?"

"Oh, you know." Joe waved at the table. "While I was working my way through that mob out there, I overheard some of what was going on, and I found out that there are totems set up to allow their people to respawn. That means that one of our biggest advantages - respawning next to the battle - is now gone, unless we can figure out a way to make that vanish."

"Again, how did you get in here?" Aten pressed the issue, "If you built secret tunnels or something, we really need to know-"

"Aten, I would never." Joe stopped him firmly. "Listen, I just wanted to warn you that nearly everyone that's ever had an issue with the guild is showing up to throw their hat in the ring, and they are pulling out every trick that they can find. Is there anyone that we can go to and ask for help?"

"There's no one." Aten waved a hand at the distant walls. "Even if there was, who is going to break through that line to come help us? Do you know anyone else that can do the ridiculous things that you do? There are hundreds of *thousands* of people out there. Mike, get someone on the lookout for those sappers. If the wall comes down, we're done."

"Yes, Commander!" Mike saluted and ran from the room. Joe had never seen the stern man act so… military.

"I've had your magical people working on defenses. You should check in on them." Aten waved Joe off, turning back to the meeting at large.

"Noticed that." Joe shook his head at his memory of avoiding the flames that had reduced hundreds of people to ashes. Now that he thought of it, he wasn't sure how his Coven would be dealing with creating that sort of massacre. Perhaps it *would* be best to check in. Joe slipped from the war room as quietly as he had arrived.

CHAPTER FIFTY-TWO

Joe jogged toward the Grand Ritual Hall, not even slightly bothered by all the smoke in the air. One of the benefits of having a higher constitution was that he was able to shrug off things such as smoke or weak poisons. Besides that, smoke inhalation was a stacking debuff, and his Neutrality Aura made sure it never had a chance to overwhelm him.

When he had departed to try to raise his luck, Joe had left the others in his Coven in charge of the defenses. As far as he could tell, they were doing a great job. However, he was certain that they hadn't had to kill a bunch of people before, and he was worried about what effects that aspect of battle might be having on their minds. He opened the path to the Grand Ritual Hall and solemnly strode down the winding ramp…

"*Cheers*!"

…only to walk in as the Coven slammed together large mugs of ale. Joe paused in shock, then started to chuckle. Soon, he broke down into full-bellied laughter, and the others were staring at him in concern.

"You… ha ha… I thought you'd all be *miserable*! You're having a party!" Joe was wheezing; he had finally realized that people were hardy, and they didn't need him to tell them that they were doing the right thing. They knew it already. "I need to learn to trust people! Ha, ha!"

Joe's mood lightened considerably, and the stress that had been causing his shoulders to knot up started to vanish. He sat down at the table and started discussing the rituals that were in use. Not only had they set up the massive flames, but there were dozens of minor rituals in use that he hadn't been expecting. Kirby gloomily informed him of the rainbows and peaceful music ritual she had accidentally meshed together, then activated in the staging area where guild members were resting until called to the walls to fight. Apparently, it boosted fatigue recovery by a huge amount.

They had also set up reinforcement rituals that added armor to the buildings they were activated on; this was a concept that Joe was *very* interested in learning, as he hadn't seen anything similar before. Of course, there were rituals meant for assault as well, and Big_Mo and Hannah had been working on a special combination of their rituals. Big_Mo explained it carefully. "So, we take the combined Ritual of Quarantine, and add it to the ritual I designed that I call 'Blood amplification'."

"All it does is absorb any blood in the area and use it to amplify the range that the quarantine impacts!" Hannah burst in enthusiastically to clarify certain points. "If we use this in conjunction with a large-scale attack, we might be able to force the entire army out there to swim through a moat of sewage to come after us!"

"How many people are going to want to do that, knowing that they'll get sicker the closer they come?" Big_Mo laughed and **clinked** his mug against Hannah's.

"This is ready? Why haven't you activated it?" Joe was *pleased* with this development. "I like this a lot. Non-lethal, really inconvenient, and the entire attacking force will help us fertilize the fields that they ruined on their way in!"

That got a laugh from the people in the room, and Hannah explained that she was still working on boosting the efficiency of the ritual, as the combination made it an Expert-ranked ritual, and she knew that she could get it down to Journeyman with enough time. Joe nodded at that. "Let me take a look; I'm sure that together we could-"

"Time!" Taka called, and a few of the people got to their feet. "Sorry, Joe; gotta bind a set of shattering, spinning, and gravity rituals on a boulder that the guild is sending over the wall via trebuchet. I call this one 'Stone Blender' for… obvious reasons."

"Less happy with *that* use of our abilities," Joe sighed as they walked out of the room, their hurried footsteps and swishing cloaks stirring up dust. "I don't think anyone remembers that rituals were once banned here, considered taboo by the Mage's College. How are we supposed to break the image that rituals are evil if we keep using them to destroy things?"

"Is that why I only ever see you using them defensively or to build things?" Hannah pulled over a few pages with spell formulae on them as she questioned him.

"I… guess so?" Joe thought about it. He really didn't use many of the more potent, darker rituals to which he had access. "I guess I'm afraid that if I use my full abilities like that, I'll be feared. I don't want our class to have to slink through the shadows. I want us to be the wise old magicians that Kings go to for ways to save their people."

"Well, I'm not a King, but I'd sure like my home saved." Big_Mo snorted at Joe's words even as he missed a flask he was pouring blood into and got it all over his hands. "Crap, that's acidic! Ow, shoot. Joe, can I ask that you go out there and do something scary so that we have time to set up more rituals?"

"No, I need to help Hannah with-"

"We got this," Hannah interrupted Joe firmly. "All I need is time to make it happen. You could be finding things to do that are more useful."

Joe looked between the two, understanding that they weren't trying to get rid of him; they really believed that he could do something. He stood straight, nodded, and marched from the room; determined to do… something! Something that would justify their faith in him. As he walked out into the Pathfinder's Hall, he went straight for the door, but paused as a whisper reached his ear.

Joe.

"Who's there?" Joe peered in the direction of the whisper, but only heard soft music and the crackling of a fire. Seeing as the building was nearly empty, that might not be a great thing. A buzzing filled his ears, and Joe followed his instincts toward the Temple. Looking around the lively room, Joe didn't notice anything out of the ordinary. Just before he left, a flash of darkness shifted the appearance of Tatum's altar. He stepped closer, and placed a hand on the stone book.

Greetings, Champion of Tatum! Your Cleric class level is considered equal to your character level, due to starting as a hidden class! As a Cleric, you gain an ability or spell every third level. Calculating… level is eighteen! You are owed an ability from level eighteen!

As you are a Champion, and not a standard Cleric, you get to choose the school that you draw your cleric abilities from! As Occultatum is a 'Neutral' deity, you can choose 'neutral', 'good', or 'evil' aligned abilities from the school of your choice. Would you like to choose your level eighteen ability? Yes / No.

"Yes." Joe perused the options that were available: abjuration, conjuration, divination, enchantment, evocation, illusion, necromancy, and transmutation. His mind reached for illusion, but he stopped himself. The recent conversation that Joe had with the Coven made him seriously consider necromancy. If there was something 'scary' when it came to spells, the undead usually topped the list. He took a deep breath, reached out… then stopped, shaking his head. Joe wasn't cut out for that type of spell. Although he *could* pick from 'evil' spells, he just… couldn't.

Joe looked at the remaining options available, and selected 'Evocation'.

Evocation is the act of calling upon or summoning a spirit, demon, god, or other supernatural agent through the power of your will, mana, and potentially various sacrifices. Choose a spell.

"Yes, that's what I need…" There were only two spells that appeared, and both were decent.

Mystical Infusion: Perform a rite that infuses your body and mind with power and knowledge pulled from an outside source. Unlike possession-style spells, there is no chance of losing yourself to an outside being, as you are taking only their power. Effect and time limit vary.

Planar Shift: Directly summon a being from behind the veil, and use them to accomplish your goals. Binding and directing are very important, as it is unlikely that you and the summoned being have goals that align. Effect and time limit vary.

Joe wanted Mystical Infusion, but the practical part of him knew that if he were using that power… he would become a front-line fighter. Then, when the spell ran out, he would be at the front of combat. It made far more sense to summon something that he could use to aid him, or be a meatshield at worst. "I choose Planar Shift."

He collapsed to the ground as information hit him right in the brain. Joe writhed in agony while darkness poured from the altar and into him. As he lay there, panting, a book materialized and dropped onto his chest; a volume so thick that it knocked the wind out of him.

Spell gained: Planar Shift (Student 0). Directly summon a being from behind the veil, and use them to accomplish your goals. You have been granted a book that will allow you to know what being you are summoning, how to control it, and how to banish it if needed. Effect and time limit of the summoned beings vary. As this is a spell granted directly by a deity and fits within your skillset, it has been increased to the Student ranks. Effect: Comparatively easy control of anything summoned below the Student rank. To increase skill level, summon and control a being that you intended to summon for one hour per skill current skill level.

Current skill progress: 0/30 hours of control.

Mind still buzzing, Joe inspected the swirling pages of the book, also handily named 'Planar Shift', and saw what appeared to be variant ritual diagrams. "I suppose I can see why I got boosted all the way to Student…"

"There he is!" Joe heard the pounding of feet just before being pulled up to his own. Two guards hoisted him upright, and they started running out of the room together. "Joe, the wall was breached. We held off three teams of bombers, but the fourth managed to take down a section of wall to the north."

"Why are we running toward headquarters?" Joe spat out a huge ball of blood and phlegm that had caught in his throat for unknown reasons.

"Aten sent for you. This… this wasn't supposed to happen." The guard on Joe's left seemed to be choking on something as well. "We were supposed to be *safe* here!"

"He has a plan." The other guard seemed far more calm. "Aten always has a plan."

CHAPTER FIFTY-THREE

"I do, in fact, have a plan." Aten told Joe, much to his surprise. "It requires a bit of legal mumbo-jumbo, so bear with me."

"*Rawr*!" Joe waved his hands in front of him like they were claws. Seeing that no one was smiling, Joe coughed into his hand and settled into a seat. "Sorry, was trying to 'bear' with you."

Aten tapped the table with his index finger a few times, then shook his head. "Just… alright, here we go. Will you continue working to get this town to town level five? Even without a tangible benefit?"

"Of course, but-" Joe was cut off as Aten waved his hand.

"Good enough; then I predetermine that your quest is complete."

Quest complete: The making of an Elder. The Guild Commander has determined that you fulfilled the spirit of this quest. You will automatically become the 'First Elder' when the guild upgrades to a 'Sect'.

Aten leaned toward him. "As First-Elder-in-waiting, you have more power than a measly Guild Commander. Do you want to run the guild? I can get the paperwork-"

"Not even a *little*!" Joe physically recoiled from the offer. The others around the table sighed a breath of relief.

"Good, because I was testing you." Aten admitted easily, ignoring the glare he got in reply. "Just like that, you are automatically considered to be at the same privilege level as mine in the guild. Here is my plan: you have all the requirements to move into your second specialization, except the raw stats. You and I are going to go to the breach in the wall, and work to plug it. If the battle is turning against us, I am going to activate the Aegis."

"What happens after that?" Joe pressed as the people stood up around him and started walking. "Guys? The rest of the plan? There was more to it than that; I know there was!"

"We'll tell you if we need to enact it," Mike grimly stated, his hands on a pair of daggers at his waist.

"This is *not* a comforting plan!" Joe yelled at the group. No one was listening, so he hurried to catch up with them. They rushed toward the sound of clashing metal, breaking stone, and harsh screams.

As they got in range, Joe felt as though his eyes were lying to him. His guild members were being pushed back by what appeared to be non-player mercenaries, and hundreds of people holding mauls were bashing on the wall. A huge chunk of wall had fallen inward, and their current actions were widening that gap every second.

The leadership rushed into the fray, and combat over the next few seconds proved that they had *earned* their high positions. They moved in delta formations of five people each, and swung their weapons in harmony, sometimes *almost* touching their comrades with naked steel. But, each time, the weapon would slide past and land only on the intended target. Arrows rained down on the enemies as the wings of the formations opened fire, and narrow openings were exploited to bring down the opposition.

The mercenaries were clearly around level fifteen, judging by their dangerous air and the power of the abilities they could use, but they were still routed quickly. They fell into an orderly retreat, even though they were being heavily pressured by the Wanderers. Joe saw a flash of something… a sigil? That was… these were mercenaries from a Noble House! The sigil was quickly obscured by combat, but Joe now knew for certain that there were enemies coming after them from all walks of life.

More good news reached him. Joe noticed that Kirby was directing a group of the builders into moving the massive stone that they had bound with a building repair ritual, and it should be close enough to fix the wall in only a few minutes. All they had to do was drive back the opposition, and they would once again have a thick wall dividing them from those that were coming after their lives.

It was just then that the leadership started dying. It began with an arrow through the eye of a mage. Joe would have chalked it up to standard combat, but her scream ended abruptly. *Too* abruptly. Catching sight of purple-robed wizards coming through the crowd, Joe understood what was happening. "This is a trap!"

Though he shouted as soon as he made the connection, it was already too late. Even as Joe responded, four more leaders on their side were killed by Jesters that seemed to appear from nowhere. The silence mages stopped anyone that seemed to be trying to shout orders, and the mercenaries surged against their lines. Joe watched person after person get cut down, and suddenly Aten was next to him. "Just like we thought. If we didn't come, they would have been able to destroy the whole wall, but if we did… they'd get the leaders."

"You knew this would happen, and you still-"

"We *thought* this might happen. We didn't know for sure." Aten grunted his words. "It is time… *Golden Aegis*!"

The reaction wasn't as instant as he had hoped it would be, but the change started soon enough. A deep **thrum** rose from the center of Towny McTownface, similar to a jet engine spinning up. Golden light began pouring out from the Guild Hall, coating everything in its path like honey pouring over a spoon.

Everything the light touched, so long as it was associated favorably with the guild, from buildings to people; started to shine with the golden glow.

It sped up as it encroached upon the edges of town, and in no time flat, it had crashed over the walls. Joe felt a glorious sense of well-being fill him, and a counter appeared in his vision.

Golden Aegis activated! Immunity to all damaging effects is in place for 24 hours, so long as you are in the town-specific territory controlled by the guild 'The Wanderers'. All damaging effects against someone under the protection of the Golden Aegis will rebound upon the attacker for double damage!

Joe jumped forward into the open, past the protections of the wall. Hundreds of arrows were aimed and released at him, dozens of spells were fired off, and fighters charged at him. In an instant, Joe was peppered with so many attacks that in any other circumstance, only the heel of his feet would have remained non-shredded. Instead, roughly forty percent of everyone who had aimed at him was slapped by a dark clone, and *all* of the enemies were slapped if their attack landed; then each assailant was dealt double damage by a golden light that rebounded on them.

Damage dealt: 83,219 Dark damage. Title effect Pierce the darkest night has come into effect: Damage increased by 10%! (All damage dealt now includes 5% armor piercing. The piercing bonus increases to 10% with dark-aligned spells and weapons.) Damage partially reduced when dealt to lower-leveled personnel, due to title effect: Tatum's Chosen Legend.

Damage dealt: 159,211 Dark damage. (Split among 312 aggressors. See full damage breakdown?)

Skill increase: Retaliation of Shadows (Student IX). It's not about the ability, it's about how you use it! Killing three hundred people within two seconds by using a single-target spell is quite *the achievement!*

"I went up *nine* ranks in that spell?" Joe gasped as he glanced at the data swarming in. Then he spotted the wave of arrows coming for him and laughed wildly. "More! Give me all your anger! Let the hate flow through you!"

In response to his taunts, hundreds, *thousands*, of attacks and attackers flew at Joe. Cone of Cold claimed the lives of dozens of fighters as they closed in, and a Dark Lightning Strike eliminated those that managed to survive. His shadowy self was everywhere at once; slapping, slapping, *slapping*. Anyone who survived a double slap—which could deal up to three hundred and ninety damage before other effects were considered—was then hit with double the damage they would have dealt. In this way, nearly two thousand people died in under thirty seconds.

More would have followed, but there were professionals in the mix as well. Before Joe could react, a net settled over him and dragged him to the ground. No damage was done, so no reaction occurred. Joe was yanked along, and though people were still dying from barraging him with attacks, he was being drawn slowly and steadily toward the enemy lines.

He couldn't *believe* that he had been captured so easily. Joe roared like a caged tiger and flung spells as fast as he could manage. Acid washed his nets, and the fibers started to wither. Rough hands grabbed him, and he was tossed to the ground. Then, seemingly from nowhere, his robe was caught and he was yanked back into Aten's embrace. The huge man sprinted for the walls, and dove through just ahead of more nets.

"You absolute *walnut*!" Aten shouted at Joe, who was spotless even though he had received hundreds of attacks. "Didn't I *tell* you that we had a plan for all of this?"

"I was able to take out over two thousand attackers." Joe's words caused Aten to blink. "I thought it was a good deal."

"What happens when they drag you off our land and toss you into a place you can't escape, one that automatically forces your bind point to that location? *Less* of a good trade, yes?" Aten took a deep breath as he saw Joe turn serious. "*Listen* to me, abyss-blast it! I need you to go and get your specialization, and I need you to do it *now*!"

"I can't-"

"Everything is set, except for your stats, correct?" Aten interrupted.

"Yes, and that's why-"

"Otherwise, you are prepared?"

"Of course-"

"Then you need to go. You need to come back, and you need to save us. In a single day, we were forced to use our final trump card. In one *more* day, it will run out, and we will be running on fumes. At that time, if we don't have something else ready… we are going to lose everything. This will last for five minutes." Aten took a deep breath and put a hand over Joe's heart. "*Might of the Guild.*"

CHAPTER FIFTY-FOUR

All the light in the area seemed to dim as Joe was bathed in eight intermingled colors, which came together into a silver stream that filled him to the breaking point and beyond.

Strength has reached the Zone maximum!

Constitution has reached the Zone maximum!

The messages continued until luck also showed that it was at the Zone maximum, which seemed to be one hundred and fifty points. His health shot over fifteen hundred points, his mana over three thousand. Joe looked at his hands, which seemed to have replaced all fat and bone with pure muscle, and turned to look at Aten. "You're out of your mind! What good is this to me? I can't use this to-"

"Jo..oo..oe, yo..oo..oou need to go..oo!" Aten's voice was so *slow* that Joe had a hard time understanding what he was saying. This must be the effect of having his intelligence and dexterity so much higher: everything else seemed to happen in slow motion.

"I'll try, Aten." Joe growled and pulled out the tablet that was in his codpiece. "Activate?"

Scanning... Base Class found: Ritualist. First prerequisite for usage met.

Scanning... Specialized class found: Rituarchitect. Second prerequisite for usage met.

Generating class selection options one through four... previously generated.

Scanning... Third prerequisite for usage met. Base class 'Ritualist' requires that Characteristics 'intelligence' and 'wisdom' be at the Mortal characteristic limit before second specialization can be applied. Scan indicates that all *characteristics are at this limit.*

Activate specialization attempt? Yes / No.

"Yes." Joe's word was too fast to be intelligible to those around him, but that wasn't on their mind. What *they* saw was a multicolored lightning that struck Joe... leaving behind a cloud of smoke with nothing in it. Their hopes died, and they thought he had as well.

Joe blinked, and gazed around the room that he stood in. It was a small, comfortable space, with four hallways attached to it, and... there was one other person in the room. "Tatum?"

Occultatum looked his way and grimaced. "You foolish mortal... activating a tablet using borrowed power? Do not talk, only listen. Choose which path you will attempt, and for all that is Celestial, finish the trial before your borrowed power fades! The tablet you activated was *single-use*!"

Four paths lead away from where you currently stand. All of them contain power enough to transform you into what you wish to be. There are three things to decide before you follow a path to the end.

Are you choosing the path that is right for you?
Are you choosing a path that you are willing to follow to the end?
Will you do what you must to attain the power at the end of the path?

Path one: Reductionist. There is more, there is always *more. More to do, more to build, more to learn. What if that can be reduced to the most basic components? The ultimate desire of the multiclasser, this path opens the way for all crafting by reducing everything to the common denominators. The path of the Reductionist is the path of industriousness.*

Path two: Reinforcer. The might of a city is not only in the buildings that it contains; it is also within the people that live there. Health, happiness, fertility, protection, empowerment. You will hold a city in your hands, and they will live or die when you decide. This path is based around protecting and enhancing structures, and allows for permanent boosts to nearly all aspects of life within its range. The path of the Reinforcer is the path of permanence.

Path three: Siegebreaker. By following this path, no defenses can stand before you. No one would dare *to hide behind a wall that you approach. Conversely, no one would dare assault a wall you have decided to protect. One way or another, the siege ends with you. Always. This path is the natural next step for a Rituarchitecht, being able to create or destroy cities practically on a whim. The path of the Siegebreaker is the path of the intransitive.*

Path four: Rarified. A rarefied being is one who has forgone other attachments, and has devoted themselves to their mental and physical perfection. Instead of focusing on what they can do for others, or what they can make for themselves, they look at what they can make of *themselves. All characteristic training is easier, all skill gain is increased. The path of the Rarified is the path of enduring.*

Joe wanted to take all the time in the world to make his choice. He wanted to ponder the pros and cons, to make a carefully considered choice. But… there had been fear in Tatum's eyes, not anger. Joe needed to make his choice *now*.

He did.

He ran.

Siegebreaker. That wouldn't do. Just like rejecting the choice to become a Waritualist, Joe didn't plan to fight forever. He didn't want to be forced into it just so that he could advance along his chosen path.

Reinforcer was a no-go, as he could create the same effects with his study into building as it was. So he might need to take longer to achieve the same effect? Worth it. The same feeling came from the Rarified; though it might take longer, the end goal was something he could do either way.

This meant that the choice was simple for him. Joe sprinted along the path of the Reductionist. Turn everything into the common denominators? Useful for all crafters? Joe was nothing if not industrious, so the description suited him perfectly. A gate appeared, and Joe slammed into it without slowing down. The heavy wooden gate shattered into splinters. There hadn't been a lock, or a key. This was a gate that had tested his strength.

Nearly two minutes had passed.

Soon, another 'gate' blocked his path. This one was intangible, and Joe sprinted through it. His nerves screamed in pain as the mist tried to tear apart his skin. His constitution held firm, and he passed through. Joe ran, pushing himself to the edge of his ability. The world *blinked*, and Joe stumbled… it seemed his luck had held firm.

Five minutes had passed.

Two gates appeared, and Joe went through the one on the left, somehow knowing that the right path held only failure. His perception and wisdom had seen him through. A narrow gate ahead, too small to fit through, too strong to smash. Joe *contorted*, screaming as his bones seemed to melt; then he was through. Jaxon would have been proud of his dexterity.

Seven minutes had passed.

A powerful saintly figure waited for him, a flaming trident poised to strike. Joe nodded politely, "Pardon me, I don't have time to fight you."

The figure cocked it's head to the side, and nodded. How very *charismatic* Joe felt right then! The figure only *slowly* got out of the way. So… so… *slowly*.

The last gate was in sight, and Joe sprinted forward, saw what he needed to do… and the knowledge was gone. He collapsed to the floor as his body screamed that it had been badly used and abused. Forcing himself off the floor, Joe confirmed that his boost from Aten was gone. He reached a trembling hand to the gate, but he no longer had knowledge of how to open it.

"I had to prove my intelligence..." Joe shook his head. "That's not something that's possible. There's no way to *show* that you are intelligent."

Joe sat and stared at the door. There was no longer a time limit. If he couldn't go forward, he was lost here anyway. The minutes turned into an hour, then two, as Joe searched every inch of the door for a clue. He slammed a fist onto it in frustration. "I chose the path that was right for me!"

Joe kicked the door. "I'm *absolutely* choosing a path that I'm willing to follow to the end!"

"What do I *need* to do to attain the power at the end of the path?" he shouted at the door. "I'll do it! I just need to know what it *is*!"

He sat and thought. He tried over and over to find a pattern, to discern some secret. Joe took a deep breath and mulled over all the information at hand... and a spark flew, a clue flashed in his mind. "This is the path of industriousness..."

"How can I show my industriousness, willingness, and intelligence all at the same time? I know I knew I could do it... extra-smart me was even *happy*... what *was* it?" Joe pounded on the floor. "There's only an eighteen-point intelligence difference. I can reach where I need to be in eighteen days. I can survive here that long; I just have to trust that the guild can hold out."

Joe pulled out his puzzle cube and worked on it, grumbling the whole time. "I'll boost my intelligence until I'm able to get through this naturally! See if I don't, *door*. I'll stay here until I'm *forced* out, or I win!"

Just under two hours later, Joe solved a question on the cube, and the entire thing locked into position and started to glow. "I *solved* it? No! I won't be able to gain intelligence through training!"

Characteristic training complete! Special reward, all characteristics +5! You have solved a tier three Puzzle Cube! You are the first to do this on Midgard. Your reward was decided long ago! Sage Treasure himself *was the one to load the interior with-*

[[Sacrifice acceptable]]

Joe was startled as the message he was reading was interrupted by a much more *mechanical* one. The cube was pulled out of his grasp, and hovered in front of the gate.

Sacrifice Unopened, Completed Tier Three Puzzle Cube to open this gate? Yes / No.

"I've been working on that since I learned that I could increase my stats!" Joe shouted at the message hovering in his face. "It was loaded by a Sage of freaking *Treasure*! You want me to give up… you want me… the third question. This is what I need to do to attain that power?"

Joe stared hungrily at the items that were *just* visible through a haze of energy. That cube seemed to have been a spatial device, or the world might be messing with his mind. "Am I willing… to do what I have to do… to attain the power I desire?"

He swallowed deeply. "Yes. Sacrifice the cube."

[[Sacrifice accepted]]

The cube vanished with a small **pop**, and Joe felt his stomach drop. The gate fell over, toppling backward and leaving the way open for Joe to walk along. In the center of the room was himself, just as it had appeared when he had originally chosen a class. This doppelganger mimicked his movements, but stopped as he got closer. Then, it reached into the surrounding air and pulled two items out of nothing.

One was a strange diagram that showed moving energy throughout all of Joe's body. Joe took it, but wasn't sure what to do with it. The other was a ritual diagram, but… there was a sense of *permanence* to this diagram that he had never felt before. The other him activated the ritual, and Joe was wrapped in potent power.

The shackles of Midgard trapping you upon the Zone break away from your limbs! You have gained the class specialization 'Reductionist'. There are three benefits to this class and two negatives that balance it out.

The first negative: You will no longer gain characteristic or skill points by leveling. Neither from character class, nor specialization.

The second negative: You can no longer use standard materials for any form of crafting.

"*Excuse* me?" Joe blanched at the words that appeared in front of him. Had his warehouse of crafting materials stored in his codpiece just become worthless?

CHAPTER FIFTY-FIVE

Joe held back his fury and read onward, hoping that the benefits would be worth it. In fact, they seemed to be more of an explanation than anything else.

Benefit one: You now have the ability to process all materials down to basic components. All raw materials, processed materials, and items are able to be 'reduced'. You are able to reduce all materials by using mana alone. There is a ritual now engraved upon your being, a ritual that only requires the empowerment of mana to function.

Benefit two: Any sensory abilities now also inform you of the value of anything that can be reduced, as well as the amount of material you will attain by reducing it.

Benefit three: You can use the reduced material in any form of crafting, as a replacement for all components, ingredients, or other required material.

After reading through everything one more time, Joe was… nonplussed. There was nothing in here that offered him or his guild salvation at this critical juncture, and nothing that looked useful in the near future. He would be able to craft more efficiently… maybe? Joe's hands started to shake as he realized that he might have just failed to save his guild.

He looked at the other item he had gained, and found that

it was a type of mana circulation, designed to grind away at the Mana Manipulation and Coalescence skills. "Breaking the Mortal limit?"

Either way, it was a system of ebbs and flows that appeared to be designed with his current mana system in mind. It *also* looked like it would take a very, *very* long time to learn and put into place. The world around him started to fade away, and Joe realized that he was returning, now that he had gained his reward.

Tatum appeared, and though it seemed that he couldn't say anything, his face showed a brilliant smile. Tears of joy had welled up in the deity's eyes, and Joe relaxed as he suddenly *knew* that he had made the absolute best choice.

Then Joe blinked, and found himself surrounded by smoke. Not a mystical smoke, but black, greasy smoke that only came from burning oily things such as pitch. Obscured movement shifted all around him, and Joe gaped in confusion at the surrounding rubble. "This… the outer wall?"

There was no golden coloration shining through the smoke, no Aegis protecting him from getting attacked. In fact, it appeared that the only thing keeping him safe was the smoke hiding his face and body from the tide of humanity. In an odd moment of deja vu, he realized that once again, he was surrounded by the huge mob of people that were attacking the town.

A gust of wind cleared the immediate area for a brief moment, and his heart lurched as he saw the charred, burnt-out buildings that had once been housing for his guild members. They were structures that he had built, now collapsing under their own weight. He let himself be carried along with the crowd, and soon found himself at the inner wall that protected the core of the guild buildings.

"You all need to surrender!" A man was shouting up to the top of the wall.

"Your *face* needs to surrender!" Jaxon called down with an

instant reply. Joe beamed at that; at least *some* of his people had survived!

"Are you qualified to speak for your guild? Can I please speak to anyone except this antediluvian madman?" The man was getting exasperated; shouting for nearly an hour already, only to get this kind of reply was apparently hard to bear.

"Are you qualified to speak for *yourself*?" Jaxon taunted him easily. "You appear sleep-deprived, and you seem to have an *ashen* complexion. Go get some food, a proper rest, and for the love of elderberries, take a shower! This is Towny McTownface, and you are Stinky McStinkface!"

"*You* have all the food!" The man self-righteously screeched. "We are here to give it to the *people*, and you can't stop us! It's only a matter of time - *peh*!"

A tomato splattered against his face, and Jaxon called down again, "There you go! Fresh salsa!"

"I'm going to make sure you die *slowly*," The man called calmly, hopping off his pedestal and vanishing into the crowd. Joe took this moment to make a plan. The inner wall was only twenty feet high, and he was certain that he could jump that. On the other hand, the wall was *bristling* with people ready to fire at any moment. He didn't like his chances of getting over the wall without getting fragged by his own teammates.

He turned his eyes toward the other place he could go: the Pathfinder's Hall. Joe made his way over to the large structure, and found that the wall surrounding the inner area had been breached and swarmed by hundreds of people. However, no one was entering the building. It was easy to see why; the entrance was just beyond a sea of blood. Tapping someone on the arm, Joe motioned at the doors. "What happened?"

Recognizing the purple robes, the man's eyes shone with vigor. "Mr. Silence wizard! There are huge golems that kill anyone that enters. They stepped out and shouted 'no admittance, no warnings', then vanished. Not sure what else is happening, but I think leadership is planning to figure this out after we own the place."

"No one has gone in?" Joe got a head shake in reply. "No one has come out either? Then I'm going in to clear out the rat's nest!"

With a small crowd cheering him on, Joe ran at the building and crossed the threshold. "Hold! Don't attack me."

A blade was at his neck just as the word 'hold' passed his lips. "Yeesh. Carry on with guarding the area; slay any that enter."

"*Understood. Thus far, five hundred and twenty-two deaths.*"

"If you weren't so effective, I'd never want you around me." Joe breathed the words *very* softly. He emerged into the huge room that was just past the entryway, and found hundreds of people waiting for him.

"No! They've broken through!"

"Kill them before they have room to maneuver!"

Joe blanched as all eyes turned hostile. "Hold on! I'm Joe! Wanderer's Guild, First Elder!"

There was a long pause as people waffled back and forth about attacking, but Everard the Weaponmaster stepped forward and looked Joe over carefully. "I know him! He's Guild!"

There was a collective sigh of relief, and the room descended into questions. "What's happening out there?"

"Has the guild fallen?"

"Did we win?"

"How did you get in here?"

Everard waved his arms, then locked eyes with Joe. "I'm glad you came here, but where have you been for the last few days? You missed one *abyss* of a battle after the Aegis fell."

"Days?" Joe shook his head and pulled up his status, trying to use the time to think of a proper answer.

Name: Joe '*Tatum's Chosen Legend*' Class: Reductionist
Profession I: Arcanologist (Max)
Profession II: Ritualistic Alchemist (1/20)
Character Level: 18 Exp: 175,220 Exp to next level: 14,780

Rituarchitect Level: 10 Exp: 45,000 Exp debt: 14,714
Reductionist Level: 0 Exp: 0 Exp to next level: 1,000
Hit Points: 732/732
Mana: 1,039/2,137 (983 Reserved)
Mana regen: 42.28/sec
Stamina: 726.5/726.5
Stamina regen: 5.94/sec

Characteristic: Raw score

Strength: 71
Dexterity: 93
Constitution: 72
Intelligence: 137
Wisdom: 112
Dark Charisma: 79
Perception: 87
Luck: 59
Karmic Luck: +18

Joe was pleased by his increases, though he knew that from now on, all stat increases would be based on hard work and not leveling. In fact, he was starting to think that his level might not matter as much as… Joe paused as he remembered a line that he had appeared when he had bound the tablet. 'New Prestige Classes' had become available. All game logic told him that prestige classes had the prerequisite of being high-leveled… perhaps there was still a benefit to leveling up.

"Aten took a chance, and sent me to reach my second specialization. I just finished ranking up, but to me it was only a few hours, not days. How long has it been?" Joe's words were met with a sharp inhalation. The people in the area knew how difficult it was to reach the *first* specialization, and so far, there had only been *rumors* of people reaching the second. Yet, here was a person claiming to have reached the *second* Specialization?

"It's been four days total, three since the Aegis failed." Everard's voice was raspy as he tried to wrap his head around Joe's information. The outer wall fell yesterday, and a general retreat was ordered to the inner area. We didn't make it over there, obviously. We got cut off, and were forced in here. Also, anyone that didn't have their guild sigil showing was cut down by those crazy metal golems."

"Aten must have requested emergency lockdown." Joe muttered, his brow furrowing. "But why would he have taken the time to come here and give that order? He would have needed to come here in person."

"He brought this." Crim stepped forward, pushing his way through the crowd. He handed Joe a small box. "Sorry it took me so long; I started crossing the room as soon as I heard you were here. Aten left this in the Temple area, with instructions to get it to you right away. He figured you would go there first; I think he thought you died."

"Thanks, Crim." Joe opened the box, and narrowed his eyes. He pulled out a note, and a large gold ingot that was three-quarters full of intricate magical glyphs. "A remote activation? Where's Hannah?"

There was no reply past a few shrugs. Joe unfolded the note and read through it as quickly as his combined intelligence and perception would allow.

Joe, as soon as you get this, we need your help. I don't know how long it will take for the rank-up to complete, and I feel like a fool for expecting it to be quick. Your Coven members got caught and killed. I'm sure of it. Not only that, but our fast-travel and respawn points in the Temple stopped working; something about a war order. Anyone coming back would need to break the encirclement and return from Ardania. One of your people made it to me in time, but she died after handing me that ingot. Good luck saving us all, First Elder. I don't know what this means, because she and Mike died when the wall dropped, but here is all she was able to tell me before she went to respawn:

Southeast side unlinked. Standing stone #16. No whitelist. Mike demanded and authorized extreme measures.

Joe read over the message once more, and realized a few things. One, it seemed that the Coven had managed to set up most of the outward-facing Ritual of Quarantine. Two, he needed to finish it, and he now knew where it was set up and waiting to be linked. Three, if he activated it prematurely, he would get hit by the effects. That was what it meant not to have a whitelist: no exceptions. Lastly… what extreme measures? Mike barely understood what Joe's group was capable of doing; how would he be able to do anything extreme?

He looked up from the paper, and met the gazes of all the people that saw him as their last hope. "Well… looks like I have some work to do. Anyone want to come with me?"

Silence filled the room, and Joe snorted softly. "That's just fine, but I'm still gonna need some help. Everard, you'll enjoy this next bit."

CHAPTER FIFTY-SIX

Joe stumbled out of the Pathfinder's Hall bruised and bloody. There were open wounds on him, and his right eye was swollen shut. He bent over and spat out a mouthful of blood, then lifted his head and regarded the horde of people staring him down. He stood up proudly, and announced, "The golems came back, so don't go in, but I've cleared out this patch of villainy! No more will we need to fear an attack on our flank as we focus on the *real* issue!"

There was a roar of approval, started by the man that had told Joe about the situation inside the building, and picked up by the others as they realized that something good had happened. That was the way of a large crowd, though. "Let's move out, and join in the encirclement of the main area!"

Dark Charismatic effects have had an exceptional effect on a large number of people at once! Charisma +1!

The area around the Pathfinder's Hall rapidly emptied, and only a few people remained nearby to protect it until the leadership had a chance to claim the area. Joe was fine with that, as it had been part of his plan from the start. He had persuaded the people in the building to beat him badly, and after the exterior was empty, they would use the open area to stage their attack.

Once Joe could get the Ritual of Quarantine to work correctly and make everyone outside the town too ill to come fight, the people staged at the Pathfinder's Hall would charge in and assault the combatants surrounding the core of the town. Then, they would work together to retake the town at large and get the walls back in place. Joe was confident that they could work together, gather all the damaged stone, and use the wall-raising ritual to put their protections back in place. The only downside of this plan was that Joe needed to survive walking through… *that* without getting recognized.

Joe gulped as he considered the seething masses of humanity that had overrun the town, knowing that this was simply the smallest fraction of the total force, which couldn't possibly fit in its entirety. He started walking nonchalantly through the area, moving toward the Southeast corner of the town.

The distance wasn't too terribly far; standing stone number sixteen was simply a temporary directional marker intended to help people find their way around. Road names had not been voted upon in the town yet, which meant no street names or addresses. Also, an *astounding* number of people simply stared blankly when instructed to go to the 'south'. So, the pillar-like rocks had numbers carved into them, which was how people found their way around.

As it turned out, they were also an excellent place to bind a ritual. The stones had been very carefully placed so that they were all equidistant from the next, which was beneficial for magic, such as rituals, that required stability and perfect proportions to use effectively. This, along with helping people find their way around town, was why Joe had been in enthusiastic agreement when a seemingly minor point like his had come up in the required-attendance leadership meetings a while back.

The hardest part of his trek was keeping his behavior natural. He was going against the stream of humanity here;

everyone else was doing their best to make their way deeper into the area, and he was leaving. That alone turned a few heads, and caused more than one person to consider him calculatingly. Joe shook his head at the unexpected gift that he had been given by the silence mage; his current robes and bearing were off-putting and recognizable. Everyone knew that the order of mages Joe appeared to belong to was cruel and efficient, which caused many of those considering, sizing-up, greedy stares… to turn into panicked 'nonchalance'.

Soon enough, the crowd parted in front of Joe like a shark fin slicing through water. The darkness in his aura seemed to be having a serious impact on the crowd, which he was both pleased and concerned with. Pleased, as he got where he needed to go much faster. Concerned, because he was gathering far too much attention. After twenty minutes, he had finally reached the stone. Normally, it was a five minute walk at worst, thanks to the speed people with higher stats were able to move.

Joe went to work right away, finding the ritual set onto the stone with ease. This wasn't something that should have needed to be hidden, as it was intended to be kept in the safe area of the guild. It was ready; Joe could see the mana contained within swirling and practically begging to be released. He held the gold ingot close to the ritual and activated the binding that would bring it all together. He breathed a sigh of relief as the binding began and his mana rushed out to put the effect in place.

"It stabilized." Joe carefully wiped the sweat off his head.

"Who are you, and what are you doing?" The sharp voice was clearly directed at Joe, but he didn't turn around. Answering right away could only make him look guilty, and he couldn't afford to be interrupted right now. "I asked you who you were! You will stop what you are doing right this *instant*, or by authority of the Floodwater family, I will end you where you stand."

"Ahh… the Floodwater family." Now the group offering money to this cause was clear. The Floodwater family had, as far as Joe knew, only a single strategic resource: Floodwater grapes. A grape that had recently been found in a second place: the Evergrowth Greenhouse. Joe replied without turning around. "You have the authority to tell *me*… to stop what I'm doing?"

"I most *certainly* do." The voice was cold, and the rasp of a blade scraping leather as it was pulled from a sheath caused chills to run down Joe's spine. He turned and locked eyes with a grizzled veteran, likely the leader of the mercenary group he had fought against when the wall had first been damaged. If that were the end of it, Joe still wouldn't have been too concerned; he would have attempted to bluff his way past as a 'respected silencer'. Unfortunately, another man in purple robes was standing nearby, obviously trying to place where he knew Joe from. His dark purple robes were *ornate*, and he was clearly a high-ranking member of the mages.

"How do I know you? No," The mage tapped his chin, "more, why do I recognize you and not know you *well*? I approve all who join my order. Why are you wearing our colors? You can only be a spy."

"His bald head sparks no joy, only furious memories of trapped brothers and sisters." A Jester stepped forward and stood next to the others.

"I know this one." A man wearing simple robes and half-moon spectacles stared at Joe over the top of his eyewear. Joe had only ever seen him once before: at the library of Ardania. "He is the one who convinced Boris that he was a scholar, and even achieved the highest rank and honor from our organization before his *true* intentions were brought to light. He is the Arcanologist that forced us to demote Boris and send him on missions like a man half his age."

"What? What did you do to Boris?" Joe stepped toward the group as he heard these words. Now that he thought about it, the 'tenured scholar' profession had vanished from his status sheet, leaving behind only Arcanologist. He hadn't thought anything of it at the time, but now…

"*We* did nothing." The scholar put his hands in the sleeves of his robes, arms crossed. "He did not do proper research; the hallmark of failure for a scholar. This is Joe, the focal point of all these disturbances within our organizations."

Joe swallowed as the area around him went still. The people in the area knew that something had just happened, but they didn't know what to make of the situation. The mercenary stepped forward. "Come with me. My employer is *very* interested in meeting you."

"No, we have the right of first blood with this one!" The silencer brandished a ball of glowing mana on his palm.

"I plan to have him dissected to find what makes him tick," The scholar announced bluntly.

Joe wanted none of this, and started backing up toward the edge of the crowd. The mercenary saw through his intent right away. "And where are *you* going, *Joe*?"

"Away from you." Joe muttered, though in the strange silence of the area, his words were heard clearly.

"I think not." The merc pulled out a second sword and started advancing.

"Let's find out, shall we? *Dark Lightning Strike*!" Joe called down the darkness, and the crowd that was starting to press in on him was fried, all lower-leveled people dropping instantly.

Skill increase: Dark Lightning Strike (Apprentice 0). Sacrificing hundreds of humans is totally what this skill was intended to be used for! At least you never flinched away from putting yourself under the effect. Because of that single fact, this spell has gained a new ability! Bonus: Call down the lightning anywhere within line-of-sight.

Joe didn't stop to appreciate how huge of a benefit he had just gained. He ran over the pile of corpses, but only made it to the far side before a sword scraped along his Exquisite Shell. Joe knew right then that he needed to fight; fleeing was not an option. He turned and released an Acid Spray, soaking the mercenary.

Well, that was the plan. Instead, a barrier appeared, and the acid slid past the man, directly to the ground. "Huh. When you've been in the business as long as I have, you make sure that liquids don't land on you. Nice try."

Planning a Cone of Cold next, Joe found that his mana fizzled and the words stuck in his throat. A bright purple glow appeared in his vision, reading 'silenced'. He glanced over and saw the other three people walking over leisurely. Joe grabbed a fallen staff, kicking a body that had collapsed on top of it, then took a ready stance.

"That's… so cute." The Jester shook his head at Joe's antics. "Leave this one to me. We need to feed the Creeping Death Squirrel."

Even the Scholar blanched at that, and the man had wanted to dissect him while he was still alive! What horror had Joe unknowingly given to the Jesters? All in return for what? Coffee…? Coffee! The silence wore off, since clearly the others weren't seeing him as a serious threat. "Mate, Over-Caffeinate!"

The others attacked, unaware of what Joe was doing. Dark liquid swirled on Joe's arm, and he felt a massive increase to his heart rate. He parried the sword coming his way with a burst of speed, then knocked the Jester's flying daggers slightly off track with a large sweep of the polearm. Using his burst of speed, Joe dropped to a knee and held up a golden coin.

"You can't *buy* your way out of this, fool!" the Jester snarled.

Joe simply smiled as he squeezed his hand and the 'coin' broke in half.

CHAPTER FIFTY-SEVEN

The mercenary was slapped away, and he went bouncing along the bodies that had piled up due to Joe's Dark Lightning Strike. Arthur the Neigh-Bear fully phased into being, instantly becoming the focus of hundreds of nearby people. On a positive note, most of them were screaming and backpedaling.

"What in the…?" The silencer took a trembling step back.

"A Neigh-Bear! How *rare* and sought after!" The Jester took a decisive step forward. "A single fang is enough to guarantee a rare-quality dagger-"

"That's not just any…" the scholar's eyes widened. "That's… that's Neigh-Bear King Arthur! Leader of the Seven Hordes, brightest light in a generation, Ember of the Flaming Berserkers! I'm sure of it, look at those markings! He even wields the claw weapon Excalibear!"

Joe jumped onto Arthur's horsey hindquarters and dug his heels in. "Giddyup."

The area descended into silence once more, this time in shock. Only the creaking of a building burning and collapsing broke the still air. Arthur growled, "*What* did you just say?"

"We need to get out of here, right now. I need you to clear a path directly to that building, and time is running out for your summoning."

"The people in the way?"

"Enemies, one and all." Joe pointed at the distant wall. "Go, now! Hurry, Arthur!"

"You will *not* use me as a mount again." Arthur rumbled as he started charging toward the core of the town.

"Deal." Joe winced as Arthur got up to speed. There was no way for people to get out of the way in time; they were packed too densely together. Arthur trampled anyone in his path, his huge hooves pulverizing everything they landed on. His paws and jaws seemed to work independently, and the Neigh-Bear sent dozens of people to respawn every few steps, and critically wounded even more. Somehow, he was able to keep increasing his speed the entire time.

"You have ten seconds remaining until I vanish." Arthur spat out the words and a hand at the same time, so the message was a little garbled.

"Understood. Get as close to the wall as possible, and jump as high as you can." Joe stared at the distant wall, then shifted from sitting into a crouching position. A dagger slammed into his arm, and a sharp **slap slap** rang out nearby.

Damage dealt: 617 Dark damage. Jester slain x1. (Retaliation of Shadows)

Joe was silenced a moment later, and a strange metal ball impacted his back and finished off his Shell, as well as cracking one of the ribs on the left side of his back. Joe silently spat out a mouthful of blood; his lung must have been punctured. Arthur jumped and started to fade. Joe felt his feet starting to slip through, so he empowered his legs and *jumped*. It was a smooth jump, and he went ten feet above the wall, clearing it easily.

He arced back down, plummeting toward the stone ground that surrounded the bathhouse. He landed badly, his legs cracking, his wrist shattering, and internal injuries stacking up rapidly, if the way he felt was any indication. The silence countdown had another ten seconds, and Joe was currently staring down a half dozen swords. He could only pray that someone would recognize him under the ash, blood, and bruises.

"U-um. Excuse me, he's my party leader." Joe managed to turn his head slightly, and saw Alexis lightly tugging on one of the men that was about to skewer him. "I really think killing him is a bad idea. Please hold off?"

"I…" the man hesitated, clearly tightly wound. If someone had harshly demanded that he step away, he likely would have finished Joe off. "Yes, miss. Just, make sure it is who you think it is. Looks like one of them mages that messed with our defenses."

The timer finished, and Joe slapped his unbroken hand to himself and cast Lay on Hands, which caused his bones to grind against each other as they aligned.

Skill increase: Lay on Hands (Student 0). You can now use each hand independently to cast this spell! This means you can have two spells ready to go whenever you need them, which seems to be pretty often! Their cooldown is determined individually.

Alexis offered her hand, and Joe took it to stand up. As he did so, the majority of the grime that had accumulated on him just… slid away. Every second, more blood flaked off, and ash slid off him as if he wasn't there. "I need to see Aten."

"I figured as much." Alexis started pulling Joe away from the still-suspicious people staring him down. "He's in the main building, coordinating the defenses. He left orders that you were to be brought straight to him when you showed up. I don't know how you did it, but that man has a crazy amount of faith in you."

Joe felt his eyes burn with shame at the undeserved praise. "I'm just a cockroach… really hard to kill, seems to survive against all odds, but not really great to have around. I've barely got any good news for him at all. I…"

"It's fine, Joe." Alexis assured him. "Even if all this goes away, all that happens is that we need to start fresh. We got here in such a short time, and next time, we will build with heavy defense in mind. We went to luxury too fast, trying to bypass security because of our life experience on earth to this point. Next time…"

Her eyes blazed with fervent belief. "Next time, we'll make them *fear* coming after us."

They crossed the remaining distance in silence, and Joe was admitted to the meeting room right away. Aten held up a hand and cut off an accounting of supplies. "Joe! Blast it, man, you *did* make it back!"

"Aten, I don't have much-"

"Quiet, Joe. I haven't pinned *all* my hopes on you." Aten could see at a glance that Joe didn't have the news that he had been hoping for. "You're one man, and *we* are a full guild. Even if you didn't come back with a miracle, we'll figure this mess out. Did you succeed? Are you third tier now?"

"Yes. but-"

"Was it worth getting?" Aten demanded with shining eyes, clearly picturing glory and battle prowess.

"I can only hope." Joe sighed and ran a hand over his bald head and down his neck. "I do have *some* good news. I cleared out the area around the Pathfinder's Hall, and our people there are ready to strike whenever we give them a proper signal."

"You made it there, too!" Aten grabbed Joe's shoulders. "Did you get the box? Did you-"

"I got it, and managed to get everything linked before I came here." Joe nodded at Aten's wide smile. "I think that we will be able to retake our town, at least for a while. This will give us a shot of getting the walls up, at least."

"Do it now." Aten demanded. "Make them start feeling it. Wait, how long will it last?"

"At least a few hours?" Joe shrugged, slightly off-put that he couldn't give a definitive answer. "I didn't set this one up; my juniors did it. Can't imagine it lasting any shorter than that."

"Do it then, we'll plan the counterattack to go out in an hour." Aten slapped Joe on his unprotected back, reminding him that he needed to get his Exquisite Shell going again. He nodded at Aten and pulled out the gold ingot.

Joe pressed the activation sequence, starting the ritual.

Ritual 'Blooded Quarantine Area' activation started x4! Players who will remain unaffected: none. All beings in the impacted area will feel sick, and gain symptoms 'vomiting' and 'no bowel control', stacking to higher ranks with increased proximity to the ritual diagram. Once active, this ritual will remain for .25 seconds per impacted living being, increasing range by one foot in radius per impacted living being. Timer does not increase if a living being leaves the impacted area and returns. Activate all four rituals now? Yes / No.

Joe selected 'yes', and flopped into a chair. His part in this war was over for now, and a nap was long past due. He blinked at the gold as his hand began to hurt, then dropped the ingot with a yelp as it turned red-hot and began to melt. "What… what was *that*?"

Ritualist Hannah has broken a vow with you, and has been given the title Warlock V!

His eyes went wide, and Joe scrambled to pull up his notifications.

Alchemical agents added to rituals have taken effect! Altering effect of ritual 'Blooded Quarantine Area'… complete. Substance 'Blood of Endless Hunger' from being 'Gameover' has significantly altered the ritual! New ritual in place, see effects?

"What? *Yes*, see the effects!" Joe's bellow attracted attention, and anyone who had interacted with him before saw that his face was pale, and his hands were trembling as he read over the information that he alone could see.

New ritual activated: Ritual of Liquifying Membranes. Players who will remain unaffected: none. All beings with less than 80 points in constitution within the impacted area will become sick, and gain symptoms 'vomiting blood', ECC, and 'damaged organs', stacking to higher ranks with increased proximity to the ritual diagram. Once active, this ritual will remain for .25 seconds per impacted living being, increasing range by one foot in radius per impacted living being. Each impacted being increases the threshold of constitution required to ignore effects by .0001 each. Does not increase if a living being leaves the impacted area and returns.

"Show status, guild contribution points!" There was only one thing this could be, but there was no way-

Contribution points: 6,189,761.

"Oh… oh my… Mike. Mike authorized extreme measures." Joe was dizzy. He nearly fainted as he read the horrifying effects that this ritual had. "See information 'vomiting blood'."

Vomiting blood: take 1 bleeding damage per second per stack, lasts 10 hours. Maximum: twenty stacks.

"Ten… *hours*?" Joe felt a tear roll down his cheek. "Damaged organs?"

Damaged organs: reduce effects of healing by 50%.

"What in the world is ECC?" Joe whispered, truly not wanting to know the answer.

ECC: Exploding Corpse Curse. When a being inflicted with this curse dies, their body explodes, dealing half their maximum health as concussive damage and inflicting all debuffs they had at the maximum possible stacks.

"I need to stop this. I need to stop this right now!" Joe stood up, and turned toward the door.

"Joe? What's going on? Joe!" Aten called as Joe ran from the room.

"Don't let *anyone* into the central area of the town! We just released a massive curse… a plague that might kill us all!" Joe bellowed over his shoulder. "Wait… the safeguard I put on all rituals! I can end this now! End ritual: Ritual of Liquifying Membranes!"

Nothing.

"End Ritual: Blooded Quarantine Area!" There was no message, there was *nothing*. That meant there was no response from the ritual; it was still starting. Why? He had always been able to cancel them before! Joe's hands slapped to the sides of his head as he remembered a past conversation with Hannah. She had said… 'She was stripping everything down to make it as efficient as possible'… she wouldn't know… the safeguard! "No! She *removed* it!"

Joe ran to the top of the ramparts and staggered over to the edge of the wall. Thousands of people were milling about, and he could hear someone give the order to launch a full-scale assault. He shouted as loudly as possible, infusing his throat with mana in an attempt to make his words reach further. "No! *No*! Listen to me! You all need to run! You need to scatter! If you stay here…"

Darkness flashed through Joe's eyes, and a shadowy version of himself appeared behind him with a sinister grin on its face. The words that rumbled out of Joe's chest were filled with dark charisma, and caused fear to run through the crowd below.

"*You're all going to die!*"

CHAPTER FIFTY-EIGHT

"Attack!" The people below charged the walls, but Joe didn't bother to watch as arrows were traded, ladders were knocked away from the wall, and fireballs burned people to charcoal. No… he was watching the rear of the lines, where ever more people were running through the active rituals.

He was waiting for it… it wouldn't be too long now… **pop**.

The sound was soft at this distance, but since the fires had burned out and smoke had begun drifting upward instead of settling, a red mist clearly showed where the first victim of what would become known as the 'Corpse Plague' had died. The sound of vomiting and screams started coming from the distance. Joe winced: the sound of *hundreds* of people puking at the same time, over and over, was going to stay with him for a very long time.

One thing that Joe appreciated was that the ritual actually killed very quickly. Mostly. The low-level people had far less than two hundred health, so with twenty health per second vanishing, they died in under ten seconds. Most fell in less than five. Hysteria began to set in, but there was nowhere to run. Within half a minute, the demands of victory, war cries, or random babble all changed to begging to be let in before whatever *that* was got to *them*.

Guild Title upgraded! Utterly Ruthless II. Show details?

Joe swiped away the message and watched the panicked crowd below. The doors stayed shut, of course. There was no way anyone was letting *that* in; orders be abyssed. If there was one positive note, it was that the sight was blocked out by the red mist swiftly, and all retching and popping sounds stopped soon after that. An eerie silence set in, but no one wanted to be the first to break it. Joe made the choice after a few long minutes. He turned and waved to get the attention of anyone in sight.

"That red mist is going to stay in place for *days*. If you touch it, you'll die from it. You'll also make it stronger. Right now, if you have less than…" Joe checked the active ritual for information, eighty point two… eighty-one… eighty-three…. Celestial…"

Guild Title upgraded! Utterly Ruthless III.

He gulped and shook his head. "If there really were a million people out there, and this doesn't go anywhere else… we will be trapped in here for sixty-nine hours. Anyone below one hundred and eighty constitution will catch *that*, and it lasts for ten hours. Twenty health a second for ten hours. *No one goes out or comes in*!"

The last sentence had been a bellow, and no one dared to let out a single peep. "On the plus side, it has now been three minutes. Anyone caught in there with less than nine *hundred* health has died. In fifteen minutes, I'll ask Aten to let most of you stand down. For what it's worth…"

"We won." Joe started walking down the stairs heavily, and no cheers rang out. Everyone wanted to win, but no one wanted to win like *that*. Starting over would have been preferable.

Guild Title upgraded! Utterly Ruthless IV.

Guild Title upgraded! Utterly Ruthless V.

The next few days passed quietly. It was tight quarters, but everyone was able to stay fed, thanks to the greenhouse, clean, thanks to the bathhouse, and calm, thanks to the sea of red mist that hovered a foot above the ground as far as the eye could see. Joe trained his stats as well as he could during those few days, and spent some time drawing up new spell scrolls. He didn't learn any of the spells, not just yet. He wanted to be ready for what came next, and he knew that people were still dying.

Guild Title has reached maximum rank! Utterly Ruthless has transformed into a new title: Ruthless.

Ruthless. When attacking a guild, town, army, or defending those, damage dealt is increased by 25%, damage received is reduced by 25%. There is now a 50% chance of an item dropping from a slain enemy when they are attacking areas owned by your guild, and it is automatically collected into the guild vaults. If no guild vault is present, the loot will accumulate in the Guild Hall.

Joe was once more standing on the walls, staring out at the sea of red. The ritual was about to end, and nine days had passed. That meant that at least three million people had been caught by the ritual's effects. He hoped that Ardania still *existed*. On the positive side, if everyone practiced social distancing and no one added fuel to the mists, it would be over in an hour.

"Everyone!" a voice broke the morning stillness, and Joe startled away from the edge where he had been leaning. Quiet voices had been the norm, so this was shocking after over a week of quiet contemplation. "It is time to make our choice! Over the last few days, I've spoken to many of you. If I haven't had the pleasure yet, allow me to do so now."

The man hopped onto a table, and continued shouting. "My name is Mr. Banks! I am one of the founders of this guild. This war… was pointless! I had secured a deal that would have left us in an advantageous position with all the poor souls that were *wiped out* by the actions and choices of the 'players' who staged a coup! Instead of calm negotiations, they ousted the council, and demanded war! Instead of taking care of all of us, and making sure we had safety, they trapped us here for the last fortnight!"

"*Banks*!" Aten appeared on the scene, looking like a thundercloud. "You have *no* right to-"

"Oh, but I do." Banks stated coldly. "Look, I'm level ten now, Guild *Commander*. It is time for cooler heads to prevail! We need to show this whole kingdom that we are going to make amends! This starts by removing Aten as a leader! I hereby call for a vote of no confidence!"

The council of the Wanderer's Guild has issued a 'No Trust' vote to remove Guild Commander Aten from his position! Should he be removed? All Guild members currently waiting on respawn automatically vote 'abstain'. Yes / No / Abstain.

"*This* again?" Aten roared as buttons appeared in the view of all currently living members of the guild. "You can't possibly believe... that they... would..."

The guild has spoken! Abstain: 18,501. Votes to remove Aten as Guild Commander: 268. Votes for him to remain: 231. Aten has been removed as Guild Commander. Per his contract, he will attain the highest position in the guild only in the next Zone, so long as a new guild area is established. If this happens, the guild in Zone one 'Midgard' will become a branch guild.

"It's just good business, Aten. Looks like the handful of people that survived under your iron fist have chosen *freedom*!" Mr. Banks' smile was more like a disturbing mask. "We need to prepare to hand over the war criminals to the crown. If they are here; Aten, Joe, Mike, come here *now*."

The last word was an order, and Aten was forced to one knee. Joe stayed where he was, staring down at the man who had decided to take command. Mr. Banks looked up, and Joe saw just a hint of fear in his eyes. "I know you're here. I said get *down here*."

"That's a big nope from me." Joe shook his head. "Just because you removed Aten from his position doesn't make *you* the guild leader. Just someone with a power complex."

Joe's words sent laughter rippling around the area. Banks' face went red. "I am the only councilman present! By guild contract, I am the highest ranking person in the guild at this moment, which means *I* set the rules!"

"No, actually." Joe shook his head. "I was recently promoted to First Elder. Technically, that makes *me* the highest ranking member of the guild."

"That's not a position! Wait... no... Aten would *never* give someone else as much power as he had in the guild!" Banks sputtered as he pointed a shaking finger at Joe. "That would make a massive breakdown in hierarchy! Aten is... he'd... grab that man!"

"Nobody move." Joe calmly ordered as a few people started toward him. Everyone stopped, a few of them shocked at the fact. Joe had just proven that he did, indeed, have the authority he claimed to have. "Aten, get up. What do I need to do to fix this?"

Aten swallowed a few times, nodded at Joe, then started walking toward the Guild Hall. "Paperwork, Joe. Then a new vote after people come back to life. Give me twenty minutes."

"Do we need *him*?" Joe waved at Banks. Aten coldly contemplated the sweating man, then shook his head 'no'. "Works for me. Over the wall he goes."

"S-stop! You can't murder me like this!" Banks fixated on the looming wall as people grabbed him and pulled him toward the edge. "It's not *legal*!"

"Hold on." Joe walked over and looked Banks in the eye. "You really are *this* dense? This isn't about business, or a game, or *legality*. This is *survival*. What we are all striving for isn't *luxury*. It's abyssal... survival. For that, this guild has proven that we are willing to be *Ruthless*. Throw him over."

There was a soft **pop**, and the ritual counter went up by a fraction of a second: too little to matter.

Days later, Joe once again stood before the Royal Court, waiting to see if his actions would cause him to be locked away. He wasn't cuffed this time, and he had been brought to join a large group to be tried all at the same time. He was led in, and found himself standing next to Aten, Mike, Hannah, and Big_Mo.

There were a slew of other people that he didn't recognize as well, but he was less concerned for them.

The King sighed, and the room seemed to freeze from that single exhalation. "Over three million dead in under half a day. Thousands more perished, due to starvation and fear of the Corpse Plague. Mass rioting was averted, at least, but for that... we look back at the fear. This attack was not just ruthless. It was vicious, and serious punishments *must* be given."

His head shifted, and it felt like Joe had been punched in the gut as his diaphragm refused to move and allow him to breathe in. "Tell me what happened on your end first, Joe. I know you, and your character. You know mine. I need the unvarnished truth."

"Why does *he* get to-"

The King cut off the new voice with a light hand wave. "Marquis Floodwater, wait your turn."

Aten stepped forward. "As Joe's superior, all of this falls upon me. Joe was only doing what he could to patch our ship as we sunk. He did nothing wrong, or even out of the ordinary."

"I was the one who authorized the use of a magical reagent that Joe had *expressly* forbidden others to use, or even know about." Mike offered, pushing Aten out of the way. "I even *paid* for it, knowing it was wrong. Please, if anything, the blame falls on-"

"Me." Hannah interrupted directly, her eyes shining from unshed tears. She looked absolutely terrible, the effect of the title Warlock V thoroughly destroying her charisma. "I was the one that redesigned the spell and pulled out all the safeties. I was the one that told Mike about the blood, and pulled the item away from the location where it had been securely stored. I put it into place without Joe's knowledge."

The King snorted at the display. "Never before have I seen so many people falling all over themselves to take the blame for a catastrophe of this scale. How about you?"

Big_Mo gulped as he found the King's focus on himself. "No, I agree with Hannah. She kinda sucks to have done all that, and I think she should be thrown into the dark for a long, long time."

The room, as well as King Henry, were silent, unsure how to react to that statement after all the pleas for blame. The King coughed and moved on. "I'll come back to this. Floodwater."

It didn't escape anyone that the King hadn't used the moniker 'Marquis'. King Henry continued, "You, in *direct* opposition to my orders of destroying monopolies and the right to work, funded a war against a Noble Guild, a war that cost over fifty million lives… over fruit."

"F-fifty million? What?" Floodwater shook his head violently. "Your Majesty, I was simply trying to right the wrong he caused me! He stole the seeds that my family-"

"Has had a *monopoly* on for centuries. Yes." The monarch growled. "Do you know what a war totem is, Floodwater?"

"I can't be sure of the *exact* details-"

"No? Because you supplied twelve of them to the 'war effort'." The King slumped into his throne. "Does everyone know that a war totem sets a bind point? Yes? Good. Did you know that it is the *only* bind point that someone can use if the conflict is ongoing, that it reduces respawn time to four hours, and that it *forces* the bound individual to respawn? All of the people that attacked… Towny McTownface… died to the Corpse Plague, on average, fifty-one times. The constant deaths and forced respawn have left their minds as wrecks, and somehow their characteristics have *all* fallen below the ten point threshold."

The room erupted in muttering as the 'over fifty million' was made clear, and the suffering was put in perspective. "For your part in this, Floodwater, you lose everything except your life, and I formally reduce all reputation you have with any crown-affiliated faction by four thousand points. Your wealth will be used in the rehabilitation of those that suffered due to your actions. Take this beggar out of my court."

Floodwater was seized and dragged from the room. The King turned to the members of The Wanderer's guild. "As for all of you, you have a choice. Imprisonment, death until level one, or-"

"Your Majesty." Joe used every bit of strength and mana he had just to get those words out of his throat while Henry was speaking, then collapsed. The King stopped, and acknowledged him questioningly. When Joe was able to move again, he pulled himself off the floor and bowed. "Your Majesty, please. So much of this fell on my guild because of my actions alone. I antagonized all of the groups that came after us. The blame for this is mine alone."

"I came into conflict with architects, and the disenfranchised workers knocked over my walls. I set myself against the assassins, and they came to extract their price in blood. The fruit, though… to be fair, that was a gift. Didn't even know it was gonna be an issue till later. Good call with that one." Joe cleared his throat and talked over the muttering members of the court.

"The spell used was my own, altered by my brilliant apprentice because I wanted to do other things, and was too lazy to carefully explain things. The blood used to cause this plague was collected and stored by me. *My* actions called the attention of these different groups onto us. Hannah, I'm sorry I failed you so badly. I formally remove the Warlock title." Joe looked at his guild members, who were still fighting his words so that he could walk away. Hannah's face literally shifted as her charisma came back into play. Now it wasn't nearly so hard to look at her. "It is hard for me to trust others, but these people have earned my trust, even if a few actions were not advisable. Still, the crimes are my own. Please allow me to be the only one to pay them."

The room was silent for a long moment. "Your spell, your blood, your actions. I know more of this chain of events than you think I do. I know *far* more about you than you think I do… and you are correct. Much of this *is* due to your actions. You just reached your second specialization, correct…? Yes, I see this too.

"Then here is my ruling." King Henry's voice echoed through the room. "Joe, you are hereby exiled from Midgard. You will be able to return to your guild to put your affairs in order, but within twenty-four hours, you will be escorted to the bifrost. You will not be allowed to take anything with you, except what you are wearing. I formally reduce all reputation you have with any crown-affiliated faction by *eight* thousand ponts. Your exile will last a year and a day."

"One more thing. As you are demanding the punishment for your entire guild, that means you are taking their share of responsibility. This court gives you the title 'Despised by Humanity'. If, after your time in exile, you come back with proof of significant efforts to promote and help humans, this title might be revoked."

You have lost the title: I'm a healer! I swear!

You have gained the title: Despised by Humanity. Effect: You cannot gain reputation with humans that are positively affiliated with Ardania.

"This court rests."

EPILOGUE

Joe stood near a double-helix of light that stretched into the sky, giving his mother one last hug. "I'll be fine! This was the plan all along, after all. I was *supposed* to go to the next Zone!"

"But… all you have is your clothes! How will you fend for yourself with *nothing*? You have nothing!" Brenda sobbed into his shoulder.

Not able to bear it any longer. Joe leaned into her and whispered. "It's all goose. I have a *Legendary* storage device, one that the guild packed *full* of anything they thought I could use. The only currency I had was contribution points, since I already gave you the extra gold I have! I *somehow* gained over six million contribution points suddenly, so I went on a shopping spree."

Mike heard that last bit, and it seemed that he might start to cry. So much lost revenue! If it weren't for the Guild Hall being stuffed with gear from all the collected loot gathered by the new Ruthless guild title, he would have been sent packing, useful to the guild or no.

Joe patted his mother on the back one last time, then addressed his party, his Coven, and his guild leaders that had all come to see him off. "I'm looking forward to seeing you all soon! I'll try to have a nice, safe location built up that we can all live in, okay? Jaxon... don't collect the warrants for your arrest. It's a bad idea."

"The wanted posters are free portraits, though! I keep artists in business!" Jaxon gave in after a stern look, sighing sadly at the lost opportunity.

"Aten..." Joe grinned at the man, a dark smile that made the newly-reelected Guild Commander shiver. "I think you'll be able to tell who isn't loyal to you by the time you return back to the guild."

"What did you do?" Aten demanded nervously. Joe just laughed, which wasn't at all comforting. "Joe? Joe!"

Joe stepped into the bifrost, and waved his hand just before being yanked into the sky. He was moving faster than a rocket, and the ground was a thousand feet away before he completed a blink. He kept traveling at that blinding pace, but decided to use his time constructively. "Reputation... reputation..."

Then he started laughing. King Henry had really known more than Joe had given him credit for. He knew about Joe's storage device, and gave Joe plenty of time to go get anything he wanted or needed. He also knew that in terms of reputation... Joe had only lost half of what he should have as punishment. Instead of being thrown into 'Hatred', his lowest reputation score was still at two thousand points, 'Reluctantly Friendly'. In a year, when he was allowed back, Joe would have plenty of opportunity to make up for the loss. Until then, he would work to become so powerful that his guild would become the number-one existence on Midgard.

Joe crested the bifrost, and saw an entire new world laid out before him. Then... he started accelerating downward. The ground came closer, closer... and Joe was suddenly slowing. He landed right between two people who were glaring at each other.

"Hello." A musical voice called over as Joe peered around from the fluffy chair that he found himself in. He blinked as he locked eyes with an Elf. "Welcome to Alfenheim. You have a choice to make."

"Welcome to *Svaltarheim*, and the choice should be an easy one!" The Dwarf on the other side called out. "Join the snooty Elves and become a sworn enemy of the Dwarves-"

"Or join the unruly mob that is the Dwarves, and become the sworn enemy of the Elves."

Joe tried to catch his breath, but every single moment felt like standing in the presence of King Henry. The Dwarf narrowed his eyes as he watched Joe struggle to breathe. "You… you didn't wait to break the mortal limit before you came here?"

"This one is *clearly* going to join the Dwarves; he must have no intelligence at all!" The Elf scoffed.

Joe had a strange feeling that the two of them being in agreement was a *very* bad thing for him.

"Cheers!" Mr. Banks was hosting a small soiree for his close allies, celebrating the deal they had pushed through while the trial was taking place. Not only was Joe out of their hair, but they had retrieved a large amount of power. Yes, Joe had been able to work with Aten to get the obstinate man reinstated, but it was only a matter of time before they had another opportunity to step forward and take their rightful place in the guild. They had certainly *paid* enough for it!

The party was going well, and they had even received a small package containing Floodwater wine that had been delivered to them, all thanks to the now ex-Marquis Floodwater. Banks chuckled at the memory of finding out that they had gained so much, and now owed *nothing* to their benefactor. Truly, things were going splendidly!

Banks finished off his glass of wine and filled it once more from the limited stock, before standing and tapping on his glass to call attention. "Thank you all for being here today! As you all know, we took some losses in the recent days. However, let me remind you of what we mang-gged to acc-ccomprish."

Mr. Banks coughed to clear his airway, then shook his head. No one's eyes were on the bottle of Floodwater wine, else they may have noticed a shifting ritual diagram spinning up the neck. "Stho sthorry about that! Asth I was stahying…"

He trailed off and clamped a hand to his mouth as pain flooded his gums. Everyone else was doing the same, and he gaped around wildly. Suddenly, his mouth felt full, and he spit out a handful of corn. Corn? No! That was… his teeth!

"Ahh!" someone shouted as they saw what was happening. "We're *ruthless*!"

"Of courth we are! We alwath have been!" Banks slammed his fist on the table. "Whath going on here?"

"No! Bankth!" The man tearfully pointed at his mouth, then to the teeth that had fallen out of the mouths of everyone present. He showed his empty, bleeding gums.

"We're *ruth*-less!"

ABOUT DAKOTA KROUT

I live in a 'pretty much Canada' Minnesota city with my wife and daughter. I started writing The Divine Dungeon series because I enjoy reading and wanted to create a world all my own. To my surprise and great pleasure, I found like-minded people who enjoy the contents of my mind. Publishing my stories has been an incredible blessing thus far, and I hope to keep you entertained for years to come!

Connect with Dakota:
MountaindalePress.com
Patreon.com/DakotaKrout
Facebook.com/TheDivineDungeon
Twitter.com/DakotaKrout
Discord.gg/8vjzGA5

ABOUT MOUNTAINDALE PRESS

Dakota and Danielle Krout, a husband and wife team, strive to create as well as publish excellent fantasy and science fiction novels. Self-publishing *The Divine Dungeon: Dungeon Born* in 2016 transformed their careers from Dakota's military and programming background and Danielle's Ph.D. in pharmacology to President and CEO, respectively, of a small press. Their goal is to share their success with other authors and provide captivating fiction to readers with the purpose of solidifying Mountaindale Press as the place 'Where Fantasy Transforms Reality.'

Connect with Mountaindale Press:
MountaindalePress.com
Facebook.com/MountaindalePress
Twitter.com/_Mountaindale
Instagram.com/MountaindalePress

MOUNTAINDALE PRESS TITLES

GameLit and LitRPG

The Completionist Chronicles and
The Divine Dungeon by Dakota Krout

A Touch of Power by Jay Boyce

Red Mage by Xander Boyce

Space Seasons by Dawn Chapman

Ether Collapse by Ryan DeBruyn

Bloodgames by Christian J. Gilliland

Wolfman Warlock by James Hunter and Dakota Krout

Axe Druid and
Mephisto's Magic Online by Christopher Johns

Skeleton in Space by Andries Louws

Chronicles of Ethan by John L. Monk

Pixel Dust by David Petrie

Artorian's Archives by Dennis Vanderkerken and Dakota Krout

Made in the USA
Middletown, DE
12 October 2021

50164639R00225